Praise for #1 *New York Times* bestselling author Sherryl Woods

"Sherryl Woods writes ~~with a warmth and compassion that~~ family, friendship an~~d community...~~"
—#1 *New York Times* be~~stselling author Debbie Macomber~~

"Woods...is noted for app~~ealing, character-driven stories that~~ are often infused with the ~~flavor and fragrance of the South.~~"
—*Library Journal*

"Woods always thrills with her wonderful characters, witty dialog and warm and loving family interactions and this O'Brien family saga is no exception."
—*RT Book Reviews* on *An O'Brien Family Christmas*

"Infused with the warmth and magic of the season, Woods's fourth addition to her popular small-town series once again unites the unruly, outspoken, endearing O'Brien clan in a touching, triumphant tale of forgiveness and love reclaimed."
—*Library Journal* on *A Chesapeake Shores Christmas*

"Woods' amazing grasp of human nature and the emotions that lie deep within us make this story universal."
—*RT Book Reviews* on *Driftwood Cottage*

"Launching the Chesapeake Shores series, Woods creates an engrossing...family drama."
—*Publishers Weekly* on *The Inn at Eagle Point*

"Sparks fly in a lively tale that is overflowing with family conflict and warmth and the possibility of rekindled love."
—*Library Journal* on *Flowers on Main*

"Timely in terms of plot and deeply emotional, the third Chesapeake Shores book is quite absorbing. The characters are handled well and have real chemistry— as well as a way with one-liners."
—*RT Book Reviews* on *Harbor Lights*

#1 *New York Times* Bestselling Author

SHERRYL WOODS

A Seaside Christmas

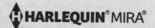

Recycling programs
for this product may
not exist in your area.

ISBN-13: 978-0-7783-1668-8

A Seaside Christmas
Copyright © 2013 by Sherryl Woods

Santa, Baby
Copyright © 2006 by Sherryl Woods

Printed in U.S.A.

A Seaside Christmas

1

Chesapeake Shores had been frozen in time, Jenny Collins thought as she turned onto Main Street toward the Chesapeake Bay. Not yet decked out for the holidays, the quaint and welcoming storefronts were the same familiar ones she'd known practically since childhood—Flowers on Main, owned by her uncle Jake's wife, Bree O'Brien, and then Shauna's bookstore, which had another family connection through the O'Briens, then Sally's café, Seaside Gifts and, finally, Ethel's Emporium, which sold everything from penny candy to gaudy beachwear.

Bree's shop and the bookstore were the newest additions. The others had been around since the town's founding. Ethel herself was something of an institution, a woman who knew everything and kept very little of it to herself.

It was Bree—as much friend as aunt—who'd lured Jenny back to town after she'd spent several years offering pitiful explanations that no one in her family had believed. First college and then her blossoming career as a songwriter in Nashville had given her more legitimate excuses, but Jenny knew they'd worn thin, too.

The truth was that she'd stayed away because her mom's marriage to the much older Thomas O'Brien and the birth of Jenny's half brother had freaked her out. The safe, secure world in which she'd grown up had suddenly changed in a dramatic way. She'd no longer known how to fit in.

At least she recognized that it didn't say anything good about her that she'd been wildly jealous about not having her mom all to herself anymore. For so long after her dad had left they'd been a dynamic duo, with only her uncle Jake as backup. She'd liked it that way, even when her mom had gotten on her last nerve being overly protective.

Rolling down the car window now, she breathed in the sharp, familiar tang of salt air and sighed. No matter how uncomfortable this visit might turn out to be, it felt amazingly good to be home. She felt settled, as if a part of herself had been restored.

Gazing out at the water, sparkling in the pale sun, she thought of the countless times her mom had talked about how lucky they were to call this town home, how the Chesapeake Bay—Thomas's passion and life's work—was such an amazing estuary and such a national treasure. She hadn't appreciated that then, but on a day like today she did. She could even admit she admired Thomas's dedication to preserving the bay.

Glancing at the car's clock, she saw that she was running later than she'd planned. She drove on to Bree's theater, the real love of her friend's professional life. She'd promised Bree she'd write a few songs for this year's Christmas play, a play Bree herself had scripted.

The prospect of such a collaboration, of possibly reaching a whole new audience with her songs, had been impossible to resist.

And it had given her the perfect excuse to flee Nashville during the holidays. She'd stuck it out there the year before after her breakup with megastar Caleb Green, mostly to prove to everyone that she was doing just fine, but a second year of loneliness during this special season? She simply couldn't face it.

Inside the cozy theater, Jenny shrugged out of her coat and headed for the rehearsal hall, which echoed with childish squeals and laughter and the occasional snatches of applause. She walked into the room just as silence fell. A sea of rapt young faces stared at Bree, her dark red hair pulled back into a loose ponytail, curls lit with sparkling highlights escaping around her pale-as-porcelain face. Though she was in her thirties, she looked younger.

"And once again the whole town felt the magic of the season," Bree concluded with a dramatic flourish.

The children, many of whom Jenny recognized as the newest generation of O'Briens, applauded enthusiastically. A smile split Bree's face at their exuberance, then widened when she spotted Jenny at the back of the room. She jumped up, leaving two young women in charge of the energetic children, and ran to embrace Jenny. When the women waved, Jenny realized with a sense of shock that they were Bree's sister Abby's twin daughters.

"Welcome home!" Bree said, enveloping her in a hug.

"Thanks," Jenny said. She nodded in the direction of the twins. "Caitlyn and Carrie?"

Bree laughed at her amazement. "Can you believe

it? They're all grown up. Abby's still reeling about that. As for Trace, I'm afraid their stepfather is having a very difficult time thinking they're old enough to date, much less be on their own at college. He has this mile-long list of rules for them while they're home on break from school. They're convinced he lives in the Dark Ages. I've read the list. Abby showed it to me. They could be right."

Jenny laughed. "I can imagine. Those girls might not be his biologically, but Trace was always as protective as if they were."

"He's much worse than their dad, who's always indulged their every whim to make up for not being around," Bree said, then winced. "Sorry. I didn't mean to be insensitive."

Jenny shrugged. "Things with my dad are what they are. I've gotten over the fact that he's not the least bit interested in me or my life. It's been years since I had so much as a birthday card, much less a call from him."

"But you have a stepfather who does care," Bree reminded her pointedly. "My uncle Thomas really wants to be part of your life."

Jenny held up a warning hand. "Don't go there, okay?"

Bree sighed. "Just saying. He's a great guy to have in your corner."

Jenny deliberately turned away and glanced around. She realized then that she and Bree were the center of attention for some of the children, including her half brother. Sean Michael O'Brien, who'd turned four a few months back, was studying her with a quizzical expression, as if not quite sure who she might be but clearly thinking he ought to know. With his bright red curls and blue eyes, he was unmistakably all O'Brien.

The Collins genes had apparently been no match for his Irish heritage.

Jenny forced her gaze back to Bree. "So you've been trying the story out on a captive audience?" she teased, determined to lighten the mood and change the uncomfortable subject.

Bree laughed, her expression unapologetic. "There are a lot of young O'Briens. They make a great test group to be sure this story will appeal to all ages. And my sisters and sisters-in-law get free babysitting. With their careers flourishing, time's at a premium for all of them this time of year. Come and say hello. Emily Rose and Sean are especially excited about seeing you."

Jenny couldn't help it. Eager as she was to see Bree and Jake's daughter, she stiffened at the mention of her own little brother. The reaction shamed her, especially with Bree regarding her with that knowing expression.

"Don't take all your misguided, conflicted feelings out on Sean," Bree pleaded quietly. "It's not fair."

"I know that," Jenny acknowledged, flushing under the intense scrutiny. "It's just that I don't know how to act around him. I don't feel like his big sister."

"Only because you've chosen to stay away," Bree said. "You *are* a part of this family, Jenny. And he *is* your little brother. Those are facts. You need to come to terms with them."

Jenny shook her head, still in denial. "I'm not an O'Brien," she said, as if that were the only thing that mattered. In many ways, to her it was.

Bree merely smiled. "Try telling my father that. Mick's been chomping at the bit for a couple of years, threatening to go to Nashville and haul you home himself. He's not fond of family rifts, especially since he and Mom have mended theirs and gotten back together, and the rest of us have fallen into line to forgive her, too. He expects peace and harmony to reign throughout O'Brien-land."

Jenny could believe that. Mick O'Brien was a force of nature. He, along with his brother, Thomas, who was now her stepfather, and their other brother, Jeff, had built Chesapeake Shores. Mick tended to think that gave him control over everything that happened not only in the family, but in the entire town.

"What stopped him?" she asked curiously.

"Not what," Bree said. "Who. Gram, of course. Nell told him and the rest of us that you'd had to face a lot of changes in your life, that you weren't the first one in this family to need some space, and that you'd come home when it felt right. I'm pretty sure that was a not-very-veiled reference to my mother's extended absence, which Gram used to make her point with Dad."

"And yet you decided to prod things along by dangling this offer to write the songs for the Christmas play in front of me," Jenny said.

Bree flushed. "Yes, well, Gram doesn't know everything. This seemed like the right opportunity and the right time. Even though you haven't said as much, I know things have been difficult for you in Nashville since the split with Caleb. The two of you were linked so tightly professionally and personally that it can't be easy moving on with everyone in the entire country music community watching you."

Jenny didn't even try to deny it. Ignoring the stares and speculation had taken a toll. Pretending that she didn't miss Caleb had been even more difficult. "I was glad for the break, no question about it," she told Bree.

"And I was tired of showing pictures of you to my daughter and your brother to make sure they'd recognize you," Bree said. "See what I mean? Perfect timing all around."

Just then a pint-sized version of Bree, red hair coming free from two braids only one of which still had a ribbon at the end, bounced over and regarded Jenny with a somber expression. She was clutching Sean's hand, her whole demeanor protective, as if she somehow understood the undercurrents swirling around them.

"You're Jenny," Emily Rose announced with certainty.

"I am," Jenny confirmed.

"That makes us cousins, just like me and Sean."

Despite her discomfort, Jenny smiled. "That's exactly right."

"You've been in Nashville writing music," Emily Rose continued as if well-rehearsed. "I've heard your songs on the radio. I can sing some of them."

"Me, too," a shy little voice piped up. "Mommy plays them at home all the time. She told me my sister wrote them. Sometimes they make her cry."

Tears of her own stung Jenny's eyes at the innocent revelation.

"How come I've never seen you before?" Sean asked bluntly.

Jenny knelt down so she could look into his eyes. "You have. You were just too little to remember," she said, thinking of the day he'd been born, her mom's labor disrupting an O'Brien family wedding, a double wedding, in fact. She recalled the happiness that had shone in her mother's eyes and in Thomas's that day, even as she'd wanted to die of embarrassment. Intellectually she knew her reaction had been childish, but she hadn't been able to move past it. Some feelings simply didn't respond to logic.

"But I've been big for a long time," Sean said, his expression puzzled.

"Yes, you have," Jenny agreed. She took a deep breath and, with Bree watching her closely, added, "Maybe on this trip we'll get to make up for lost time."

"Are you going to stay at our house?" he asked. "Your room is next to mine. Mommy said so. I'm not allowed in there. She's afraid I'll mess it up. She says it's just like the one you had when you were my age."

Startled, she turned a frantic gaze to Bree. That wasn't what they'd agreed. She still needed distance and time to get used to the changes that had taken place in her family the past few years. Coming to town was just the first step. She wasn't yet ready for the next one.

Bree put her hand on Sean's shoulder. "Jenny's going to stay at my house, but you'll see her all the time," she promised.

"Yea!" Emily Rose shouted triumphantly even as Sean's face fell.

"Sweetie, why don't you and Sean go and grab one of Grandma Nell's cookies before they're all gone," Bree said. "Jenny and I have some things we need to figure out."

Jenny watched them walk away, then faced her friend. "I only agreed to come because you invited me to stay with you and Uncle Jake. You're not changing your mind, are you?"

"Of course not," Bree said. "I just thought maybe you might want to reconsider. You know your mom is going to be crushed if you don't come home."

"That house isn't my home," Jenny said stubbornly, thinking instead of the small house in which her mom and Jake were raised and where she, too, had grown up. "I've never spent a single night in it."

"And whose fault is that?" Bree asked reasonably. "It's the house that Thomas built for your mother and his family. No matter how you might try to deny it and hold yourself aloof, you're part of that family, Jenny."

"I'm also a part of *your* family," Jenny reminded her. "I'd rather stay with you and Uncle Jake."

Bree nodded, though she didn't even try to hide the disappointment in her expression. "Whatever you want. You're always welcome to stay with us. You know that."

"Thank you."

"No problem." She smiled. "But if you think I'm being pushy, just wait till you see your uncle. Jake isn't one bit happy about any of this. He thinks it's way past time for you and your mom to mend fences."

"I'm sure he thinks this is all my fault, that I'm being stubborn and immature."

Bree tried and failed to contain a smile. "Your words, but, yes, he's made similar comments."

Suddenly the prospect of staying with her uncle's family didn't seem much more enticing than going home. "Maybe I should book a room at the inn," she said. That, too, belonged to yet another of the O'Briens, but it still seemed more likely to be neutral turf.

"Absolutely not," Bree said. "I guarantee you wouldn't even get your bags unpacked before Jake would be over there dragging you back to our place."

"Can't you call him off?" she asked Bree plaintively. "I know he listens to you."

Bree merely laughed. "I might be the O'Brien with

meddling in my DNA, but Jake is no slouch. He knows exactly how to get what he wants, and heaven help anyone who gets in his way. Since I actually agree with him about this, I won't even try."

"All that shows is that you're highly susceptible to his charm."

"Of course I am," Bree admitted readily. "But stronger women than I have been persuaded to change their minds once Jake starts working on them."

Jenny merely rolled her eyes. As much as she'd idolized her uncle growing up, she was pretty sure she could hold her own against him.

"Bring it on," she said.

The truth was she was actually looking forward to a good test of wills. Maybe it would keep her mind off the emotional roller coaster she'd been on from the moment she'd driven into town and experienced the first powerful tug of homesickness she'd felt in years.

Caleb Green, once a partner in one of the hottest groups in country music and winner of half a dozen CMA Awards and two Grammys, sat in the shadows of a crowded club outside of Nashville. He'd come to listen to a young acquaintance perform in a showcase they both hoped would result in a recording contract. The showcase ritual was a way to get agents and record labels to take a listen to up-and-coming talent.

Though Caleb had hung around for a few of Ricky Nolan's rehearsals, he'd never before heard the mournful ballad Ricky was performing now to close out the show.

As he listened, Caleb sat up a little straighter. There wasn't a doubt in his mind who had written the song. Only Jenny Collins could rip out a man's heart and fill it with regret. Hadn't she done just that on more than one of his group's hit songs? Their collaboration had been pure gold. Every song they'd done had shot straight to the top of the charts, crossing over between country and pop to find huge audiences.

Caleb relaxed—or tried to—as the showcase ended and Ricky was surrounded by well-wishers, including a man Caleb recognized as one of country music's top agents. He'd asked Ken Davis—an agent he knew well, but had never worked with—to stop by as a personal favor to him, but he hadn't been at all sure he'd had any chits left to call in. A lot of people in Nashville had written him off this past year. The fact that Ken had taken his call had been encouraging. The fact that he'd shown up tonight, persuaded by Caleb's praise for Ricky's voice, gave him hope for his own future in the business. Maybe not everyone considered him a pariah. Apparently one person still trusted his judgment, at least when it came to recognizing talent.

Unfortunately, pleased as he was for Ricky, his gut filled with envy just thinking about that heart-tugging song that Ricky had performed. Caleb knew instinctively it was exactly what he needed to get his career back after a whole host of mistakes, including walking away from Jenny and breaking her heart. Unfortunately, he couldn't imagine a way she'd ever forgive him for their very public breakup. Cheating had been awful enough. Adding humiliation to the mix had been unforgivable.

As soon as things in the club settled down and another performer was onstage, Ricky joined Caleb in the back.

"What did you think?" he asked, all the bravado

he'd displayed onstage now gone. He was just a nine-teen-year-old kid looking for reassurance from some-one he trusted.

Ricky had been only sixteen when Caleb and Jenny had first heard him in a club outside Charlottesville, Virginia. At eighteen and just out of high school, he'd turned up in Nashville, taking Caleb up on his offer to put him in touch with the right people. A year ago, though, Caleb hadn't even been able to help himself, much less anyone else. Now he was making good on his promise, trying to earn back the reputation he'd once had as a good guy who was always ready to help a new artist.

"You knocked 'em dead," Caleb told him honestly. "I imagine that's exactly what Ken Davis told you, too."

Ricky's eyes lit up at the mention of the agent. "He wants to talk. We're meeting tomorrow."

"That's great," Caleb said with total sincerity. "You get him on your team and you'll go places fast. He has the respect of everyone in this town. He's honest and he doesn't take on just anyone. If he's braggin' on you to the labels, I guarantee you'll be under contract in no time. He'll line up a tour before summer, too."

Ricky looked a little dazed. "I can't believe it's really happening. Everyone back home kept telling me I was crazy, that making it was a long shot at best."

"You haven't made it yet," Caleb cautioned. "But with Ken in your corner, your chances have definitely improved."

"It's because of you, Caleb. You got me in here to-night. And I know for a fact you said something to Ken, too. He'd never have shown up otherwise. I owe you."

Caleb drew in a deep breath. "You don't owe me a

thing. If Ken hadn't liked what he heard, my getting him here wouldn't have meant a thing."

"I owe you," Ricky repeated.

"There is a favor you could do for me," Caleb admitted, still weighing whether he had any right to ask.

"Anything. Just name it."

"That song, the one you sang at the end. Jenny Collins wrote it, didn't she? I recognize her style."

Ricky nodded, his expression chagrined. "I know you and she... Well, I know it ended badly, but we ran into each other a while back. She remembered me from that night in Charlottesville. She said my voice was perfect for a song she'd just written. The minute I heard it, I knew I couldn't turn it down. Songs like that don't come along every day. Ken said the same thing. He said it was a guaranteed hit."

That gave Caleb pause. How could he ask for a song that could kick-start this kid's career in such a big way?

Ricky studied him intently. "You want the song, don't you?"

Caleb nodded. "I think that song is the one that could put my career back on track, this time as a solo artist, but Jenny gave it to you. Ken thinks you could turn it into a hit. I have no right to ask you to give up that shot. I should leave well enough alone."

"No way, man. It's yours," Ricky said without even a moment's hesitation. "Like I said, I owe you. There will be other songs for me, but, to be honest, I knew when I heard that one it should have been yours. You're really the one who could do it justice. Having a newcomer like me do it could be a big risk. It deserves to be played on every radio station across the country. Jenny put a whole world of hurt into that song. Anyone hearing it can tell it's real personal."

Caleb sighed, a year's worth of guilt washing over him. "Yeah, she did. And that pain? It was all my fault—every bit of it."

"All the more reason for you to be the one performing it," Ricky said, then asked worriedly, "What's Jenny going to think about my letting you have the song?"

"Now that is the sixty-four-thousand-dollar question, isn't it?" Caleb responded candidly. "Obviously, I'll have to work out an arrangement with her." He allowed himself a rueful smile. "And if Jenny hates my guts these days, her agent probably has tar and feathers nearby with my name on them."

Ricky chuckled. "Yeah, I definitely got that impression when your name came up in the conversation I had with Margo when we made the deal."

"All I can do is try to make things right," Caleb said.

Unsaid was that maybe, just maybe, negotiating for the song could open a door for him to patch things up with Jenny, too. Or at least to make amends for the way he'd treated her.

"She's out of town, you know," Ricky mentioned casually. "I heard she went to that town in Maryland where she grew up. Word around here is that she needed to take some time off. Rumor has it she's hooking up with somebody in her family to write some songs for a Christmas play."

"That must be her uncle's wife," Caleb said, surprised. In all the time they'd been together, Jenny had refused to set foot in Chesapeake Shores. Why had she gone back now? He doubted it was simply to write a few lyrics for some rinky-dink local Christmas production, even at the request of Bree O'Brien, a woman he knew Jenny loved and admired.

Only one way to find out, he decided. He sure as heck couldn't convince Jenny to make a deal for that song he wanted over the phone. This required a face-to-face meeting. He'd just have to pray that she'd been infected by the holiday spirit and wouldn't slam the door on him.

Mick stared at his brother. Thomas, usually a pretty optimistic guy, especially since he'd married Connie and had a son, looked as if the weight of the world were resting squarely on his shoulders.

"What do you mean, Jenny's staying with Bree and Jake?" Mick demanded, indignant on his brother's behalf.

"Just what I said. And it's breaking Connie's heart, I'll tell you that," Thomas said, his misery plain. "It's all my fault. I should have done a better job of winning Jenny over before I married her mother. I knew she felt as if I stole Connie away from her, but that was never my intention. I wanted to have a family with Connie and in my mind that always included Jenny. The last thing I wanted was to drive a wedge between them."

"You ever tell Jenny that?" Mick asked.

"How was I supposed to do that?" Thomas asked with frustration. "Every single time I tried, she'd give me one excuse or another. Then it was too late. She found out in the worst possible way that we were expecting a baby, right in front of the whole family on that trip to Ireland. It rocked her world. Not only had I displaced her in her mom's affections, but there was a baby on the way. It shouldn't have been a competition between her and Sean, but I know that's how Jenny felt, and she decided she'd come out the loser."

"You have to admit some of that goes back to that father of hers who abandoned her and Connie. The man should have been shot, if you ask me," Mick said. "Whatever the issues were between him and Connie, what kind of man leaves town and doesn't even stay in touch with his own daughter? It's little wonder the girl has abandonment issues or whatever it is they call that kind of insecurity."

"You're right about that," Thomas said.

"And now you're paying the price," Mick concluded. He shook his head. "As understandable as it might be, that hardly seems fair."

"I don't think fair has much to do with it. I doubt Jenny would trust anyone who came between her and her mother."

"Probably not," Mick conceded. "But she's an adult now. She needs to suck it up and deal with the situation. I've known Connie for a lot of years. You've made her happier than I'd ever seen her before, and you know I don't throw compliments your way lightly."

"Believe me, I know," Thomas said wryly. "What the heck am I supposed to do now, though? I can't go over to Jake and Bree's and drag Jenny home. It's a little late for me to throw around my weight as her stepfather."

"Want me to go over there?" Mick asked eagerly. He'd had far too little to do lately, with almost everyone in the family happily married and settled down.

Thomas fought a smile, but Mick caught it. He couldn't say he blamed his brother for being amused.

"As generous as that offer is, you don't have the finesse for this," Thomas said. "Ma was very clear that I was to leave you out of it. She recommends being patient. She says if you try bossing Jenny around, she'll only dig in her heels."

"You talked to Ma and she said that?" Mick said.

Thomas chuckled. "And a lot more about bulls in china shops and lack of diplomacy. Dillon agreed with her."

Nell O'Brien certainly had clear-eyed vision when it came to her family, Mick thought, much as her assessment might rankle. He put almost as much weight behind Dillon's opinion. Since Dillon O'Malley and Nell had reunited in Ireland and married less than a year later, they tended to be in lockstep on this kind of thing.

"Okay, I'll stay out of it for now," Mick conceded reluctantly. "But you need me, say the word."

Thomas stood up. "Thanks for listening, Mick. That's what I really needed. I can't let Connie see how frustrated I am. Then she goes and blames herself for putting me in the middle. It just complicates an already messy situation."

"How about this?" Mick said. "You bring Connie and your boy here for Sunday dinner, like always. I'll see to it that Jenny's at the table."

Thomas frowned. "Didn't you hear a word I just said? No meddling."

"I believe my instructions were to stay away from Jenny," Mick said, satisfied that he'd found the perfect loophole. "Doesn't mean I can't put a bug in Bree's ear about getting that girl over here for a family dinner. I'll speak to Jess, too. We'll make it a welcome home celebration. It'll be downright rude of Jenny to refuse the invitation, especially if the gathering is in her honor. I know her mama raised her better than that."

Thomas's expression turned thoughtful. "I think you're bending the spirit of Ma's edict, but I'm willing to risk it," he said eventually. "I want to see my wife smiling again. I thought just having Jenny back in town would do it, but not like this. Earlier, I asked Connie if she'd seen Jenny yet. She burst into tears and left the room. There wasn't a thing I could do to comfort her."

He sighed. "Just as bad, Sean knows something's going on, too. He ran into Jenny at Bree's theater this afternoon and came home with a thousand and one questions about his big sister and why she wasn't coming to our house. Since I couldn't answer most of them and Connie wasn't up to dealing with his curiosity, I dropped him over at Kevin and Shauna's to play with their kids. I need to get back over there and pick him up."

"You go, and stop your worrying. We'll fix this," Mick said confidently. "It's Christmas, after all, and don't the O'Briens specialize in Christmas miracles?"

2

It only took a couple of calls for Caleb to confirm what Ricky had told him. Jenny had, indeed, gone to Chesapeake Shores, and was expected to be there through the holidays. The second confirmation had just come from her agent, who wasn't one bit happy about having inadvertently pointed him toward her whereabouts.

"Do not go anywhere near that town or Jenny," Margo Welch warned him. "I swear, I'll advise her to get a restraining order."

Despite the unlikelihood that Jenny would do such a thing, Caleb was shaken. "On what grounds?" he asked, wondering exactly what Jenny had told people after the breakup. Hadn't those tabloid pictures of him with another woman told the story clearly enough? Had she felt the need to elaborate? Didn't it take some pretty serious accusations to justify a restraining order? Just being lower than pond scum in someone's opinion usually wasn't enough.

"You broke that girl's heart," Margo said, her raspy voice fiercely protective. "I won't let you get close enough to do it again."

"That's really up to Jenny, isn't it?" he said mildly. "Look, Margo, I know you only have her best interests at heart. You always have. Believe it or not, so do I. I'm not going over there to cause trouble, I swear it."

She sighed heavily. "But you are going to Chesapeake Shores? There's nothing I can say to talk you out of it?"

"Nothing," he confirmed. "And, just so you know, I intend to try my best to talk her into selling me the rights to record that ballad she wrote and sold to Ricky Nolan."

"There's a contract, Caleb. If that song is what you're after, you can forget it. When I write a contract, it's airtight. You should know that."

"Believe me, I do. But Ricky and I have already agreed to this. He'll relinquish his rights. To tell you the truth, he could probably make a deal with me on his own, but I didn't want to go behind Jenny's back. I want to do this in a straightforward way, by convincing her I'm the right man to record this song. If you're honest, Margo, you know that's true."

"That song will be a hit no matter who does it," she contradicted. "I've already spoken to Ken Davis. He wants to make it Ricky's first single. Are you going to strip that boy of the opportunity to go platinum right out of the gate? That just proves every rotten thing I've been thinking about you."

Caleb decided it was best not to remind her how eager she'd once been for him and Jenny to work together. She'd been even more ecstatic when their relationship had become personal. It had provided a publicity gold mine that had benefited Jenny and, by extension, Margo herself, quite nicely.

Instead, he said, "Ricky has the talent to go platinum with any song he chooses. He recognizes that this particular song was meant for me. It's a done deal, Margo. I just need to work out the details with Jenny."

"And if she says no?"

"I'm hoping she won't, but if she does, that's that," Caleb said. "I'll be disappointed, but I won't pressure her."

"I'll advise her against it," Margo informed him. "Jenny listens to me, Caleb. You know she does. I'll do whatever I can to prevent her from hooking up with you again, professionally or personally."

Even though it wasn't in his own best interests, Caleb actually respected her more for protecting Jenny's back with such maternal ferocity. "I wouldn't expect anything less."

"Caleb, please don't do this," she requested quietly. "It's taken Jenny a long time to get over what you did to her. If you ask me, the only reason she's in Chesapeake Shores right now is to get some distance from Nashville and all her memories of you."

"Then it's past time I apologized for the pain I caused her," he countered. "Maybe that will give her the closure she needs to move on."

"If that's all you intended, I might not argue," Margo said. "But you want more. You want that song and, unless I'm a whole lot worse at reading you than I used to be, you want Jenny back, too. I was there when you staged that full-court press to win her the first time. That's what you're planning now, isn't it?"

He hesitated, then decided now wasn't the time to add a lie to his sins. "Can't deny it," he admitted.

He thought back to the first time he'd laid eyes on

Jenny. His manager had brought her over to his place, but he'd been hung over and miserable. While he'd pulled himself together, his manager had sent her onto the patio to wait.

A half hour later, showered and in a more receptive mood, Caleb had found her strumming her guitar, bathed in sunlight. She'd looked ethereal. The music had been just as heavenly, striking an immediate chord in him.

When she hadn't noticed him, he'd continued listening, falling just a little bit in love with the songs and the woman. It was hard to say which had grabbed him more. The music, more than likely, because his work was his life at that point. His feelings for Jenny had deepened with time.

And then he'd gone and ruined it all.

He sighed, remembering.

"Oh, Caleb," Margo murmured, real pain in her voice. "If you still love her, can't you leave her in peace?"

Long after he'd hung up the phone, he thought about Margo's heartfelt request. The older woman was probably right. The kind thing to do would be to let Jenny go to start over with someone more deserving. And if it was all about a song, perhaps he could do that, but it wasn't. It was about reclaiming the missing piece of his heart.

When Jenny left Bree at her theater, she walked along the waterfront trying to get her emotions under control. Leave it to Bree to call her on her behavior in the gentle, chiding way that forced her to see herself more clearly. It hadn't been an entirely comfortable confrontation.

Not that she could argue with a single thing Bree had said. She'd struggled with herself over those very things for a long time now. Each and every time reason had lost out to emotion.

Chilled after just a few minutes in the icy breeze off the water, she crossed the street, walked briskly back toward Main and went into the café. Her cell phone rang, but a glance showed that the call was from her agent. Right this second, business was the last thing on her mind. She let Margo's call go to voice mail and settled into a booth.

"Jenny Louise Collins!" Sally said, a smile spreading across her face. "It's been way too long since we've laid eyes on you in this town. Welcome home!"

"Thanks, Sally. This place hasn't changed a bit."

Sally glanced around at the worn, but comfortably familiar decor and shook her head. "It could use a good sprucing up, if you ask me, but every time I mention making a few changes, the customers carry on as if they're afraid I'll turn it into some highfalutin gourmet restaurant and raise my prices."

"It's reassuring to know that it's just the same," Jenny admitted. "Any chocolate croissants left? I know it's late in the day."

"I must have had some idea you'd be home today. I held one back just in case someone special came in."

Jenny didn't believe her for a minute, or at least not that she'd been the *someone* Sally had been expecting. Still, she was grateful for the sentiment. The prospect of the treat had her mouth watering. "I'll take it, and a cup of coffee. It's colder out there than I was expecting. It almost feels like snow in the air."

"That's what I was thinking, too, but there's none in the forecast. Hard to believe we actually had a warm spell just a week ago. It was sixty on Thanksgiving. Didn't feel much like winter coming on then."

Jenny smiled, remembering how many times she'd heard similar comments over the years. Once the calendar flipped over to November and all the leaves were on the ground, it seemed everyone in Chesapeake Shores started watching the skies and hoping for snow. Sadly, though, white Christmases were few and far between. That made the ones that did come along that much more magical.

"Let me grab that coffee and croissant for you," Sally said, hurrying off to fill the order.

She'd just returned when Jess O'Brien came in on a blast of frigid air, shrugged out of her coat and slid into the booth opposite Jenny without waiting for an invitation.

"I heard you were back," Jess said, reaching across the table to give Jenny's hand a squeeze. "I stopped by the theater, but Bree said you'd taken off. Since your car was still in the lot, I thought I might find you inside someplace getting warm."

"I had a sudden craving for one of Sally's chocolate croissants," Jenny admitted.

Jess, who was Bree's younger sister and the owner of the Inn at Eagle Point, regarded the croissant enviously. "Any more?" she asked Sally hopefully.

"No chocolate, but there is one raspberry croissant left."

"I'll take it, and a coffee, too," Jess said eagerly.

"How'd you know I was back?" Jenny asked.

Jess laughed. "It's Chesapeake Shores and the O'Brien grapevine is a thing of wonder. I doubt you'd crossed the city limits when word started spreading."

Jenny wasn't entirely sure she believed her. Oh, she knew gossip spread quickly here, but she also knew how clever O'Briens were about recruiting help with their missions. She suspected her relationship with her family was high on everyone's to-do list at the moment.

"I spoke to Dad a little while ago," Jess said, her tone a little too casual. "He's rallying the troops for a welcome home dinner for you on Sunday at his place."

Sunday dinners at Mick's were an O'Brien tradition, one Nell had insisted on. They'd been initiated to get her three sons—Mick, Thomas and Jeff—and their families under one roof in an attempt to mend fences after they'd battled over the development of the town. More recently, they'd simply been occasions for huge, rambunctious gatherings that had always made Jenny feel like an envious outsider on the rare occasions when she'd gone with her mom.

If this one was being held in her honor, Jenny had a hunch it was Mick's way of trying to bring her face-to-face with her mother and Thomas in a friendly setting.

"You've got that look on your face," Jess said. "Like a deer in the headlights."

"I'm not ready for a big O'Brien family gathering," Jenny told her frankly.

"Hey, I get that," Jess said sympathetically. "Sometimes my family is a little overwhelming even for me. I even had the joy of undergoing an occasional so-called intervention. Those were fun."

Jenny smiled. She could imagine it, all those O'Briens

focused on making some point about the way one of them was behaving. "Heaven save me from that," she said.

"I'd try, but I know Dad," Jess said sympathetically. "This is going to happen sooner or later. You might as well get it over with. Just think of it this way. It's a big house. There are lots of places to hide out and still be on the premises."

Jenny laughed despite herself. "Voice of experience?"

"You bet. I can give you some tips. In fact, I might hide out with you. Everyone's bugging Will and me about when we're going to have a baby. Wouldn't you think there are enough O'Briens in this town without the whole family being so blasted eager for another one?"

"You and Will don't want to have kids?" Jenny asked, surprised.

"Sure we do," Jess said a little too quickly.

Jenny frowned. "That didn't sound convincing."

"Okay, Will's eager. I'm terrified."

"Why?"

"What if the baby has the same attention deficit disorder I have?"

"It's not a fatal disease," Jenny said, not entirely understanding. Though she knew Jess had struggled with her ADD, she seemed in command of her life these days.

"No, but I've dealt with it my whole life," Jess replied. "No question it shaped who I am, and not always for the better."

"Then you'd be quick to recognize the signs and to get your child any help he or she needs," Jenny told her. "Plus Will's a shrink. He'd be able to help, too. Are you sure there's not some other reason you're hesitant?" As soon as the question was out of her mouth, she winced. "Sorry. None of my business."

"No, it's okay. I made it your business by bringing it up. I guess it's just on my mind so much lately it popped out." Jess sighed. "And you're right. Maybe I am worried about whether I've got the skills to be a good mother. Even with all the systems I have in place for myself, I can still be pretty scattered from time to time."

"You're forgetting that I've seen you with your nieces and nephews," Jenny said. "You'd be an incredible mother, Jess. I don't think you need to worry about that."

"Thanks for saying that."

"I mean it."

Jess tore off a piece of croissant and chewed slowly, then closed her eyes. "These are so good. They practically melt in your mouth."

"It's all the butter," Jenny said.

"I'd give anything to have them on the menu at the inn, but Sally won't part with even a dozen of them. She says they're her claim to fame, the one thing she learned to make at some expensive cooking class she took in Paris years ago. She says the inn has its own culinary reputation without stealing hers."

"She has a point."

"I know, but it's frustrating just the same." Jess finished off the last bite of her croissant, then stood up and tugged on her coat. "So, you'll be there on Sunday, right?"

"Are you assigned to report back to your father?" Jenny asked, amused despite the beginnings of a stress headache starting to throb at the back of her head.

"Something like that. I'm sure others have a similar assignment, but I got to you first," she said triumphantly. "Yea, me!"

"Has anyone mentioned that the O'Brien competitiveness takes a backseat only to their meddling?"

"On several occasions," Jess said, then leaned down to give her a hug. "It's good to have you home, Jenny."

Jenny noted that she didn't wait around for Jenny to confirm that she'd be there on Sunday. It was taken for granted. After all, when Mick O'Brien set a plan into motion, it generally worked out exactly the way he intended it to.

Jenny was beginning to feel as if everyone had a plan for her life. Her uncle had been on her case ever since he'd put Emily Rose to bed and joined her and Bree in the kitchen for a late dinner. At first he'd tried reason. Then he'd cajoled. Now he was resorting to threats.

"You'll be in my truck at six forty-five tomorrow morning or I'll drag you out of bed, throw you over my shoulder and haul you out the door myself," Jake said, his expression as fierce as Jenny had ever seen it, except, perhaps, for that time he'd caught her making out with Dillon Johnson after hours in his office at the nursery he owned on the outskirts of town.

Between the nursery and his landscaping business, Jake was always on the go soon after dawn. His sister—Jenny's mom—dealt with all the paperwork and scheduling for the company. A couple of years back he'd given her some sort of title and a salary increase because they both understood that it was Connie who had the patience to deal with all the details that Jake hated. He loved the outdoors and the backbreaking landscaping work.

Jenny tried to stare him down. "But, Uncle Jake—"

He cut off the protest. "Your mother doesn't deserve the cold shoulder you've been giving her. Neither does Thomas, but I'll leave that for another time. You're coming to work with me in the morning, and you and your mother aren't walking out of there till you've made peace."

Jenny looked to Bree for backup, but Bree had suddenly become engrossed in loading the dishwasher with their dinner dishes. Sighing heavily, she gave up the fight. "Fine. Whatever."

"Spoken like the sulky teenager you no longer are," Jake said, a teasing glint in his eyes. "I only want what's best for you, you know that."

"This is not about me," Jenny countered. "You want to keep the peace with Mom. Otherwise, she'll make your life miserable at work."

He shrugged. "Okay. That, too. I hate it when she cries or even looks like she's about to." He stood up and dropped a kiss on her forehead. "Glad to have you home, kiddo. I've missed you. I'll see you first thing in the morning."

"At six forty-five. Got it."

She watched her uncle head upstairs, then rested her head on her arms. When she looked up, she said, "Coming home was a bad idea."

Bree joined her at the kitchen table. "No. Coming home was an excellent idea. Deep in your heart, you know that. It's just hard to see everyone at first. That's why this Sunday dinner thing Jess told you about will be great. You can see everyone at once, get any awkwardness behind you and then enjoy the holidays."

"I'm delighted to see that your father got you on

board so quickly. Jess, too. I imagine he'll be sending Nell out to track me down next. There will be a steady stream of O'Briens in my face until I capitulate and say yes."

Bree merely laughed. "More than likely. He knows as well as anyone that none of us can say no to Nell, you included."

"I could be the first," Jenny grumbled, though she knew Bree was right. There was something so warm and wise about Nell, that no one ever refused her requests. If it weren't for the anticipated additional pressure, Jenny might actually look forward to seeing her. She would have loved to have a grandmother like that.

"Nah," Bree said confidently. "You're as susceptible to Nell as the rest of us." Bree slid Jenny a sly look. "Especially now that she's technically your grandmother, too."

Jenny gave her a startled look, then sighed as she considered the connection through Thomas. "I suppose so."

"Why don't you look happier about that? I know how much you adore her."

"Because despite what she said about my needing time to deal with all these changes, I know she probably thinks I'm a terrible, selfish brat for leaving and not coming back," Jenny said. "She's bound to think I was trying to punish Mom for marrying Thomas."

Bree gave her a knowing look. "Weren't you?"

"I wasn't, not really," Jenny said earnestly. "I just felt lost, like an outsider in my safe, secure world. For all those years after my dad left, it was just my mom and me and Uncle Jake."

"You didn't blame me when I married Jake," Bree noted.

Jenny flushed. "Sure, I did," she said candidly. "But you'd gotten Uncle Jake to lighten up on me and Dillon Johnson, so it balanced out somehow."

Bree smiled. "Ah, so that's how I escaped your wrath."

"Pretty much. I figured you were my one ally back then." She gave her a resigned look. "Now, not so much."

"Leave me out of it," Bree commanded. "Let's stick to the real issue. Thomas came along and you were no longer the sun in your mother's universe. Is that how you felt?"

Jenny nodded. "Ridiculous, I know. I was going off to college, for heaven's sake. I didn't want her to be all alone. I should have been thrilled that she'd fallen in love. I wasn't blind. I could see that Thomas adored her, that he wanted to do everything in his power to make her happy. She was glowing when they got married. And then, just when I was coming to terms with that, she got pregnant...."

Jenny shook her head at the memory of the way she'd taken that news, as if it had been a personal betrayal. She'd fled the Christmas celebration at their Dublin hotel the moment she'd heard the announcement. "God, I behaved so badly."

"Everyone understood you were upset," Bree consoled her. "You should have found out before the rest of us. They both should have been more considerate of your feelings. I just think they were so excited, it kind of came out."

"I get that and I had no right to ruin that moment. It

just hurt to see how happy they were, as if they'd been given a miracle."

"They had been," Bree said, then added gently, "But that made you realize that your mom was a woman, that you alone weren't enough for her. It must have come as a rude awakening."

Jenny gaped at her. "You get that?"

"Sweetie, observing human beings and all their frailties is what I do. You can't write plays that mean anything without that kind of insight." She grinned. "And I write halfway decent plays."

"They're more than halfway decent," Jenny said with total sincerity.

"You have the same sort of insight," Bree noted. "It shines through in your songs. How do you think you came up with so many hits? People respond to the sensitivity and truth in your lyrics."

"I thought it was because I've been fortunate enough to have them sung by some of the hottest guys in Nashville."

"Well, that, too," Bree said with a grin. Her expression sobered. "I know I've said this before, but I'm truly sorry about you and Caleb. I know that breakup hurt."

"Over and done with," Jenny said, not even trying to hide her bitterness over that fact. "I haven't heard from him since he went into rehab for alcohol abuse. If I never hear from him again, it will be too soon."

"Said exactly like a woman who's still fighting her feelings," Bree commented. "Unless I'm mistaken, you two never talked about what happened, about those pictures that were splashed all over the tabloids. He went straight into treatment."

Jenny thought back to those devastating days. There

hadn't been one single phone call, no attempt to apologize or explain. "We never talked, no."

"Then you could probably use some closure," Bree suggested.

Jenny gave her a startled look. "No way," she insisted. "Caleb is history. I have no idea where he is. I don't want to know. He trashed his career, right along with our relationship. Forget closure. If I ever take a chance on love again, it won't be with another bad-boy singer, that's for sure. Nice, stable and boring. That's the way to go."

She reminded herself of that every single night as she lay all alone in the bed she and Caleb had once shared.

If Bree had something to say about her fierce declaration, she wisely kept it to herself. Jenny was in no mood to hear her defend the man who'd chosen a bottle over her.

She stood up abruptly. "If I'm supposed to be up before dawn, I'd better get some sleep." She gave Bree a hug. "Thanks for taking me in and for being so understanding."

"Always," Bree said. "And, sweetie, cut your mom some slack when you see her. She loves you so much."

Because she knew in her heart it was true, Jenny nodded. "I'll do my best."

"You'll come by the theater after you've seen her?" Bree asked. "We can talk about the songs for the play, maybe bounce around a few ideas?"

"Sounds good. I read the script and I've made some notes. I even have a few preliminary lyrics jotted down."

Bree grinned. "I knew you would. I should probably call your agent tomorrow and work out a deal with her."

Jenny regarded her with dismay. "No deal necessary. I'm doing this for the chance to work with you."

"Sorry. You're a professional songwriter now. You write songs, then you get paid. Given the kind of fees you can probably command these days, I might ask for the friends and family discount, though."

"I'll send an email to Margo and let her know," Jenny said. "Come to think of it, she left me a message earlier, but I'm too beat to deal with it tonight. I'm actually surprised she called. I told her when I left that I was officially on vacation, that there was nothing that couldn't wait till I get back to Nashville after the first of the year. I need a complete mental break from everything. I thought she understood that."

Bree frowned. "If you told her that and she called anyway, maybe it's important."

"There aren't a lot of emergencies in my line of work," Jenny told her. "Tomorrow will be soon enough. Whatever it is could probably wait till after New Year's, for that matter."

"Your call," Bree said.

In the guest room, Jenny took her cell phone from her purse and deliberately placed it in a dresser drawer. She piled a few sweaters on top of it for good measure. She'd meant it when she'd told Margo she wanted an uninterrupted break for the next few weeks.

Though she'd worked through the breakup with Caleb and the resulting fallout, enduring the pity and even a fair share of gloating from women who'd once envied her, there was no denying the stress of the past year. Since coming back to Chesapeake Shores was likely to be stressful in its own way, she didn't need to have it compounded by professional obligations that could be put off.

As she shut the drawer on that part of her life, she smiled. If only it were that easy to lock away the memories. Unfortunately, there was no place to shove those. They were destined to keep on haunting her until she opened her heart to someone new. Right now she was thinking that wouldn't happen till hell froze over.

3

Caleb left Nashville as soon as he could throw some clothes into a suitcase. Since he tended to live in jeans, T-shirts and his leather jacket, packing didn't take long. He threw his bag and several of his favorite guitars into the back of his 4x4 truck and headed east.

He liked driving at night, partly because there was less traffic, but mostly because it was what he'd gotten used to on tour. The band would finish a concert, party for a couple of hours, then head out on their bus for the next city on the tour. Of course, someone else was paid to drive them then, but he'd never tired of staring out the windows at the passing landscape, the lights of shadowy towns in the distance.

He'd always wondered what it would be like to settle down someplace, put down roots. The closest he'd come had been the couple of years he'd been with Jenny in Nashville, though he suspected if he counted up the nights they'd spent under that roof, it would have been less than half of those he'd spent on the road. And he'd never given up his own place, made the commitment to living with her. In retrospect, he wondered if he hadn't known from the first that sooner or later he'd mess up what they had together.

Maybe he'd gotten his wandering gene from his father, who'd taken off when he was still in grade school and who was still wandering, as far as Caleb knew. To his everlasting regret, on his rare visits home he still caught his mother gazing out the window sometimes, her expression wistful, as if she thought there would eventually come a day when Noah Green would turn up again.

Caleb knew better. Wanderers never settled in one place for long. If they were anything like him, they had the same problem being faithful. He'd always believed, though, that if it was possible to make a lasting commitment, to live happily-ever-after, Jenny was the woman he'd want by his side.

It was ironic in some ways that their absentee fathers had drawn them together. When they'd first met, they'd spent long hours talking about that. Though Jenny claimed she didn't care a bit about the man who'd fathered her, he'd known by seeing the hurt in her eyes that it wasn't true. He'd seen that same pain in the mirror a time or two. He'd been just as clever about denying it, though.

But if the pain had given them a connection, it was music that had brought a shared passion into their lives. Caleb lived to be onstage, to entertain an audience. Jenny lived to create lyrics that people could relate to, to touch a place in their hearts or express a profound sense of joy. Her music could tug at the heartstrings or lift the spirits better than anything he'd ever heard.

At times in rehab, when he'd been struggling to break the hold alcohol had over him, he'd worried that what he'd done to Jenny would somehow silence that amazing creativity. Instead, if the song he'd heard Ricky sing was an example, the heartache he'd inflicted on her had been a source of even deeper inspiration. It was possibly the only good thing to come from his despicable actions.

Reflecting on what a mess he'd made of things was bringing him down, so he flipped on the radio, found a country station and let the music wash over him as he drove from Tennessee to Maryland.

Unfortunately, this habit he had of hitting the road late at night put him into Chesapeake Shores before dawn. Since it was apparent that the town rolled up the sidewalks long before midnight and the nearest motel had been miles back, he was momentarily at a loss.

Then he thought of the Inn at Eagle Point that Jenny had mentioned belonging to someone in her family, or in that big extended family that put a faraway look in her eyes whenever she mentioned them. Using his cell phone, he found the address and directions, then made his way along a winding waterfront road that emerged on a point of land overlooking the Chesapeake Bay. The inn stood before him with welcoming lights beckoning from the downstairs windows.

He hauled his bag and guitar to the front door, only to find it locked. A small, handwritten sign posted under a bell beside the door read Ring for Assistance, so he did exactly that. Again and again, he pressed the button, then watched through the glass panels on either side of the door for some sign of activity.

A harried-looking woman who was surprisingly young eventually padded down the stairs and unlocked the door. She was barefoot, wrapped in a thick robe and clearly annoyed, but beautiful just the same.

"It's the middle of the night," she pointed out unnecessarily.

"Exactly why I need a warm bed," Caleb told her, turning on the smile that he'd been assured could melt the coldest female heart. Women the age of this one — early thirties—were reportedly especially susceptible. This woman, however, seemed to be immune. In fact, her gaze narrowed and she drew the robe even more tightly around her as a breeze swirled around them.

"You're Caleb Green," she announced as if he might not be aware of it.

"Guilty."

"I'll say," she muttered.

Her reaction didn't bode well, he concluded. Of course, anyone in this town who knew Jenny was likely to be on her side. He should have thought of that.

"Look, I've driven a long way tonight. I know I'm inconveniencing you by arriving at this hour, but I really would like to book a room, if you have one available." Since he hadn't seen a single car parked in the lot, he waited to see if she'd flat-out lie and send him away.

She frowned at him, clearly torn. Apparently, an innate sense of hospitality eventually kicked in. "One night," she said at last.

"Indefinitely," he countered.

Her frown deepened. "Why? If you're here to cause trouble for Jenny, you're not welcome, not at the inn, not in town." The warning proved she knew the whole history and had already chosen sides.

Caleb smiled. "I see what Jenny meant about this town getting in her business."

"We take care of our own. And Jenny's not just a local. She's family."

He recalled the connection he should have made the instant the door opened. "You're an O'Brien," he concluded.

"I'm Jess Lincoln now, but, yes, I'm an O'Brien."

"Which makes you what? Jenny's cousin?" Not that Jenny had embraced being an O'Brien, as far as he could remember. She'd felt alienated from the whole lot of them, even as she'd longed to be one of them. Though she'd denied it, he'd recognized that yearning in her eyes whenever she talked about them.

"Exactly. Jenny and I are cousins, at least I like to think of us that way."

He decided to forget charm, which was likely to be wasted, and go for being direct. "Okay, Jess, what's it going to be? Do I get that room? Do you want to call around and take a family vote, while we both stand out here freezing, or what?"

Though there was no mistaking her reluctance, she stepped aside. "I suppose you might as well come on in, but if I find out later that Jenny wants you gone, you're history."

He nodded, accepting where her loyalties would naturally lie. "I wouldn't have it any other way."

Jess pulled a key off the rack behind the desk and handed it to him. "We'll deal with the paperwork tomorrow. I'm going back to bed before my husband comes down here, sees you and tells me what a huge mistake I'm making."

Caleb chuckled. "A risk taker. I think I like you, Jess O'Brien Lincoln."

She shook her head. "Save that smile for someone who'll appreciate it," she said. "The room's up the stairs and to the left. We serve breakfast from seven to nine. Miss that, you're out of luck unless you head into town."

"Got it."

As he climbed the stairs he wondered once more about Jenny's refusal to come back here for so long. Sure, he knew there were all sorts of unresolved family dynamics at work, but he'd gotten the sense from Jess that any distance was all on Jenny, not the O'Briens. Jess, like Margo Welch, was a woman who'd always have Jenny's back. Multiply that by what he recalled was a very large O'Brien clan and he wondered how much more difficult that was likely to make his mission to mend fences.

Connie paced the office at the nursery, her gaze going to the clock that seemed to be moving at a snail's pace this morning. Jake had promised to get Jenny over here one way or another, and her brother always kept his word. But Jenny was no slouch when it came to stubbornness. He might have hit a snag when it came to persuading her to come to work with him.

She finally heard the crunch of tires on gravel outside and glanced out the window. When her daughter emerged from the passenger side of the pickup, Connie's heart nearly stopped.

Jenny had changed so much, from a college girl to a woman. Some of that, she knew, was simply the natural result of reaching her early twenties. Some, she suspected, came from heartbreak. Though she'd reached out to Jenny when she'd learned of her shattered romance, she'd been rebuffed, turned away with the obvious lie that Jenny was doing just fine, no motherly comfort needed.

This morning there was no mistaking Jenny's reluctance as she crossed the parking lot. She dragged her feet like a toddler heading for a shot at the doctor's office. Jake leaned down, murmured something in her ear, then all but shoved her toward the door. Connie flung it open, half-afraid that Jenny would turn tail and leave before they'd said a word to each other.

"Hi, sweetheart," she said, tears stinging her eyes. "Welcome home." She lifted her arms, then let them drop back to her side, when Jenny remained right where she was.

"Hi, Mom. You look great," Jenny said, her tone stilted, her gaze directed everywhere but at Connie.

"You look fantastic," Connie said, hating the awkwardness of the moment. She stepped aside and let Jake by. Jenny followed reluctantly behind him.

"I brought coffee," Jake said, stepping into the silence that fell. He handed out disposable cups from Sally's, along with a bag of raspberry and chocolate croissants meant to smooth over any tension in the reunion, then headed right back to the door. "Gotta run. I'm on a job this morning."

"Hey, wait," Jenny protested, looking panicky. "How am I supposed to get back into town? Bree and I have a meeting this morning. We have a lot of work to do if this play's going to be ready for Christmas week. I need to hitch a ride back with you."

"I don't think so," Jake said. "Your mom can take you whenever you're ready." He walked out and let the door slam behind him.

Jenny turned to Connie then, and gave her a hesitant smile. "Not exactly subtle, is he?"

Connie grinned at the massive understatement.

"He never was. Frankly, right this second, I'm grateful for that." She studied her daughter's face. "I can see, though, that you're not."

Jenny was silent for so long that Connie thought maybe Jake's efforts had been wasted. She sighed.

"I can take you to your meeting now, if that's what you want," she offered.

Jenny flinched. "It's okay. I have a little time," she admitted. "Bree wasn't even dressed when we left the house. She was still groaning about being up at all."

Connie smiled. "It's a wonder she and Jake ever see each other. He's always been a morning person, and she's such a night owl."

"But they make it work," Jenny said. "I can see how happy they are. And they both dote on Emily Rose." She smiled. "She's very precocious. If Uncle Jake thought I was a handful as a teenager, he's really going to be in for it when Emily Rose hits her teens."

"We've all told him that," Connie said, laughing. "He swears it won't be a problem, because he intends to lock her in her room and nail the windows shut for good measure."

"Which only means she'll grow up to excel at carpentry or lock picking," Jenny said, then predicted, "She will get out."

"No question about it," Connie agreed. She held her daughter's gaze. "I've missed you, baby."

At first she thought Jenny wasn't going to respond, but then she said in a voice barely above a whisper, "I've missed you, too."

This time when Connie opened her arms, Jenny flew into them. After too many years of strained conversations and deafening silences, Connie's world was finally right again. She wasn't going to delude herself that everything between them was fixed. It took time to heal old wounds, but this moment with her firstborn back in her arms was a start.

For an hour as Jenny and her mother drank coffee and ate the croissants her uncle had brought along, it felt a little bit like old times. Jenny told her about her life in Nashville, the people she'd met and worked with, all the while carefully avoiding anything too personal. Caleb's name never came up. Nor did her mother ask if there was anyone special in her life. It was as if there were an unspoken agreement to keep this first real conversation in such a long time light and superficial. In a way it felt more like catching up with an old acquaintance than the kind of mother-daughter talks she recalled. That saddened her.

Still it went well until her mom brought up Thomas.

"We're so anxious to have you see the house," Connie said with undisguised excitement. "Matthew designed it and Mick's crew built it. There's a view of the bay from your room. I've put all your things in there, but I thought maybe you'd like to redecorate it while you're here. We could go shopping, pick out paint and curtains, a new bedspread."

Jenny frowned. "Mom, I'm staying with Bree and Jake. I thought you understood that."

"I know that was the plan, but I'd hoped maybe, now that we've talked, you'd want to come home, at least for a while. Thomas is so anxious to get to know you better. And your little brother is over the moon that you're back. He thinks it's very cool having a big sister."

Jenny shook her head. "I can't," she said. "Not yet."

She hated the unmistakable sorrow her response put into her mother's eyes. "I'm sorry. I just wouldn't be comfortable there."

"Why not?" Connie pressed. "It's your home."

Jenny shook her head. "Grandma's house where I grew up, where you and I lived when it was just the two of us—that was home. I imagine you sold it, though," she said, unable to keep a note of bitterness out of her voice.

"No, I kept it," her mother said softly. "Jake's kept up the yard. Thomas has had Mick come in and make a few repairs and updates. He had it painted." She held Jenny's gaze. "He thought, we both did, that you might like to have it someday if you ever came back here to live."

Jenny's heart seemed to go still at the enormity of the gesture. "You saved Grandma's house for me?" she whispered, incredulous. "Even though you knew I might never come back here?"

"I always hoped you would," her mother said simply. "Maybe not to live, but it's a great town for vacations." She shrugged, looking embarrassed. "And Chesapeake Shores is home. At least I hope you'll always think of it that way. I hope you'll remember how much you once loved it here."

"Jake and Bree never said a word," she said, amazed. "And just now, until I mentioned it, you were pushing for me to stay with you."

"Bree and Jake knew I wanted it to be a surprise. Plus, I guess I was hoping to maybe have you under my roof for just a little bit before you went off to your own place. If you want the keys now, though, you can have them. I brought them with me this morning."

"Mom, I honestly don't know what to say," Jenny

said, filled with a mix of gratitude and dismay that she'd thought her mother didn't understand how she felt about that old house. She didn't even want to think about what it meant that Thomas had understood as well. That he had shown such kindness to her, despite how aloof she'd remained, gave her a rare bit of insight into why her mom had fallen for him so hard.

Her mother's smile was tinged with sorrow. "I take it you want the keys."

"Absolutely," she said at once. Not only was that house the only home she remembered, it would provide a refuge as she tried to figure out how to fit in with this new and overwhelming family.

Her mother fished in her purse and came up with a set of keys on a Chesapeake Shores souvenir key ring. She pressed them into Jenny's hand, then enfolded it in her own. "We'll transfer the deed into your name while you're here, if you decide you want to keep it. Connor can take care of the paperwork."

"Can we go see it now?" Jenny asked, unable to contain her excitement, even though she could see that her reaction was hurting her mom. Connie might have made this magnanimous gesture, but it was clear she'd hoped Jenny wouldn't want to take advantage of it so quickly. Though she hid her disappointment reasonably well, Jenny could see through her act.

Because she didn't want to deal with all the undercurrents, she forced a smile. "I rode by yesterday and saw that it looked like it had a new coat of paint. I was glad to see that someone was taking good care of it."

"Then you can thank Thomas and your uncle for that when you see them." Connie hesitated. "Will you at least think about coming to dinner at the new house tonight, so you can do that? I'll make spaghetti or a pot roast, whatever you want, though I think pot roast is probably on the menu at Mick's for Sunday dinner."

Jenny desperately wanted to put off her first encounter with her new stepfather until Sunday when they'd at least be surrounded by a crowd of O'Briens, but maybe this would be better. There'd be no watchful gazes, no people ready to jump in to defend Thomas from any cutting remark she might make. Not that she would do such a thing intentionally. They'd both walked on eggshells whenever they were together for her mother's sake. It would almost have been better if they'd blurted out whatever was on their minds and then dealt with the fallout.

"What time?" she asked her mother eventually.

The smile that spread across her mother's face was worth any discomfort the evening was likely to bring, Jenny concluded, glad that she'd said yes. Now she just had to make a real effort to open her heart to the man who'd given her mom the bright future she'd never dared to envision.

"How about seven? Thomas is usually home from Annapolis by then. Now that he has Kevin on board, Thomas runs the foundation from home a lot of the time. Today just happened to be one of the days he needed to go into the office for meetings."

"Has Mick finally accepted the fact that one of his sons is working for Thomas?" Jenny inquired curiously. "I know he hated it when Kevin first said that's what he wanted to do, rather than working with Mick or doing something else right here in Chesapeake Shores."

"Oh, Mick blustered for a few months, but he's admitted more than once that he's proud of the work both of them are doing to preserve the bay."

"And he didn't choke on the words?" Jenny asked incredulously.

"No. Mick's mellowed now that he's back with Megan and mostly retired. You'll see."

Jenny found it hard to imagine that the hard-driving man she'd known had eased into retirement that readily. "I'll bet he's still in his office poking around whenever he can."

Connie laughed. "Matthew can attest to that. He says his uncle drives them all crazy. He still wants status reports on every development project they have going around the country."

"His name is on the company," Jenny said, understanding that sort of pride of ownership. She often found it painful to relinquish control of her songs once she'd sold the rights. One of the great things about collaborating with Caleb had been his willingness to let her hang around through the recording sessions. He'd claimed to appreciate the occasional insights she'd dared to offer about phrasing or holding a note for emphasis.

"Your uncle's the same way about this place," Connie acknowledged. "Jake put me in charge of operations and I know he trusts me to get the job done, but he does have his moments when he tries to micromanage every detail."

"Will you ask him and Bree to come to dinner tonight, too?" she said, needing the reassurance of familiar faces. "I'll want to thank him for what he's done to the house."

"Anything you want," Connie agreed readily. "If that will make you more comfortable, I'll see to it they're there. With Sean and Emily Rose around, the adults may not get a word in edgewise. Maybe that's for the best for now."

"Thanks." She knew it wouldn't completely quiet her nerves, but it would be comforting.

Connie gave her a knowing look. "It's going to be okay, sweetie. I promise. We're family. You've known Thomas most of your life."

But he'd only been her stepfather for a few years, most of them in her absence. That was a huge adjustment to make when she thought about him and one she had yet to fully accept. Clearly, though, the time had come to make a real effort.

Bree tucked her cell phone back into her pocket and regarded Jenny curiously. "Dinner at your mom's tonight?"

Jenny nodded. "I couldn't say no. It would have been like kicking a puppy or something, especially after she told me about renovating our old house and keeping it for me."

Bree's eyes lit up. "She finally told you about that? Keeping quiet when you and I have talked these past few weeks has been killing me. Have you seen it?"

"We walked through on the way over here. The renovations are amazing. It's a lot more than a fresh coat of paint, which was what I'd been expecting. They even put in a whole new kitchen with granite countertops and stainless-steel appliances. And the bathrooms are straight out of a design magazine."

"Isn't the whole place amazing?" Bree said. "Dad thought of every detail. There are advantages to having a famous architectural genius in the family."

"I'll say. He even managed to expand the master bath and put in a huge walk-in shower, plus a Jacuzzi. When I look at it, it's hard to remember how tiny the old one used to be. I can hardly wait to climb into that tub with a glass of wine and soak till I shrivel up like a prune."

"It's big enough for two," Bree commented. "Jake and I tested it."

Jenny laughed. "Of course you did."

"Well, I needed him to see how essential it was to have one put into our house."

"The experiment paid off?"

"Oh, yeah," Bree said, her cheeks turning pink. "Just so you know, we raced home to our own bed. That fancy king-size bed in your place hasn't been slept in."

"Good to know," Jenny replied, amused by their sense of decorum. "Now, can we focus on these lyrics? What do you think of what I've written so far?"

"They're amazing," Bree said enthusiastically. "They capture the tone of the play and the whole holiday spirit in exactly the right way. I can't wait for the cast to hear them. The professionals will be here next week. I've already been doing readings with the locals since it takes them a little longer to nail down their lines. Think you can have these songs polished up by Monday? That'll give us three full weeks of rehearsals. We open three days before Christmas and run through New Year's Eve. No shows on Christmas Eve or Christmas day, though."

"Even so, that's a lot of performances," Jenny said, surprised. "You can fill the theater that many nights?"

"And two Saturday matinees," Bree confirmed. "We're virtually sold out. We have a lot more season ticket holders than I ever imagined and the Christmas play always draws from the entire region. People are anxious for a holiday event the whole family can enjoy at a reasonable price."

"Bree, that's fantastic! Congratulations!" she said, genuinely thrilled for her.

Bree grinned. "I have to say when Jake and I first talked about my opening a theater here, I wasn't a believer. I wasn't convinced it would last a year. Yet here we are in year five. We've even gotten some great reviews from critics in Washington and Baltimore, too."

"Okay, I know you're not one to rest on your laurels. What's next?"

"I want to write an original play with Broadway or at least off-Broadway potential," Bree said at once, then grinned. "When I dream, I dream big."

"Nothing wrong with that," Jenny said. "And that's not exactly a new dream. You've been working toward it your entire career. You deserve whatever success comes your way."

"Thanks." Bree glanced at her watch. "I need to get onstage and start running lines with the cast. You're okay here in the rehearsal hall?"

"I have my guitar and some paper. That's all I need," Jenny confirmed. "Go create magic."

Bree laughed. "You do the same."

Jenny thought of all the times when she'd struggled to find the perfect word or the perfect note. And it still thrilled her when she heard one of her songs on the radio. Now *that,* she thought with a smile on her lips, truly was magic.

4

"I always knew you were going to be a big-time song-writer," Dillon Johnson said, stepping into the rehearsal hall just as Jenny set aside her guitar. "That was incredible."

A smile spread across Jenny's face at the sight of her first real boyfriend. He was taller now and had filled out his lanky frame. The boy she'd last seen years ago was now a man, and a good-looking one at that.

"Dillon! Where'd you come from?" she said, jumping up to give him a hug. "And look at you, wearing a suit and tie and all grown up. How'd that happen?"

He laughed. "Time passes, at least for most of us mortals. You, however, look exactly the same. Still beautiful."

Jenny doubted that. It had been hours since she'd run a comb through her hair, and her lipstick no doubt was history. She'd chosen her most comfortable pair of jeans and her warmest sweater this morning, but neither was exactly fashionable.

She had a real superstitious streak about that sweater, though. She'd worn it when she'd written her first big hit, scribbling lyrics onto scraps of paper late into a cold, snowy night in Nashville. For every song thereafter, she'd made it a point to pull on the same sweater when she'd first started writing down ideas and words. This morning she'd wanted to bring that same luck to everything she wrote for Bree's holiday production.

"Liar," she teased. "But thank you for the compliment just the same. What brings you by?"

"Ethel mentioned that you were in town—"

"Of course she did," Jenny said, surprised there hadn't been a banner announcing her arrival on Main Street.

"She does like to be the bearer of good tidings," Dillon said. "Anyway, I had a few minutes between appointments. You probably heard I'm working with my dad now in his insurance business."

"I did hear that," Jenny confirmed. "I have to say I was surprised."

His expression turned sheepish. "You mean because I always swore I'd rather die than sell insurance?"

"You were pretty emphatic about it," she recalled.

"When I got out of school, there weren't a lot of jobs around. I needed to work."

"That's right. You're married and the father of a little girl," Jenny said. Bree had hesitantly passed on that information, clearly uncertain how Jenny would feel about the news. She'd had a momentary twinge of regret, but that was all.

"Mostly true," he said, a shadow passing over his face. "Deanna moved out and filed for divorce a few months ago. She said she was tired of competing with my past."

Jenny frowned at that. "Meaning?"

"You, of course. She said she could tell that every time one of your songs came on the radio, I started thinking about what might have been. It probably didn't help that they were all downloaded onto my iPod, too."

Shocked, Jenny sat back down, picked up her guitar and held it protectively in front of her, her fingers idly strumming as she bought time to consider what he'd said.

"But, Dillon, surely that wasn't true," she responded eventually, hoping his wife had been wrong. "You and I called it quits when we left for college. That was a long time ago. We hadn't even been in touch."

"I told her that." He shrugged. "She didn't believe it, especially after we moved to town and everyone she met mentioned our history. I don't think they did it to be cruel. It's just that people in Chesapeake Shores have long memories, and you've become a celebrity in the music world. Everyone in town is so proud of knowing you."

Jenny shied away from the description. "A celebrity? Hardly. Most people have no idea who wrote the songs. The focus is on the artist who performs them."

"Unless the writer is romantically involved with the performer, I imagine," he suggested quietly.

Jenny sighed. He was right about that. Because of her relationship with Caleb, she'd been in the public eye more than most songwriters who weren't performers themselves. "I'm really sorry."

"Not your fault. And, to be honest, maybe Deanna was right. Maybe you never entirely get over your first love."

Jenny had. She'd moved on with Caleb and, in the rare moments when she allowed herself to be completely truthful, she knew that was the relationship that still lingered in her heart. Bree had been right about that. She was determined, though, not to listen to that traitorous bit of nostalgia. She'd left Caleb in the past. He needed to stay there.

"What about your little girl, though?" she asked, thinking of her own parents' divorce, her father's disappearance from their lives and the scars that had left. "Don't you owe it to her to try harder?"

Dillon seemed taken aback that she would expect that. "Lori's okay," he insisted, his tone defensive. "She's only two. She knows she has two homes, one with Mommy and another one with Daddy. They're not far away. They're living in Annapolis."

Jenny started to argue, then waved off what she'd been about to say. "Never mind. It's not my place."

Dillon sat down beside her, then nudged her with an elbow. "That never stopped you before. Say what's on your mind."

"Just that I remember what it was like when my dad left. I'm not sure I ever got over it."

He frowned at that. "That was completely different. He moved to another state. You never saw him. You barely even heard from him. And then you found out he'd never wanted kids in the first place."

"That was a kick in the pants, all right," Jenny acknowledged. "From then on I figured it was all my fault that he'd left, that if my mom had never gotten pregnant with me, they'd have stayed married."

"You knew better, though," Dillon reminded her. "Your mom wouldn't have traded having you for anything, not even keeping your dad around. I heard her say so myself."

"Sure, that's what she always said. Still, it's hard not to wonder. She must have been in love with him at the beginning."

"I'm sure she was, but didn't she tell you that they'd fought over having children, that he knew how important it was to her but refused to even consider it? Despite how he felt, she never even gave a moment's thought to having you when she found out she'd gotten pregnant. There were choices she could have made." He met her gaze. "Personally I think it's one of those things people take for granted when they're dating, assuming they're on the same page about everything. When they discover otherwise, it changes how they feel."

"I suppose," Jenny conceded.

"Well, in my case, I'm right here. Lori will never have to wonder the way you have. She'll always know how much I wanted her and love her."

"Maybe it is different," Jenny agreed. "Maybe I just feel a little guilty."

"What on earth do you have to feel guilty about?"

"I don't like thinking I might have had even a tiny part in your breakup with Lori's mom."

Dillon shook his head. "Deanna and I shouldn't have been together in the first place. I knew better, but from the minute you and I split up, I was a little bit lost. I know we agreed it was for the best, that we were way too young to be serious, that it was crazy to try to maintain a relationship when we were at different schools, that we should be open to new people." He gave her a rueful look. "Turned out I wasn't all that eager for new experiences."

Jenny regarded him with regret. "I'm sorry."

"Yeah, me, too." He stared straight ahead, then said, "I heard you broke up with Caleb Green."

Jenny felt herself smiling at his attempt to make the comment appear casual. "Gee, you mean you saw the tabloid headlines at the supermarket and the clips all over the entertainment shows when the whole thing blew up after a photographer caught him with his hands all over another woman?"

"Something like that," he said with a grin that faded quickly. He regarded her soberly. "That must have been hard. You doing okay?"

"I'm getting there," she said, convinced if she said it often enough it would be true. Maybe if people stopped mentioning Caleb in those hushed, worried tones, she would be fine.

"So, want to have dinner sometime while you're in town?" Dillon asked.

She gave him a startled look, thinking that even something as simple as having dinner with an old friend had complication written all over it under these circumstances.

"Oh, Dillon, I don't know if that's such a good idea," she protested. "Wouldn't it just confirm what Deanna thought?"

"It's a little too late to be worrying about that," he commented. "Come on, just two old friends catching up. What's the harm in that?"

"Maybe lunch sometime," she countered, thinking that would be easier somehow, not as subject to misinterpretation by the meddling folks in Chesapeake Shores. Of course, tongues were going to wag no matter when they were seen together. Hadn't he just said that no one in town had forgotten their history?

"Whatever you want," he said eagerly, then stood up. He hesitated, then dropped a quick kiss on her forehead. "It's real good to see you again, Jenny. I'll be in touch about that lunch."

"Bye," she whispered, watching him go and wondering why she no longer felt even the tiniest whisper of longing.

She knew the answer, of course: Caleb. That didn't mean she had to like it.

Caleb had been just outside the door when he'd seen the man walk into the rehearsal hall to join Jenny. He wasn't ashamed to admit that he'd eavesdropped on their conversation, at least enough to know that he was an old flame.

That had ignited a flash of jealousy so powerful he'd finally stepped away. He knew he couldn't walk into that room with a chip on his shoulder and an angry outburst on the tip of his tongue. Jenny didn't owe him a blessed thing anymore. He had to keep reminding himself of that. When he saw her, it had to be with hat in hand.

After the man left, he waited a suitable length of time before stepping into the rehearsal hall. By then, Jenny was sitting in a chair, strumming her guitar lightly, fine-tuning the lyrics to a Christmas song of some kind. Something for the play, no doubt.

He listened to the refrain a couple of times, then joined in, his voice blending with hers in perfect harmony. Her gaze shot up then and for an instant, he was sure he saw naked longing in her eyes right before her expression shut down. Her words, when she spoke, were cold enough to make him shiver.

"You're not welcome here," she said flatly.

He took another step into the room just the same. "I didn't expect to be," he said, holding her gaze.

"Then why come?"

"I have a whole list of reasons, beginning with needing to tell you how sorry I am about everything that happened," he said quietly. He gave her a long look, surprised that she'd seemed so startled to see him. "You weren't expecting me?"

"Expecting you? Hardly. I never thought you'd have the audacity to show your face around this town."

"I thought maybe Margo would have warned you," he admitted.

Her eyes widened at that. "You spoke to Margo?"

"Yep. Just so you know, she wasn't one bit happy about my coming here. That's why I was so sure she would have been on the phone to you two seconds after she'd hung up on me."

Jenny closed her eyes. "She probably was," she admitted with a sigh. "I had a voice mail from her, but I tossed my cell phone into a drawer without listening to it. I figured it was about work and I could deal with whatever was on her mind once I got back to Nashville."

"You always did have a habit of tuning out the world when you were caught up in a new project," he commented.

"Obviously a habit I need to overcome," she said wryly.

"It worked out better for me that you haven't made that change just yet." He regarded her curiously. "No call from Jess O'Brien, either?"

Her jaw dropped. "You've seen Jess? Why?"

"She let me stay at the inn last night. Just so you

know, she wasn't very happy about it, either, but she didn't have it in her to turn me away."

"Unfortunately, most women find it impossible to resist you," she said with a touch of bitterness. "I found that out the hard way."

Caleb winced at the direct hit. "I'm sorry. I know my apology is late in coming, but I never meant to hurt you. I wasn't thinking straight back then. You know that as well as anyone. You told me often enough to get some help with the drinking. Unfortunately, for way too long, I didn't think I needed help. I figured I'd earned the chance to unwind after a concert. Then I needed a little something to relax before going onstage. Pretty soon I had a rock-solid excuse, or so I thought, for every drink I took."

She heard him out, but nothing in her expression softened even a tiny bit. "Is that part of the program?" she asked. "You're supposed to acknowledge your mistakes, make amends? Fine. You've apologized. You can leave now."

Instead, he pulled over a chair and sat next to her. "I said I had a list of reasons for being here. That's just the number-one item on it. The rest could take a while."

"That list couldn't possibly be long enough to cover everything you'd have to say to make me not hate the sight of you," she declared, her expression unyielding.

So, he thought, this was going to be a little tougher than he'd imagined. He'd always known she had a stubborn streak, but this was the first time she'd directed it at him. He'd always been able to coax a smile from her, to charm her back into his bed, no matter how furious she'd been. He'd known how to deal with the heat of her anger, how to redirect it into passion. This chilly distance, though, was new.

"I deserve that," he conceded.

"That and a lot more," she said with candor.

"Also true," he said. "No excuses, Jenny. I'm not even going to try blaming my mistakes on the alcohol. The reality is I screwed up big-time. I know I hurt you and I know you didn't do a thing to deserve it. We were friends a long time before we were lovers. I'd like to find a way to make things right between us, to get that friendship back again."

She regarded him with an incredulous expression. "Right? What on earth does that mean? You cheated on me. You chose booze over me. You drowned your career in a bottle and let your entire band down. How are you going to make any of that right?"

Caleb winced at the fury in her voice. "I don't know," he said honestly, looking into her eyes. "I guess only time will tell if I can."

"You're fresh out of time with me," she said flatly.

But even though her voice was steady, her words unyielding, Caleb found a shred of hope when he looked into her eyes. There, he was almost certain, he saw regret. He was going to use that, as fragile a thread as it might be, to bind them together once again. Heaven knew there was nothing more important in his life right now. And in that instant the song he'd come to plead for became secondary to what he really wanted: Jenny.

As hard as she tried, Jenny was pretty sure she hadn't been able to draw in a single deep breath since she'd looked up and straight into Caleb's eyes. She kept trying to remember that Dillon had been in the room only a moment before, that he was the kind of guy who never would have betrayed her, but it wasn't working.

She'd had to cling to her anger for dear life to keep from throwing herself straight into Caleb's arms. Worse, he was saying all the right words, taking responsibility, apologizing with no excuses, asking for nothing, not even forgiveness, if she was reading him correctly.

But when was the last time she'd read him correctly? He'd sworn he loved her—and she'd believed him—just days before those awful pictures had appeared in the tabloids. The irony had been that he'd sworn he had no memory of the incident or the woman. That had made it worse, somehow.

She glanced over and noted that he was waiting patiently beside her, not so much as a muscle twitching to indicate any nervousness. That infuriated her all over again. Shouldn't he be at least a little anxious? Instead, she was the one whose nerves were shot, who couldn't seem to catch her breath.

She forced herself to draw in a deep, calming breath, then said quietly, "You need to leave, Caleb. You've said what you came to say or at least the only part that matters. I've heard you. Now go."

He glanced sideways at her. "I told you, Jen. I'm just getting started."

"There's nothing more I want to hear," she said, feeling a little desperate to make him leave—the room, the inn, the town—before she did something insane and let him get to her.

He smiled at that. "But there's so much more I need to say. You can put in earplugs for all I care, but I'm not leaving till I've said my piece."

"Everything always has to be on your terms, doesn't it?"

He only lifted a brow at that. "Seriously, you did not just say that," he said. "The entire time we were together, you had me twisted around your little finger. Do you have any idea how much grief I took from the band over that? They thought it was pitiful how much I loved you."

"Until you didn't," she said wearily.

He shifted until he faced her, then tucked a finger under her chin when she would have looked away. "I never stopped loving you," he said softly, but emphatically. "Never! If you believe nothing else I say, believe that."

Even as the words warmed her stupid heart, Jenny regarded him with shock. "Putting your hands all over some other woman in public is how you show me your undying love?"

"That was a mistake, one I'll regret till the day I die. I don't know what I was thinking."

"You weren't thinking," she accused. "Wasn't that the real problem?"

He nodded. "That was the real problem," he confirmed.

"Caleb, I can't do this. I'm here to do a job. I have family issues to resolve. I just can't add you into the mix It's too much. Please, go back to Nashville or wherever you're calling home these days."

His look was long and steady, maybe even tinged with regret. "I can't do that."

"Why?" she asked in frustration. "We'll get together when I get back to Nashville. We can have that long talk then." They'd have it, she thought, when hell froze over.

Caleb chuckled. "I know better. Once you're back in Nashville, you'll surround yourself with an entire army of people whose sole purpose will be to keep me away from you."

Sadly, he knew her too well. That was exactly what she'd had in mind.

"So, how do you see this playing out?" she asked.

"We could start with dinner tonight," he suggested. "What's that restaurant you used to talk about, the one on the water? Brandon's? Brady's?"

"Brady's," she replied, surprised he'd remembered. "Sorry. I have dinner plans with family."

"Breakfast tomorrow at the inn," he countered.

Though Jenny was thankful he hadn't suggested that he be invited to join her family tonight, breakfast at the inn was a terrible idea, too. If the two of them were spotted at a cozy table in the inn's dining room first thing in the morning, who knew what people would make of that. There might not be a lot of paparazzi in Chesapeake Shores, but that was the sort of news that could have the tabloid stalkers here in a heartbeat.

"I don't think so," she responded flatly.

"Then you tell me," he said.

"Nashville," she repeated, though without much hope that he'd agree to postpone this conversation he was so dead-set on having.

"Try again."

Jenny caved in. He clearly wasn't going away anytime soon, at least not without this chat that had brought him to town. "Lunch here tomorrow," she said eventually. "Have Jess's chef at the inn pack up something or stop at the pizza place up the street. I don't care."

"In other words, you don't want to be seen in public with me," he said, clearly amused. "Don't you think if people around town recognize me, they're going to put two and two together anyway? Why else would I be here, if not to see you? Or were you thinking I should stay in my room and avoid all contact with the public?"

"I suppose that would be asking too much," she said, unable to keep a wistful note from her voice.

"Yes, it would. As long as I'm here, I want to see the town you were always talking about. I'd like to meet your family, too."

She regarded him with dismay. "Why? They don't like you any more than I do right now." Or at least they surely wouldn't if she made her case to them.

"Exactly why I'd like the chance to change their minds. I made a mistake, Jenny. A terrible one, but I'm not evil incarnate."

She knew that all too well, at least about him not being evil. That was the real problem, wasn't it? If he stuck around here long enough, she might start to remember all his good qualities—his sensitivity, his kindness, his humor and, okay, the way he'd once made her toes curl with little more than a look.

And that, she thought with an edge of desperation, simply couldn't happen.

"If I agree to this talk tomorrow, you have to promise that you'll leave," she told him.

He shook his head. "I'm not going to lie to you, Jenny. Leaving's unlikely."

"But why? You always claimed to feel claustrophobic in small towns like this. You said they reminded you of all the tiny bars and low-rent honky-tonks you played when you were scrambling to make it."

He shrugged. "Chesapeake Shores doesn't feel that way," he claimed, then met her gaze. "Maybe that's because you're here and this town means something to you."

"Stop it!" she ordered. "Stop trying to charm me or seduce me or whatever it is you're trying to do."

He laughed. "It would only upset you if it were working." He stood up, dropped a quick kiss on her forehead, then headed for the door. "See you tomorrow. I'll be here at noon."

Jenny watched him leave, her pulse racing in a way that was all too familiar. She tried blaming it on annoyance, but she knew better. He'd gotten to her, all right. Blast the man!

Regretting that she didn't have her cell phone with her, she went in search of Bree and borrowed hers. Without thinking of the possible consequences of being overheard, she found the number for Jess's private line at the inn and hit speed dial.

"You let Caleb stay at the inn?" she said to Jess without preamble.

"He showed up in the middle of the night," Jess confirmed. "It was freezing outside. What was I supposed to do?"

"Tell him to go jump in the bay," Jenny suggested. "That might have solved a lot of problems."

Jess started to laugh, then stopped herself. "You know you wouldn't have wanted him freezing to death on your conscience. I certainly wouldn't have wanted it on mine. However, if you want me to kick him out today, I will. Something tells me, though, he'll just find someplace to stay outside of town. I don't think he's going far until he's accomplished whatever he came here to do."

Jenny sighed. "Yeah, that was my impression, too."

"So, does he go or stay?"

"One more night," Jenny said reluctantly.

"I'll hold the room for him indefinitely," Jess said. "I know you didn't ask for my opinion, but maybe you should give him a chance to explain what happened. Maybe that will at least give you closure if you decide it's not going to work out."

"It's not going to work out," Jenny said emphatically. She simply would not allow herself to take that kind of risk with her heart again, not with a man who'd already proven he couldn't be trusted.

5

No sooner had she handed Bree's cell phone back to her than Jenny realized Bree had overheard every word of her conversation with Jess. It was clear she had a million questions on the tip of her tongue.

"Caleb's here? In Chesapeake Shores? And he was here to see you a few minutes ago?" Bree said, her expression stunned. "Why? No, scratch that. We all know why. He's here to win you back. How do you feel about that?"

"How do you think I feel?" Jenny asked. "I want him gone. But he says he's not going and Jess says he's booked himself into the Inn at Eagle Point and that he seems to be here for the long haul unless I tell her I want him gone. She doesn't think he'll leave the area even if she does kick him out. Unfortunately, I think she may be right. When we talked just now, he seemed pretty determined to stick around. He wants to prove he's changed."

"Oh, my," Bree said.

Jenny gave her a wry look. "Oh, my, indeed."

Bree's expression turned thoughtful, usually a sign

of her creative mind kicking into high gear. Then she got a glint in her eyes that Jenny didn't like one bit.

"I wonder," Bree began, her tone a disturbing combination of nerves, caution and excitement as she studied Jenny, clearly watching closely for her reaction. "I mean, if Caleb is determined to stay, of course, I wonder if maybe he'd—"

Jenny figured out exactly where Bree was heading and cut her off before she could overcome that very bad case of nerves and complete the sentence.

"Oh, no," Jenny declared forcefully. "Bree O'Brien Collins, you are not getting Caleb Green involved with this Christmas play. Please tell me that idea did not cross your mind for one single second."

"But—"

Jenny resorted to the only threat she thought might work. "No way, not if you expect me to write the songs," she warned her. "Or to spend the holidays here. Or ever to speak to you again, for that matter."

"Come on, Jenny," Bree cajoled. "Just think about it. If Caleb would agree to sing just one or two songs, imagine the publicity we'd get. I could get this show seen by producers in New York. It could become a staple of the Broadway Christmas season. You know they've been trotting out *White Christmas* the past few years. How dated is that?"

If Jenny hadn't already steeled herself against any and all arguments, she was forced to admit that Bree's enthusiasm might be a little contagious. Broadway would definitely be a new world for both of them to conquer. But she couldn't say yes. She just couldn't, not and have a moment's peace of mind. The few minutes she'd spent with Caleb earlier had proven just how sus-

ceptible she still was to him. Being forced to see him
day after day would ruin the tiny bit of hard-won se-
renity she'd achieved.

"*White Christmas* is a classic," Jenny argued hurriedly, determined to blast holes in Bree's scheme. "It
deserves to be revived. It puts people into the holiday
spirit. They leave the theater humming."

"They'll leave this theater humming your songs,"
Bree countered.

"Nothing against this play of yours, but even if I
knock these lyrics out of the park, it's not the same
thing."

Bree lifted a brow. "Did you just insult my play?"

Jenny winced. Inadvertently, that was exactly what
she'd done. "I didn't mean to. I was talking about my
music as much as the play. *White Christmas* summons
up memories of Bing Crosby and songs by Irving Ber-
lin. It's a holiday tradition, like *Miracle on 34th Street*
or *It's a Wonderful Life.*"

"Old traditions were new once," Bree argued. "And
if one of the best lyricists in country music—that's
you—were to team up with one of the biggest country talents—Caleb, especially if he's making his big
comeback—this show would be the talk of Broadway
next season. Backers would be lining up to produce it.
It would be a guaranteed sellout." Then, with a decid-
edly wistful expression that couldn't be faked for effect,
she added, "And I'd finally have my shot on Broadway."

Jenny sighed heavily. The woman did not play fair.
Still, she had to resist.

"I hate to burst your bubble, Bree, but Caleb's not
exactly reliable. Even if he were to say yes to this crazy
idea, there's a very good chance he'll vanish before

opening night. Then where would you be? And if the man can't be trusted for a few weeks now, who knows where he'll be a year from now. You'd have a show with an understudy and crowds demanding their money back. Ask his managers about the kind of fallout there was when he bailed on his last tour after showing up late or not at all for three concerts in a row."

Bree, the perennial optimist, clearly wasn't deterred. "But you said he swears he's turned over a new leaf."

"That doesn't mean I believe it," Jenny said. "You shouldn't either, especially for something that's this important to you."

Bree gave her a knowing look. "Okay, I hear you," she said solemnly. "And if you tell me not to talk to him, I won't."

"Haven't I just said that half a dozen different ways?" Jenny asked in frustration. "You're as bad as Jess, forcing me to be the bad guy. Can't you just make the decision yourself because you know I'm right?"

"Nope," Bree said. "There's more at stake here than the play and you know it. I want to hear you flat-out tell me to send him away, that you don't want him here. If that's what you really, really want, I'll back you up and drop this."

Jenny opened her mouth, sure that the dismissive words would come easily, but for the second time in just a few short minutes she couldn't seem to force them out. Either she was completely nuts, or Caleb had somehow managed to bewitch her in the fifteen minutes they'd been in the same room earlier.

"Talk to him," she bit out reluctantly. "If he says yes—and I can't imagine why he would want to be in some little local Christmas show, rather than performing a concert in some huge amphitheater—I'll figure out how to work with him." Her expression turned sly. "In fact, I might insist that you be our go-between. I wonder what Jake would think about that."

"Jake would want me to do whatever it takes to have the success I want," Bree declared confidently.

Jenny had her doubts, but she caved. "Okay, then. I guess you're talking to Caleb," Jenny said, fighting the desire to sigh heavily.

To her dismay, the instant she agreed to letting Caleb stay there was no mistaking the immediate flutter of anticipation that stirred in her stomach. Blast love! It wasn't supposed to outlast heartbreak.

A few hours after his visit to Jenny, Caleb sat in the lounge at the inn and listened to Bree O'Brien's proposition with a sense of wonder. She was offering him the chance to work with Jenny, giving him the perfect excuse to stick around Chesapeake Shores. And she was doing it with Jenny's blessing, at least he assumed she was. Given his own encounter with Jenny, this woman had to have some powerful mojo going for her.

"Jenny's okay with this?" he asked, just to be sure.

"She has reservations," Bree admitted. "But she's also smart enough to see the potential of the two of you collaborating again."

"Really?" Caleb said, finding that hard to believe. She hadn't even wanted to be in the same room with him a few hours ago.

"Okay, she's going along with it for my sake," Bree conceded. "She knows having you in the production will drag producers from New York down here. I have connections, of course, but this could take my theater credentials to a whole new level. I'm convinced we could get this produced on Broadway for the holidays next season. You'd have to commit to that, though."

There was very little Caleb wouldn't agree to if it meant working with Jenny again. "Draw up a contract. I'll get my agent and manager to take a look, but it won't be a problem. I want this." He knew perfectly well they'd see what a boon this could be to kicking off his comeback.

Her eyes lit up. "Fantastic!"

"Jenny must really owe you," he said. "I'm still a little stunned that she's willing to sacrifice her own comfort to do this for you. I'm sure you're well aware that I'm not her favorite person."

"Believe me, I know. I had to do some pretty fast talking to convince her." Her expression suddenly turned fierce. "So help me, Caleb Green, if you do one single thing to hurt that girl again, especially in this town, there won't be any place on earth you can hide. The entire O'Brien clan will descend on you like a pack of vultures."

Caleb nodded, hiding another smile. Jess O'Brien had said something very similar an hour ago when she'd reluctantly agreed to let him check into the inn for an undetermined length of time during the increasingly busy holiday season which had already started picking up just since he'd arrived. He'd noticed that she seemed to take a certain amount of devious pleasure in tucking him into an out-of-the-way room with no charm and faulty heating.

"Duly noted," he told Bree as he had Jess. "I'm not here to upset Jenny. I want to make peace with her."

"Then we understand each other," Bree said, a glint of satisfaction in her eyes.

"Perfectly," he agreed. "I'm grateful for the opportunity."

She looked surprised. "You almost sound sincere."

"I am sincere," he assured her. "I know my reputation stinks these days. You're taking a chance on me. I appreciate that."

"You're grateful for the chance to sing a couple of songs in a local Christmas play?" she asked, her doubts still plain. Then understanding apparently dawned. "Or is it for the chance to spend more time with Jenny?"

"Both," Caleb responded without hesitation. "I have to start my life and my career over somewhere. Why not in Chesapeake Shores? As for the possibility of Broadway a year from now, that could be an unexpected bonus. I've always been open to new challenges."

Of course, the bigger challenge was going to be Jenny. That's the one he intended to devote himself to 1,000 percent.

Sitting in his sister's living room, Jake regarded his wife with dismay. "Let me get this straight, Bree. You encouraged that no-account scumbag Caleb Green to stay in town by asking him to perform in the Christmas play?"

Jenny recognized the sparks of anger in her uncle's eyes and saw an already tense evening at her mom's going downhill in a hurry.

"Uncle Jake, it's okay," she said quickly. "Bree and I talked about it first. If it will be good for the production and draw the kind of attention Bree's work deserves, I'm okay with this. I can make it work."

"Oh, sweetie, are you sure?" her mother asked, her frown every bit as deep as Jake's. "It seems to me as if this is just asking for trouble. Even though you swore to me you were fine, I could hear the pain in your voice after Caleb betrayed you in public the way he did."

"And I know you listened to her crying her eyes out more than once," Jake said to his wife. "This is nuts!"

Bree remained astonishingly calm in the face of their doubts. "Caleb will be making his comeback on my stage, in my play, singing Jenny's songs. Do you have any idea how much attention that will bring to this production? It's going to be a huge win-win for everybody."

"Except Jenny," Jake complained bitterly. "You need to send him away, Bree. Nothing is more important than Jenny's peace of mind."

"And I'm saying I can work with him," Jenny repeated. "Let it go, Jake. I appreciate the backup, but it's a done deal. Nobody's going to get hurt. I've taken my shots. I'm immune to Caleb's charm. Honest."

Okay, so that was a big fat lie, but she had to say something before this situation caused a huge rift between Jake and Bree. It wasn't worth that. Her mother was looking none too pleased with Bree at the moment, either. If things got out of control, the situation could put quite a damper on the holidays, with tension coming from every direction.

Bree faced both of them down. "You heard her. Jenny's a strong woman. She can handle this. If she couldn't, she would have said so. And if she had, I wouldn't have spoken to Caleb about staying. Jess wouldn't be allowing him to remain at the inn, either."

Jake's expression turned incredulous. "He's staying at the inn, too? I thought O'Briens put family above all else. What's Jess's angle? Is she hoping the presence of a big celebrity will boost reservations?"

Bree scowled at him. "The inn is already sold out for the holidays and for most of the spring and for next summer," she replied. "Jess doesn't need the attention. The man showed up on her doorstep in the middle of a freezing-cold night. She took him in."

"If the inn was sold out, where'd she put him?" Jake asked. "I don't suppose she told him to sleep in the stables."

Jenny bit back a laugh. "The inn doesn't have stables," she reminded him. "Jake, you need to settle down. I know you're just trying to protect me, but give it a rest, okay?"

He scowled at the request, but he did fall silent just in time to have Thomas walk into the room. He dropped a kiss on his wife's lips, then glanced around, his expression instantly filled with concern.

"Okay, what's the problem?" he asked.

Jenny's mom gave his hand a squeeze. "Don't worry, this isn't about you. It seems Jenny's ex, Caleb Green, has turned up in town and Bree hired him to be in the Christmas play."

Thomas nodded slowly, his expression vaguely confused. "Sounds like a smart move to me." When Connie poked him sharply in the ribs, he added, "But I gather it's not."

"Of course it's a smart move," Bree said. "Everybody's just a little freaked that Jenny won't be able to deal with working with him."

"But I am totally okay with it," Jenny said. "Mom, is dinner ready? Now that Thomas is home, maybe we should eat."

"Good idea," her mother said, jumping up eagerly. "I made pot roast." She gave Thomas an apologetic look. "I know Nell's probably making it on Sunday, but it's Jenny's favorite."

Thomas winked at Jenny. "You can never have too much pot roast, if you ask me."

Jenny managed a weak smile. "I couldn't agree more."

When Bree and Jake followed her mom toward the kitchen to help get dinner on the table, Thomas beckoned for Jenny to stay behind.

"Thank you for agreeing to this dinner, Jenny. It means the world to your mom. To me, too."

Jenny drew in a deep breath. Apologies had never come easily to her, but she knew she owed him one. With effort she could even make it sound sincere. "I'm sorry I've stayed away so long and I'm sorry for taking out all my insecurities on you. I know how happy you've made my mother. I'm grateful for that."

She finally looked him in the eye. "And I'm genuinely grateful for everything you did to renovate our old house for me. I can't tell you how much I appreciate that you understood how important that house is to me."

"It's your home," he said simply. "After so many years of living alone in a small apartment in Annapolis, I can't say I totally understood the importance of that. Then I built this place for your mom and me. It's where Sean will grow up, where our memories will be. As much as I'd hoped you'd be comfortable here, I'm aware that your memories are in your grandmother's house. You'd think I'd have gotten that before, given all the time I've spent at Mick's surrounded by the whole family. That environment is something special. Still, it took marrying your mom to make it clear to me that the house in which you build your life is the one that will always feel like home."

"This is a beautiful house," Jenny said, but couldn't help adding, "So is my grandmother's, thanks to you and Mick."

He gave her the same sly look she'd seen more than once on his brother Mick's face. "You planning to stick around long enough to spend some time there?" he asked.

"Through the holidays, for sure. Then I guess we'll see."

"But you do want to keep it?"

She nodded. "No question about that."

"That will make your mom very happy."

"Me, too. I don't think I realized how much I missed home until I drove into Chesapeake Shores yesterday."

"This town does seem to have a hold on people," Thomas said. He stood up and held out a hand. "Let's go and dig into that pot roast. Ma gave your mom the family recipe. Don't tell Ma, but I think your mother's is even better."

Jenny smiled at the biased comment. "I imagine Nell would say it's because it has that special ingredient."

Thomas looked perplexed. "Special ingredient?"

"Love, of course. Nell says that's the one thing that can't be replaced."

Thomas chuckled. "You know, I think maybe she's right."

Hours later Jenny left with Jake, Bree and an exhausted Emily Rose who'd fallen asleep right after the meal.

No sooner were they in the car than Jake started to bring up Caleb yet again. Jenny immediately silenced him.

"We're not debating that again," she said firmly.

"I'm just saying there's still time to rethink this."

"Give it a rest, Jake," Bree commanded. "I don't come to the nursery and tell you which plants to order."

"But if you did, I'd listen," he said.

"No, you wouldn't," Bree countered. "That's your domain and rightfully so. The theater is mine."

"There should not be dissension between the two of you over me and Caleb," Jenny said. "I swear if this keeps up, Jake, I'll head back to Nashville and fax my songs to Bree. Then I won't have to listen to you or deal with Caleb."

"Maybe that would be for the best," Jake said.

"Jake Collins, what would your sister say if she heard that?" Bree demanded. "We all want Jenny right here— Connie most of all. Now, behave!"

To Jenny's amusement, her uncle fell silent. She doubted that was the end of it, though. He'd probably be popping into the theater unannounced a dozen times a day to keep an eye on things. It would be a lot like old times when he hadn't trusted Jenny and Dillon out of his sight for a single second.

When they arrived at Jake and Bree's, Jake carried the still-sleeping Emily Rose to her room, leaving Jenny alone with Bree.

"I'm going to move into my house tomorrow," she told Bree.

Bree regarded her with disappointment. "Are you sure? Your mom got rid of all the old furniture. There's not much more than the new bed in there. And if you go right now, you know Jake's only going to freak out over who's sharing that bed with you."

Jenny grinned. "I'm trusting you to keep him from

sneaking over there in the middle of the night to check it out."

Bree studied her knowingly. "You planning to invite Caleb to share that bed?"

"Absolutely not," Jenny said at once, though the image that immediately came to mind had her catching her breath.

"Look, sweetie, you're a grown woman. You know your own heart better than any of the rest of us possibly could. Listen to it. If Caleb's the man for you, we'll all deal with it, even Jake."

"He's not the man for me," Jenny insisted. If determination alone were enough to make that true, she'd be a lot less anxious, though.

"What about Dillon?" Bree asked. "You haven't mentioned a word about it, but I know he stopped by to see you today. Any old sparks?"

"Not a one," Jenny said regretfully. "I wish there had been. He's exactly the kind of man I should be looking for. He's dependable and kind, and we have this great history." She smiled. "He was the first person who believed I could be a songwriter."

"I remember," Bree said. "That night Jake and I took the two of you to a concert, on the way home Dillon told Jake about your songs. He was so proud of you. You could hear it in his voice."

"Definitely my biggest booster," Jenny agreed. "We are planning to have lunch sometime while I'm here. Maybe if I spend a little time with him, I'll remember why I was so crazy about him."

"But you don't have to think about it as far as Caleb's concerned, do you?"

Jenny sighed. "Sadly, no. He walks into a room and

my brain shuts down. My libido kicks into overdrive. That can't possibly be a good thing."

Bree smiled. "It's not necessarily a bad thing, either. Jake has the same effect on me."

"But Jake isn't Caleb. He never ripped your heart out the way Caleb did mine."

Bree fell silent for a surprisingly long time. Jenny studied her sad expression. She knew there had been a breakup and some bad blood, but she'd never heard any explanations.

"Bree, he didn't, did he?"

"No, it was the other way around," Bree said. "I nearly destroyed him." She met Jenny's gaze. "In a lot of ways my betrayal was much worse than what Caleb did to you."

"How so?" Jenny frowned. "Why don't I remember any of this?"

"No one knew the details, not back then."

"What happened?"

Bree drew in a deep breath, obviously struggling with the memory. Jenny stepped in. "I'm sorry. We don't have to talk about this."

"No, it's okay. I just find it upsetting, even after all this time." She met Jenny's gaze. "The truth is that I got pregnant. I was a wreck about it, because the timing couldn't have been worse. I had this theater apprenticeship in Chicago that I really wanted. But Jake was over the moon about the baby, so I tried to push my own plans to the back burner. He started planning for a wedding."

Jenny was terrified she knew what had happened next. "You didn't have an abortion, did you?"

"No, I couldn't have done that, but I did lose the baby."

Jenny heard the pain in her voice even after all these years. "Oh, Bree, I'm so sorry."

"Me, too," Bree said softly, then sighed. "It wasn't that I miscarried our baby. That was no one's fault. What Jake blamed me for was leaving town right afterward, taking that apprenticeship. To him that said neither he nor the baby had meant a thing to me."

Jenny regarded her with dismay. "He must have been crushed."

"He was," Bree said simply. "And angry, especially when I left. Not long after that he came to Chicago and caught me with my mentor there in what he thought was a compromising situation, even though at the time there was nothing between Marty and me. That was the end for Jake."

"And that explains why he was so furious with you when you first got back to town," Jenny concluded. "My God, his attitude makes so much more sense now. I thought he was just being stubborn."

"The important thing is that he found a way to forgive me," Bree told her. "We put our relationship back together and it's stronger than ever. That's something for you to think about."

Jenny thought about second chances all the time. She'd written songs about them. She just wasn't sure she was brave enough to give Caleb the one she was pretty sure he'd come here looking for.

6

Despite Bree O'Brien's assurances that Jenny was on board with this plan for the two of them to work together again, Caleb had a hunch he didn't dare walk into the theater empty-handed. There was a good chance she might need a little more persuasion.

Jenny had never been interested in jewelry or fancy cars. He knew because he'd offered her both. She was, however, a sucker for flowers. She claimed it went back to her days helping out at Flowers on Main back in high school. She'd apparently seen firsthand the way a fragrant, simple bouquet, sent with a heartfelt apology or a loving note, could touch a woman's heart.

He'd noticed the day before that Flowers on Main was still open. What he hadn't remembered was that it belonged to Bree. She eyed him with curiosity when he walked in the door.

"Were you looking for me?" she asked. "Is there something more you need to know about the offer I made?" Alarm flitted across her face. "You haven't changed your mind already, have you? Jenny warned me you weren't reliable."

Insulted, even though he shouldn't have been, Caleb held up his hand. "Whoa! No change of heart. I need flowers, that's it."

Bree's expression immediately brightened. "For Jenny?"

"Of course."

Bree studied him so intently, he started to wonder if she was going to refuse to sell him any. He waited while she made up her mind.

"Anything in particular?" she asked eventually, making the question sound like a dare.

He laughed now that he knew what was on her mind. She wanted to know how well he really understood Jenny.

"Are you thinking I'll go the trite route and order a dozen red roses?" he asked. "I know Jenny better than that, Bree. Yellow roses are her favorite, and not long-stemmed, either. She likes tea roses, in a bouquet with baby's breath. She says that reminds her of the old-fashioned arrangements your grandmother used to make from her garden. She told me they were something of a specialty in this shop."

Surprise lit Bree's eyes, and maybe even a hint of approval. "You must have done a lot of apologizing during your time together."

"Nope. No reason for it. I was pretty good at courting her, though. A smart man pays attention."

"Is that what you're doing now? Are you courting her?"

"Trying to," he replied, taking a chance by putting his cards on the table. He wondered if she'd be an ally in his quest to win Jenny back or a roadblock.

"She won't make it easy," Bree warned.

"I wouldn't expect her to. That just means I'll have to try harder and be persistent."

She gave a nod of satisfaction. "Okay, then. One yellow rose bouquet coming up."

"I'm surprised to find you in here this morning," he said as she went to work on the arrangement, her hands deft as she settled the flowers into a simple but elegant crystal container. To his surprise, she seemed to know exactly what she was doing.

"The woman who runs the shop for me had a doctor's appointment," she explained. "She'll be here in an hour or so. I like to help out from time to time, anyway. I learned how to arrange flowers from my grandmother. I feel close to her when I work in here. There's nothing she loves more than her garden and sharing her flowers with others."

"I'm looking forward to meeting her. Jenny talked about Nell a lot. She sounds like a special woman."

"Nell is something, all right," Bree said.

Her expression turned thoughtful. Yet again, it was clear she was weighing something. Caleb waited for her to decide.

"If you're really serious about courting Jenny, maybe you should come to Sunday dinner. The entire family gathers at my parents' house. You can get the inquisition—and believe me, there will be one—out of the way all at once."

Caleb debated declining. He thought maybe it was an invitation that should come from Jenny.

Bree smiled at his hesitation. "If you're thinking you should wait until Jenny asks you, you should know she's not all that thrilled about being there herself this week.

You'll be taking some of the attention and pressure off her. She might even be grateful for that."

Caleb frowned. "What sort of pressure is she going to be under? I thought the family would roll out the welcome mat. Isn't that what you all do?"

"Usually, but Jenny's stayed away a long time." She studied him. "You know about her mom marrying my uncle, right?"

"And that Jenny resented it," he confirmed. "Mostly she clammed up whenever I asked why she didn't want to come back here, since it was clear she loved everything about this town and the people in it."

"My family can be pretty overwhelming," Bree explained. "As much as Jenny envied us for our closeness, she felt like an outsider. None of us ever felt that way about her, but I can understand why she stayed away. It was even harder because her mom and Thomas had a new baby. She saw Sean as a real O'Brien and as a threat to her relationship with her mother."

Caleb nodded slowly. The situation was a lot more complicated than he'd imagined. It explained a lot about Jenny's dark moods when holidays rolled around or the subject of home was broached. He suddenly understood, too, why the pictures of Sean her mother sent invariably brought on tears she denied shedding. A whole pile of those snapshots had accumulated in her nightstand drawer. She wouldn't look at them after a first brief glimpse, but she couldn't throw them away, either.

"So when she shows up on Sunday, she expects everyone will judge her for staying away?" he guessed.

"It's mostly in her head, but, yes, that's what she's afraid of."

"And you really think having me there will make it easier for her?" he asked doubtfully.

Bree grinned. "If nothing else, she'll be so furious at me for inviting you and at you for showing up that she'll forget about being nervous. It has the added benefit of giving everyone in the family a chance to freak out over your daring to show up in Chesapeake Shores."

"Gee, you make it sound like a fun time," he said dryly.

"It will be," she said, clearly pleased with her devious plan. "At least once everyone settles down. Just so you know, while I always had the reputation of being the quiet one in the family, I have been known to stir the pot from time to time. This seems to be one of those times that calls for it."

Caleb was willing to take a little heat if it would help smooth the way for Jenny. "Okay, then, I'll be there. Thanks for inviting me, and for the flowers," he said. The bouquet was one of the prettiest he'd ever bought for Jenny with the unexpected touch of a few blue flowers.

"What are these?" he asked, pointing.

"Forget-me-nots," she said with a smile. "They seemed fitting."

Caleb laughed. "I know when push comes to shove, you're on Jenny's side, Bree, but something tells me you don't exactly hate my guts."

"Not at all," she said, then added, "Just remember that warning I gave you yesterday— one wrong step and that could change."

"Got it," Caleb assured her, pulling out his wallet. "How much do I owe you?"

"That one's on the house. The next one will cost

you. I'm thinking you're going to become one of our best customers."

"No matter what you charge, if the flowers put a smile on Jenny's face, they'll be worth every penny. See you at the theater later?"

"Count on it," Bree said. "I'll be anxious to see for myself if the flowers have any impact."

"Pretty as they are, they're a token, not a miracle."

"Surprisingly, I'm relieved to know you understand the distinction."

Though he wasn't about to admit it to Bree, Caleb was very much afraid it was one of those lessons he'd learned the hard way.

Jenny's gaze narrowed when Caleb walked into the rehearsal hall bearing a stunning bouquet of her favorite flowers, along with a large shopping bag with the Inn at Eagle Point logo on it.

"What are you up to?" she asked suspiciously.

He held out the flowers. "An apology bouquet," he said at once. He lifted the bag. "And, as promised, lunch. Jess had her chef prepare a feast for us. She took pity on me when I explained that you didn't want to be seen in public with me."

Jenny groaned. "Please tell me you did not say that to her."

"Wasn't I supposed to?" he inquired, his expression entirely too innocent. "I told you I'd turned over a new leaf. I vowed to always tell the truth."

"I imagine Bree knows all about the flowers, too. I heard she was filling in at the shop this morning."

"Afraid so."

"And now they both think you're sweet and thoughtful."

"I didn't ask for testimonials, if that's what you're thinking. I imagine they'd still side with you, if it came down to making a choice."

Jenny sighed. "I don't think I'll test that. They're both highly susceptible to roguish charm."

"You hungry yet?" he asked, pulling a loaf of French bread, a bottle of wine, some cheese and roasted chicken from the bag. "There's some kind of gooey chocolate cake in here, too. Jess said it's a favorite of yours."

"Anything from the inn is a favorite of mine. The chef is amazing," she said.

"Then I hope you'll eventually agree to have dinner with me there," he said. "I mean once people in town have digested all the gossip about my being around."

Jenny regarded him with alarm. "There's gossip? Already?"

"You're the one who predicted it. I'm just assuming you know this town better than I do. I haven't spoken to anyone other than O'Briens so far."

And wasn't that bad enough? Jenny thought. Rather than saying it, she looked at the food he'd spread out. "I'm not hungry yet. If you are, go ahead and eat."

"I'm good with working first," he said readily. "Any thoughts about which songs you want me to sing in the play?"

"I'm still reeling from the fact that you agreed to be in it," she said. "You realize it's going to tie you down until after New Year's. And if Bree has her way, you'll be tied up for a few months over the holidays next year, too."

"No place I'd rather be," he claimed. "And, speaking of surprises, I'm still trying to figure out why you went along with this."

She gave him a wry look. "You've met Bree. Can you imagine saying no to her? You didn't, and you've only known her for a day. I've known her my whole life. She knows exactly which buttons to push."

"I could back out," he offered. "She wouldn't be shocked. You made sure of that."

Jenny winced. "Well, you weren't all that responsible right before you made a shambles of your career. She needed to know that."

"True enough," he said without hesitation, once again startling her with his candor.

Jenny hesitated, then risked asking, "What about your music, Caleb? Shouldn't you be in Nashville trying to get your career back on track, making peace with the band?"

"I've worked things out with the group," he told her. "They've moved on. They're doing better than ever these days with the new lead singer. I'm sure you know that. Breaking up was for the best for all of us. I just wish it hadn't happened the way it did."

"You mean with your setting bridges ablaze in your wake?"

He gave her a rueful look. "Yes, that way."

"So what's next?"

"This play of Bree's," he said at once. "Then I'll see what I can work out with the old record label. My agent says they're interested, but I'll need to put together a new band, a backup band this time."

"You're going solo?" Jenny asked, surprised. He'd never wanted that before. He'd liked being surrounded by guys he'd known forever.

"That's the plan."

"Was that really your decision? Or did you get backed into a corner because your friends moved on without you?"

"It was my decision, Jenny. A couple of the guys came to see me in rehab to talk about it. I wished them godspeed. I knew it was time for me to make a change, that if I came back again, I needed to be in charge of my own career. No more group decisions. This way I get to set the pace. I'll tour, but it won't be the kind of grueling schedule we were doing. That's what got me into trouble before. I didn't much like being in a different city every night."

The admission startled her. "I thought you thrived on it," she said.

"So did I," he said. "Then I realized I was on the run, just like my dad, trying to get away from having to ask myself the serious stuff, like what I really wanted out of life."

"You wanted to be a superstar," she said readily, sure that she knew that much about him at least.

He shook his head. "That was great, no question about it, but I realized that all that attention didn't matter one single bit without someone to share it with me. I figured out a lot about myself in those first weeks after we broke up and before I went into rehab. Even drowning my sorrows in alcohol wasn't enough to keep me from seeing that I'd lost the most important thing in my life. I vowed if I ever got that lucky again, I wouldn't throw it away."

Jenny steeled herself against the words. She had to. Otherwise she might have allowed the tears stinging her eyes to fall. She could not let him get to her, no matter how sincere he sounded, no matter how deeply his words touched her.

She concluded that it was time to stop talking about a past that couldn't be changed. They needed to stay in the here and now. She drew in a deep breath and forced herself to look him directly in the eyes without so much as a hint of sympathy. "We need to get to work."

He nodded at once. "You're the boss."

She handed him the lyrics she'd been writing all morning, then strummed a few notes so he could hear what she had in mind. He grinned at once.

"I imagine you intend to have all the children in the show singing backup on this one," he said.

"Yep," she said happily, thinking how much he'd hate the lack of perfection that was likely to elicit. "Think you can handle being upstaged by a bunch of kids who may not be able to carry a tune?"

"If just thinking about my discomfort puts that huge smile on your face, then I'll do my best to pull it off," he said with surprising ease.

She frowned at his uncharacteristic reaction. "You're not to tell the ones who can't sing to be quiet and just mouth the words," she warned him.

"Of course not," he agreed solemnly.

Jenny studied him, then laughed. "This could turn out to be a lot more fun than I was imagining."

Caleb winked at her. "I'll certainly do my part to make sure it is."

And that, she thought, her smile fading, was troubling. Because when Caleb threw himself into something, he generally got exactly what he wanted. At the moment, his goal seemed to be to totally charm her once more.

* * *

Caleb had always admired Jenny's work ethic as much as he'd appreciated the results of her intense determination to nail down the perfect word or the right run of notes. She'd always listened to his thoughts, but in the end she'd had an innate sense of what worked and what didn't. She'd won more arguments than he had, because he'd trusted her gut. It had never steered either of them wrong.

When he popped the cork on the bottle of wine, her head shot up.

"Really?" she demanded, disappointment written all over her expressive face.

He held the label out so she could read it. "Nonalcoholic. I'm not an idiot, Jenny."

"Sorry," she apologized at once. "I just panicked for a minute."

"Understandable. Now, do you want a glass with lunch? It's time to take a break."

"I just want to get this last couple of lines right," she protested.

He reached for her guitar and moved it away from her. "They'll come to you a whole lot better if you give your brain a little time off. You know how important it is to relax and take a breath."

She regarded him with amusement. "I said I'd work with you, not take orders from you."

"It wasn't an order. It was a gentle reminder that I actually do know a few things about your working habits. Once you tense up and start pushing, the lyrics are never as good as when you get away from them for a little while." He held out a plate with roasted chicken, cheese and bread on it. "Eat!" He grinned at her. "And that *was* an order."

Jenny accepted the plate, but feigned a scowl. "I'll eat, but not because you say so. It's only because that chicken looks amazing."

"Whatever you need to tell yourself," he commented.

They ate in companionable silence for a while. Eventually, Caleb couldn't take another moment of the quiet. "This morning wasn't so hard, was it? Working with me, I mean."

She glanced sideways at him. "It wasn't horrible," she conceded. "You were on very good behavior."

"It reminded me of old times."

"Don't go there, Caleb."

"We had a lot of good times, Jenny. You can't deny that."

"I can't deny it," she agreed. "But I don't want to think about them."

He regarded her knowingly. "Why not? Afraid you'll let down your guard?"

"That's not going to happen," she said fiercely. "If you're thinking it will, you're in for a rude awakening. The past—*our* past—is behind us, Caleb."

"Doesn't feel that way to me," he insisted.

"Well, it is."

He figured that he'd pushed hard enough for now. "How late are you planning to work today?"

"Do you have someplace you need to be?" she inquired tartly. "You can leave anytime."

"No, but I was thinking that you've been at this for hours."

"We don't have a lot of time. The professional actors Bree hired get to town on Monday. I know she wants to run through the songs with the locals at least a few times before that."

"Makes sense."

"What about you? Has she told you how she's going to work you into the script? You can't very well just pop up and sing a song here and there."

Caleb shrugged. "I figured she'd spell it out for me when she has it nailed down. She's the playwright. We just agreed to do this yesterday."

"Which means she's probably written you in by now. Maybe you should look for her and find out what she has in mind."

"Trying to get rid of me, Jenny?"

"Just being practical. As I said, there's not a lot of time."

He regarded her with amusement. "And you don't think Bree knows exactly where to find me if she needs me?"

She frowned at his logic. "More than likely," she conceded. "But I'm not going to be around much longer, anyway, so you might as well look for her."

Now it was Caleb's turn to frown. "Hot date with that ex-boyfriend who was here yesterday?"

She ignored his reference to the old flame. "If you must know, I'm going to move my things from Jake and Bree's tonight."

For a moment, Caleb's heart stuttered. "To the inn?"

She shook her head. "You wish. No, my mother and Thomas kept our old house for me. I'm going to move in there. Of course, the furnishings are a little sparse, so I'll need to spend some time shopping for furniture, but I won't need much, at least not on this trip."

Her words stirred a memory. "Remember when we

shopped for furniture for your place in Nashville?"
Caleb asked. She'd insisted on buying the town house
out of her first big paycheck, rather than agreeing to
move in with him.

"I thought we weren't going to walk down memory
lane anymore," she said, her frustration plain.

"Your plan," he said. "I like memory lane, especially
when we picked out the bed. I thought the saleswoman
was going to have a heart attack when we both climbed
into it. I'm stunned there weren't pictures on the internet within seconds."

"She knew better," Jenny said, a smile tugging at her
lips. "She wanted the big fat commission she stood to
get because you insisted on buying up half the store."

"Admit it, though. We had fun that day."

"Yes, we did," she acknowledged grudgingly.

"Then you should let me come shopping with you,"
he suggested. "You already know I have excellent taste,
especially when it comes to the perfect mattress."

"This house already has a new bed," she told him,
then shrugged. "It's the only thing it has, in fact."

"Then get out your credit card, sweetheart. Let's go
shopping!"

She regarded him with astonishment. "You may be
the only man on the planet who actually sounds excited
about the prospect of shopping."

"That's because we'll be doing it together," he told
her. "Just like before."

He could see the precise instant when she gave in,
even before she said, "Okay, fine." She gave him a stern
look. "But do not get any ideas about moving in with
me the way you did in Nashville. You were practically
delivered to my doorstep there along with the furniture."

"Okay," he agreed readily. "We'll talk about that later."

Alarm spread across her face. "No. No talking. No cajoling. You are not moving in, Caleb, and that's final."

"You sure about that?"

"As sure as I've been about anything in my life," she said forcefully.

"Then I guess we'll just have to wait and see."

"Caleb!"

"Here, try a little of this cake. You always feel better once you've had a chocolate fix." He held out a forkful of the decadent cake.

"You are not getting around my decision with cake," she said, then moaned when she took the bite he'd offered. "Oh, sweet heaven! It's as good as I remembered. Better, even."

"Have some more."

She took the outstretched plate eagerly and finished it off amid sighs of pleasure. Caleb regretted that the cake was responsible for her current state of ecstasy, rather than him, but it was a start. If making her moan and call out his name was his endgame, he was pretty sure he was on the right track.

7

"You know, it would help if I saw this house of yours before we go furniture shopping," Caleb told Jenny as they drove away from the theater in his pickup. He'd only managed to convince her to take that by pointing out that there might be a few purchases they could bring home in the bed of the truck without having to wait for a delivery. She had, however, insisted on driving.

"I know the roads," she'd argued, planting herself outside the driver's-side door in a display of the control issues she swore didn't exist.

Caleb had given in readily and flipped the keys to her. "Whatever makes you happy."

"Your staying home would make me happiest of all," she'd countered.

"Debated and decided," he'd retorted.

He glanced over at her now. "About my seeing the house—"

She immediately cut him off. "I've already told you, you are not crossing the threshold of my house."

"No, what you said was that I could forget about moving in. I'm just suggesting that I'll be more help with choosing furniture if I have some idea what the place looks like, the proportions of the rooms, that kind of thing." He met her gaze. "Look me in the eye and tell me that doesn't make sense."

She scowled at him, but finally agreed, "Okay, it does make sense."

"Then why are you so resistant to the idea?" He suspected it was because she wanted to keep the house devoid of any and all memories of him, to make it her personal Caleb-free zone. Since he wanted just the opposite, he pushed a little harder. "Stop being stubborn, Jenny. A ten-minute walk-through." He winked at her. "I promise not to linger in the bedroom."

"As if I'd let you anywhere near the bedroom," she muttered.

"Okay, agreed. What's the harm in letting me take a peek at the rest of the place?"

"None, I suppose," she replied with unmistakable reluctance.

A few blocks later, with daylight fading fast, she turned down a neighborhood street that looked as if it would be shaded by giant oaks in the summer. Right now, though, the branches were bare, at least those that hadn't been strung with white Christmas lights. It was a little like driving into a holiday theme park with every house already lit up brightly and every lawn outfitted with displays ranging from gaudy North Pole scenes to more tasteful religious figures. Only one house in the middle of the block was eerily dark.

"Yours, I assume," he said even before she turned into the driveway. "You need to get with the program, Jenny."

"I just found out this house was mine yesterday. It's

not as if I've had a lot of time to decorate. It probably doesn't even make sense to bother now," she said, though there was an unmistakably wistful note in her voice.

"We could decorate the yard, too," he suggested. "It would be fun."

She immediately shrugged off the offer. "I suppose if I decide I want outdoor lights, Uncle Jake can do it. Mom's bound to have saved all the decorations." Her expression turned nostalgic. "We always did Santa's workshop with these giant candy canes and the ugliest elves you've ever seen. I have no idea where on earth they came from, but we kept them because I absolutely knew nobody else would want them. I felt bad thinking about them being relegated to the dump."

Caleb smiled, thinking about the compassionate child she must have been. He wondered how much that had to do with the rejection she herself had felt at her father's abandonment.

"What else did you have in the yard?" he asked.

A smile touched her lips. "My favorite was the toy train that wound around the whole yard with Santa riding in the caboose," she said.

She turned to him suddenly, her eyes bright. "Can I borrow your cell phone? Mine's still buried in a drawer at Bree and Jake's."

He handed it over, then listened as she spoke to her mother. After what sounded to him like some fairly awkward pleasantries, she said, "I'm at our house. The neighborhood's already lit up like some crazy wonderland. It made me think about the old decorations, especially the train. Where are they? Did you leave them in the attic?"

Caleb watched as her face fell.

"Oh, of course. That makes sense," she said flatly. "No, no problem. I'll see them next time I'm over there, then. Gotta run. I'm going to look for furniture."

She hung up and handed the phone back to him. When she was about to start the car and pull away without ever setting foot into the house for their walkthrough, Caleb reached over and covered her hand with his.

"What?" he asked softly, though he was sure he already knew.

"They're putting the decorations up at the new house this weekend," she said, her tone emotionless. "It makes sense. I mean, they didn't even know if I was going to keep the house or even be here for the holidays. No sense in letting the decorations go to waste. And Sean apparently loves the train as much as I did."

A tear leaked out despite her best attempt to keep her voice casual and breezy. Caleb rubbed it away with the pad of his thumb.

"I'm sorry."

She managed a smile, though there was little question it was forced. "No big deal," she insisted.

He could tell, though, that it was.

"Change of plans," he said then. "The furniture can wait."

"No, it can't," she said, frowning. "I can't live here with just a bed."

"You can for a day or two or you can stay at Jake and Bree's a little longer. Tonight we're shopping for new decorations."

"That's crazy. I'm only going to be here for a few weeks," she said, but there was a spark of interest in her eyes. "Besides, people buy this stuff before Thanksgiving. Everything will be picked over by now."

"Which means there will be some great bargains, and who has more creative genius than the two of us. We're going to have a display that people will drive for miles to see. Forget the train. That is so old-fashioned. We'll have a rocket ship with Santa on board. Maybe some little Martian elves."

She started laughing then, her somber mood broken. "You're nuts."

Caleb thrilled to the sound of her laughter. "Maybe just a little," he agreed. "Don't tell. I'm trying to repair my reputation, not add to the talk."

She met his gaze. "Caleb, do you really want to decorate the house?" she asked, genuine yearning in her voice.

If he hadn't wanted to before, he did now. "I do," he told her solemnly. "And think of all those rejected decorations we're going to find. You'll be giving them a home."

She lifted a brow. "Seriously, you're going to play on the sympathy factor for the decorations?"

He shrugged. "Whatever works."

"Have you ever done over-the-top Christmas decorations in your entire life?"

"Nope, but I can get into the spirit of it," he assured her. He could do anything that might make the two of them close again.

"But can you do it without falling off a ladder and breaking your neck?"

He held her gaze. "I guess we'll see."

"Okay," she said eventually, her expression turning thoughtful, "but we'll need a theme."

"I gave you a great theme," he said, feigning indignation.

"No Martian elves," she replied. "No rockets. I'm a traditionalist."

He smiled at her. "Could have fooled me."

She laughed. "I'm a little surprised by it myself." Her grin spread. "Let's do it. Let's turn this house into something magical."

Studying the light in her eyes as she gazed around, apparently imagining the transformation, Caleb thought what was happening was already just a little magical.

Jenny hadn't laughed so hard in a very long time. Suddenly the past—her own, his or even theirs—wasn't even part of the equation as they hit a half-dozen stores to pick through the outdoor decorations until they'd assembled more than enough to turn two or three yards into the gaudiest of all wonderlands.

"If we use all this, the house won't even be visible," she protested as Caleb found yet another Santa figure, this one sitting in a giant sleigh that played music as it appeared to lift off toward the sky. "And we can't have three Santas."

"Why not?"

"It'll be confusing to the children. They think there's only one." As soon as she'd said the words, she caught him struggling with a grin. "What?"

"Sweetheart, even toddlers have to know that all these Santas hanging out in the front yards of every house in the neighborhood are not the real thing," he explained patiently. "For one thing, they're plastic. For another, everyone knows that the real Santa lives at the North Pole. So what if we have a Santa family? Has

anyone ever said for sure that there aren't Santa trip-
lets? Or clones, even? I mean, he does manage to hit a
whole lot of places in one short night."

"Please do not share these ideas of yours with Bree,"
she begged. "With the way she delights in doing things
that are cutting-edge, she's liable to turn this Christmas
play into some sci-fi holiday adventure that will have
the audience totally bewildered."

"So we can get this Santa?" Caleb asked, studying
the rosy-cheeked figure and the gold-trimmed sleigh
with lights and bells on the reins. "He's the best one
yet."

"By all means, let's take him home," Jenny relented,
delighted by this playful side of Caleb she hadn't seen
in far too long.

By the time they were finished, the bed of the pickup
was jammed with outdoor lights and displays.

"One more stop," Caleb announced. "If we're going
to do this job tonight, we'll need hot chocolate, marshmallows, a boom box and some Christmas CDs."

Jenny smiled, thinking of the years when she, her
mom and Jake had worked on the yard with exactly the
same things to set the mood. "Big marshmallows, not
those little miniature guys," she told him when he offered to run inside yet another big box store to get their
supplies. "We'll need some popcorn, too. And make
sure you get the traditional Christmas CDs by Johnny
Mathis and Tony Bennett, as well as all the latest ones."
She frowned. "Maybe I should come, too. You'll never
remember all that."

Caleb merely lifted a brow. "You questioning my
musical taste *and* my memory?"

She hesitated, thinking of their arguments over various singers. His taste was far more eclectic than hers. "Could you at least avoid the rappers?"

He winked at her. "That I can do. And I promise not to forget a single thing. If I do, you can send me back for it."

She leaned back in the warm cab of the truck, listening to the local country station, her eyes closed.

It had been a surprisingly pleasant evening. She'd let down her guard. Caleb hadn't been trying too hard to prove he'd changed. He was just Caleb, the way she remembered him from before he'd started drinking too much and lost his way.

He'd always been able to make her laugh. He'd delighted in provoking her with outrageous comments that he knew wouldn't fail to elicit a strong response. He'd claimed he liked to see the fire flashing in her eyes. And that he'd liked even more stoking that fire by making love to her.

That memory had her sitting up straight. *No, no, no,* she warned herself. She couldn't go there. She couldn't start remembering how it had felt to have his hands all over her or his mouth covering hers, how he'd coaxed her along until she could barely remember her own name for all the sensations he was stirring up. She needed to be steeling her resolve, not getting weaker. Hadn't she come to Chesapeake Shores at least in part to forget about him once and for all?

A tap on the window scared her to death. "Jenny, open the door," Caleb said. "My keys are in the ignition."

Her nerves jumpy—and definitely not just because he'd startled her—she unlocked the door to let him in.

"Find everything?" she asked, her voice surprisingly breathless.

"As promised," he said, then studied her. "You okay?"

She forced a smile. "Perfect."

His expression remained worried. "But?"

She drew in a deep breath. "I'm thinking it's already late. Jake can do the decorations tomorrow or the next day. He does it for a lot of people this time of the year, so he knows exactly what to do. I should probably get some sleep. We still have a lot of work to do on the music for the play."

Caleb stilled, his frown deepening. "What the heck happened while I was inside that store, Jenny?"

"Nothing. Honest. I just realized it was late, that's all."

He sighed. "If you say so," he said, though it was evident he wasn't buying her explanation.

He pulled out of the parking lot and drove back to her house in silence, breaking it only to ask for directions once or twice. In the driveway, he said, "You go on inside and get some rest. I'll unload everything and leave it on the porch."

"I can help," she offered, filled with guilt over ruining the evening by cutting it short simply because she'd panicked. After all, he hadn't tried anything. She was the one who'd suddenly gotten all nostalgic.

"No need to help," he told her. "I can do it. Just take the CDs, the CD player, and the popcorn and hot chocolate inside when you go."

She took the bags and started for the house, then turned back. "Caleb, I'm sorry."

"For what?"

"Spoiling things." Avoiding his gaze, she said, "I had a good time tonight. I really did."

He walked over to her then and ran a finger along the curve of her jaw. "Too good?"

That he understood that surprised her. She dared to look into his eyes. "Maybe."

His gaze remained steady, locked with hers. "I won't apologize for that."

"You shouldn't. It's me. This feeling scares me."

"I don't want you to ever be scared of me or with me," he told her solemnly. "You take all the time you need, Jenny. I'm not going anywhere."

This time when he said it, it didn't sound so much like a warning. It sounded like a promise. And that scared her most of all.

Even though it was Saturday, Caleb knew he'd find Jenny, and most likely Bree, at the theater first thing in the morning. He risked a stop at Sally's café for coffee and some of the chocolate croissants she assured him were Jenny's favorites. He smiled as she put them into a bag. His girl—and she would be his again, he vowed—sure did love her chocolate, apparently in whatever form it took.

He'd admittedly been disappointed the night before when she'd put on the brakes to end their evening, but he had understood the sudden panic that had obviously washed over her. He'd come back into her life knowing exactly what he wanted. He'd grown more certain of it with every minute he spent with her. She needed some time to catch up.

When he arrived at the theater, he heard voices in the rehearsal hall where Jenny had set up camp the day before. One was low and definitely masculine. He knew even before he glanced into the room who it was—the ex-boyfriend.

"Today's great," Jenny was telling him. "I should be able to break free by noon. Shall I meet you at Brady's?"

"I can pick you up," the man offered, but Caleb saw Jenny shake her head.

"It's easier if I just meet you there," she insisted.

Her response and the uneasiness he heard behind it made him wonder if she was feeling just a little guilty about accepting the date. Good, he thought. She should.

But as soon as those thoughts crossed his mind, he sighed and stepped away, then went back outside and sat on the front steps of the theater, sipping one of the coffees. He needed to settle down before he walked into that room. Jenny wasn't doing anything wrong, not really. Making her feel guilty wouldn't help him win her back.

Bree found him there when she arrived at the theater a few minutes later. She was bundled up in a thick down coat, a scarf and mittens.

"You're going to freeze to death," she said. "What on earth are you doing sitting outside?"

"Jenny has company," he said simply, offering her one of the coffees. "The ex-boyfriend."

Understanding dawned. "Dillon dropped by again?"

He nodded. "They're making plans for lunch."

A smile tugged at her lips, but she made an obvious effort to fight it. "And you're out here so you won't make a scene."

"Something like that," he said. "So what's the scoop with those two, anyway? Were they serious?"

"They were in high school," Bree told him as she

sipped the coffee. "But they broke up before they left for different colleges. Jenny's idea, by the way. She didn't want to be tied down. I think even then she was being honest enough with herself to see that he was the wrong guy for her."

"She doesn't seem so sure of that now," he suggested.

This time Bree didn't try to hide her smile. "It's lunch, Caleb. Broad daylight. Don't you think if they were starting something, they'd be getting together in the evening, maybe even having dinner at her place?"

"She doesn't have a table at her house," he said, though that was hardly the issue. They'd shared some pretty intimate dinners on a blanket in front of the fireplace at her house in Nashville, even with lots of comfy furniture around them.

Bree merely lifted a brow. "A table? Do you really think that matters?"

Caleb chuckled. "Okay, no. But lunch isn't exactly a guarantee that they're not going to start crawling all over each other after dessert."

"Voice of experience?"

"I'm not saying," he demurred.

"My point is, Jenny told me herself that when Dillon first mentioned getting together, she insisted they stick to lunch to avoid any hint of gossip." She leaned into his side. "Come on. This is no big deal. Stop sulking."

He frowned at her. "I do not sulk."

"Then prove it. Come inside with me. Despite this lovely coffee you brought along with you, I'm freezing to death. I'll introduce you to Dillon myself. You can size up the competition."

Caleb laughed. "Did you just insinuate that I'm intimidated by a guy who looks as stuffy as this guy? Or are you implying I'm a coward?"

She gave him an innocent look. "That word never crossed my lips."

"But it's exactly what you meant. You think I'm hiding out here because I'm scared of a little competition. What does he do, by the way?"

She barely contained a smile. "He sells insurance, if you must know."

"Well, there you go," he said. "Nothing scary about that." Suddenly eager to get a better fix on this guy who'd once owned a piece of Jenny's heart, he stood up and held out his hand to Bree. "Let's go inside and make some music."

Bree tilted her head to study him, a frown on her lips. "Why did that sound more like you intend to stir up trouble instead?"

"Not at all," he vowed. "Just a polite meet-and-greet. I excel at those, especially with insurance salesmen." He held up the tray with one more container of coffee and the bag of treats from Sally's. "Besides, I'm armed with coffee and chocolate croissants. The guy doesn't stand a chance."

Bree laughed. "Then it's definitely not a fair fight. Even if you weren't sexy as sin, you'd steal Jenny's affections with those croissants. She made me ship her a box every few weeks. She swore she couldn't find any half as good in Nashville."

Caleb frowned at that. "There was an excellent French bakery right in her neighborhood. She was a regular."

"She claimed they weren't the same as Sally's," Bree told him. "Personally I think she just liked knowing they came from Chesapeake Shores. As much as she denied it all those years, she missed home, Caleb. I, for one, hope she sticks around for a while."

"You'll get no argument from me," he said. He could see how this charming town—and even the slightly overwhelming O'Briens—could weave a spell around anyone.

There was another reason he was happy to have Jenny back on her home turf. Despite the presence of the ex-boyfriend, he figured he had a better chance with her here than he ever would back in the town where everyone knew their history, and all his mistakes besides. Here, he might even have a shot at reinventing himself, at reclaiming her heart before all the demands of the music business started tearing away at the fabric of the life they could have together.

"Look who I found sitting outside," Bree announced, cheerfully leading Caleb into the rehearsal hall where Jenny had been working on lyrics while Dillon listened.

Jenny frowned at him. "Why were you outside? The door wasn't locked."

"Just enjoying the view of the bay," Caleb claimed.

Jenny knew it was a lie and immediately guessed why he'd felt the need to utter it. He'd overheard her and Dillon earlier making their date for lunch. He must have had a pretty strong reaction to walk away, rather than join them.

"Dillon, this is Caleb Green," Bree said, stepping into the awkward silence. "Caleb, Dillon Johnson, an old friend of Jenny's."

The scowl on Dillon's face proved there was no need to explain about Caleb. Besides, he'd already acknowledged a few days before that he knew the whole story of the breakup. Now he looked as if he were about ten seconds away from punching Caleb just on principle. Jenny stepped between them before he could give in to the impulse.

"Okay, we'd better put in some serious work if I'm going to be able to break for lunch. Dillon, I'll see you at Brady's at noon."

Dillon looked a little startled by the firm dismissal, but he nodded and grabbed his jacket. Then, to her shock, he crossed to her and planted a solid kiss right smack on her lips.

"See you," he said, his tone casual, but an unmistakable glint of triumph in his eyes as he shot a look toward Caleb on his way out.

Caleb took a step in his direction, but Bree's hand on his arm stilled him.

"There will not be any turf wars in my theater," she said quietly. "Understood?"

Caleb drew in a deep breath, then nodded.

She turned to Jenny. "You might suggest to Dillon that he call you instead of dropping by. We have a lot to get done and not much time to accomplish it."

Jenny bristled at the suggestion that Dillon wasn't welcome here, but then she, too, drew in a deep breath. "You're right, of course."

"And I can leave you two alone in here without worrying about an argument breaking out the instant my back's turned?"

Caleb chuckled. "Yes, Mama Hen. Your chick will be safe with me."

Jenny gave him a wry look. "Don't be so sure about your rooster," she retorted.

"Jenny Louise!" Bree said firmly.

"Okay, okay. We'll both behave."

"And focus a hundred percent on the music for this play?" Bree encouraged.

"A hundred percent," Jenny confirmed.

After Bree had gone, Jenny dared to look at Caleb. "Were you really jealous?"

"Didn't you want me to be? You had to know when I was likely to turn up. Didn't you make that date with Dillon just to make a point to me?"

"First of all, it's not a date. It's lunch with an old friend. Second, I had no idea you were in the building."

"Not even with that clear view you have of the front sidewalk?" he suggested skeptically, nodding toward the window directly across the room with its excellent view of the sweeping lawn, the walkway and the water.

Jenny winced. He was right. She had seen him coming, had heard the theater's front door open and close. Even though she hadn't invited Dillon to come by, she'd considered his presence a chance to make a point to Caleb, to remind him that he no longer had any claim on her, no matter how strong the feelings had been between them the night before. Those had been a fluke, an old habit not yet broken. At least that's what she'd told herself as she'd tossed and turned through the night.

"Okay, you're right," she said. "Maybe I did take advantage of the situation."

"No more games, Jenny. Whatever else happens between us, let's at least keep it honest, okay?"

He was right. "Okay," she promised.

"Will you break your lunch date with the ex?"

"Would you, if you were in my shoes?" she asked, turning the tables on him.

"No," he conceded grudgingly. "But it's the last time, okay? Like it or not, we have things to work out. We can't do it if you're going to throw him in my face whenever the mood strikes you."

Jenny smiled at that. "It's not all about making you crazy, you know. Dillon and I were good friends once. He knows my history. He gets me."

Caleb locked gazes with her. "But I'm the one who knows who you are now, Jenny. History's all well and good, but make no mistake about it, your future's with me."

She trembled under the intensity of his words and his gaze. She didn't doubt for a second that he believed exactly that. What worried her was that she might start believing it, too. All the more reason to go on this date with Dillon and see if she couldn't fan a few of *those* old flames.

8

Since there was clearly no way Jenny was going to break the date she'd made with Dillon, Caleb needed to find something to do at lunchtime to keep himself from losing it. He thought of all those decorations he'd left stacked on the front porch the night before. While he had plenty of ideas for where they should go, he didn't have a ladder or the expertise to make sure they stayed put once he'd created the scene he had in mind.

He poked his head into Bree's office, thinking maybe he could kill two birds with one stone—get those decorations up and maybe make some inroads with someone else in the family.

"Jenny said something about Jake being an expert at installing outdoor Christmas decorations," he said to her. "Do you happen to know if he's tied up this afternoon?"

"I can call and ask," she said. "What did you have in mind?"

He explained about all the old decorations going up at Jenny's mom's, what a downer that had been for Jenny, and about their shopping binge for new ones. "I have some ideas for how the house should look, but not a lot of practical experience at hanging lights."

A smile spread across Bree's face. "What a great idea! Jenny will love it. And you're so sweet to want to surprise her by having it all done when she gets home tonight."

"Ulterior motive," he confessed.

"Of course," Bree said knowingly. "But it's a good motive, I think." Her smile spread. "You're starting to grow on me, Caleb. I can see now why Jenny fell so hard for you. At heart you're a pretty thoughtful guy."

He shook his head. "You're seeing the new and improved me. I'm not so sure the old Caleb had a lot to recommend him aside from some hit songs and a loyal fan following."

"No way," Bree contradicted. "Jenny could have had her pick of sexy country superstars. She chose you because of what she saw in you. She believed in you, Caleb, not just in your talent, but in you."

He was touched by her comment. "If that's true, I hope I don't let her down this time."

"You won't," she said with surprising conviction, then gave him a stern look. "You know the consequences if you do."

"I'll have O'Briens chasing me from here to Kingdom Come," he said. "I get it. Now, do you think Jake would be willing to help me this afternoon, or am I still his sworn enemy? If he's as protective of Jenny as I've been led to believe, I doubt he's mellowed half as much as you have."

"You leave my husband to me," she said confidently. "Head on over to the house. I'll have help there within the hour. You might pick up some barbecue—a lot of it, in fact—and some sodas." She handed him a note with directions to a barbecue place on the outskirts of town.

He took the directions, but regarded her with suspicion. There was a worrisome glint in her eyes. "You sending an army?"

"Something like that."

An hour later Caleb wasn't all that surprised when pickups started arriving at Jenny's. His head swam as he tried to keep not only the O'Briens straight, but several others who'd apparently married into the family. The one person he had no trouble identifying was Jake Collins. Despite Bree's assurances, Jenny's uncle was regarding him as if he'd been personally responsible for spreading a plague.

"I don't much like you," Jake said by way of introduction.

Caleb nodded and stood his ground. "Understandable."

"I'm only here because my wife insisted on it." Jake's scowl deepened. "And because I don't trust you. I intend to keep a very close eye on you while you're in town."

"Also understandable," Caleb told him.

"Back off and leave the man alone," the man who'd identified himself as Mick O'Brien told Jake. "He's here trying to do a nice thing for Jenny. You should be thanking him."

"It's not what he wants to do this afternoon that worries me," Jake said, his scowl firmly in place. "It's what he has in mind for later tonight and tomorrow and the next day."

"Then you can come back later and keep a close eye on him then," Mick said. "I'll be right here beside you, if you want. There's not an O'Brien here right now who won't do the same if we feel it's necessary to protect Jenny. We all know the story, Jake. None of us want to see Jenny hurt again. I'm just thinking that maybe the man deserves a second chance to get it right. We've all had our share of those."

"You especially," an older man commented, slapping Mick on the back. "I'm Jenny's stepfather, by the way. Thomas O'Brien." He held out his hand and shook Caleb's, a hard look leveled directly into Caleb's eyes. "Don't let Mick's soft attitude fool you. He'll be the first one in line to punch you out if he doesn't like what he sees or hears about the way you're treating Jenny."

"Got it," Caleb said. "I'm glad to know so many people have her back." He regarded Thomas curiously. "Jenny's mentioned you. I didn't get the impression you were close."

Thomas flushed. "We didn't get off to the best start. In fact, it's certainly likely that you didn't get a glowing endorsement of me from Jenny. I'm working to rectify that."

Caleb took pity on him, since he was so obviously troubled by the bad blood between them. He knew better than most that there were two sides to every story.

"I doubt anyone who married her mom would have fared any better," he told Thomas. "I'm just starting to figure out all these complex family dynamics."

Mick interrupted. "Okay, enough chitchat," he announced. "Jake, you, Mack, Will, Matthew, Luke and I can start stringing lights on the eaves. Thomas, you and Caleb can open boxes and figure out where you want the lawn display, then Jake and I will hook things up." He turned to a younger man. "Connor, why don't you run to the hardware store and buy some outdoor extension cords?"

Connor frowned at that. "You don't need my help here?"

Jake laughed. "Connor, listen to Mick. Your father has a lifetime of experience with your construction skills or lack thereof. We want this display to work, not cause a neighborhood blackout."

Connor scowled at him. "Thanks, pal. I'll remember that next time you call and need an extra pair of hands to assemble something."

"Stick to law," Jake taunted. "That's where your real skill lies. Let the rest of us do the manly things."

"Oh, brother," Mack muttered under his breath, stepping between the outraged Connor and Jake.

"Settle down," Will said quietly, clearly in peacemaker mode. "Connor, you know perfectly well Jake is just trying to yank your chain. Don't let him goad you into brawling with him. We have a lot to do. It requires teamwork."

Connor and Jake exchanged a malevolent look, then chuckled.

"Spoken exactly like a shrink in that soothing, professional tone that sets my teeth on edge," Jake said.

"Bite me," Will retorted, but he was grinning.

Caleb listened to the teasing, amazed by the affection behind even the sharpest barbs. No wonder Jenny had been in love with this family. He'd never known a tight-knit group like them himself. Even his old band, as well as they'd known each other, hadn't been this free and easy. Nor had they been as deeply committed to one another. He'd been as much to blame for that as any of them. He'd tested the limits of the friendship too many times.

With peace restored, Will, Mack, Matthew, Luke, Mick and Jake went to work hanging the lights.

Thomas led the way onto the porch, then pulled a box cutter from his pocket and handed it to Caleb. He opened a second one for himself. "Let's get busy. Bree's going to do her best to keep Jenny at the theater until after dark, but if I know Jenny and she starts getting suspicious, there won't be a thing short of tying her down that Bree will be able to do to keep her there."

"You've got that right," Caleb said. "Hey, I thought you were supposed to be putting up decorations at home today."

Thomas nodded. "Connie thought my time would be better spent over here. She heard the disappointment in Jenny's voice when she found out we'd claimed the old decorations." As they started up the porch steps, Thomas stared in amazement at the boxes piled up. "Do you think you two might have gone a little overboard?"

Caleb shrugged. "As her mom said, Jenny was a little bummed out about the old decorations. Finding all this stuff cheered her up. And, I have to admit, I was having a little trouble controlling myself, too. I never lived in a house with outdoor decorations for Christmas. I always envied the families who had them."

Thomas nodded. "Welcome to Chesapeake Shores. This time of year I feel as if I've made a wrong turn and landed at the North Pole. My parents didn't waste money or electricity on outside lights back in the day, though Ma has recently become a convert. Wait till you see her cottage. It's like an enchanted gingerbread house on the cliff overlooking the bay."

"You're talking about Nell, right?"

"That's right," Thomas confirmed. "She's still going strong. She had this same crew over at her place last weekend climbing on ladders while she supervised the placement of every strand of lights. Jake took it in stride, but Mick almost had a coronary trying to keep his temper under control. He loves her to pieces, but he likes doing things his own way."

"I take it you're almost as new to the tradition as I am," Caleb said.

"Absolutely. After living in an apartment with an artificial tree as my only concession to the season, it was a tough transition for me when I married Connie. She wanted every tree in the yard dripping with lights. And that train..." He glanced at Caleb. "I imagine Jenny told you about the train."

"That's what set her off," he confirmed. "She loved that train."

"Everybody loves that train," Thomas said, "except for the poor soul stuck with trying to get the blasted track together and keeping the thing from derailing every twenty minutes and tossing Santa out on his behind. That poor soul would be me, by the way. Jake and Mick and the rest of these guys may have a knack for assembling things, but I do not. Connie didn't want to ask for their help. She said it should be our family tradition. I think she just didn't want to expose me to their ridicule."

"I'm confused," Caleb said. "Didn't you, Mick and your other brother build Chesapeake Shores?"

Thomas immediately shook his head. "We had a partnership, that's true, but Mick built it. Jeff sold the properties as we developed the town. My task was to keep as many trees in place as humanly possible, to keep the whole thing environmentally friendly. That put me and Mick at odds more than once."

"Ah, now I remember," Caleb said. "You have a foundation that works to protect the bay."

Thomas nodded. "And Mick, for all his grumbling back then, finally gets how important it was that I stuck to my guns, even when it was a major inconvenience to his plans. His son, Kevin, is working with me now. Kevin would be here today, but he's giving a speech to a civic group. We never miss a chance to spread the message."

Caleb thought of the brief glimpses he'd had of the bay's beauty in just the past few days. "I don't suppose you'd want to do a benefit concert sometime," he suggested. "I could probably enlist a few of my buddies in Nashville and put something together."

Thomas regarded him incredulously. "Seriously? You think you could pull that off?"

"I don't see why not," Caleb told him, warming to the idea.

"Just how long are you planning to stick around?"

Caleb smiled. "As long as it takes."

"Well, to be honest, I don't care if your motive has more to do with Jenny than it does with protecting the bay, I'll accept your offer. Connie's been coordinating a lot of special events for us. Would you mind sitting down with her to work things out?"

Caleb regarded him skeptically. He had a hunch Jenny's mom wouldn't be all that thrilled about working with him. "Are you sure that's a good idea? She might drive a stake through my heart instead."

Thomas laughed. "She might," he admitted. "But I'll

see that she doesn't do it till after this concert you just suggested. That'll buy you some time to win her over."

In Caleb's experience, mothers were sometimes easier to win over than their daughters. He suspected that might be the case with Connie O'Brien and Jenny. Since he needed both of them on his side, he accepted Thomas's terms.

By now they'd opened all the boxes and haphazardly set the multiple Santas, a gingerbread house, a few giant candy canes and a family of elves on the lawn.

"There's one more thing," Caleb said. "It's still in my truck. I went back for it after I dropped Jenny off last night."

Thomas followed him over to the pickup, then chuckled when he saw the boxes. "You found her a train."

Caleb nodded. "I've never seen the old one, so I don't know how this compares, but it does have Santa riding in the caboose. She said the old one did, too."

Thomas clapped a hand on his shoulder. "Son, even if this one weren't a new and improved version of the one she remembers, the fact that you found it for her will go a long way toward making her happy."

Caleb couldn't seem to keep the hope from his voice when he asked, "You think so?"

Jake wandered over just then, his eyes widening when he saw the train. He shook his head. "Ah, man, just when I really wanted to hate your guts, you had to go and do this."

Caleb looked from Thomas to Jake and back again. "Then you're agreed the train will be a hit?"

"It's going to knock her socks off," Thomas confirmed.

Jake's gaze narrowed at that. "But that's all. Only her socks. Understood?"

Caleb laughed. "No promises, but I'll keep your warning in mind."

In the end, though, it was going to be up to Jenny just how far things went between them, not only tonight, but in the future. He understood that, even though it grated on him that this was one time when he wasn't guaranteed he'd get what he wanted.

Jenny's lunch with Dillon had been surprisingly tense. She figured out right away that he was still upset about the encounter with Caleb earlier.

"I just don't understand why he's here, Jenny," he said finally. "Okay, maybe I can see why Bree wants him around, but what about you? How can you even stand the sight of him after what he did to you?"

"Dillon, it's not that big a deal. Caleb and I are over," she said, even though a part of her knew that was a flat-out lie. "This is about work. Haven't you ever had to work with someone you didn't particularly get along with?"

"You're the talented songwriter," he argued, not giving her a direct answer. "Bree needs you. Shouldn't you get to call the shots?"

"Bree needs my music," Jenny agreed. "Or I should say she wants it. She could always hire another songwriter. What she can't do is replace the kind of buzz that having Caleb in the play will create. His presence could help to take her career to a whole different level."

"Never mind the strain it puts on you in the meantime," he said bitterly.

"Dillon, she and I talked about this before she ever

made an offer to Caleb," Jenny explained, then added as she had to her uncle, "If I'd said no, she wouldn't have asked him."

"Then why didn't you say no?" he asked, studying her. Understanding apparently dawned. "Oh, my God, you want him here, don't you?" He sighed heavily. "I should have seen it right off. You're not over him."

"Yes, I am," she insisted, refusing to acknowledge that Dillon might be right.

His smile was tinged with sorrow. "Give it up, Jenny. I could always tell when you were lying, even to yourself. Even though Caleb humiliated you and broke your heart, you still want him."

She started to deny it yet again, then shrugged. "Okay, maybe there are some old feelings left, but I don't want there to be."

"That's not quite the same thing as being over him, though, is it?"

"No, but I'm not going back there, Dillon. I've learned my lesson."

He studied her, clearly unconvinced. "Good luck with that."

Despite her very firm declaration that there would be no future with Caleb, she couldn't help feeling that she owed Dillon an apology for the future that wasn't in the cards for them, either. "I'm sorry."

"Why are you sorry?" he asked, though his expression was sad. "You broke up with me years ago." He gave her a rueful look. "Unfortunately, that didn't stop me from hoping that maybe we were going to have a second chance."

"Dillon—"

"Stop. No need to be upset," he told her. "It's not as

if you made me any promises. Heck, you didn't even want to have dinner with me."

"Only because I didn't want anyone, least of all you, to get the wrong impression," she said gently. "You were my best friend once. I'd like to think we're still friends, but that's all it will ever be. And despite what you think, that has nothing at all to do with Caleb. I know you probably don't believe that, but it's true."

"You're sure of that?" he asked, clearly disappointed.

"Afraid so." She looked into his eyes. "I wish it were otherwise. I really do. This situation with Caleb would be a lot easier if I were falling madly in love with you."

"You're positive there's no chance of that?" he asked.

"I'm sorry," she said again.

He shrugged. "Getting rejected is not going to stop me from worrying about you, you know."

"You don't need to worry. I know exactly who Caleb is. He won't get a second chance to break my heart."

Dillon smiled at that. "Tough talk, Jenny, but something tells me it's way too late. Despite everything, it's evident to me that he already has a pretty solid grip on your heart again."

Jenny knew she could deny it all she wanted, but the sad truth was that he might be right. That didn't mean she had to listen to her heart, not when she knew so well how much pain could follow.

Dusk was falling when Jake and the rest of the extended O'Brien clan left Caleb alone on the porch to await Jenny's arrival. He'd settled into an old swing hanging from the ceiling, the control for the lights in his hand. For now, though, the yard was in shadowy darkness. Bree had called fifteen minutes earlier to alert him that Jenny was leaving the theater and heading for the house.

"She was a little peeved that you never came back this afternoon, in case you're interested," Bree said. "I think she was wondering what you were up to. Jake says the yard looks amazing."

"He's the expert," Caleb said. "Please tell him again how grateful I am for the help."

"Will do. Enjoy the evening."

He set the swing in motion as he waited, his nerves jittery as he anticipated Jenny's reaction to the surprise. When her car turned the corner at the end of the block, Caleb sat up a little straighter. He watched as she hesitated at the end of the driveway when she saw his truck parked there. He could imagine her drawing in a deep breath, then deciding not to let his presence chase her off.

It still took a few minutes, though, before she finally cut the engine and stepped out of the car.

"Caleb, what are you doing here?" she asked as she closed the car door.

"Just a few odds and ends," he called back, then hit the switch.

Lights came on everywhere. White lights wound through the trees. Colored lights outlined the house. Spotlights shone on the figures in the yard, at least on those that weren't lit up themselves.

"Oh, my heaven," she said, her hand over her mouth, her expression stunned as she stood at the edge of the driveway. "What have you done?"

He flipped a second switch and the train whistle blew. It chugged around the yard, then stopped in front of her, giving her a clear view of Santa in the caboose.

"Jake and Thomas seemed to think this is pretty close to the one you loved so much," he said, stepping off the porch and crossing to where she seemed to be rooted in place.

Jenny turned to him, her eyes shining with unshed tears. "You found another train," she whispered.

"Is it okay?"

In response, she threw her arms around him and kissed him squarely on the mouth, her face damp with tears. "It's the most perfect, the most amazing thing anyone has ever done for me," she said. "I can't believe you went to all this trouble. Where did you find the train? When?"

"I spotted it last night and managed to steer you to another part of the store before you got a glimpse of it," he said, one arm holding her snugly against him. "After you went to bed, I went back to get it."

The twinkling lights in the yard were reflected in her eyes. "You can't possibly have done all this yourself in one afternoon," she said.

"I had help," he confirmed. "Bree rallied the troops."

Jenny's expression turned incredulous. "She called Jake?"

"And Mick, Thomas, Mack and Connor and a slew of others," he added. "We've had quite an afternoon. Ate a whole lot of barbecue and drank a whole lot of soda."

She regarded him with amusement. "And now you have the whole O'Brien fraternity on your side," she guessed.

"Well, the train seemed to make an impression on your uncle, that's for sure, but believe me, I have been duly warned that I am not to hurt you ever again. The entire contingent, led by Mick, is probably lurking in the bushes right now to be sure that you're fully in control of the situation."

She sighed as she leaned into him. "I want to be in control," she said wistfully. Then she met his gaze. "But you seem to have a knack for taking my breath away, Caleb Green. It's really annoying under the circumstances."

He couldn't seem to stop himself from smiling. "So you like the surprise?"

"I love the surprise," she said. "And if I weren't trying so darn hard to hang onto my last shred of sanity, you'd be getting very lucky about now."

"Sanity's overrated," he suggested, holding her close.

"It probably is," she agreed. "But I have to, Caleb. I can't take another chance. Not yet."

"I get that," he told her. "I really do. I have to earn your trust again, Jenny. I understand that."

"Just so you know, though, this..." She gestured around at the colorful display of lights. "It goes a long way toward telling me how you feel."

"More effective than a kiss?" he wondered, thinking he might not be able to survive much longer if he couldn't capture her mouth beneath his.

"Much more," she said, then smiled. "But one little kiss might not be entirely out of order."

She didn't have to say it twice. Caleb lowered his head and touched his lips to hers, savoring the sweet surrender.

And for the first time since his life had fallen apart by his own doing, it suddenly felt as if it might be on its way to being right again.

When Jenny finally made herself step away from Caleb, she was trembling from the inside out. There was nothing she wanted more desperately than to take his hand, lead him upstairs to that king-size bed and make love with him again.

Instead, she gave his hand a squeeze and said only, "How do you feel about cold pizza? There's a large one in the front seat of the car."

Even inviting him inside for warmed-up pizza was a risk, but she couldn't bear the thought of sending him away after what he'd done today just to make her happy.

"You sure about that?" he asked, his expression knowing. "It's not far from the kitchen to your bed."

"Far enough," she said with determination. Her emotions might be out of control, but she was made of sterner stuff.

"Okay, then. Pizza sounds good. I'll grab it. You go on inside and turn on the oven."

"There's a bag with paper plates and napkins in there, too," she called after him.

"Got it," he said.

On her way to the kitchen, she tossed her coat at the foot of the stairs, then deliberately turned on every light in her path in the hope that all that brightness would keep both of them from getting any romantic notions.

She flipped on the oven, then spotted plastic cups on the counter along with a few unopened bottles of soda. Her hands shook as she put ice into the cups, then poured the drinks. By the time Caleb joined her, she was convinced her nerves were under control, but one glance into his eyes told her otherwise. She didn't give two hoots about soda or pizza. She wanted him.

But she wasn't going to give in, she told herself staunchly. She just had to keep remembering all those lectures she'd been giving herself, all those claims she'd made to Dillon. She needed to remember every heart-breaking second of Caleb's betrayal.

Suddenly she realized that Caleb was regarding her with amusement. "What?" she demanded.

"Did you win the struggle just then?" he asked. "Or did I?"

She frowned at his conviction that he knew what had been going on in her head. "You have no idea what you're talking about," she said. "I was just trying to figure out where we were going to eat, since we don't have a table."

"If you say so," he replied, clearly unconvinced. "I have a blanket in the truck. Why don't I grab that, make a fire, and we can eat in the living room?"

So much for avoiding a romantic ambiance, Jenny thought, remembering a few too many occasions when lovemaking had followed a meal in just such a setting back in Nashville. She couldn't let him see that the notion rattled her, though.

"Sure," she said breezily. "Sounds perfect."

But a few minutes later when she walked in the living room with the pizza and found the atmosphere every bit as romantic as she'd feared, her heart stuttered. This was a bad idea, she told herself, even as she handed Caleb the hot pizza and settled beside him in front of the fire.

Or maybe it was the best idea either of them had had in months.

9

"How'd the work go this afternoon?" Caleb asked Jenny as they finished up their pizza in front of the fire. He'd picked the topic mostly to distract himself from the way the firelight played over her skin and danced in her eyes. He was starting to want her way too much.

"It would have gone better if you'd been around to run the lyrics with me," she told him, as if he were the one who'd run off and cut the session short.

He smiled but didn't call her on it. "Since when do you really want my input at this stage? You mostly grumble that I'm messing with your creative process."

"Okay, that's true," she conceded. "But I couldn't seem to get focused. I really should have insisted you come back after lunch. After all, this show's success depends as much on you as it does on me."

He had a hunch her irritation had nothing to do with him or his failure to return to the theater earlier. "What's this attitude really about, Jenny? Didn't lunch with the ex go the way you wanted it to?"

"Lunch with Dillon was just fine," she said a little too quickly.

"But he was unhappy to discover I was hanging around, wasn't he?" he asked, taking a certain amount of masculine pleasure in that. How could he not? Dillon's mere existence made him crazy. Why shouldn't he return the favor?

"It's not up to him to approve or disapprove," Jenny responded.

"That doesn't mean he's happy about it," Caleb told her. "Can't say that I blame him. I'm not overjoyed about bumping into him at the theater all the time, either." When she would have snapped back a retort, he held up a hand. "Not that I have any right to complain."

"No, you don't. And how many times have you actually bumped into him there, anyway? He's only been by twice, and the first time..." Her voice trailed off and her eyes widened. "You were there that day, too?"

"I was."

"And what? You stood outside the door and eavesdropped on a private conversation?"

"I overheard enough to figure out who he was, then I left," he replied.

"How discreet of you."

He smiled at her annoyance. "I thought so." He hesitated, then asked, "How did the two of you leave things? Again, not that it's any of my business."

"It's not your business," she agreed, "but if you must know, I told him that nothing's going to happen between us again, that I think of him as a friend." She leveled a determined look into his eyes. "I'm not interested in a relationship with anyone at the moment. I've had enough drama to last a lifetime."

Caleb shuddered at the firm declaration, empathizing with Dillon for being blown off so emphatically. "That must have stung," he said, as if he didn't know perfectly well that she'd intended the same message for him.

"I also told him nothing was going to happen with you again, either," she said, intent on clarifying the point he'd deliberately ignored. "You can wipe that smug look off your face. You were behind all the drama, so I'm definitely immune to you."

He laughed. "Here's the difference, sweetheart. He probably took you at your word. I know for a fact you're just saying that because you know we're going to get back together eventually and you're hoping to postpone the inevitable."

"Caleb, you don't know everything," she said, clearly frustrated by his refusal to take her seriously. "I said I'm immune and I meant it."

"If you say so," he agreed solemnly.

That said, he decided a timely retreat was in order and stood up, then gathered the pizza box, paper plates and cups. Jenny regarded him curiously.

"Since when do you clean up after a meal?"

"I'm trying to make a good impression, remember?" He winked at her. "See you tomorrow."

Her expression faltered, proving that despite her very stern reminder about her lack of interest, she wasn't half as certain about what she wanted as she claimed. "You're leaving?"

"I am," he said. "If I don't, I can't promise I won't try something. Since you're so sure that's not what you want, it's best if I go rather than proving you wrong."

"As if you could," she muttered.

Caleb gave her a long look. "Is that a challenge, Jennifer Louise? Do you want me to try?"

"Absolutely not," she said at once, but there was no

mistaking her disappointment. Acting and lying weren't part of her skill set.

"Okay, then," he said agreeably. "See you tomorrow."

"It's Sunday. We won't be working," she reminded him.

"I know. I'll still see you," he said, thinking of the invitation he had to join the family at Mick's. Jenny apparently didn't know about that. It was probably better that way. She might warn him off and he'd feel obligated to comply with her wishes.

He could feel her watching him as he walked away. Once he'd dumped the trash in the kitchen, he went back and found her still sitting where he'd left her, looking a little lost and a whole lot perplexed.

"Something wrong?"

She glanced up at him. "You're a very confusing man, Caleb."

He laughed. "I'll consider that progress, Jen. It's much better than anything you were saying about me as recently as last week."

And if he had his way, she'd have reasons to sing his praises in the not-too-distant future.

A family dinner at Mick's was an O'Brien Sunday tradition, one that Jenny had actually enjoyed when she and her mom had gone along with Jake and Bree. For an only child of a single mom, being around such a large, rambunctious family had given her a taste of a life she'd only dreamed about. Even now she saw the irony of not fully embracing the chance to be part of this one once it had become a reality. But when her mom and Thomas had gotten together, it had felt weird.

Today, unfortunately, was no different. She still felt

like an outsider. With children running around underfoot and the kitchen overloaded with too many cooks, Jenny grabbed her jacket and escaped to the porch where she could stare out at the bay and think about something besides family dynamics. Instead, she pondered the odd note on which she and Caleb had parted the night before.

Sadly, after a half hour of grappling with the possible reasons for his unexpected departure, she was no closer to figuring out what he was up to or why she wasn't as immune to him as she'd imagined herself to be. She told herself that the time in this serene setting on a surprisingly mild day might be better spent trying to work out the troubling second verse of the song Bree wanted to end the first act of the play.

She ran out to her car, grabbed her guitar and settled again in the rocker. Unfortunately the instant she'd strummed the first few notes, she glanced up and into Caleb's dark brown eyes. A shudder swept over her that had nothing to do with the chill in the air.

"You!" she said, startled. How in heaven's name had he wangled an invitation to a family dinner?

He didn't seem unduly bothered by the lack of warmth in her voice. "Such a lovely welcome!"

She sighed. "Sorry. My manners seem to desert me when I'm caught off guard. I'm guessing Bree invited you. She has a habit of taking in strays, even if nobody wants them around."

Caleb only smiled at the intended barb. "She did."

"And it didn't occur to you that she was only being polite?"

"Of course it did, but since you and I seem to be getting along okay these days, I figured you wouldn't object to my turning up. Is it a problem?"

"Of course not," she said. "Why didn't you say anything last night?"

"I thought it might be more fun to take you by surprise."

She knew better. "You thought I'd tell you to stay away, didn't you?"

He shrugged. "That was always a possibility and, as I told you the other day, I always wondered about this family you were trying so hard to leave behind. I wanted to come today."

"A lot of them are going to hate you on principle," she commented, taking a little too much delight in that. She could recall the last time Bree had invited an outsider, a former lover who'd come to town to win her back. The entire family had been stunned. Jenny's uncle had walked out in a fit of jealous rage. It had taken days for the uproar to die down. Today promised to have a similar outcome. Amazingly, Caleb didn't seem concerned.

"I'm pretty sure I won over most of the men yesterday," he told her.

"That still leaves the women," she reminded him. "We have longer memories, and we're not all bound by some kind of testosterone oath."

"I can take it," he assured her.

"Really?" she asked skeptically. "You used to thrive on adulation, especially of the female variety."

"Still do, but I'm not worthy of much of that these days, especially when it comes to folks who care about you. I have a lot of work to do to earn that back."

She was stunned by his candor. It demonstrated a

surprisingly new level of self-awareness. "Wow, if you truly believe that—"

"I do."

She met his gaze for the first time, studying the face that she'd once known so well. "I want to believe you've really changed, Caleb. For your sake. That self-destructive path you were on was going to ruin you, right along with your career."

"No doubt about it," he agreed. "If I learned nothing else in rehab, at least I figured out just how close I'd come to hitting bottom. I imagine I'll stumble from time to time, but I *have* changed, Jenny. You can count on that. I will never hurt you again."

"No, you won't," she said quietly. "I won't let you get close enough to hurt me."

"So you keep saying." A smile tugged at the corners of his sensual mouth. "I guess we'll see about that."

Just then the front door opened and Carrie and Caitlyn, Abby's teenage twins, peered out at them.

"Oh, my God!" Carrie exclaimed. "It really is him. I didn't believe Aunt Jess when she told us that Caleb was actually here at Grandpa Mick's."

While Carrie appeared to be awed by his presence, Caitlyn's expression was indignant. "Jenny, how can you even stand to look at that man after what he did to you?" She whirled on her twin. "And you, get over the starry-eyed, hero-worship thing. He might be the hottest thing in country music since Tim McGraw or Kenny Chesney, but you know he's a creep."

Despite her own misgivings about the situation, Jenny stepped in.

"It's okay, Caitlyn. Caleb's not here because of me.

Your Aunt Bree asked him to perform a couple of songs in the play. You know how persuasive she can be."

"Well, I can't imagine what she was thinking," Caitlyn said. "Did she invite him here today, too?"

"Of course she did, you ninny," Carrie said. "Remember that guy from Chicago? She hated his guts, but she asked him to come to Thanksgiving dinner. Unlike you, Aunt Bree doesn't hold grudges."

Jenny glanced at Caleb and noted that he seemed more amused than distraught by the debate over his presence. "Caleb, I want you to meet Carrie and Caitlyn. Their mom's an O'Brien. Abby. She's bound to be inside somewhere."

"Twins?" he guessed.

"Yes, but we're nothing alike," Caitlyn was quick to declare.

"Are you really going to be in the Christmas play?" Carrie asked Caleb.

"I've agreed to take a small part," he said. "I'll be singing a couple of Jenny's songs."

"I told you we should be in the play," Carrie said to her sister. "It would be awesome to tell the kids at school we were onstage with Caleb Green. They would totally freak out."

"And I told you to go ahead," Caitlyn reminded her. "I have too much studying to do."

Carrie rolled her eyes. "She could make straight A's without cracking a book. She'll probably graduate from college in three years instead of four."

"While you'll drag it out as long as possible because you like the parties," Caitlyn countered.

Jenny laughed, but Carrie didn't even bother trying to deny it.

"So what if I want to meet someone and get married?" Carrie said. "That's what you're supposed to do in college. Half the seniors in our sorority are already engaged and planning June weddings."

"If Mom heard you say that, she'd have a heart attack," Caitlyn responded.

"Mom's been married twice," Carrie countered.

"But she has a great job and is totally capable of being an independent woman. That's what she wants for us, to be able to stand on our own two feet. You'll be happy to marry some rich guy and let him pay the bills."

Carrie shrugged, clearly unoffended. "There could be worse things."

"Like having no job skills when he divorces you," Caitlyn suggested.

It was obviously a long-running discussion between the two young women. Jenny dared to step in. "For whatever it's worth, I'm with your mom," she said.

"So am I," Caleb added, drawing a shocked look from Carrie and the first approving one of the encounter from Caitlyn.

"People should always know who they are and what they're capable of accomplishing before they get into a relationship," Caleb said. "You don't want to live in someone else's shadow."

"Exactly," Caitlyn responded. She hesitated, then glanced at Jenny. "Is that how it was with you two?"

"Jenny was already successful when we met," Caleb said before Jenny could try to explain the complexities of their relationship, probably in more detail than either girl needed to hear.

"But you took her talent to another level when you

started collaborating," Carrie said, her gaze on Caleb. "Isn't that true?"

It was Jenny who answered. "Yes," she said.

"But she would have done incredible work even if I'd never come along," Caleb insisted.

"But together you were magic," Carrie said dreamily.

Jenny bit back a sigh. Most of the time they had been.

Carrie looked from Jenny to Caleb and back again, then said softly, "I hope you will be again. I bet this play will rock because of the two of you. Come on, Caitlyn. We should leave them alone."

Caitlyn rolled her eyes. "Now you're Miss Sensitivity." She glanced worriedly at Jenny. "Do you want us to go?"

"Why don't we all go inside?" Jenny suggested. "Dinner's bound to be ready soon."

With any luck, she could find a place at the table far, far away from Caleb. Unfortunately, steering clear of all the likely matchmakers was going to be more difficult.

Nell O'Brien was everything Caleb had heard her described to be, a petite matriarch who ruled over the household with a great deal of love and wisdom. Dillon O'Malley, who'd once been an old flame in Ireland and was now her second husband, sat beside her and quietly looked after her every need, putting a little extra food on her plate, keeping her water glass filled.

What really touched Caleb, though, was not the attentiveness, but the unmistakable tenderness in his expression as he watched Nell's interactions with this huge, rambunctious family. He was clearly prepared to jump in at the slightest hint of disrespect, though it seemed unlikely to Caleb that the need would ever arise. Everyone clearly adored Nell.

"They're remarkable, aren't they?" Jenny commented.

Despite her very deliberate attempts to find a place at the far end of the massive dining room table, Jenny had landed in the seat beside him. Caleb had noted the precise instant when she'd realized that changing places would cause more commotion than it was worth.

"Theirs is such a romantic story," she said, her expression wistful. "They fell in love as teenagers while she was visiting her grandparents in Ireland, but she came back to the States to marry someone else. Then, years later, she went back with the whole family at Christmas…" She looked at him. "I told you about that trip, right?"

Caleb nodded. What he remembered, though, was that she'd found out on Christmas Day that her mom and Thomas were expecting a baby. That news had left her reeling. He was a little surprised that she remembered other events of the trip with such distinct fondness.

"Anyway, Nell went to the old tobacco shop that had been run by her grandfather. Dillon had worked there during the summer, and he was still there. He owns it now, along with a ton of other businesses. He was a widower, and he'd never forgotten her."

She smiled. "Mick nearly had a heart attack over his mother dating an old flame. You'd have thought she was an errant teenager, rather than in her eighties," she told Caleb. "Everyone else thought it was fantastic. Dillon came here for a visit a few months later, they got married in the garden at Nell's cottage on the same day his granddaughter married Luke, Nell's grandson. Now they live there."

"That is pretty amazing," Caleb said. It was proof of just how long love could endure when it was right. He could only hope his and Jenny's was that strong.

He noticed that on Jenny's other side, her little brother was trying to get her attention. More than once, he'd noticed how difficult it seemed to be for Jenny to warm up to the boy who clearly craved her affection.

"Hey, buddy," Caleb said. "What's up?"

There was no mistaking the frown on Jenny's lips, even though it came and went in a heartbeat as she reluctantly turned to Sean.

"Guess what, Jenny? Mommy and Daddy bought me a guitar so I can learn to play music like you," Sean announced excitedly. He'd clearly decided music might be the link to tie him to his big sister.

"Wanna hear me play?" he asked her.

When Jenny remained silent a beat too long, Caleb jumped in. "Absolutely," he said at once. "We can have a jam session after lunch, you and me. How about it?"

Sean looked confused. "What's a jam session?"

"We'll play something together," Caleb explained. "Maybe I can teach you some chords or one of Jenny's songs."

"One of Jenny's songs," Sean said beaming. His expression faltered as he turned to her. "Would that be okay?"

Caleb awaited her reply with almost as much nervousness as Sean did.

"Of course," she told him.

"Me, too. Me, too," Emily Rose announced when she overheard them. Her face fell. "But I don't have a guitar."

"I have a spare," Caleb said at once. "It might be a

little too big for you, but we can figure out a way to make it work."

Jenny seemed startled by his response. She leaned over. "Caleb, you don't have to do that," she told him quietly. "I know how expensive those guitars of yours are. They're not toys."

"It's no big deal," he insisted. "I want to do this." Maybe she hadn't seen the hope in that little boy's eyes, but he had. And who could turn a blind eye to Emily Rose when she was filled with such boundless excitement? Somebody had to build a bridge between all of them. Maybe he could at least get it started.

Jenny shrugged. "Up to you."

He gave her a long look. "You'll be joining us, right? We need Jenny to play, too, don't we, Sean?"

The boy's head bobbed enthusiastically. "Please, Jenny."

"Yes, please, Jenny," Emily Rose echoed.

Jenny hesitated, then nodded. "Sure."

Over Sean's head, Connie caught Caleb's eye. "Thank you," she mouthed.

He merely winked back.

He'd wondered when he came to Chesapeake Shores if he could possibly make peace with Jenny, wondered, too, if he'd ever find a way to fit in. Day by day, though, it was increasingly clear that while they might not entirely trust him yet, Jenny's extended family had warm hearts and were eager to welcome him. He might even have a role to play in at least one little boy's relationship with the big sister he so desperately wanted to impress.

Caleb had run out to his truck to retrieve his guitars after lunch while Jenny hid out in the kitchen helping the women clean up. She'd harbored the faint hope that he wouldn't come looking for her on his return.

"I like your young man," Nell said to her as they put away the dishes while Jess, Abby and Bree finished drying them. "I'm aware he made some mistakes, but I can tell how fond he is of you."

"He's not my young man," Jenny told her. "Not anymore."

Nell chuckled. "If you've told him that, he doesn't seem to be buying it."

"Because he's stubborn," Jenny said in frustration.

"Well, for whatever it's worth, I don't think you should be so quick to write him off."

Jenny regarded her curiously. "Why? You've barely exchanged more than a few sentences with him."

"I saw how kind he was to Sean," she said simply. "For a man who's new to all of us to see what that child needed—what you need—demonstrates a depth of sensitivity I don't see all that often." She smiled. "Except in my own family, of course. I like to think I've had a little influence with them."

Just then Caleb came back into the kitchen, Sean and Emily Rose hanging on his every word. He'd made conquests, Jenny thought, not entirely certain how she felt about that. How was she supposed to hold out, to cling to her well-deserved anger, when everyone else was giving Caleb the benefit of the doubt?

Caleb bent down and whispered something to Sean. A shy smile spread across her little brother's face, though there was uncertainty in his eyes as he approached Jenny and Nell. As if she understood, Nell put a reassuring hand on his shoulder.

"Jenny, Caleb wants to know if you're ready to play music now," Sean asked, his expression hopeful.

Aware that everyone in the kitchen had gone silent awaiting her reply, she bit back any last trace of resentment and forced a smile she hoped looked genuine. "Absolutely," she told him. She glanced at Nell. "Do you suppose Mick would mind if we used his office, so we don't drive off the rest of the guests? This could be more noise than music."

Nell immediately shook her head. "I think we're all going to want to hear. You'll play in the living room." She glanced toward Caleb. "If you happen to play a few old Christmas carols, I might even be tempted to join in on the piano."

Caleb grinned at her. "Now we have ourselves a real jam session, Sean."

Sean ran back to him and slapped his hand in a jubilant high five.

Jenny shook her head. "The man is full of surprises," she commented under her breath.

Nell laughed. "Take a word of advice from someone who's been around a very long time. Surprises are essential. Not a day goes by that Dillon doesn't find some new way to take my breath away. Whoever thought that at my age, with all I've seen and done, anyone would be able to do that again?" She glanced toward the doorway to the dining room, spotted the man in question, and blushed like a girl.

"I hope I can find someone like that someday," Jenny said.

Nell pointedly looked in Caleb's direction. "Not that my opinion is the one that counts, but it seems to me you already have."

Jenny had a huge amount of faith in Nell's wisdom, but this time? She told herself Nell wouldn't have sounded half so certain if she knew everything Caleb had done not only to destroy his own life, but to rip her heart to shreds, too.

Of course, the real problem was that even though she'd lived through the experience, she was starting to have trouble remembering just how devastating it had been. And that, she warned herself, certainly wasn't good.

10

Just a few notes into one of the first hits that Caleb had recorded of one of Jenny's songs, Emily Rose picked up a pink princess hairbrush and began belting out the lyrics like a little pro. She missed the notes more often than not, but made up for it in flair and enthusiasm. Caleb accompanied her with an expression of astonishment on his face. As she strummed along, Jenny couldn't help laughing at the two of them. She wasn't sure which one was having more fun.

When they'd finished their duet, everyone in the room burst into spontaneous applause and cheers. Emily Rose bowed deeply from the waist, a huge grin on her face. Caleb leaned down and kissed her cheek, whispering something into her ear that had her laughing, then scampering away to climb into Jake's arms.

Caleb and Jenny put down their guitars then, since it was evident that nothing could top that performance. As the family slowly started to disperse, Caleb moved closer to Jenny. He gave her a peck on the cheek no friendlier than the one he'd given Emily Rose.

"A pleasure performing with you again," he said, his voice solemn, but a twinkle in his eyes.

"Is that what you said to Emily Rose?"

"Nah. I told her I was thinking we ought to team up," he said. "I said I'd have my people speak to her people."

Jenny laughed at the outrageous suggestion. "Watch it, pal. That little girl is already smitten. If you're not careful, she's going to expect you to take her on the road on your next concert tour."

"I could do a lot worse for an opening act," he said. "Or a duet partner. She'd have the crowds eating out of the palm of her hand."

"Bree and Jake might object," Jenny said, though she actually wondered about that. Bree might be all for her daughter being a superstar by age six.

"I imagine I could convince them," Caleb said confidently. His gaze narrowed and he studied her more intently. "How about you, Jenny? Did you have fun this afternoon?"

"Surprisingly, yes," she admitted.

"You made Sean happy, I know that."

"He's a good kid," she acknowledged. She might not entirely feel the family connection the way everyone wanted her to, but she certainly wasn't immune to his bright smile and eagerness to please.

"He adores you," Caleb reminded her. "Your mom has obviously made sure he thinks of you as his big sister, even though you haven't been around much."

"I haven't been around at all," she corrected. "I'm still embarrassed by that. Maybe if I had been, I'd feel a stronger connection to him."

"Instead of that last little bit of lingering resentment?" Caleb asked with surprising insight.

"Okay, yes. A part of me does resent him, but I do know that's wrong. None of this was his fault. It's nobody's fault. Mom and Thomas fell in love. They had a child together, which is an incredible gift. I need to grow up and get over it. I realize that my attitude stinks," she said, unable to keep a defensive note from her voice. "And I know everyone is still judging me for that."

"I haven't heard a single critical word," Caleb told her. "In fact, it seems to me the only person who hasn't understood how hard this has been and forgiven you for taking the time you needed to adjust is you."

"Everyone's just too discreet to say anything in front of you," she insisted. "For all the inroads you may have made with your charm, you're still even more of an outsider than I am."

Caleb frowned. "Why do you keep saying that? You're not an outsider, Jenny. These people are family, or at least they're willing to be. Can't you at least meet them halfway?"

She was startled by the impatience in his voice. Now he, too, was judging her? What right did he have? He hadn't been here, hadn't known the bond she'd had with her mom before Thomas and then Sean had taken her place.

"You don't understand," she said, blinking back tears.

"No, I don't," he acknowledged. "I've heard the longing in your voice, the admiration, when you talked about the O'Briens. I assumed they were the ones who hadn't accepted the situation, that you were like a kid locked outside a candy store with all those wonderful treats just out of reach. Instead, you've had the key all along."

She knew he was right. Why couldn't she accept that

she had a rightful place in their midst? Was she simply scared they'd take that love away as her father had? Did she think it was better never to experience it than to want it so badly, then lose it?

"I can't think about this now," she said. "It's too confusing."

For once Caleb didn't push. "Want to take off? Maybe get a burger or something?"

She wasn't sure which startled her more, his sensitivity or his suggestion that they grab a bite to eat. The latter was less dangerous.

"You can eat again already?" she asked incredulously. "After all that pot roast? You ate as if you'd never had a home-cooked meal before."

"I haven't had many like that," he said. "My mom wasn't much of a cook. There aren't a lot of home-cooked meals to be had on tour. As for you, you were the queen of takeout. You had a drawer filled with menus from every place in a ten-mile radius that delivered."

She gave him a wry look. "You always seemed eager enough for pizza."

"One of the staples of life," he agreed. "I'm not complaining, just observing." He regarded her curiously. "Can you cook?"

"Sure," she said a little too quickly. "If I have to. Play your cards right and maybe I'll show you one of these days."

"I'll look forward to it. For now, how about that burger?"

"No food," she said. "But I will go along if you're starving." Anything to get away from here and all the spoken and unspoken questions for which she had no ready answers.

They said their goodbyes then, thanking both Mick and Megan for including them, and then spending a moment with Nell.

"We'll expect to see you here again on Christmas, if not before," Nell told them. "Is that understood?"

"Yes, ma'am, and thank you," Caleb said.

Nell regarded Jenny intently. "And you?" she prodded gently.

"I'll be here," Jenny promised, then acknowledged to her as she had to others, "I know how wrong it was to stay away so long."

"You stayed away as long as it took to get your feet back under you," Nell corrected. "Now you can concentrate on looking forward."

Relieved by the apparent understanding which confirmed Caleb's earlier observation, Jenny enveloped her in a warm hug. "Thanks."

"No thanks needed, precious child. I consider you as much my granddaughter as anyone else in this family."

Tears stung Jenny's eyes at the comment. She didn't want Nell or even Caleb to see how touched she was. Understanding was one thing, but unconditional acceptance? It was such an unexpected blessing.

She quickly turned away and hurried to the door. When she glanced back, she saw Caleb give Nell's hand a reassuring squeeze. Even from the doorway, she could overhear him telling her that she'd said exactly the right thing.

"I hope so," Nell said, sounding worried. "She shouldn't be walking through life alone when there are so many of us who love her." She gave him a pointed look. "I count you among them."

"You can," he said.

She nodded. "Then do whatever it takes to make certain she knows that."

Jenny saw the glint of determination in Caleb's eyes and knew then exactly how much trouble she was in. Up until now, Caleb had been pushing gently to make his way back into her life. Now, with Nell's apparent blessing, she had a hunch he was going to launch a full-court press. And no matter how many misgivings she might have, she wasn't sure she'd be able to resist.

"Boy, your string of conquests in Chesapeake Shores keeps getting longer and longer," Jenny said as she and Caleb sat at a table overlooking the bay in Brady's. "Bree, Emily Rose, the guys, Sean and now Nell."

Caleb shrugged. "That's just because I didn't break their hearts," he said simply. "That doesn't mean most of them aren't angry about what I did to you or wary about my intentions toward you from here on out." He gave her a questioning look. "Are you upset about their accepting me? Do you feel as if I'm doing an end run around you?"

She shook her head at once. "I'm not really upset, just surprised."

"You were hoping for tar and feathers, weren't you?" he teased.

"Well, they could at least have made a pretense of hating you for my sake," she grumbled. "At least for one afternoon."

"How would that have made things any better? Would it have justified your holding me at arm's length longer? Helped you to reinforce all those defenses you put into place after I hurt you?"

"Something like that."

He held her gaze. "You do know that your opinion is the only one that matters to me, right? I like this huge extended family of yours, no question about it. They're good people. And I'm glad they seem willing to give me a chance. In the end, though, you're the one who counts, Jenny."

She gave him a perplexed look. "Why do you want me back, Caleb? Is it that you can't stand the thought of losing? Are you trying to prove something to yourself?"

He didn't like what she was implying. "Do you honestly think I'd come after you and court you, not because I love you, but just to see if I could get you back?"

"Anything's possible," she said.

Caleb realized that she wanted to believe he was that shallow. It would make it easier for her to keep withholding her forgiveness.

"Then what?" he prodded. "Do you think I'll humiliate you again? Walk away, satisfied that I've still got what it takes to get a woman, even one who has every reason to hate me?"

She winced at that. "It sounds horrible when you put it like that," she said.

"It sounds horrible no matter how I say it," he said. "Don't you know me better than that?"

"I did once," she said softly. "Now I don't know. Maybe you're just taking the whole making amends thing to a new level."

Caleb's temper stirred. He tried telling himself she had a right to be suspicious, a right to distrust him, but that didn't mean it didn't sting like crazy.

Fighting for control, he sat very still and leveled a look directly at her. "Look at me, Jenny," he commanded very quietly, then waited until her reluctant gaze finally lifted to meet his.

"I am not playing games with you," he said. "For all my flaws, and I have a whole ton of them, I have never used you or even deliberately hurt you. What I did was incredibly stupid and wrong and I've paid for it in ways you can't possibly imagine. I want to make that up to you, not because of any program, but because I owe that to you."

"Fine," she said, seemingly eager to slam the lid on the can of worms she'd opened. "Sorry."

"No, wait a minute. You started this. Now hear me out. I loved you even though it must not have seemed that way, given the thoughtless stunt I pulled. I still love you," he declared forcefully. "I came to Chesapeake Shores hoping to apologize. I've stayed, not just because Bree offered me an interesting opportunity to try something new, but to try to earn your trust again. Maybe even your love."

She opened her mouth, but he cut her off again.

"Hold on," he said. "You need to hear the rest. I want all of that, not to prove some point to myself, but because it physically hurts to think about going through life without you."

There was a sheen of tears in her eyes when he finished and he felt guilty about that, but he'd said what he needed to say. She could believe him or not, but he knew in his gut that this was a turning point. If she truly believed what she'd implied before, that he was up to no good, or only here for some selfish reason, then he'd lost. They'd never get back what they'd once had.

He thought of the song that had initially sent him to Chesapeake Shores. Amazingly, it was the first time it had crossed his mind in days. He was glad he hadn't mentioned it to her. She'd only see that as proof that his motives for being here weren't as straightforward as he'd led her to believe. Losing that song, letting Ricky Nolan go right ahead and turn it into a hit, was a small price to pay if he could reclaim Jenny.

After he'd said his piece, he sat back. "Your turn."

A tear streaked down her cheek. "I don't know what to say, Caleb. I want to believe you. I really do. Since you've been here, I've seen so many glimpses of the man I fell in love with. I've seen new sides to you, too. The way you were with Sean and Emily Rose today…" She smiled tremulously. "I had no idea you could be so sweet and patient."

"I like kids. I wouldn't mind having a whole houseful, if I could have them with you."

She gave him a startled look. "We never talked about having kids."

"I thought you understood that's where we were headed, at least until I went and ruined everything."

"Kids, Caleb? Really? How would that work with all the touring and the late nights in the studio?"

He chuckled. "It probably wouldn't, the way I was going after everything full throttle. I told you, though, that being a solo act will be different. My priorities are going to be different. There are plenty of musicians and singers who can balance a career and family."

"Are you one of them?" she asked skeptically. "You don't do anything by half measures. Look at how you've been since you got here. You're throwing yourself into courting me. You've embraced this Christmas play. And I have no doubt if your agent called and said he could get you a concert gig during the holidays, you'd find some way to give your all to that, too."

He shook his head. "That was the old me, trying to grab everything out of fear that it would disappear if I didn't seize it right then and there. I know better now. I've learned to prioritize." He shrugged. "I might even have learned a little bit about patience."

"Seriously?"

"Hey, have I been giving you time or not? The old me would have had you in bed by now."

She laughed. "That's what you think. I've learned a few things, too. I won't rush into some hot and heavy romance a second time."

"And I accept that," he said, a note of triumph in his voice as he added, "See what I mean? Patience is my middle name."

"Caleb, what on earth am I going to do with you?" she murmured.

"Anything you want to," he suggested. "I'm open to all sorts of possibilities." He held her gaze. "Are you?"

She drew in a deep breath. "I guess we'll have to wait and see."

"But you're not closing any doors?"

She hesitated, then shook her head. "I'm not closing any doors."

"Okay, then," he said, satisfied for now. "Why don't I get you home to get some rest? Tomorrow's going to be crazy with the rest of the cast hitting town and rehearsals going into full swing. You ready for that?"

"As ready as I'll ever be," she said, though her nervousness was plain.

"You worried about something?"

"This is a play. I've never written music for a play

Sherryl Woods

before. And the actors coming in—they're professionals. What if they think the songs are all wrong?"

"No way, sweetheart. I predict they're going to be
holiday classics the minute they're released."

Her eyes widened. "Released? What on earth are
you talking about?"

"Bree mentioned something to me earlier about putting out a single of one of the songs in time for the holidays. She spoke to your agent and mine about it. Didn't
she mention it to you?"

"She did not," Jenny said. "Neither did Margo."

"I gather your cell phone is still stuffed in a drawer
somewhere. Apparently Margo's been calling for days.
She even complained to me about your ignoring her
calls."

"*You* spoke to Margo, too?"

"She called me when she couldn't reach you," he
said. "I think she was afraid I was holding you hostage
and trying to brainwash you."

"And of course you convinced her you were behaving in an entirely proper way," she said, a bitter note
in her voice. "The newly reformed saint of Nashville."

Caleb laughed at her evident annoyance. "Hardly
that, sweetheart. And Margo still hates my guts, if that
makes you feel any better."

"Marginally," she said.

"I'm sure if you returned her call, she'd deliver all
sorts of stern warnings about getting mixed up with the
likes of me again. Or I could just repeat what she said
to me. None of it was flattering."

She leaned forward and propped her chin on her fist.
"Tell me," she said, looking intrigued.

Instead, he took his cell phone from his pocket and held it out. "I think it'll be better coming from her."

Jenny seemed surprised. "You're not scared she's going to succeed in warning me off?"

"Nope. I think you're made of tougher stuff than that."

"No, you just think you already have me right where you want me," Jenny corrected.

"If I had you where I wanted you, we'd be back at your place in that big king-size bed of yours," he said. "You're still holding all the cards." He winked at her. "But I am hopeful that you're coming around."

Even after the contentious way the evening had started, he was counting on it.

Jenny sat in the shadows at the back of the theater and listened as the cast ran through their lines from start to finish. There was only piano accompaniment to the music, at least until Caleb performed his two songs, when he added his guitar to the mix.

As the second act drew to a close, Bree slipped into the seat beside her. "What do you think?"

"For a first full rehearsal with actors who've just arrived, I thought it was pretty amazing," Jenny said honestly.

"And Caleb? How'd you think he did?"

"The man's a pro," Jenny acknowledged. "He knocked those songs out of the park."

"I'm going to expand his role a bit," Bree said. "I think he can handle it. I may add a couple more songs, too."

Jenny frowned. "Whose songs?"

"Yours, of course. Think you can do it?"

"We're cutting it awfully tight," Jenny protested, then rose to the challenge. "But I can try. What did you have in mind?"

Bree described the places in the play where she could envision adding songs. "I'll leave it up to you and Caleb. You both have great instincts about this. I truly am impressed by how well you work together, especially under less than optimum conditions. I can see now why your collaboration was such a success."

Jenny studied her with a narrowed gaze. "Why do I think this is more about throwing us together day and night than it is about what the play needs?" She gave Bree a stern look. "I heard about the whole single release you want to pull off practically overnight. A very sneaky tactic to go to our agents and get them on board. Even Margo's a little wild for the idea, and she can't stand Caleb. She'll move heaven and earth and the entire music industry to make this happen, even if the song only gets play on YouTube before the holidays. The woman knows a great public relations opportunity when it comes along."

"That's her job," Bree said. "I'm glad she's excited." She beamed at Jenny. "This whole thing is coming together in ways I never envisioned."

"You sure about that?" Jenny inquired.

"I had no idea Caleb would follow you here," Bree insisted. "Pure happenstance."

Jenny believed that much at least. It didn't mean her friend wouldn't take advantage of the happy serendipity once it was smack in front of her. As exasperating as that might be, she had to admit that there were a whole lot of positives to be gained for everyone.

Jenny glanced away from Bree just in time to see

the leading lady—Helena McGuire, a Tony-winning ingenue a decade ago—clinging to Caleb as if he were the absolute love of her life. The kiss she planted on him was hot enough to turn the entire auditorium into a sauna. Jenny whirled around to meet Bree's innocent gaze.

"That's where you're going with this? You're turning it into a romance between Caleb and that woman?"

"It's perfect, don't you think? They seem to have a lot of chemistry. I asked them to try the scene that way so I could see if it worked."

"I'm sure you must be thrilled with the results," Jenny said irritably.

Bree chuckled. "Well, I'm certainly thrilled to see the impact it's had on you. You might want to think about why you're acting as if Caleb is cheating on you all over again. It's a play, Jenny. They're acting."

Jenny sucked in a deep breath and tried to calm her fury. Bree was right. It *was* just a play. It shouldn't matter that the last time she'd seen Caleb draped all over another female like that it had been on the front page of a tabloid. This woman, at least, was wearing more clothes.

"I don't like it," she said, despite all the rational thoughts she'd tried to embrace.

"Because you're still in love with him," Bree suggested. She gave Jenny's shoulder a squeeze. "You have a lot to think about. I'll leave you to it."

"Talk about hit and run," Jenny muttered as Bree headed down front to give notes to the cast.

"I heard that," she called over her shoulder. "I'd love to hear those new lyrics tomorrow, by the way." She turned her attention away from Jenny and beckoned for Caleb. His new costar sashayed over right along with him.

"See me in my office in an hour," Bree told him. "I want to discuss a couple of ideas I have for expanding your role. In the meantime, maybe you can get together with Jenny and go over some ideas for those new lyrics you and I talked about earlier. She's going to want your input, I'm sure."

Jenny cursed the excellent acoustics of the theater because she heard every sneaky, conniving word out of her friend's mouth. She was aware of the precise instant when Caleb glanced her way. Was his expression smug? It was, she decided, her annoyance growing.

And that woman's hand had strayed to his backside, too. She had to be at least ten years older than Caleb. What was she thinking? Her behavior was embarrassing, especially since the two of them had met only hours earlier.

"I'm out of here," she muttered under her breath. If she didn't get away from here, there was every possibility she'd head for the stage and rip that woman's hair right out of her head. She'd do it without the tiniest hint of regret, too, or concern for the impact on the play. After all, weren't wigs totally commonplace onstage? She thought the actress would look especially lovely in a gray one with some heavy-duty wrinkles on her face. She wondered what Bree would think about her big romantic ending then.

Of course, what really ate at her was the worry that Caleb might not be put off in the slightest. For all she knew he was an equal opportunity philanderer who had absolutely no age restrictions at all.

She was still pacing and muttering in the rehearsal

hall when the door opened and closed quietly. She knew without turning exactly who it was and clamped her mouth firmly shut. She tried plastering a smile on her face, but she couldn't quite pull it off.

"You seem upset," Caleb said mildly.

"Nope. Just a little stressed by this latest idea of Bree's."

"Which one, to expand my role, add a couple of songs or end the show with a kiss?"

She whirled on him then. "You're loving this, aren't you?"

"The chance to have a bigger part? Sure. The possibility of another couple of songs? Absolutely."

"And the kiss? What about the kiss, Caleb?"

He took a step closer, then another. Only when he had her backed against the wall so she had nowhere to go did he touch a finger to her lips, the caress gentle, but enough to have her breath hitching.

Then he leaned in, covered her mouth with his and took his sweet time about reminding her of what a kiss could be when two people loved each other. She was trembling by the time he released her.

With his gaze locked on hers, he said softly, *"That's the only kissing I'm interested in, Jenny. That other stuff? There's no comparison."*

"Okay, then," she said, still trying to catch her breath. "Good thing."

"Why is that?"

She thought of her desire to rip the actress's hair out. "You don't want to know."

He laughed. "You may not be saying the words, sweetheart, but you can't hide the temper in your eyes.

You're jealous. Since I've been in the same place all too recently, I recognize the signs."

"I might have been," she conceded. "A tiny bit." She frowned at him. "Don't let it go to your head."

"Wouldn't dream of it," he said.

His tone was absolutely, 100 percent serious. The twinkle in his eye, however, was anything but. The blasted man knew her way too well.

11

Connie tapped hesitantly on the door of the house that had once been home to her family. She and Jake had grown up in this house. When her parents had left town and she'd been recently divorced, she and Jenny had moved in, grateful to be in familiar surroundings while they'd adjusted to life on their own.

She could hardly believe that her own daughter was now all grown up and living here, at least for the time being. She'd been waiting for Jenny to ask her over, but when the invitation hadn't come, she'd sucked in a deep breath, put together a welcome basket of some of Jenny's favorite homemade treats and come calling.

The door eventually swung open. Jenny regarded her with unmistakable surprise. "Mom! What are you doing here?"

"I thought I'd bring you a few things," Connie said, holding the basket aloft. "I have some of that strawberry jam we used to get at the farmer's market in the summer. Some local honey. There's peach preserves in here, too, and a jar of country relish."

Jenny's eyes lit up. "Your country relish?"

Connie laughed at her eager expression. "Yes, mine. I know how much you love it, so I found time to make a batch this summer just in case you got home. So, is this enough to get me invited in?"

Jenny stepped aside, her expression stricken. "Sorry. Come in. I wasn't expecting company."

"Since when am I company?" Connie asked, hurt by the comment but trying not to let it show.

"I just meant that I'm not really set up for people stopping by," Jenny explained. "Not anyone. You'll see." She beckoned Connie in.

As soon as Connie moved through the small foyer and looked around, she gasped. "There's no furniture."

"Exactly," Jenny responded.

"But I thought you and Caleb went shopping," Connie said, confused. "Hasn't the furniture been delivered yet? You should have put a rush on it. I can call and take care of that first thing in the morning."

"Slow down, Mom. There is no furniture on order." Jenny looked faintly chagrined. "We got a little caught up in buying Christmas decorations instead." Her expression brightened. "The yard's really something, isn't it? I can't recall ever having a better display out there. The neighbors have been stopping by to say so, too. Mrs. Walker says she sits at her front window and stares at it while she listens to Christmas music. Of course, I think she sits there all year long just to see what's going on in the neighborhood the way she always did."

Connie glanced out the window at the blinking explosion of colors on the lawn, then laughed. "I always knew you'd never get over being a kid at Christmas. I don't think it would have mattered if there was food on the table or even presents under the tree, what you cared about was the wonderland outside."

"Still true," Jenny said.

"Sean's the same way," Connie said, then immediately regretted it. Making comparisons, no matter how innocent, was no way to mend the gap between those two.

As if she'd sensed Connie's dismay, Jenny put a hand on her arm. "It's okay, Mom. I think I like knowing that Sean and I have that in common. You said he loved that old train as much as I did. You'll have to bring him over to see the new one. Caleb found it. He kept me from spotting it, then went back to the store and brought it home as a surprise."

Connie studied her and noticed the unmistakable brightness in her daughter's eyes when she mentioned Caleb. "Caleb is becoming a real fixture around town," she noted, ever so casually. "Even Ethel mentioned to me the other day what a down-to-earth guy he seems to be. She'd heard about the train, too. Apparently it's the vote-getter of the week as the most romantic gesture."

Jenny flushed. "It was sweet," she agreed. "As for Caleb being down-to-earth, he was never one to put on airs. That's one of the things I always liked about him. He was already a superstar when we met, but he didn't act like it. He's kind to everyone, not just in the business, but waiters, waitresses, store clerks, whatever. I was pretty green back then, scared to death that I wasn't good enough, but he treated me like an equal. Thanks to him, I finally started believing in myself and my music. Sure, you and Jake had faith in me, even Dillon, but this was an honest-to-goodness musician who loved what I was writing."

"Just shows what great taste he has," Connie said. "He not only saw how talented you are, but what a wonderful woman, too. Still thinks that, if what I saw over at Mick's is any indication."

She regarded her daughter with curiosity, wondering how far things had gone between them since Caleb had followed Jenny to town. "Seemed to me on Sunday that you might be mellowing toward him just a little, as well."

"Afraid so," Jenny said, looking more resigned than excited about it. "But don't worry. I'm not about to rush into anything. He's got a lot to prove to me before I'll take another chance. I'm not sure I'll ever be able to trust him entirely again. I was so sure of him before and just look what happened."

"Admittedly I don't know him all that well, but he seems to genuinely regret hurting you."

"Seems that way to me, too," Jenny replied. "But how am I supposed to know if it's real?"

"You'll figure it out," Connie said confidently.

Jenny merely shrugged. "Maybe."

Connie recognized the signal that Jenny was ready to put the topic of Caleb behind them. She glanced around at the empty living room then. "Sweetie, you can't live like this. Don't you want to go shopping for a sofa, maybe a couple of comfortable chairs?"

To her surprise, Jenny didn't seem interested.

"It hardly matters. I'm at the theater most of the time anyway. I have a bed. That'll do for now."

Connie frowned. "You're not thinking of giving this place up, after all, are you?"

"Absolutely not," Jenny said. "I just can't come up with a spare minute, much less a few hours to shop for furniture. I don't want to grab the first thing I see just to have something to sit on. I want to take my time. If this house is going to be my own little safe haven, it has to be perfect."

"I could help," Connie offered hesitantly. "Maybe take a look around, show you some pictures of what I've found so you can make the final decision. It would be fun, sort of like old times."

"You and me shopping together would be like old times," Jenny said, a hint of censure in her voice as if Connie had deliberately kept her at arm's length, rather than offering a well-meant hand.

Connie winced. Once again she'd inadvertently landed in a minefield. What on earth had happened to the days when she and Jenny had been totally in sync? Despite the strides they'd made on this visit, they obviously still had a long way to go before they got back there.

"I didn't mean..." she said, beginning yet another apology.

Jenny sighed and waved it off. "Don't apologize, Mom. That was a stupid thing for me to say. You were just trying to help."

"I was, you know."

"How about this? The first time I see a break in the schedule, I'll call you and we'll go together, even if I can only manage a couple of hours." A smile spread across Jenny's face. "Remember when we bought the new kitchen table, the one we both loved in the store, then discovered it had to be assembled? Two days later it was still in parts on the kitchen floor because you didn't want to admit to Uncle Jake that we couldn't figure it out."

"He would have gloated from then till doomsday," Connie said. "Thank goodness for Dillon. That boy had a knack for that kind of thing and he wasn't a blabbermouth." She gave Jenny a sly look. "I heard you had lunch with him at Brady's on Saturday."

"Just lunch," Jenny said. "Don't make anything out of it, Mom."

"I'm not the one who needs to be warned about that," she said.

"Not to worry. I made it clear to Dillon, too."

"Okay, then," Connie said, letting it go. "Now I'd better get home before Sean convinces Thomas that it's okay to have a banana split before bedtime. When it comes to ice cream, they're two of a kind."

She hesitated, then said, "You could come with me. Maybe I'd make an exception about that ice cream for once. You always wanted your share before bedtime, too."

"Still do," Jenny told her. "But tonight I need to get straight to sleep. Bree's turned out to be a very tough taskmistress. She keeps adding songs to the play. I think now that she's got Caleb locked in, she wants to take full advantage of it."

"She's not expecting too much of you, is she?" Connie asked worriedly.

Jenny shrugged. "Maybe a little, but I love the challenge. Don't tell her that, though. She'll turn this into a full-scale holiday operetta or something and I won't get a wink of sleep before New Year's."

Connie gave her a hug. "You speak up if she's asking too much, you hear me?"

"Promise," Jenny said. "I'm glad you came by. Next time I hope I'll be able to offer you a place to sit down. Maybe even some toast to go with that jam."

"I'll look forward to it, and to that shopping trip," Connie told her.

She walked slowly back to her car, satisfied that there had been a little more progress in getting her relationship with her daughter back on track. In a way it was ironic that the rift seemed to have happened in a heartbeat, but the repair was clearly going to take time. Thankfully, because of Brec and her play, she finally had that chance.

"You can't put a romantic ballad into the middle of a Christmas play," Jenny argued, sparks in her eyes as she faced down Caleb. "Or are you just eager for an excuse to play a little love scene with your costar? I'm sure Helena would be ecstatic about that."

"You know better," Caleb responded calmly.

"Then why are you pushing so hard for this?"

"Because it makes sense," he said. "Have you even read the most recent update of the script?"

"When would you suggest I do that? During the two hours I currently devote to sleep?"

His patience snapped and he stood up. "Okay, that's it, Jenny Louise. We're quitting for the night. Let's get out of here."

"Caleb, no way," she protested. "There's too much left to do. If you want to leave, go, but I'm staying right here until I have this figured out. I know the scene needs something, but a romantic ballad isn't it. This is a Christmas show, not a Broadway musical."

"If you took a break and got some sleep, you'd be more reasonable," he said, only to get a look that could have frozen an entire garden of fresh vegetables.

"Are you suggesting I'm refusing just to be stubborn?" she asked, radiating exasperation.

He merely lifted a brow. "Think about it, Jenny. Weren't there romances in a lot of the great Christmas movies? We're not performing the story of the birth of Jesus. The way I read Bree's play, it's about redemption and hope and forgiveness." Something Caleb thought reflected his situation with Jenny pretty accurately.

To his delight, they'd been arguing like this for a couple of days now. It had been like old times, when they'd been trying to come to a meeting of the minds over the lyrics of a song for his group's latest album. Jenny could string pretty words together, imbue them with soul and meaning, but Caleb had always pushed for more. He knew instinctively what would touch the heartstrings of an audience. Right now, he believed this show needed a romantic ballad, something to make the adults leave the theater with the same sense of holiday magic the kids would experience.

Or maybe what he really wanted was a chance to work on a song like that with Jenny again.

"You're not scared of working on a romantic ballad with me, are you?" he asked, a daring note in his voice. He knew Jenny couldn't resist a challenge.

"Why would I be?" she asked, an indignant flare of color in her cheeks.

"Because you remember what always happened after

we'd gotten a song like that just right," he said, his voice low and deliberately laced with seduction. "We'd get all caught up in the emotions and the next thing we knew, we'd be all over each other."

"That was then," she said fiercely, but there was more telltale color in her cheeks when she said it. "Those days are behind us, Caleb. Far, far behind us. Ancient history."

He smiled at her vehemence. "Okay, then, if you're not scared of what might happen, why not just give it a try? You'll write it, I'll perform it and we'll let Bree decide if it goes or stays." There wasn't a doubt in his mind what Bree would say. His respect for her had deepened over the past few days. He'd come to realize she was a woman who truly knew her stuff when it came to producing a show that would bring an audience to its feet.

"Okay, fine. Whatever," Jenny finally conceded. "I'll see if something comes to me."

"So gracious in defeat," he teased.

"You didn't defeat me," she countered stubbornly. "I said I'd give it a try. If you gloat, I could easily change my mind."

"No gloating, I promise," he said.

At least not till he was alone.

"Now let's get out of here and get something to eat."

"I'm not hungry."

He nearly rolled his eyes at the petulant tone. "Well, I am. I'll pick up a pizza and be back in twenty minutes. You want mushrooms, onions and peppers on yours?" Before she could respond with another claim of not being hungry, he answered his own question. "Of course you do. Back in a few."

He smiled to himself as he left the theater. Sometimes Jenny made taking care of her next to impossible. He'd learned a long time ago to ignore what she claimed aloud and act on what he saw in her eyes. Back then the tactic hadn't steered him wrong. He'd gotten pretty good at reading her and anticipating her needs. He thought about his unspoken plan for working that ballad into the play—the one he intended to discuss with Bree at the first opportunity—and hoped that he'd gotten it right this time, too.

Jenny walked into the rehearsal hall the next morning, new lyrics scribbled in a notebook. She'd spent the whole night trying to get the words just right. They'd flowed more easily than she'd expected on the first draft, but the fine-tuning she required of herself to seek perfection had taken a lot longer.

Entering the room, she stopped in her tracks. Caleb was sitting on the floor with Emily Rose cuddled in close on one side and Sean on the other. Her breath caught in her throat at how natural he looked with them, how at ease he was reading from a picture book.

How many times had she wondered about whether he was marriage material, much less father material? Though she'd tried to live in the moment when they were together, never entirely believing that their love could possibly last, she'd wondered about the future, imagined scenes a little too close to this one for comfort. Now, here he was for the second time lately, proving that she hadn't been entirely wrong to believe in that particular happy ending.

He glanced up and saw her. "There you are," he said, his eyes lighting up. "You're late."

"Sorry."

"No problem. I figured that meant you'd gotten an inspiration that kept you up half the night."

"You know me too well."

He held her gaze. "I did...once upon a time."

Emily Rose stared up at him, her eyes filled with adoration. "Is that the beginning of a story, Caleb?"

"It is," he said. "It's a story about a princess who fell in love with a man with many flaws."

"Is Jenny the princess?" Sean asked.

Caleb grinned. "She is, indeed."

"And you're the man," Emily Rose said, bouncing up and down with excitement. "But you fall in love and live happily ever after."

Caleb's gaze was on Jenny now. "I hope that's how it turns out," he said quietly.

Jenny released a sigh. She was very much afraid that her silly, sentimental heart was going to lure her into finding out for herself.

Once Sean and Emily Rose had gone off to play with the other children in the cast, Caleb held out his hand for the lyrics that had kept Jenny up all night.

"Let me see."

"They probably suck," she said, though she reluctantly handed them over. "It was the middle of the night. I was so exhausted I could hardly see straight, much less think."

He laughed at the litany of familiar excuses. "We both know that's when you do some of your best work, darlin'. Now hush and let me read."

She stood anxiously by as he read through the first verse, the refrain and then the second verse. She'd scribbled enough notes on the page for him to get the idea of what she had in mind for the tune.

"Well?" she prodded.

Rather than answering, Caleb picked up his guitar and strummed a few notes. "Like this?" he asked.

She dropped down beside him and picked up her own guitar. "More like this."

He smiled, figuring out what she'd had in mind, then joining his sound to hers. On the second run-through, he sang the lyrics, adjusting the tempo from time to time.

When the song ended, he glanced at her to find her eyes bright, her expression faintly uncertain.

"It works, doesn't it?" she said hesitantly.

"It's amazing," he said. "Bree is going to go crazy for this."

"Are you sure you're not saying that just so you'll win?"

He leaned over and kissed her cheek. "I'm saying it because the song is fantastic. It's going to have the audience on its feet. I may not know as much about theater as Bree does, but I know a showstopper when I hear one. There won't be a dry eye in the house."

He looked away, then turned to her. "Is this how you really feel, Jenny? About me? About forgiveness?"

"It's a song for the play," she insisted, not meeting his gaze.

"Jenny," he commanded softly, then waited.

She finally met his gaze.

"Is it how you feel?" he asked again.

She nodded slowly. "I want those old feelings back, Caleb. I want to believe that our happily-ever-after is still possible."

"But you're scared," he guessed. How could she not be?

"Of course. You nearly destroyed me when you cheated. How can I give you a chance to do that again?"

"Sometimes we don't have a choice," he said simply. "Sometimes love is so strong that we just have to take a leap of faith."

"That's so much easier for you to say," she argued. "You didn't have your heart ripped out."

He gave her a startled look. "Do you really believe that, Jenny? Just because I caused the breakup doesn't mean I didn't get hurt. I never left you and moved on to someone new. I made a stupid mistake that cost me the woman I loved. It might have been my own fault, but it still killed me. Maybe it was even worse in some ways, because I had to live with the guilt of knowing how badly I'd hurt you."

Her eyes flashed then. "You do not seriously want me to feel sorry for you," she said.

"Of course not. I'm just saying I paid a price, too." He regarded her earnestly. "The only good thing to come out of it was that I woke up to the mess I was making of my life. I'm working my tail off now to get a second chance—with the music, with you. I won't blow things again, that's for sure, because I really get the value of what I lost."

He could see how badly she wanted to believe him. The yearning in her eyes touched him, but there were doubts there, too, doubts he hadn't entirely erased. He was smart enough to know that only time and patience could accomplish that.

He risked putting an arm around her shoulders,

drawing her close. She hesitated, then leaned into him. "We have time, sweetheart. I'm not asking you to make a decision about me just yet."

She regarded him with regret. "I wish I could. I wish I were ready, Caleb."

He smiled at the wistfulness in her voice. It echoed his own. "Me, too, darlin'. Me, too."

But the hard truth was, forgiveness took time. Worse, sometimes forgetting took even longer.

"I swear to goodness, if that woman does not get her hands off Caleb, I am going to do some serious damage to her," Jenny muttered from the wings where she'd been watching rehearsal.

Beside her, Jess chuckled. At Bree's request, she'd stopped by to deliver lunch from the inn for the cast.

"Oh, this is wonderful," Jess said with obvious delight. "Bree told me you were green-eyed with jealousy, but I didn't believe her."

"I'm not jealous," Jenny replied. "It's just unseemly, that's all."

"Why?"

"It's a Christmas play, not some X-rated movie," Jenny replied. "This is supposed to be family entertainment."

Jess struggled to swallow a laugh, but in the end the sound erupted.

"What?" Jenny demanded. "You think this is funny?"

"I think it's hilarious," Jess confirmed. "You remind me of my cousin Susie and the way she reacted when Mack's ex-lover came to work for him." Her expression suddenly turned dark. "Of course, that woman was a she-devil, so Susie wasn't entirely to blame for how she reacted."

"And you don't think that woman onstage is a she-devil who'd haul Caleb off to bed at the first opportunity?" Jenny demanded.

"I'm sure she would. I doubt there's a woman still breathing who wouldn't be delighted to haul Caleb off to bed. The real question is whether he'd go. Caleb's the kind of guy in the kind of profession who's always going to face temptation. You know that. What's really important is that I've seen no evidence that he's interested in anyone's bed other than yours."

Jenny was slightly appeased by Jess's assessment. "Seriously?"

"Seriously," Jess said. "So, any inclination to take him home with you?"

Jenny sighed. "Of course I feel the inclination. Sometimes I want the man so badly I actually ache with it. I've been through three pints of Ben & Jerry's in the past two nights trying to get him out of my head."

"Any luck?" Jess inquired, her expression amused.

"No, but I am making an excellent start on working my way through the flavor selections at the grocery store."

"It might make more sense to stop fighting so hard and just invite the man over for an evening of hot lovin'."

"So delicately put," Jenny commented. She shook her head. "I can't, Jess."

"Because you're too stubborn to give in?"

"No, because once I give in, it will be all over. There will be no going back. I'll be hooked, just like before."

"You're already hooked," Jess suggested. "Maybe you should just enjoy it."

"And risk getting my heart broken again?"

"Okay, in my role as devil's advocate, let me ask you this. If Caleb left town tomorrow, if he never called you again or crossed your doorstep, would you be any less heartbroken?"

"No, but…"

"But what?" Jess pressed.

"I wouldn't be humiliated," Jenny told her. "Not like before. And it would be worse this time because the entire family has been standing on the sidelines watching all this unfold."

Jess nodded. "I thought so. Pride's a wonderful thing, Jenny. We all need a healthy dose of it. We need to believe in ourselves, nurture our self-respect, not let others take advantage of us."

"That's all I'm trying to do," Jenny said.

"And bless you for having that strength and belief in yourself. Sometimes, though, you need to have a little faith in the honorable intentions of others. I'm no expert on Caleb, of course, but it seems to me he's trying to do the right thing, that he's a man who's made mistakes, tried to rectify them and knows what he wants. I guess it all comes down to whether you're more interested in protecting yourself or grabbing the dream."

Jenny heard what Jess was trying to tell her. She turned her gaze to the stage where Caleb was pouring heart and soul into the lyrics she'd written. Though his attention was meant to be on his costar, who was once again draped all over him, his gaze sought out Jenny in the backstage shadows. There was no question to whom he was singing.

A sigh rippled through her then and when she released it, the last of her reservations left as well. Jess was right. Starting over again with Caleb was a risk. It would take work to get it right. But playing it safe would never get her what she really wanted—another chance with the man she loved.

12

Caleb saw Jenny rush out of the theater just as his big scene ended. He started after her, only to be stopped halfway up the aisle by Bree.

"We need to go over my notes, Caleb," she told him. "I'd like to see you try a couple of things differently. Give me ten minutes before you take off, okay?"

He shook his head. "Not okay. I will be right back, though," he promised. "Something's up with Jenny. I need to see what happened."

Bree looked for a minute as if she were going to argue, but Jess joined them just then and said, "Let him go. They need to talk."

Caleb studied Jess. He knew that she and Jenny had become confidantes lately, even if they didn't appear to be as close as Jenny and Bree were. "You know what this is about? What upset her, Jess?"

Jess looked more amused than disturbed by whatever she was about to reveal. Caleb took heart from that.

"I'd say it's a toss-up between your costar crawling all over you and her own panic that she's falling in love with you again."

A smile immediately spread across Bree's face. "Really?"

"Oh, yeah," Jess confirmed.

Caleb glanced at Bree. "Well?"

"Go," she said at once. "Be back in an hour. Believe me, I have plenty of notes for everyone else I can go over in the meantime."

"Better make it two hours," Jess said. "Something tells me this could take a little time." She grinned at Caleb. "That is, if you don't blow it."

Caleb didn't intend to blow anything. "Any idea where she was headed?"

"She didn't say, but back to her house would be my guess," Jess said. "I'm sure she wanted to be someplace she considers a safe haven."

Caleb grabbed his jacket and bolted from the theater. He jumped in his truck and headed toward Jenny's, noting that snow was starting to fall. The flurries were light right now, but given the clouds banked overhead, there was a good chance of a nice accumulation before the storm passed. He couldn't help imagining what it would be like to be snowed in with Jenny for a couple of days. Of course, knowing the sorry state of her cupboards, they'd probably starve to death, but it might be worth it to have her all to himself.

He was on Main Street when he spotted Jenny on the town green, sitting on a bench. Even bundled up, she had to be freezing, but her rapt gaze was pinned on the Chesapeake Shores community tree, which had been lit the night before. Even from the truck, he could see the smile on her face. He thought maybe the sight of the tree might have soothed her temper, at least a little.

He angled into the only open spot he saw, a space

designated No Parking. A ticket would be a small price to pay, if it came to that, he decided as he walked slowly in her direction.

He dropped down onto the bench beside her. "Lovely day to sit outside," he commented, drawing a startled look.

She laughed. "It's actually my favorite kind of day." She tilted her face to the sky. "It's snowing and the tree is lit. I wish I'd been here last night. The lighting of the tree is one of the best events the town has. There are carols and hot chocolate, and then the mayor flips the switch. It's always so beautiful." She turned to him. "Isn't it wonderful? It feels just like Christmas."

"You know what I think is wonderful? Seeing how happy you look right this minute." He stroked her cheek, felt her tremble. "Are you happy, Jenny?"

"Sure. Of course," she replied a little too quickly.

"Then why did you run out of the theater?"

"I needed to think," she told him.

"About us?"

She nodded.

"Want to go back to your place and talk about it?" he asked. "I don't know about you, but my butt's about to freeze on this bench."

"Your own fault. If you had more meat on your bones, you wouldn't be cold."

"If you kissed me, that might help, too," he suggested.

Her expression sobered at once as she seemed to consider the idea. "I suppose it's worth a try," she said solemnly, placing a hand on his cheek. The tentativeness of the touch was telling. It was as if this were the first time there had been any intimacy at all between them.

Caleb left it up to her what happened next. She leaned in so slowly he thought his heart might stop as he waited. Then her soft-as-velvet lips, cool as ice, were against his. Damp with snow, they warmed as the kiss deepened.

"I've missed this, Jenny," he murmured against her lips. "More than you'll ever know."

"Me, too," she said with a sigh, returning for more.

Caleb would have happily stayed right there with the snow falling, the tree lights twinkling and the sudden scratchy notes of Christmas music swirling in the air from what sounded like a fairly antiquated speaker system, but Jenny shivered in his arms.

"That's it," he said, pulling her up. "We need to go inside." He looked into her eyes. "Your place or the theater?"

She glanced away and hesitated for so long, he thought for sure they'd be heading straight back to rehearsal. Instead she eventually lifted her gaze to his. "It's up to me?"

He nodded. "Always has been."

She drew in a deep breath then and whispered, "My place."

"You're sure?"

"Not entirely," she said candidly. "But it's what I want."

He looked into her eyes and made a solemn vow. "You're not going to regret it, Jenny. Swear to God."

No matter what effort it took, he was never going to let her down again.

Jenny was pretty sure she must have lost her mind for just a minute back there on the town green. Had she seriously invited Caleb to her home with the clear intent that the invitation included a lot more than hot chocolate and conversation?

At the front door she swallowed hard and tried to get the key in the lock, but her hand was shaking so badly she couldn't do it.

"Nervous?" he asked, taking the key from her.

"Of course not," she insisted. "Just cold. I think my fingers are frozen. First thing inside, I'm going to make hot chocolate."

He studied her, amusement sparkling in his eyes. "First thing, huh?"

She refused to blink or look away. "First thing," she said firmly.

"What's the second thing on your agenda?" he asked as he opened the door to let her inside. "Just out of curiosity."

"Still working that out in my head," she acknowledged.

"In my experience it's sometimes possible to overthink things," he said.

"A convenient philosophy under the circumstances," she replied as she tossed her coat aside in the kitchen and pulled cups from the cupboard. She was about to fill a pot with water and grab the hot chocolate packets when Caleb's hand covered hers.

"Wait," he commanded quietly.

"You don't want hot chocolate?" she asked, her nerves back. Even if he were absolutely desperate for hot chocolate, it wasn't what he wanted right this minute and they both knew it. It wasn't what she wanted, either. That didn't mean it made sense to give in to temptation. She understood on some level that if she was this conflicted, making love with Caleb right now might not be wise.

"Hot chocolate is optional," he said, holding her gaze. "What I want is you, upstairs, in bed."

"Oh." She exhaled softly as her pulse raced. The rational side of her was rapidly losing the fight. Desperate yearning was winning.

"But," he said, his thumb grazing her lower lip, "if that's not what you want, if you're not ready, just say the word. I promised you time, Jenny. I'm not going back on that now."

She frowned at him. "Why can't you be more unreasonable?" she asked in frustration.

"And take the decision out of your hands?" he asked, chuckling. "No way. Not this time. I won't have you throwing it in my face from now till doomsday that I took advantage of you when you were feeling all sentimental about the holidays. You need to be ready to take responsibility for this decision the same way I'm trying to take responsibility for mine in the past."

She stood there shivering under the intensity of his gaze, then sighed. As badly as she wanted this man, as desperately as she wanted to forgive and forget, she wasn't ready yet. She hated that, too, because right this second with her blood humming and her pulse scrambling, jumping into bed with him held a whole lot of appeal.

Caleb must have sensed her struggle, because in the end, he took a step back. "Hot chocolate, then back to rehearsal," he said briskly.

Relief washed over her, right along with bitter disappointment. She wasn't sure how the two could coexist, but she felt both. "I'm sorry."

He touched a finger to her lips. "Don't you dare be sorry. This takes as long as it takes. I'm not going anywhere."

"Not even to that woman's bed?" she grumbled before she could stop herself. "I'm sure Ms. Broadway Hottie would be eager to share her room at the inn with you."

He laughed. "Not a chance. I know what the stakes are, sweetheart. You're the woman I want and you're worth waiting for."

"You could at least tell her to keep her hands to herself."

"I believe Bree is the one who's directing her on where her hands should go," Caleb said. "Does it really bother you?"

She shrugged, trying to feign indifference, but she could see he wasn't buying it. "Makes me crazy," she confessed.

"I know this is going to make me sound like a total guy, but I'm not entirely unhappy about that," he told her. "Not that I would deliberately set out to make you jealous, of course. That would be an incredibly lousy strategy."

"But if the green-eyed monster just happens to take over my body and make me completely irrational, you won't object," she said, shaking her head. "You *are* such a guy."

At the moment, though, he seemed to be hers. But she knew in her heart that as patient as he swore he would be, sooner or later that could change, especially with a whole world of willing women ready to take her place. He might not want them…now. He might be totally committed to her…now. That didn't mean he'd remain immune to their charms forever.

"Caleb," she said softly as he mixed boiling water with the packets of hot chocolate.

He glanced at her. "What?"

"I do love you."

"I know."

"It's not about that," she said, needing him to understand.

"I know that, too."

She studied his face, saw the tenderness in his eyes, the genuine caring and gave a little nod of satisfaction. "I just want to be sure."

"The love's a given," he said. "It's the trust that's a work in progress."

"Exactly. But I'm almost there," she said. "Honestly."

He brushed a strand of hair from her cheek. "Take your time. I've got nowhere else to be."

That wasn't entirely true, Jenny thought to herself. Once this Christmas play was over and done with, the music world would be rushing back to his doorstep with new demands on his time and attention. Suddenly the pressure to take a leap of faith was overwhelming.

Rushing a decision this huge, though? How could she do that and be true to herself? Because once she made her choice to let Caleb back into her life, she'd have to be all in. And even though they'd come such a long way, the prospect of giving herself so completely still scared her to death.

"Things seem to be going well between you and Caleb," Bree said casually, her gaze on Jenny.

They were at Flowers on Main, Bree's other business, making flower arrangements for a wedding on Saturday, just a few days before Christmas.

"I suppose," Jenny said, reluctant to admit that she'd fallen hard for a second time with a man she didn't entirely trust. Not that her feelings would come as any surprise to Bree. She'd been right there when Caleb and Jenny had returned to the theater two days before, her expression a little too knowing.

"I wanted to talk to you about something," Bree said.

"About Caleb?"

"In a way. It's a request, really."

"Don't you know by now that there's nothing I won't do for you?"

"Good to know," Bree said. Her expression innocent, she inquired, "Would you consider taking a small part in the play?"

Startled, Jenny stared at her. "At this late date? You can't add another part. You'll make the cast crazy."

"Just one scene at the end of Act I," Bree explained. "No big deal. It's too late for me to find someone else."

"Do it yourself, if it's no big deal," Jenny suggested. "At least you've been onstage before. I'm not an actress. I never aspired to be one, either. Performing in front of people is not my thing. Caleb tried to drag me onstage at a concert once and I came close to passing out in his arms. It wasn't pretty."

"It's nothing to worry about," Bree assured her. "It's a nonspeaking role. By the time you get nervous, it will be over."

"Are you kidding me?" Jenny protested. "I'm already nervous just thinking about it. No. Find someone else."

"You're the one who's right for the part. You have to trust me on that."

Jenny frowned. "Bree, I don't get it. You have a whole family to pull from. Why am I the only one who could possibly do it?"

That facade of innocence, never terribly believable, slipped ever so slightly. "As a matter of fact, Caleb suggested it."

Jenny's suspicions went on high alert. "Since when do you listen to Caleb when it comes to making changes to your work?"

"I think his instincts about this are right on target," Bree said. "He's surprisingly insightful about what will work. I've come to respect his instincts. We make a good team."

Jenny could add two and two as fast as the next person, especially on the sneakiness scale. "You want him to sing that love song to me, don't you?" she said flatly. "You figure the audience will go wild at the implication, an implication that has nothing to do with the play and everything to do with our personal lives. Buzz on the internet to follow, of course."

Bree didn't waste time trying to deny it. "All I care about is that it would be a showstopper," she insisted just the same.

"I doubt the actress who's been playing his love interest for the whole production would agree," Jenny said dryly, thinking it might just serve Helena McGuire right to be kicked out of his arms at the last minute.

"I made a minor change to the script to make it work," Bree explained. "You haven't seen rehearsals for a couple of days now."

That much was true. Jenny had steered clear because listening to Caleb sing her songs had reminded her a little too much of what might have been, especially when it came to that ballad. And now Bree was asking her to let him sing it to her onstage with the whole world—or at least one small part of her world—looking on.

"Bree, you don't know what you're asking of me," she whispered. She'd poured her heart into that song. She'd never intended to let an entire audience, especially comprised of people who knew her so well, see how deeply it touched her. The emotions were still too raw.

Bree touched her cheek. "Oh, sweetie, I know exactly what I'm asking. So does Caleb. He loves you. And you still love him. He wants to celebrate that."

"You of all people know what this town is like once they get the bit in their teeth as far as romance is concerned. We won't have a moment's peace. So far they've been giving us time, but once Caleb sings that song, makes that public declaration, our relationship will be fair game. To say nothing of what the media's likely to do if they get wind of it."

"Are you really worried about people here in town or even the media?" Bree asked. "Or are you just scared that he'll knock down the last of your defenses?"

"Okay, that, too."

"Sweetie, whether you say yes or no to what I'm asking, don't shut the door on a future with Caleb, not because of what happened in the past. Believe in the here and now. Believe in everything he's done these past couple of weeks to prove how much he's changed, how much he loves you."

"I'm trying to," Jenny said, tears gathering in her eyes. "I'm just not there yet."

"Then think about what I'm asking. Can you do that much? Not for me. Not even for the play. Or for Caleb. Do it for yourself."

"I'll think about it," Jenny agreed at last. In fact, she doubted she'd be thinking about much else.

Bree studied her. "I know you're not entirely convinced that I don't have an ulterior motive when it comes to you and Caleb. Your getting back together works out for me in terms of publicity—no question about it—but I'm your friend first and foremost. I truly want to see you happy. That's my bottom line here. You do believe that, don't you?"

Jenny nodded, knowing that Bree had always been in her corner.

"How about this, then? Talk to your uncle," Bree suggested.

Jenny was taken aback by the suggestion. "You want me to talk to Jake about Caleb? Why? I know he's mellowed toward the man, but he's not as gaga as you are."

Bree laughed. "I certainly hope not, but what I meant was, talk to Jake about forgiveness and moving on. I've told you my side of what happened between us. He might be able to give you some insight into how he was able to forgive me."

Jenny tried to imagine bringing up such a touchy subject with her uncle, but couldn't. Jake was no more inclined to be open about his innermost feelings than most men.

"Want me to pave the way?" Bree asked as if she'd read Jenny's mind. "Or do you want me to back off and leave you alone to figure things out?"

While it might be a lot more comfortable to be left alone, Jenny knew she needed help. She trusted her uncle Jake to be honest with her, even if baring his soul was difficult for him. He'd do it if he thought hearing what he had to say mattered to her peace of mind.

"It's okay," she said eventually. "I'll talk to Jake."

Bree gave her a fierce hug. "Good."

"You seem awfully certain things will work out the way you want them to if I talk to him," Jenny said.

"Because no matter what his personal reservations about Caleb might be, my husband is as fair as they come. He's going to do what's best for you, even if it goes against the grain."

"In other words, you intend to coach him on exactly what's best for me," Jenny said, suddenly getting it. "The way you did with Dillon years ago when Jake wanted to rip his heart out for messing with me in his office at the nursery. You calmed him down, made him get to know Dillon."

Bree grinned. "Can't deny it. But my influence will only go so far. The man is stubborn as a mule. He'll say what's on his mind, no matter what I want him to do."

Jenny drew in a deep breath. She was counting on that. Maybe some straight talk from the male perspective was exactly what she needed.

Jake sat in his usual booth at Sally's expecting the arrival of Will and Mack for lunch. He was stunned when Jenny slipped in opposite him.

"I don't usually see you in here this time of day," he said. "What brings you by? Did my wife give you a well-deserved break or did you escape on your own?"

"To be honest, I was looking for you. I know this is your regular lunchtime and I was just up the street at the flower shop helping Bree with the flower arrangements for a wedding on Saturday."

"Oh? And my name happened to come up?"

Jenny squirmed uncomfortably, but nodded. "I was hoping we could talk," she said.

"Sure, but Mack and Will should be here soon."

She shook her head. "Bree called them and told them to give me some time with you."

He blinked at that. "Bree shooed them away?"

Jenny laughed. "She was pretty adamant, in fact."

"Boy, this must be important. Why does that make me nervous?"

"It shouldn't," she said. "I just need some advice."

"No, you shouldn't have sex until you get married," he said flatly.

Jenny smiled. "I'm afraid that ship has sailed and I wouldn't come to you about advice like that, anyway. You're an old stick-in-the-mud, at least when it comes to me and men."

Jake picked up his soda, suddenly wishing it were something much stronger. He sipped slowly and regarded her with a narrowed gaze. "So, what sort of advice are you looking for?" he asked eventually.

"The big stuff," she said. "Betrayal, forgiveness, that kind of thing."

Jake barely contained a groan. He did not want to go down that road, not with his niece. "Since when do you want advice from me? You're usually all too eager to run off when I start to tell you what to do."

"I'm hoping you'll make suggestions, not give me the kind of orders that set my teeth on edge," she told him, grinning.

"Okay, fine. You're asking a lot, but I'll try," he grumbled. "What's up?"

"I'm having a little trouble letting go of all the anger

I'm feeling toward Caleb over what he did to me," she explained.

"Good for you," Jake said automatically, then winced as her expression shut down. "Sorry. What's the question?"

"How did you forgive Bree for what she did to you?"

Jake set down his drink so hard ice bounced out of the glass. "You know about that?" he demanded. "I mean the details? How? Who filled you in?" He shook his head. The answer was obvious. "Never mind. It could only have been my wife. And I'm sure she had her reasons."

She nodded. "I know how hurt you were back then, how angry. I saw that much for myself. Bree explained why."

"Did she now?" he said, unable to keep the annoyance from his voice.

"Come on, Jake. Don't get all worked up. She was trying to point out that people do get past betrayals. You did." She studied him hopefully. "How'd you do it?"

He finally managed to put aside his exasperation with his wife for sharing such an intimate story and focused on what his niece really wanted to know—if forgiveness was possible. "I had no choice," he told her. "I loved Bree more than I hated what she'd done. I believed her when she said she was sorry. I made a conscious decision to let it go."

Jenny looked skeptical. "Just like that? I don't remember it that way."

"Okay, it took time. And Marty showing up here to try to win her back didn't help. Eventually, I had to decide if I was going to be happier taking a risk on loving her again or if I was going to play it safe and spend the rest of my life without the woman I loved. Safe and alone didn't hold a lot of appeal."

Jenny sighed. "You make it sound easy when you put it like that."

"No way, kid. There's nothing easy about it. I'm not going to sit here and tell you doubts never crop up, because they do. Not because of anything Bree's done," he said hurriedly. "I guess a certain amount of insecurity never dies. It's just outweighed by all the positives in our life together."

He waited, studying Jenny's expression as she considered his words. He could see how hard she was struggling with whatever decision she felt she had to make.

"Is Caleb pressuring you about this?" he asked. "I can tell him to back off."

She smiled. "You'd love that, wouldn't you? But, no, he's not pressuring me, at least not the way you mean. He's just here, being all charming and sweet and sensitive and so blasted patient it makes my teeth hurt from gritting them."

"And you're falling for him all over again," Jake concluded.

"Afraid so," she said wryly.

"Then, as reluctant as I am to say this, it sounds as if you're where I was with Bree. You have to take that leap of faith, kiddo. If it's any comfort, there are a whole slew of people who'll be here for you if he dares to let you down."

"I don't want to start something thinking it's going to fail," she said. "That's way too fatalistic."

"Then believe in it with everything you've got until the very second that you can't," he advised.

Her eyes were shimmering with tears when she met his gaze. "Thanks, Uncle Jake."

"You just let me know if you ever need me to punch his lights out," he told her.

She reached across the table and squeezed his hand. "You'll be the first person I call." She slid out of the booth. "Now I'd better run. We have rehearsal soon."

Jake nodded. "Send Mack and Will over on your way out. They've been watching intently from the counter for the past fifteen minutes. I'm sure they'd like to add their two cents, so you might want to say hello and goodbye in a very big hurry unless you're up for a full-scale counseling session."

Jenny shuddered. She loved both men, but she'd already gotten the advice she'd come for. "Not so much," she told Jake. "See you, and thanks."

"Anytime, kiddo."

Jake shook his head as she paused to speak to his friends, then hurried on.

This role of advice giver was a new one for him. This was Will's stock-in-trade. Most worrisome of all was that he had a daughter of his own at home. He had a hunch this was just the first of many uncomfortable conversations he was likely to face in his lifetime. He couldn't help wondering if he'd passed the test on this trial run or if he'd just set Jenny up to get her heart broken all over again.

13

Caleb walked into Flowers on Main, hoping to ask Jenny to join him for lunch at Panini Bistro, which he'd heard was one of her favorite places along the waterfront. Instead, he found Bree in the shop all alone, practically buried in a sea of red and white roses.

"You just missed Jenny," she said.

"Oh? Where'd she go?" he asked, watching as she worked quickly with florist tape, wires and streaming satin ribbons to make what he assumed were to be bouquets for the bridesmaids for the wedding he'd heard was taking place this weekend.

"She's over at Sally's having a talk with my husband."

Caleb frowned. "Should I be concerned about that?"

Bree looked amused by the question. "Why? Have you done something to feel guilty about? Something new, I mean?"

"Not a chance." He spotted the twinkle in Bree's eyes. "You've been matchmaking, haven't you?"

"Trying to," she confessed readily. "I gave her a

nudge in your direction. I'm hoping Jake will push her the rest of the way."

As much as he appreciated the support, Caleb worried that the pressure would backfire. "Bree, I think I have this covered. Jenny needs to come to her own conclusions about the two of us."

"I agree, but she's having trouble getting there. I'm not telling her what to do, just helping her cut through all the chatter in her head. She's listening to logic instead of her heart." She gave him a hard look. "*That* won't turn out well for you."

He laughed. "Nice spin. You're meddling."

"Oh, so what?" she said, waving a red rose in his direction in a dismissive gesture. "I'm a rank amateur compared to my dad. Be glad he's not on the case."

Caleb merely shook his head. "Have you had a chance to talk to Jenny about being in that scene with me?"

"That's what we were talking about when I concluded that she needed to have a chat with her uncle."

"I don't get it," Caleb said, confused. "You think Jake will convince her to come onstage with me?"

"No, I think Jake will convince her to take a blind leap of faith back into your arms when you sing that ballad to her." She studied him over the lovely bouquet of flowers she'd just created. "That is what you're counting on, isn't it?"

"Of course, but I don't think Jake's one of my biggest fans. He's mellowed toward me, true, but asking him to give Jenny a push in my direction? I don't see it happening. Jake doesn't strike me as a softhearted romantic."

"Oh, he's most definitely not, and I doubt he'll push," Bree agreed. "What he will do is say exactly what she needs to hear about forgiveness. I'm counting on that to make it possible for Jenny to do what her heart is telling her to do."

"Let me back into her life," Caleb concluded.

"Yep," Bree said. Just then a smile broke across her face. "And here she comes now. Unless I'm way worse at this than I think I am, we'll know if it worked when she spots you."

Caleb turned toward the door and saw the precise instant when Jenny noticed him. Color flared in her cheeks. A once-familiar spark lit her eyes. As skeptical as he'd been about Bree's plan, he had to admit that it appeared to have had an effect, perhaps even a positive one.

"Bingo!" Bree said softly, apparently seeing exactly what he saw.

"What are you doing here, Caleb?" Jenny asked, a surprisingly breathless hitch in her voice.

"I came by to see if you'd have time for lunch."

Jenny glanced toward Bree, who immediately nodded.

"Sure, if it's okay with Bree, I can spare a half hour."

"Take longer," Bree encouraged. "I'll get Abby and Jess over here to help me. I can call Gram, too. After all, she's the one who taught me everything I know. You come back whenever."

"A half hour," Jenny repeated firmly. "I promised to help. Besides, it's fun doing these fancy arrangements and bridal bouquets again."

Caleb figured he'd better take what he could get. "Let's go, then. Is Panini Bistro okay?"

"Perfect," she said, following him out. "It's one of my favorites and I haven't had time to stop in on this trip."

As they walked down Main and turned the corner toward the restaurant, Caleb kept glancing over, trying to read Jenny's mood.

"Everything okay?" he asked eventually.

"Great, actually."

"You and your uncle Jake had a good talk?"

She frowned. "You know about that?" She shook her head. "Of course you do, Bree told you."

"Got it," he said, then switched gears. "Have you given any thought to doing that scene with me in the play?" he asked. "Bree seemed to think it was a great idea."

"Bree's a romantic," she said. "Apparently, she's also a publicity hound. If it was good for publicity, she'd try to convince you to streak across the stage naked."

Caleb laughed. "We both know that would be flat-out *great* for publicity, but she hasn't mentioned it."

"Just wait. Maybe I'll plant the idea in her head. You look pretty darn good in the buff, as I recall," she said, giving him a lingering once-over.

Caleb stared at her in astonishment. "Jenny Louise, are you flirting with me?"

She slanted a half smile in his direction. "Could be."

"Maybe you should spend more time with your uncle."

"Not necessary. We wrapped things up today."

Since he had a hunch the conversation had gone in his favor, Caleb let the subject go and returned to the issue of the play.

"You're avoiding my question," he accused lightly. "Are you going to do that scene with me?"

Her smile faded. "I'm thinking about it."

"Aside from your advanced case of stage fright, what's holding you back?" he asked.

She frowned at him. "We both know it's about more than my panicking over the thought of being onstage. If you sing that song to me, word will spread ten seconds after the final scene on opening night. It's going to be plastered all over the tabloids and the entertainment shows. People will assume we're back together."

"And we're not," he concluded, knowing it was true, but not all that happy that despite the change in attitude he'd just witnessed, they still hadn't managed to get over whatever last hurdle was holding Jenny back.

"No, we're not," she said without hesitation. "We're getting there, Caleb. Maybe we're even there, but once that particular cat is out of the bag, the pressure will come from every direction, including my family here. We won't have a minute's peace to work things out in private. You know how it was when we first started dating. It turned into a circus everywhere we went."

Silent after her explanation—especially since he couldn't think of a single valid argument to contradict what she was saying or her memory of the early days of their relationship—he made his way to a table that was away from most of the prying eyes in the small restaurant.

"We could always work things out in private now," he suggested hopefully after the waitress had taken their order. "It's noisy enough that I doubt anyone can overhear us."

"A preemptive strike?" she said, seemingly willing to consider the suggestion.

He nodded. "So to speak."

"Sorry, but I don't think so. The kind of work we

need to do to resolve things is going to take longer than a half hour of hurried conversation over a sandwich," she said.

"We could at least take a stab at it," he said, struck by a sense of urgency that had nothing to do with the play and everything to do with his fear that Bree had been right, that the more thinking Jenny did, the less likely things would work out as he hoped they would.

Her frown returned. "Caleb, you said you were willing to give me time. What changed? Why are you suddenly in such a rush to make our relationship official again?"

"It's an opportunity, that's all. I saw the potential in that scene with that song and wanted to make the most of it."

As soon as the words were out of his mouth, he knew what a mistake they'd been. It was entirely the wrong tactic to use. She was regarding him now with deepening suspicion.

"Have you run the idea by anyone else?" she asked, her tone cool. "Aside from Bree, I mean?"

"Such as?"

"Your agent? Margo?"

He felt a moment's guilt. "I did mention it to my manager," he acknowledged. "He thought it might jump-start things for me again in Nashville, but I swear to you that's not what this is about, Jenny."

"Of course it is," she said with a sigh. "I'm sure he thought it was a fantastic idea. Even I can see that much." She gave him a weary look. "Thank you for being honest about talking to him."

"I told you I'd never deceive you again. It's not as

if this wouldn't be a win for everybody. Bree stands to get a huge amount of buzz from it, too."

"I know that. It's one of the reasons I promised to consider doing that scene." Her expression troubled, she looked into his eyes. "It just makes me feel so exposed to think about our relationship being front and center again. Sure, right now all the reports will be positively giddy with excitement, but everyone will be watching for the first misstep. You know they will."

Caleb understood what she was saying. He wasn't happy about it, but how could he deny the role the tabloid media had had in tearing their lives apart before? Not that he hadn't done the deed, so to speak, but the photographers who always seemed to be lurking in the shadows had been right there to capture it for Jenny and the rest of the world to see. When it came to this kind of stuff, there was no such thing as neutral objectivity in the reporting. It was all about sensationalism. Thankfully they'd lost interest while he was in rehab, giving him this breathing space, but it wouldn't last.

He studied her with regret. "You really hate this idea, don't you?"

"Not entirely," she said softly. "I like the thought of your singing that song to me." A grin spread across her face. "Especially if it means you won't be singing it to Ms. Broadway Hottie."

At her nickname for his costar, Caleb chuckled. "I hope you don't call Helena that in front of other people."

"Why not?"

"She's really a very nice woman."

"Who has the hots for a man who professes to want me back."

"I *do* want you back," Caleb assured her. "Badly. And I want the whole world to know just how badly."

"Is it a deal breaker for you if I don't want the world to know just yet?" she asked.

"Absolutely not," he said hurriedly. "All I care about is getting us back on track. I thought the song might be a way to do that and give the show a boost, too."

To his relief, she at least looked as if she wanted to believe him.

"I told Bree I'd think about it, and I will," she promised. "That's the best I can do right this second."

Their order came and after they'd taken a few bites, Caleb dared to ask, "So, what did you and Jake talk about? Bree said you'd gone to him for some advice."

"We talked about forgiveness," she said. "And betrayal."

"Ah, I see. The little, inconsequential stuff. Did he help?"

She smiled. "He did. He helped me to realize something, something I should have known from the second you turned up in Chesapeake Shores."

"What's that?"

She looked into his eyes. "That, despite what happened and how much you hurt me, my life is so much better with you than without you," she said simply.

Caleb felt the knot in his chest loosen at her admission. That was huge and he knew it.

"I was trying so hard to pretend that wasn't true so it would be easier to send you away." She regarded him with apparent frustration. "But you wouldn't go."

He smiled. "I'm afraid that was never an option."

"And here we are," she said, a mix of resignation and something else in her voice.

"Good thing or bad?" he asked.

"Good for you," she said, a smile tugging at her lips. "It remains to be seen if it's good for me."

"I have another chance?" Caleb said, his tone cautious. He didn't want to misread what she was saying.

A full-fledged smile broke across her face. "You have another chance," she confirmed. "Crazy as it may be, I don't want to go through life without you."

Caleb let out a whoop that had the other customers turning to stare. He didn't care. He was on his feet, scooping Jenny into his arms and twirling her around. Sure, they still had a ton of things to work out and a long time before she truly put the past behind them, but she was willing to work at it. That was huge!

"So much for discretion," she said, laughing as he finally set her back down. "I suppose now it hardly matters whether I let you sing that song to me. I saw half a dozen cell phones snapping pictures of this happy little scene."

"Oops!" Caleb said, not very contritely. He did stand again and shout for attention over the excited chatter in the place. "I know it's asking a lot," he said to his immediately attentive audience. "But would you mind not sharing any pictures you took just now? As you can imagine, Jenny and I have a huge beef with the tabloids and we'd really prefer not to see our faces on their front pages again."

Suddenly Mick O'Brien, who'd apparently arrived after they had, was on his feet at the front of the room. "I'd consider it a personal favor, too," he said. "These two deserve to patch things up without the whole world watching every little kiss, right? Let's keep this between us right here in Chesapeake Shores. This town knows how to protect its own."

Though there was no mistaking the disappointment on some of the faces, most everyone nodded.

"I'm deleting the picture right now," one woman said.

"Me, too," her companion added.

While others did the same, Caleb suspected it was too much to hope that everyone who'd snapped the telling photo would comply. All he could hope was that, with Mick's help, he'd bought a little more time and privacy for him and Jenny before the world intruded.

Jenny knew both Caleb and Bree were anxious about her answer when it came to whether she'd appear in that scene with Caleb, but she simply couldn't decide. She'd almost been prepared to give in and say yes, when all those cell phone cameras had started snapping pictures at lunch earlier. It had reminded her of what the frenzy would be like if she agreed to go onstage with him.

Since she wasn't getting anywhere wrestling with her own thoughts, she called her mom.

"Are you free to do a little shopping?" she asked Connie. "I won't have long, but I'm thinking it would be nice to have a sofa at least in the living room before Christmas."

"I'll pick you up in twenty minutes," Connie replied eagerly, then ticked off her personal to-do list to make the logistics work. "Just let me tell Jake I'm taking a break. Thomas is working at home, so he can pick Sean up at preschool and drop him off at the theater for rehearsal. I'll remind him there's lasagna in the freezer in case we're gone longer than you're planning."

"Great," Jenny said, biting back a chuckle at her

mom's organizational skills. No wonder Jake wanted to keep her happy working at the nursery. "See you in a few minutes. I'll be out front."

When she'd hung up, she realized with a sense of shock that she hadn't suffered even a twinge of resentment at the mention of Thomas or Sean. Maybe she was healing after all. Or growing up, she thought wryly. Either way, she seemed at peace with the way things were. She could honestly see now that she'd never lost her mom. She'd pushed her away.

After Connie picked her up, she drove straight to the store where they'd found the few pieces of new furniture they'd splurged on over the years. Each one had been chosen with extra care, because replacing the old, functional but hardly stylish pieces had been such a luxury.

"We're just looking for a sofa this afternoon?" her mother asked as they walked to the entrance.

"Unless we stumble across something else I can't live without," Jenny said. "There's not enough time to pick out everything I need, so we have to stay focused."

"Any particular style? That could save some time."

"Big, comfortable, maybe leather," Jenny said, thinking of the sofa Caleb had in his huge Nashville home. Though it wasn't to her taste, she had to admit it *was* comfortable. And it suited him.

Her mom gave her a knowing look. "Is this for you or Caleb?"

Jenny shrugged. "Maybe a little of both."

"Is he moving in with you?"

She immediately shook her head. "We haven't discussed that."

"But it looked to me as if you discussed something

and reached a consensus at Panini Bistro earlier," her mother said.

Jenny frowned. "How do you know about that?"

"Ethel sent a photo, then swore she was deleting it from her cell phone, per Caleb's request."

"And Mick's," Jenny said. "I think Mick's carried more weight."

"Not with Ethel," Connie insisted. "She's a big fan of Caleb's and has made it plain she's rooting for a reconciliation. She seems to think she has the inside scoop on one. Is she right?"

Jenny debated trying to equivocate, then nodded. This was her mother, after all, the woman she'd confided in all her life. "She's right."

Connie smiled. "And you're obviously happy about that."

"Happy. Terrified. It's hard to say."

"Don't I know those feelings," her mom said. "That's how I felt when Thomas asked me to marry him."

Jenny regarded her with surprise. "Really? I thought you were ecstatic."

"Oh, in a lot of ways, I was. I certainly never expected to fall in love again. He's an incredible man and we have so much in common. He treats me like I'm the best gift ever to come his way." She gave Jenny a rueful look. "But it meant a lot of changes, you know? Not the least of which was what it was going to do to you and me."

Jenny blinked at that. "You felt that way, too?"

"Of course. We'd been a team, sweetie. I didn't want anything to shake up our relationship. I loved that strong bond we had, stronger than most mothers and daughters, at least when the daughter's a teenager. Thomas and I talked about it. He made it clear that we were a package deal, you and me. He never saw it any other way. He's been beside himself thinking that he caused this rift between us."

"I should have cut him more slack," Jenny said. "He didn't make all the mistakes. Neither did you. I probably made the most of anyone."

Her mom squeezed her hand. "Water under the bridge," she assured her. "We're good now, right?"

Jenny smiled and let go of the last of her hurt. "We're good."

"Then let's turn our attention to finding the perfect sofa. I'm personally voting for something other than leather." She grinned. "Not that I get a vote, of course. I just know your taste."

"Flowered upholstery," Jenny said at once. "Bright, casual, comfortable, cozy."

Connie laughed. "Exactly what I was envisioning, and I think I see the perfect thing right over there," she said, pointing. "And it won't be all bad for Caleb. It's long enough for him to stretch out on. Maybe that will make up for it not being dull and brown and leather."

"Oh, I think I can convince him that it'll accommodate the two of us very nicely," Jenny said, thinking of the similar sofa in her Nashville home. He'd certainly gotten accustomed to that one quickly enough.

"Too much information," her mom scolded, already beckoning for a salesman. She pointed to the rest of the display. "Those oversized chairs look as if they're meant to go with it. Interested?"

"Perfect," Jenny said at once. She could already envision them in front of the fireplace. "The lamps and tables, too."

The delighted salesman wrote the order up quickly and promised delivery for the next day, first thing in the morning.

"They can't be even a minute late," Jenny cautioned. "I have a rehearsal at the theater at ten."

His expression brightened. "You talking about that play over in Chesapeake Shores? My wife got tickets for the whole family."

"Great," Jenny said. "You're going to love it."

"My daughter wrote the music," Connie told him proudly.

His eyes widened at that. He glanced at the credit card she'd given him, then up at her. "You're Jenny Collins?"

"I am," she confirmed.

"And you were involved with Caleb Green," he said. "I think he's the reason my wife bought the tickets. She's crazy for his music. I know you wrote a lot of it."

"It was a great collaboration," Jenny said. "It's been fun to work together again."

He handed her the sales receipt. "The delivery will be right on time," he promised. "I don't think I'm going to tell my wife about meeting you till tomorrow afternoon. Otherwise, she might stow away on the delivery van in the hope that she'll catch a glimpse of Caleb."

Jenny laughed, but sadly, she was well aware that devoted fans were capable of far worse. "I'd appreciate that," she told him. "But come backstage when you come to the show. I'll see that she gets an autographed picture of Caleb."

Outside, her mother was frowning. "Is it always like that?"

"Like what?"

"People going a little crazy when they realize who you are."

Jenny shook her head. "Him? The salesman? He was sweet and thoughtful compared to a lot of fans. Of course, none of it happens much if I'm out on my own. People rarely recognize me or even my name. When I'm with Caleb, it's another story. Some women have absolutely no sense of boundaries at all. And he can draw a crowd in nothing flat."

"Like today in Panini Bistro."

"Pretty much." She tried to shrug it off. "It comes with the territory."

Her mom shook her head, clearly not buying her blasé attitude. "And you're ready to face all that again?"

"I don't have a choice. Not if Caleb is the man I love, and he is."

She wasn't half as calm about that as she'd sounded. It was just something she had to come to terms with. She'd done it before. She could do it again. The payoff—being with Caleb—had been worth the sacrifice of privacy, at least till it had exploded in her face. God willing, that wouldn't happen again.

Despite her promise to give the two of them another chance, Caleb knew he wasn't off the hook with Jenny yet. He knew her reluctance to do that scene with him spoke volumes about the doubts she still harbored when it came to the unavoidable spotlight always being directed on their relationship. And the fact that she'd disappeared right after lunch, rather than coming to the theater said a lot, too. She'd clearly been worried that he and Bree would gang up on her.

When he finally got a break, he walked into the otherwise empty rehearsal room and spotted Jenny pacing as she talked on her cell phone. Apparently she'd finally dug it out of that drawer. He wasn't sure what it was going to take to convince her that he was 100 percent trustworthy, but he wasn't done trying.

Unfortunately, the expression on her face when she ended the call and caught sight of him wasn't promising. Whatever ground they'd made up seemed to be vanishing before his eyes. The last time he'd seen that particular look on her face was when she'd seen the first tabloid exposé of his betrayal.

"Something wrong?" he asked carefully, walking over to join her.

"I suppose that depends," she said, her voice chilly. "That was Ricky Nolan. I had a half-dozen messages from him when I finally retrieved my cell phone. He wanted to know if I'd agreed to let you have the song I gave him. Funny how you hadn't mentioned anything about that song, not even once in the past couple of weeks."

Caleb groaned. Ricky's timing couldn't have been worse. Caleb understood how the situation must look to Jenny, as if he'd come to town with an ulterior motive. And while it was true that the song had sent him here, Jenny was the reason—the only reason—he'd stayed.

"Is that song the reason you came to Chesapeake Shores, Caleb?" she persisted. "Is that why you've been so accommodating to Bree and everyone else in my family? Was it all about getting the rights to that song so you could launch your career again?"

Caleb cursed under his breath. "It's not like that, Jenny. I swear it. Yes, I heard that song and I wanted it, but it's not the only reason I came to Chesapeake

Shores. I wanted you back more than any song, but I didn't think I stood a chance of making that happen. The song just gave me the excuse I needed to come."

Hurt darkened her eyes. "And to think I was almost ready to forgive you. I really am a fool," she said with self-derision.

"You are not a fool," Caleb said fiercely. "I never mentioned the song because once I got here and saw you, you were the only thing that mattered. Ricky's welcome to the song. You can call him back right now and tell him that or I will. All I need is you."

"Me and the exposure this play will give you and that oh-so-revealing ballad you want me to let you sing to me," she said. "I don't think so, Caleb. I won't let you use me like that."

She turned then, grabbed her coat and purse, and left the room. Caleb's heart shattered as he watched her go, every hope for a reconciliation dashed. And, once again, it was his own stupid fault.

14

Jenny had Christmas carols turned up to the highest volume on the small CD player Caleb had bought. She was on her third cup of hot chocolate, which she had to admit was having some sort of weird effect between the caffeine and the sugary marshmallows. She'd lit a fire in the fireplace and had Jake set up a tree in her living room. She was going about capturing the Christmas spirit with a determination she hadn't shown since she'd set out to weather Caleb's first massive betrayal.

When first Jake and then her mom and then Jess had offered to help decorate the tree, she'd turned them down. Help would come with prying questions, questions she had no intention of answering. She'd actually been surprised by the offers of help from Jake and Jess, who had to know she'd blown off Bree's request to appear in the play.

Jake had shown up with the tree and a worried frown on his face, just the same.

"You want to talk?" he'd asked.

"Nothing to talk about," she'd assured him.

Though he'd still looked concerned, he was obviously relieved that she wasn't going to burst into tears on his watch.

Jess had been less circumspect. She'd come with cookies and questions, and clearly hadn't intended to leave without answers.

"What's Caleb done now?" she'd asked. "Do I need to get Dad to run him out of town?"

Jenny had smiled at the sincerity of the offer. She knew Mick was capable of doing exactly that and probably much worse.

"Leave it alone, Jess. Bree needs him here. I'll be fine," she'd assured her.

Jess hadn't looked as if she believed her. "I could send Will over. He's neutral, and a shrink to boot. He could be exactly the person for you to talk to about whatever happened, maybe give you some perspective."

"I don't need to talk," Jenny insisted. "I don't need perspective." She knew without a doubt what she had to do. She had to forget Caleb once and for all, even if that was a whole lot easier said than done. She'd failed miserably at it the first time he'd betrayed her. This time she intended to get it right. After all, practice was supposed to make perfect, wasn't that the old adage?

Jess had looked unconvinced. "Are you sure? You look miserable."

Jenny had even smiled at that. "You're not too great at cheering a person up, if you don't mind my saying so."

"You're right," Jess said. "I'm no good at this. What will help?" Her eyes lit up. "One of Gail's chocolate decadence cakes from the inn, all for you?"

"I don't think cake, even that one, is the answer. There's nothing I can think of that will change what happened," Jenny told her. "Thanks for coming by, though."

Though she'd sighed heavily, Jess had finally taken the hint and left.

Which meant Jenny was now all alone with her thoughts and a dozen boxes of decorations she'd bought on sale in a frenzy of holiday shopping. Unfortunately, none of it—not the decorations or the music or the hot chocolate—was helping to dispel her very unholiday-like mood.

She might have slammed a door on her relationship with Caleb, but the man sure as heck wouldn't stay out of her head. She kept thinking about the night they'd shopped for outdoor decorations, about the huge train he'd bought as a surprise and about the way he'd reached out to her family for help in turning her yard into the kind of wonderland she'd remembered. The sweetness of that gesture reminded her of why she'd fallen in love with him. The man actually listened, and he knew how to make dreams come true.

But she didn't need to keep remembering the good things, she told herself sternly. She needed to focus on all the bad, including how he'd lied to her about his reason for coming to town. It had been about a song, about his career.

No matter what he said now, no matter how he tried to spin it, she couldn't make herself believe he'd come here for her the way he claimed he had. How could she when the evidence of that phone call from Ricky Nolan was still ringing in her ears? Ricky had been genuinely shocked that she hadn't known. He couldn't have faked his reaction, would have had no reason to.

So, bottom line? She wasn't going to be taken in by the sweet-talking Caleb again, she thought fiercely. Never again.

"Stop it, stop it, stop it!" she ordered herself. "Why are you even thinking about this? You've made your decision. Now move on."

Her house was shaping up quite nicely now that she had furniture in the living room. It was cozy and warm, exactly the way she'd envisioned it. A few pictures on the walls, a few aromatic candles, and it would feel like home whenever she had the time to spend here.

For now she had a beautiful tree, its scent filling the downstairs rooms. It needed just a few final touches to be the best tree ever. She had music and an endless supply of hot chocolate. She even had a mountain of presents to wrap. Taking off from the theater as she had had given her plenty of time to shop. She didn't need to be wasting time thinking about Caleb and what might have been.

When the doorbell rang, she groaned. More company was the last thing she needed. She opened the door to find Sean on the stoop, shockingly all alone from the looks of it. He was bundled up in a winter coat, a bright green scarf, a knitted cap and gloves. She was surprised he could move. She could recall being sent out to play in the snow dressed almost exactly like that. Obviously, some of her mom's habits hadn't changed.

"Are you by yourself?" she asked worriedly, glancing around for some sign of her mother or Thomas.

"I came to visit," Sean told her solemnly. "Mommy said maybe I could help put decorations on your tree. Can I?"

Jenny hesitated, still trying to figure out how he'd gotten himself over here. "We'll see."

"She said you'd probably have hot chocolate, too, and maybe some cookies." His eyes brightened at the possibility. "Do you?"

Jenny smiled despite her sour mood. "Mommy seems to know me very well. Where is she?"

He gestured toward the street. "Down the block, waiting, just in case."

"Just in case what?"

"You don't want company," he said, then regarded her hopefully. "Do you want company?"

It was the very last thing she wanted, but she couldn't send him away when he was so clearly eager to spend time with her. Maybe this visit was exactly what she needed after all.

"I'm thrilled to have company, as long as it's you," she told him, injecting a note of enthusiasm into her voice and stepping aside so he could enter.

A smile broke across his face and he turned to yell exuberantly, "It's okay, Mommy. I can stay."

Jenny spotted her mom's car and her thumbs-up gesture as she drove away. Nice move, she thought. She hadn't realized that her mother's level of sneakiness was so evolved. Must be the O'Brien influence, she decided.

Sean lifted the shopping bag she hadn't noticed before. It was almost as big as he was and he struggled to carry it across the threshold.

"I'll take that," Jenny offered. The bag weighed a ton. Was he moving in with her, for heaven's sake? "What on earth do you have in here?"

Sean stripped off his jacket and tossed it on the floor, then grinned at her. "It's my train set," he said. "For under your tree. I want you to have it this year, 'cause Mommy said you've been sad and that you really like trains, too."

Jenny's eyes filled with tears at the sweetness of the gesture. "I love trains," she told him solemnly. "How about some hot chocolate and then we'll get this set up?"

"All right!" he said with a fist pump. "Cookies, too?"

"Of course, though I might have to save a couple for Santa on Christmas Eve."

His eyes brightened. "You believe in Santa?"

"You bet," she said.

In the kitchen she made his cup of hot chocolate, then put some of Jess's cookies on a plate and carried them into the living room.

Sean studied the tree, his expression puzzled. "Did you forget to put lights on?"

She smiled. "No, they're on there. I just haven't turned them on yet."

"Daddy says you should turn them on before you add anything else in case they need to be moved around."

Jenny smiled. She had a hunch Thomas had gotten that tip elsewhere, from Jake more than likely. From what she'd heard from Caleb, Thomas didn't have a lot of personal Christmas decorating experience.

"He's absolutely right," she told Sean. "And I did that. You want to take a look in case I missed something?"

He nodded solemnly. "I'd better. Daddy says I have a good eye."

Once Sean had approved the placement of the lights, he threw himself eagerly into adding the last of the decorations, then said, "Can we do the train now?"

"You'll have to teach me how," she told him.

"I can do that," he said proudly.

On his hands and knees with his tongue caught between his teeth and his brow furrowed in concentration, he assembled the track into an oval around the base of the tree.

"See how easy it is?" he said.

"You certainly made quick work of it," she said.

"And the cars go together like this," he told her, putting them onto the track, then showing her the battery-operated on-off switch. He sat back on his heels.

"You can do it," he said.

She accepted the offer for the honor he clearly meant it to be and flipped the switch, watching as the small train began to chug around the track under the tree. In that instant, with an expression of innocent delight on her brother's face, Jenny's holiday spirit stirred.

Sean gazed up at her. "It's great, huh?"

"It's fantastic!" she agreed.

But what was most fantastic of all was sharing this moment with her little brother.

"You will be in that theater tonight if I have to drag you there myself," Bree said, her gaze on Jenny unrelenting.

Jenny hadn't left the house for days, despite repeated invitations from various family members trying to coax her out. Instead, she'd sat on her new sofa, hot chocolate in hand, and stared at the lights on her tree. Sean's little train had chugged around the track so many times, she'd had to change the batteries.

Now it appeared that Bree didn't intend to take no for an answer. That didn't mean Jenny was going to give in without a fight. She was comfortable in her isolation, happy to be away from the prying eyes and the worried frowns.

"Not a chance," she told Bree emphatically. "If Christmas weren't three days away and my mom not counting on my being here, my bags would be packed and I'd be loading up my car right this second."

"Well, Christmas *is* three days away, your mom *is* counting on you, and so am I. Producers from New York are going to be here and they're going to want to meet the lyricist. And you deserve to bask in all the accolades. Your songs have made this production into something special. Thanks to you and Caleb, this has become a big deal, Jenny. It's putting my theater on the map."

Jenny noticed that Bree was no longer insisting that she be onstage. Once she'd learned about what had really brought Caleb to town, she'd been as indignant as Jenny. And while Jenny personally didn't care about any praise her work might garner, she knew she owed it to Bree to be there to help her celebrate this success. She understood that family loyalty demanded that much of an effort. She also knew that if she didn't give in now, Bree would be only the first in a long line of people pestering her today. The possibility that Caleb himself might be one of them was most worrisome of all.

"I'm not setting foot backstage," she said eventually, accepting the inevitable.

"Fine."

"Or onstage," she added, just to be clear.

"Not a problem. Believe me, I understand. Though I do expect you to attend the after-party at the inn. You don't have to stay long, just put in an appearance, meet a few people."

Jenny stilled at the idea of being in the same room with Caleb, even if the crowds of people invited were likely to provide a halfway decent buffer. "Don't push your luck," she warned. "The last thing you need is a scene, and I can't promise I won't cause one."

"I know you better than that. Besides, you need to greet the potential backers," Bree insisted. "We'll all do our best to keep you and Caleb apart." She gave her a questioning look. "If that's what you really want."

"It's what I want," Jenny told her emphatically.

"Okay, then. I'll enlist the rest of the family and we'll make it happen," Bree promised.

"Thank you," Jenny said. "As for tonight, I'll sit in the audience, in the back, preferably beside total strangers, not anyone in the family." She didn't want anyone watching her to see how she was handling Caleb being onstage. If her expression turned wistful for even a second, they'd catch it and make way too much of it.

Bree grinned, obviously delighted to have gotten her way. "I already have the seat reserved."

Jenny shook her head. "If I didn't love you so much, I'd hate you for being so blasted sure of yourself."

Bree's grin merely spread. "Your uncle's not the only one in the family with excellent powers of persuasion. Besides, I had a secret weapon."

"What's that?"

"I knew you wouldn't be able to stay away. Deep down, tonight means as much to you as it does to me."

Sadly, Bree was exactly right. Jenny wanted to see how people responded to the play, to her music. And, she thought with a sigh, to Caleb. As badly as a part of her wanted everyone to hate him on sight, she knew with absolute certainty that, just like her, they were going to fall in love with him.

Caleb had only one chance to get things right with Jenny, to convince her that she was the most important thing in his life. After tonight there'd be no more excuses to see her, no more support from the one ally he had left in her family.

Somehow he'd managed to convince Bree of his total sincerity when it came to his feelings for Jenny. She was taking a huge chance on him. She was putting her whole play on the line by making a few changes to accommodate his determination to get through to Jenny. She'd even hired extra security to be sure no obvious paparazzi slipped into the theater. One camera flash could ruin everything.

The Chesapeake Shores Playhouse was packed for tonight's performance. Clearly it was a friendly audience, with the entire O'Brien clan in attendance. While that might work in Bree's favor, it could be a hostile crowd for Caleb if he didn't pull this off.

Jenny had missed most of the final rehearsals, so she had no idea about the adaptations that Bree had made. He exited the stage after performing his second song, walked outside, then came into the theater's lobby and waited just outside the door for his cue.

When it came, he stepped into the aisle, knelt down beside the seat Bree had reserved for Jenny and began to strum his guitar. The spotlight found him and the audience turned their way. He heard the collective gasp when the O'Briens especially realized where he was and to whom he was about to sing. Jenny's eyes had filled with alarm, but there was no escape, not without causing a scene. He was counting on her innate sense of decorum, or perhaps her fear of another tabloid frenzy to keep her in her seat at least long enough to hear him out.

The words he sang then weren't those of the song she'd written to close the first act, but those of the song she'd given to Ricky, the one filled with heartache and longing. He knew that singing it was a risk, a huge one, but he needed her to understand just how deeply those words had touched him, why he'd wanted so badly to sing them. He put every ounce of emotion he could summon into the lyrics, needing her to hear him, not as a singer, but as a man who'd loved and lost and wanted desperately to have a second chance.

Tears welled up in her eyes as he poured heart and soul into the song. When he'd sung the final note, the audience, sensing there was much more than a performance going on, went wild with cheers and applause, but Caleb was oblivious to everything except Jenny. Tears were streaming down her cheeks, but the look of abject misery was gone from her eyes.

Her hand shook as she touched his cheek. "You were right," she whispered. "You were meant to sing that song."

"That's not important," he insisted. "This is the one and only time I intend to sing it. Ricky's already in the studio recording it."

Surprise flashed in her eyes. "What?"

"You gave it to him. Ken Davis believes it will launch his career and make him a star. He deserves that chance. The only chance I want is to get back with you. Will you give me that second chance, Jenny? The way we talked about a few days ago?"

She gave him a look filled with what he hoped was feigned exasperation.

"You won over an entire audience, including my own family," she said. "Isn't that enough for you?"

"It will never be enough until I have you." Knowing that his pride and his future were at stake, he pulled a ring from his pocket. "What do you say, Jenny? From here on out we're a team. Even if you never write another song for me, that's okay. It's you I need. Only you."

Her smile broke then, wobbled a bit, but her eyes were shining. "Don't think for a minute I'm letting anyone else write for you," she scolded. "You have a bad habit of falling for songwriters."

"Only for one," he said, standing and pulling her into his arms. "Only one."

As he sealed his mouth over hers, the lights dimmed and the audience went into a frenzy. Over the shouts, he could have sworn he heard Mick O'Brien declare loudly, "And Merry Christmas to all!"

Emerging from the kiss, Jenny met his gaze and laughed. "Bree's second act is going to have a heck of a time trying to top that."

"Which is why you're coming onstage with me so we can sing the finale together," he said. "That ought to send everyone out of here smiling."

Jenny looked into his eyes. "You and Bree definitely share a sense of the dramatic."

"And we both love you," Caleb declared.

Eyes shining, Jenny whispered, "It really is going to be a merry Christmas, isn't it?"

"The absolute merriest I've ever had, that's for sure."

He couldn't recall ever being more certain that not only this Christmas, but every holiday to come would be perfect as long as he had Jenny by his side.

Epilogue

One year later

The curtain fell on Act II of *A Seaside Christmas* on its opening night on Broadway, and the audience was on its feet. Sure, it was a smaller, older theater, but it was *Broadway!* Bree's dream had come true. Caleb couldn't have been happier for her, though he did have his own big plans for the night.

"I think we have a major holiday hit on our hands," Bree exclaimed to Jenny and Caleb, her eyes bright with excitement. "I can't thank the two of you enough for working with me on this."

Caleb looked down at Jenny. "I don't know about you, but I have someplace I need to be."

She smiled up at him. "Right beside you," she said.

Bree regarded them with confusion. "You're not coming to the after-party?"

"There's been a slight change of plans," Jenny admitted.

"Not that we wanted to steal your thunder, but we figured nobody would be paying much attention to the traditional after-party on opening night," Caleb explained.

"And everyone we love will be there," Jenny added.

Bree frowned. "Meaning?"

"We thought we'd get married, that is if you don't mind," Caleb said.

"We were going to elope," Jenny added quickly. "But we figured somebody would spot us and that would be the end of that. Where better to pull off a secret ceremony than at a party that's already planned and closed to the media?"

Caleb watched Bree's expression closely to see if she minded sharing the spotlight. A smile spread across her face.

"I love it," Bree exclaimed delightedly. "Does anyone else know?"

"Mom does," Jenny told her. "I knew she'd go nuts if she wasn't wearing the absolutely perfect dress for a wedding. She had her hair done and a mani-pedi. I think she's going to look better than I do."

"Nobody can hold a candle to you," Caleb assured her.

"Spoken like a man who wants to get married as quickly as possible," Bree said. "So let's do it." A frown crossed her face. "Does the hotel know? Will there be a wedding cake? You can't get married without a cake. And what about flowers? I wanted to do the flowers for your wedding. I've been thinking about that ever since you two got back together."

"Which is why I had them deliver the flowers to the hotel without assembling them into a bouquet," Jenny said. "I worked with you enough to know exactly what you'd need. Just a bouquet, Bree. Everything else is done. Will you do it?"

"I'd be honored," Bree assured her.

Fifteen minutes later, they'd made their way to the hotel just up the street where the entire extended O'Brien family was waiting. Caleb followed Bree to the private room that had been reserved for the party, while Jenny disappeared to meet her mother.

"Don't take too long," he pleaded, kissing her cheek. "It's been too long already."

He watched her go, his heart in his throat. He might have stood there forever, but Bree touched his arm.

"Let's go and make things pretty for the bride," she said.

"No matter what we do, she'll outshine it all," he said.

Bree laughed. "There's that charm I've grown to love. Are you sure you're not a little bit Irish?"

Caleb laughed. "No, but the O'Briens are definitely rubbing off on me."

The party was in full swing when Jenny came back downstairs with her mother. She could hear the music, a sound track from the play, the minute they exited the elevator.

"Sounds good, doesn't it?" Connie said. "I am so proud of you." She studied her daughter with a worried look. "Are you sure you want to get married here tonight? I always dreamed of you walking down the aisle at church back home."

Jenny shook her head. "This is perfect," she said. "It's private. My family is here. And as long as Caleb and I get to say our vows in front of the people who matter, I'm happy."

Connie kissed her cheek. "Then I'm happy, too. He's a good man, sweetie."

"He's flawed," Jenny corrected. "Which makes him human." A smile spread across her face. "But he's the perfect man for me."

When she and her mom walked into the room, it was Mick who caught sight of her first. Though she'd chosen a simple white dress, there was no mistaking that she was dressed for a wedding.

Mick hurried over with Thomas right behind him, a questioning look in his eyes.

"Seems we're having a wedding," Connie told them, linking her arm through Thomas's.

"So that's why Caleb's been looking so nervous," Mick said. "I thought he was worried about the reviews."

Caleb crossed the room, never taking his eyes off Jenny. "You ready to do this?" he asked quietly as he handed her the bouquet that Bree had created with yellow roses and baby's breath and white satin ribbons. A few forget-me-nots had been tucked in as well.

Jenny turned to Thomas. "I don't have the right to ask this, but would you consider walking me down the aisle?"

"Shouldn't Jake be doing that?" he asked.

"I think he'll understand," Jenny told him. "I want this to be a fresh start, not just for me and Caleb, but my whole family."

There was no mistaking the sheen in Thomas's eyes as he nodded. "It would be my pleasure."

It took only moments for most of the other guests to

figure out what was going on. And when the wedding march replaced the sound track from the play, the rest glanced around, then gasped.

"You're getting married?" Carrie asked, rushing over, her eyes bright with excitement.

"We thought we would," Jenny confirmed.

"This is totally awesome," Carrie said. "Wait till my friends hear that I was at Caleb Green's wedding."

Jenny gave her a stern look. "They can hear about it," she said, then warned, "But no pictures, not a one."

For an instant disappointment flashed in Carrie's eyes, but then understanding apparently dawned. "Got it. If there's a leak, it won't be from me."

"Thank you," Caleb said, kissing her cheek.

For a minute, Jenny thought the teen might pass out, but then she rallied and rushed off to find her twin.

Seconds later Jenny and Caleb were standing in front of a minister, repeating the vows they'd written themselves, vows that acknowledged all they'd been through and all they hoped for in the future.

"No matter how I falter, I will always be certain of this one thing: that I will always love you above all else," Caleb said. "I want you to carry that promise in your heart every single day."

Jenny smiled at him through her tears. "And I promise you that I will always try to be the best wife I can be, that my love will be unconditional and that each day will be blessed because we're facing it together."

As soon as the minister declared them to be husband and wife, Caleb swept her into his arms and kissed her until she came close to forgetting her own name...the old one or this new one she'd agreed to take today: Mrs. Caleb Green.

Then toasts were being made, a late supper was served and the cake was brought in, a towering confection that could have served ten times the number of people in attendance.

Jenny saw Sean's eyes widen.

"Wow! Is that all for us?" he asked excitedly.

"One piece of it is for you," Connie told him firmly.

Jenny leaned down to whisper in his ear. "I'll make sure there's some for you to take back home."

He grinned and slapped her hand in a high five. "Awesome!"

Caleb pulled her aside. "I know it's traditional to hang out a little longer, but I'd really like to be alone with you."

She gave him an impish look. "You're expecting a honeymoon?"

"I'm expecting a wedding night," he corrected. "The honeymoon comes later, once the holidays are over and the play closes for the season. I'm going to sneak you off to a private beach somewhere. For now, I have this lovely suite of rooms with a very large bed that's calling our names. What do you think?"

"I think we're wasting time," she told him.

He grabbed her hand and tugged her toward the door. Jenny made him wait while she said a quick goodnight to her mother and thanked Bree for sharing this special night with her. She and Caleb had almost made their escape when Carrie stopped them.

"Aren't you going to toss the bouquet?" she asked, stars in her eyes.

"It is a tradition," Caleb reminded her.

Jenny regarded the bouquet with regret. She'd really wanted to keep it.

"You'll get it back," Caleb assured her. "Just ask whoever catches it if you can have it as a memento."

"You can," Carrie said at once, obviously intending to be the lucky person who nabbed it.

Caleb tapped on a glass for attention. "Gather round, all you single women," he called out. "Jenny's about to toss her bouquet."

Of course, Jenny realized, in this very large family there were only a few single women and a lot of very young girls. Carrie made sure she was at the very front of the crowd, clearly counting on the bouquet to help her marriage prospects.

But when Jenny turned her back to those gathered and tossed the yellow roses into the air, the catch was greeted by a yelp of shock, or perhaps dismay.

She turned to find Caitlyn holding the flowers as far away from her body as she possibly could, an expression of abject terror in her eyes.

"No way," she muttered, trying to pass them off to Carrie.

"It doesn't work like that, you ninny," Carrie told her. "And if I have to wait for you to get married first, I'm probably doomed."

Jenny glanced at Caleb and laughed. "Now that's an interesting turn of events," she commented as she studied Caitlyn's shell-shocked expression.

"I'll say," he replied. "I can hardly wait to see how it turns out."

If Jenny knew nothing else about Chesapeake Shores and the O'Briens, she knew this. It would turn out exactly the way it was supposed to.

* * * * *

Want more of Sherryl Woods'
heartwarming holiday storytelling?
Turn the page for a bonus Christmas story—
SANTA, BABY.

1

Amy Riley had a fever of 102, globs of oatmeal all over her face, hair that desperately needed washing, a screaming baby and a five-year-old who was regarding her with such reproach that she wanted to sit down and cry herself. It was not a promising start to the holidays.

"But, Mom, you said we could go to the mall today and see Santa," Josh whined. "You promised."

Amy clung to her patience by a thread. "I know, sweetie, but I'm sick. I'm sorry."

"But it's Christmas Eve," he persisted, clearly not hearing or at least not caring about the state of her health. "We *have* to go today. If we don't, how will Santa know what to bring us? He doesn't even know where we live now. What if he takes our presents to Michigan and we're not there?"

"He won't," Amy assured him.

"But how do you *know*?"

"Because I sent him a letter," she claimed in desperation.

"What if he didn't get it? Mail gets lost all the time."

"He got it," she reassured him, thinking of the small

stash of gifts in her closet. Tomorrow morning, they would provide proof for her doubting son, but today he'd just have to take her word for it.

Thanks to the expense of relocating, she hadn't been able to afford much this year, but she was determined Josh would have at least a few packages from Santa to open on Christmas morning, along with a handful from her folks and the one from his dad that she'd picked out just in case Ned didn't bother sending anything. Unless a miracle occurred and something turned up in an overnight delivery on Christmas morning, she'd pegged her ex's lack of consideration exactly right.

With Josh in her face this morning, she had to keep reminding herself that it wasn't his fault that she and his father had gone through a nasty divorce and that she'd packed up with him and his baby sister and moved to a suburb outside of Charlotte, NC, far from family and friends back in Michigan. Everyone had tried to talk her into waiting until after the holidays, but the thought of spending one more minute in the same town as her ex had been too much. Maybe by next year the wounds would have healed and she and the kids could spend the holidays with her folks, but this year staying there a few weeks longer or making a quick trip back had been out of the question. Amy hadn't had the stomach or the money for it.

She'd convinced herself that things would be better after the first of the year when she started her new job at the headquarters of the same bank she'd worked for back home. At the time she'd been offered the transfer, it had seemed like a godsend, a way to get a fresh start with the promise of some financial security in the very near future.

This morning, though, she was regretting the hasty decision. Money was tight and emotions were raw. She was far from home with no new support system in place. And if it was tough for her, it was a thousand times worse for Josh, who felt cheated not to be with family for Christmas.

But, she reassured herself, Josh was an outgoing kid. He would make new friends in kindergarten. In a few more weeks tantrums like the one he was pitching now would be a thing of the past. They just had to survive till then.

"I hate this place," Josh declared, pressing home a point with which she was already far too familiar. Not a day had gone by in the last week when he hadn't expressed a similar sentiment.

Fighting for patience, Amy lowered the now-quiet baby into her portable playpen, then sat her son in her lap and gave him a squeeze. "It's going to get better," she promised him.

He nestled under her chin in an increasingly infrequent display of affection. "When?" he asked plaintively.

"Soon," she vowed. No matter what it took, she would make this work.

"There's not even any snow in this dumb place. At home, we always had snow for Christmas and Dad would take me out on my sled." He sighed dramatically. "I miss Dad."

"I know you do, sweetie. And I'm sure he misses you, too," she said, though she was sure of no such thing.

Ned had been all too eager to see them gone so he could get on with his new life with another woman and the baby that was already on the way by the time his divorce from Amy was final. He rarely spared more than a couple of minutes for his calls to his son and even those brief bits of contact had become less routine. Ned was an out of sight, out of mind kind of guy, which was pretty much how he'd gotten involved with a woman he'd met on his business travels. Amy—and his marriage—had definitely been out of sight and out of mind during those trips.

Amy resolved not to dwell on her many issues with her ex today. Even though she felt awful, she was going to do whatever she could to make this first Christmas in their new home memorable for Josh. Emma was still too young to notice much more than the bright lights on their skinny little tree, but Josh needed more. He needed to believe that life in North Carolina would eventually be much like his old life in Michigan. Perhaps even better.

She tousled his dark brown hair, which badly needed a trim. "We can bake cookies later," she told him. "We'll play all the Christmas CDs and tonight I'll make hot chocolate with lots and lots of marshmallows and we can watch Christmas movies on TV. How about that?"

"Sure," he said wearily. "But it won't be Christmas if I don't get to see Santa. We *always* go on Christmas Eve."

Amy bit back her own sigh. That's what came of creating a tradition for your children. They clung to it tenaciously, even when circumstances changed. And seeing Santa was such a little thing for him to ask for. He hadn't requested a million presents. He didn't make a lot of demands. He even helped with Emma as much as he could. He'd rock her to sleep in her carrier or even show her his picture books accompanied by dramatic reenactments of the stories. He was a great big brother and, most of the time anyway, a big help to Amy.

How many more years would he want to climb up on Santa's lap, anyway, she asked herself. How much longer before he stopped believing?

Maybe if she took a couple more aspirin and a hot shower, she could manage the trip to the mall, she thought without much enthusiasm. Her head throbbed just thinking about the crowds. Still, one look into her son's disappointed eyes and she knew she had to try.

"Will you stay right here and watch your sister?" she asked Josh. "Keep her entertained, okay?"

"How come?"

"So I can take a shower," she told him without elaborating or making another promise she might not be able to keep.

Josh's eyes lit up in sudden understanding, anyway. "And then we'll go see Santa?" he asked excitedly.

"*Maybe* we'll go see Santa," she cautioned. "If I feel better."

He threw his arms around her neck and squeezed. "You will, Mom. I know you will."

He scrambled down, knelt beside the playpen and peered through the mesh at Emma. "We're going to see Santa, Em. You're gonna love him. He's this jolly old guy, who goes ho-ho-ho real loud." He demonstrated, holding his tummy, as he bellowed ho-ho-ho. "He's all dressed in red, and you tell him what you most want for Christmas and then, if you've been good all year, he brings it to you. Santa's the best." He grinned up at Amy. "Next to Mom, of course."

Amy couldn't help grinning back at her budding young diplomat. How could she resist giving him anything he asked for, especially this Christmas? She just hoped she didn't throw up all over jolly old St. Nick.

Nick DiCaprio was not having a good week. Hell, he wasn't having a good life. The police department psychologist had informed his superiors on Monday that he was burned out, that he had anger management issues, that letting him go back on active duty in the immediate future would be irresponsible.

Well, duh! After being forced to stand by helplessly while a deranged man had terrorized his own kid to get even with his ex-wife, who wouldn't have anger issues? Nick had wanted to pound heads together that awful day, especially those of the SWAT team who wouldn't allow him to intervene. He couldn't imagine that talking that whole disastrous scenario to death with some shrink was going to improve his mood.

As if all that psychobabble weren't annoying enough, it was Christmas Eve. The whole world was all caught up in the commercialized holiday frenzy. If he heard one more Christmas song, he was going to turn on the gas and stick his head in the oven. Or just get blind, stinking drunk. Yeah, he thought, that was better. Saner. The stupid shrink would be delighted to know he wasn't completely self-destructive.

When his phone rang, he ignored it. There wasn't a single person in the universe he wanted to talk to this morning. Not one. There were even more he wanted to avoid completely, namely his family, almost all of whom seemed to be possessed by unrelenting holiday cheer. The answering machine clicked on.

"Nick, answer the phone!" his baby sister commanded, sounding frantic. "Dammit, I know you're there. Pick up. I'm desperate."

Nick sighed. When Trish hit a panic button, the whole world was going to suffer right along with her. She'd be over here banging on his door, if he didn't answer the phone. Or, worse, using the key he'd given her for emergencies to barge in and turn his world as topsy-turvy as her own apparently was.

He yanked the phone out of its cradle and barked, "What?"

"Thank God," she said fervently, oblivious to his sour mood. "Nick, I need you at the mall right now!"

"Not in a hundred million years," he said at once. "Are you crazy?"

Just because her duties as a mall events coordinator required Trish to be at a shopping mall on Christmas Eve didn't mean he intended to get within ten miles of the place. He wouldn't have done it when he was in a good mood. Today, it would border on turning him homicidal.

"I'm not crazy," she insisted. "I'm desperate. Santa called in sick. If you ask me he took one look outside at the lousy weather and decided to stay home in front of a warm fire, but the bottom line is it's Christmas Eve and I don't have a Santa."

"Hire another one," he said without sympathy. "Gotta go."

"Don't you dare hang up on me, Nicholas DiCaprio. If you do, I swear I will tell Mom and Dad all about this burnout thing."

Nick hesitated. The only thing worse than having Trish nagging him to death would be to have his parents all over his case. They weren't that happy about his decision to become a cop in the first place. They'd see this so-called burnout thing as the perfect excuse to harangue him about getting off the force for good. If his sister was annoyingly persistent, his protective mother was qualified to drive him right over the brink into insanity.

"What about Rob?" he suggested, referring to their older brother. "He'd make an excellent Santa. He loves the holidays."

"Rob and Susan are taking the kids to cut down a tree today. It's their Christmas Eve tradition, remember?"

Nick groaned. How could he have forgotten that? Last year he'd gone along. It had taken the entire day, because everyone in the family, including one-year-old Annie, had a vote and there hadn't been a single tree on which they could all agree. How they could gauge Annie's vote, when she only knew one discernible word—mama—was beyond him. By three in the afternoon, he'd vowed not only to never begin any Christmas traditions, but to never have a family.

"And Stephen?" he asked hopefully. His younger brother had no traditions that Nick had ever noticed. No family, either. In fact, he was the DiCaprio black sheep, but surely Trish could corral him for the day. She was the only one in the family who seemed to understand his need for rebellion. In return Stephen did things for her that no one else could persuade him to do. She could even coerce him into showing up for holiday meals and tolerating their mother fussing over him.

"I actually spoke to Stephen. He's a little hung over," she admitted. "I don't think that's a good quality for a Santa."

Nick regretted not getting drunk when he'd had the

chance. "Okay, fine," he said, his tone grim. "What exactly do you need from me?"

"Isn't that obvious? I need you to substitute for Santa," Trish said sweetly, obviously sensing victory. "It won't be hard. Just a few ho-ho-ho's for the kids. Listen to their gift lists. Don't make any promises. Get your picture taken. That's all."

"How long?"

"I need you here ASAP and the mall's open till six. It's a few hours, Nick. How bad can it be?"

It sounded like hell. "Come on, Trish. This is so not me. There has to be someone else," he pleaded. "Don't they have agencies for this kind of thing? Rent-a-Santa or something?"

"Are you nuts? It's Christmas Eve. All the good Santas are already working. I don't have time to hunt down the last remaining qualified Santa in all of North Carolina. And why should I, when you have absolutely nothing to do today? Please, Nick. You're good with kids."

Once upon a time he had considered himself to be good with kids. He'd been a doting uncle to Rob's kids, taking the older boys to ball games, even babysitting Annie a time or two. But after what had happened with freckle-faced Tyler Hamilton less than a month ago, Nick didn't trust himself to be within a hundred miles of a child. He didn't even want to be anywhere near Rob's kids this Christmas, at least not without backup.

Still, despite his reservations, somewhere deep down inside—very deep down—he wondered if this wouldn't be a chance for some sort of redemption. He hadn't been able to do much to help Tyler, so he could spend all day today making up for it.

No, he thought wearily, this was more like payback.

Like some sort of giant cosmic joke, asking a man with his complete and total lack of holiday cheer to spend a whole day faking it for the sake of a bunch of greedy little brats.

"You'll owe me," he told his sister eventually.

"No question about it," she agreed. "Won't that be a nice change?"

"I beg your pardon."

"I have a list of the favors I've done for you, big brother, beginning with getting you your dream date with Jenny Davis."

"You did not get me a date with Jenny," he snapped, thinking of the redheaded teenager who'd been able to twist his insides into knots at seventeen.

"Did, too. She wouldn't give you the time of day, till I told her what a terrific guy you are. I also offered to loan her my cashmere sweater and to give her my new Kenny Chesney CD."

"You bribed her?" he demanded incredulously. If that wasn't the most humiliating piece of news he'd heard lately, he thought with a shake of his head.

"It was the least I could do for my favorite brother," she said.

"Well, given how badly that relationship turned out, I wouldn't be bringing it up now, if I were you," he muttered. Jenny, whom he'd dated all through his senior year in high school only to be dumped by her the day before prom, had been the first in a long string of disastrous mistakes he'd made when it came to women. At least Trish hadn't had a hand in any of the rest. He'd made those absurd choices all on his own.

"Not to worry, Nicky. My list of the favors I've done for you goes on and on. I keep it posted right beside my desk for times like this," she said cheerfully. "See you in an hour. Come to my office. I have Santa's costume here. This is going to be fun."

"Torture," he mumbled. "It's going to be torture."

"What?"

"Nothing. I'll see you in an hour."

"Love you, Nicky."

Normally he would have echoed his sister's sentiment, but at the moment he was more inclined to throttle her.

2

The parking lot at King's Mall was already a zoo by the time Amy had showered, dried her hair, packed up the kids and found it after taking several wrong turns. A line of cars waited at the entrance and more inched up and down each aisle looking fruitlessly for someone who might be about to leave. Heavy, dark clouds were looming overhead, almost completely blocking the sun. She couldn't be sure if they were threatening rain or even snow. Though snowfall here was rare, it certainly felt cold and raw enough for it to Amy.

Just a year ago, when she'd been eight months pregnant with Emma and totally exhausted, she'd still felt the excitement of the last-minute holiday crush. Today, all she felt was tired, and the gloomy sky wasn't helping.

"Over there," Josh shouted from the backseat. "Mom, see that lady with all the bags? She's gonna leave. You can get there."

Amy spotted the woman two aisles over. "Sweetie, there are already half a dozen cars waiting for that space. Don't worry. We'll find one. It's always like this on Christmas Eve. We just have to be patient."

"What if Santa's not even here?" Josh asked worriedly. "I mean, he's in Michigan, right? How can he be in two places at once?"

"He's here. I called."

"Maybe he gets off early on Christmas Eve, you know, so he can start flying all over the world. We usually go first thing in the morning back home, then Dad and me shop to buy your presents."

Amy bit back a grin at her pint-size worrier. That, at least, was a trait he'd gotten from her. It probably wasn't the best one she could have shared. "I checked on that, too," she told him. "Santa will be here till the mall closes at six."

"What time is it now?"

"Two thirty. We have lots of time."

"Not if we don't find a parking place *soon*," Josh warned grimly.

Amy was forced to admit, she was beginning to have her doubts about that ever happening, too. People were nuts. Two cars were currently in a standoff over a space in the next aisle, both so determined to grab it that the poor driver trying to get out couldn't even move.

"People in Michigan were nicer," Josh declared from the back.

"No, they weren't. These people are nice, too. Everyone gets a little stressed out on Christmas Eve." A fat drop of rain splatted on the windshield and her mood deteriorated even further. She envisioned whatever bug she'd had this morning turning into pneumonia.

"I'll bet Santa won't come see them," Josh predicted direly. "Not when they say bad words and stuff. Look at that guy over there. He said something bad and he did that thing with his finger that you told me never, ever to do."

Amy regretted that her five-year-old had ever seen that gesture, but unfortunately it had been one of his father's routine actions behind the wheel. She'd been forced to discuss its inappropriateness on numerous occasions.

"I think that's enough play-by-play commentary on the parking lot," she told Josh just as a space right in front of her opened up. The driver even backed up in a way that guaranteed Amy would be the one to get it, then waved cheerfully as she drove off.

"See, she was nice," she told her cynical son. "Now let's get your sister into her stroller and go see Santa before it really starts raining."

Unloading the stroller, then getting Emma settled into it took time. Emma liked being carried. She hated the stroller…or thought she did. She kicked and screamed until Amy thought her head would split. Once she was in, though, and they were moving, Emma beamed up at Amy with the sort of angelic smile that made Amy wonder if she'd imagined all those heart-wrenching sobs only moments before. That was the joy of Emma. She could switch moods in a heartbeat.

As they reached the mall entrance, Amy gazed directly into Josh's eyes. "No running off, okay?" she said sternly. "You don't know this mall, so you have to stay with me and hold on to my hand."

"Mom!" he protested. "I'm not a baby."

"It's either that or we go right back home," she said in her most authoritative, no-nonsense tone. "I don't want you getting lost on Christmas Eve."

He rolled his eyes, but he took her hand. As soon as

they were inside, he began to hurry her along past the shoe stores, lingerie shop, dress boutiques, cell phone kiosks and jewelry stores. Amy thought it was ironic that with all the big-name chain stores in the mall, it seemed every bit as familiar as anyplace they'd shopped back home. Maybe that's why Josh thought he knew where he was going.

When she was tempted to linger in front of a toy store, Josh barely spared a glance at the games in the window, then tugged her back into motion.

"Mom, come on," he urged. "Santa's gotta be right up here. See all those people? He's there. I know it! Hurry."

"Sweetie, he's not going anywhere. Slow down."

"We gotta get in line, Mom," he countered. "I'll bet it's really, really long."

Before Amy could argue with that, with some sort of child's radar, Josh spotted Santa.

"There he is," he shouted. "See, Mom. He's right there in the middle of all those Christmas trees! It's like a whole Santa's workshop around him." His eyes lit up. "Wow! That is totally awesome! It's better than anything I ever saw in Michigan! Did you bring the camera? We gotta send pictures to Dad."

His excitement was contagious. Even Emma seemed captivated by the glittering sea of lights ahead.

"I gotta see," Josh declared.

And with that he let go of Amy's hand and bolted into the frenzied crowd that was swirling all around between Amy and Santa.

It took less than a second for him to disappear in the crush of people. Excitement and anticipation died. Panic clawed its way up the back of Amy's throat. Instinctively, she gathered Emma out of her stroller and clung to her as she shouted over and over for Josh, pushing her way through the crowd, the stroller abandoned.

Most people were oblivious to her cries, but finally a young woman stopped, alarm on her face.

"What's happened?" she asked, placing a comforting hand on Amy's arm. "Can I help?"

Amy was shaking so hard, she couldn't seem to form a coherent sentence.

"It's okay," the young woman soothed. "Take a deep breath and tell me. I'm Trish DiCaprio." She gestured toward her name tag. "I work for the mall. What can I do to help?"

"My son," Amy whispered. "He spotted Santa and took off and now I can't find him. There are so many people and we don't know anyone here and he's never been in this mall before." She was babbling now, but she couldn't seem to stop.

"When did you lose track of him?"

"A minute ago at the most."

"Then he can't have gone far. It's going to be okay," Trish reassured her. "My brother is playing Santa. In real life he's a cop. He'll know exactly what to do. I'll talk to him and we'll find your son in no time. Will you be okay right here for a minute till I can get to him?"

Amy nodded. She was clinging so tightly to Emma that the baby began to whimper. Someone appeared at her side just then with the stroller. Dazed, Amy stared at it, wondering where on earth she'd left it.

"I saw your boy take off and then you ran after him and left this behind," the woman said, her voice gentle. Her blue eyes were filled with concern. "Are you okay? Shall I stay with you till that young woman comes back?"

Tears stung Amy's eyes at the kindness in the woman's expression. "Thank you for rescuing the stroller. I don't know what I was thinking."

"You were just trying to catch up with your boy. What's his name?"

"Josh."

"Oh, my," the woman said with a smile. "I have a Josh, too. Of course, he's all grown-up now." She gave a rueful shake of her head. "My kids used to pull this kind of stunt on me all the time when they were small. Trust me, they all turned up. Now they have children of their own putting them through the same thing. What do they call that? Karma, isn't it?" She patted Amy's shoulder. "Don't you worry. Your boy will be back any minute. He'll probably find you before they can even get a search going."

She spoke with such conviction that Amy felt her panic slowly ease. "You're very kind. I really appreciate it. If you need to get your shopping finished, I'll be okay now."

"I have time," she said. "I'm Maylene Kinney, by the way. I'll just wait with you till that nice young woman comes back with help. I heard you say that you're new to Charlotte. Is that right?"

Amy nodded.

"What's your name?"

"Amy. Amy Riley."

"Well, welcome, Amy. I know this isn't the way to get off to a good start in a new place, but you will laugh about it someday, I promise you that." She smiled. "Maybe not till that boy of yours is grown and his son is doing something just as bad, but you will laugh."

Maylene's soft, Southern voice and friendly chitchat kept the panic at bay, at least for now, but Amy couldn't seem to stop searching the crowd for some sign of Josh. She ought to be looking for him, not just standing around waiting. She was always so careful to make sure he stayed in sight, to hold tight to his hand in unfamiliar surroundings. Now he could be anywhere, with anyone. This was her worst nightmare come true.

Her imagination immediately went into overdrive, envisioning every dire fate she'd ever read about. This time when the tears started, she couldn't seem to stop. Apparently sensing her mother's despair, Emma began to howl, too. Maylene put an arm around Amy's shoulder and murmured reassurances.

"I can't do this," Amy said finally. "I shouldn't be standing around crying. I have to do something constructive. I should be looking for Josh."

"You will," Maylene said. "Help will be here any second. They'll know exactly what to do. If you go running around every which way and getting lost yourself, what good will that do?"

Amy knew she was right. She drew in a deep breath and accepted the wad of tissues Maylene handed her. "You're right. I have to be smart about this."

But she'd never felt so helpless in her life.

If Nick had to utter one more ho-ho-ho, he was going to scream. It had been 9:00 a.m. by the time he was decked out in this ridiculous red suit with all the fat man pillows stuffed into it. The stupid beard itched like crazy and the too-big hat kept sliding down over his eyes. If he was fooling one single person in this mall into thinking he was Santa Claus, he'd eat the oversize hat. Even the littlest kids were eyeing him with skepticism.

Even so, the line waiting to see him was endless. It had been nonstop since he'd settled onto Santa's red velvet throne, which he intended to tell his sister was uncomfortable as hell. No wonder Santa hadn't reported for duty.

He'd managed to eat two cookies and sneak a sip of a soda for lunch before Trish had snatched them out of his hands to have his picture taken with a dad and three teenage boys. He was so hungry he was about to snatch a candy cane out of the pile being handed out to the kids. And he was just about blind from the flashbulbs going off in his eyes. Every parent clearly wanted to record the scene.

At least the job didn't require much acting on his part. Aside from trying to inject an unaccustomed note of cheer into his voice, his dialogue was pretty much limited to the ho-ho-ho's and asking what the tiny monsters wanted Santa to bring them. He'd done okay with that, he thought. None of them had run off screaming that he was an impostor. Not yet, anyway.

"You go on being a good girl," he told the shy imp sitting rigidly on his knee. "If you do everything your mommy and daddy tell you to do, Santa will bring you that doll you've been asking for."

Her sky-blue eyes went wide. "Really?" she asked with such amazement that Nick wondered if he'd made a serious blunder. Never promise anything, Trish had warned him. Why hadn't he listened? He cast an anxious glance toward her mother, who gave him a surreptitious wink. He sighed with relief. Thank goodness he hadn't set the kid up for disappointment.

Just then his sister, who'd been suspiciously absent since she'd parked him here in Santa's workshop, except for the photo-op with some contest winners, appeared at his side. He immediately noted the complete lack of Christmas cheer in her expression. She looked pale and even more harried than she had earlier.

"Something up?" he asked.

She leaned down and whispered, "We have a problem, Nicky. I've got a panicky mom back there who can't find her little boy."

Nick's gut began to churn. "Call security and the cops."

"I've already called security," Trish told him. "But I'm worried she's going to pass out or something. She just needs some reassurance that everything possible is being done. Can't you help? It would make me feel a lot better if you would. You're trained to deal with situations like this. And I'd rather not call the police in unless it's absolutely necessary."

"Why the hell not?"

"I'd just rather not, okay?"

He gave her a hard look. "Are you worried about how this would play out on TV or something?"

She frowned at his scathing tone. "Don't look at me like that, Nicky. It's part of my job to worry about things like that."

A missing child scenario barely a month in the past played itself out in Nick's mind. That one hadn't come to a good end. He didn't want to be in the middle of another one with a tragic outcome. And, goodness knows, he knew how stories like that played in the media. He'd seen his face on the front page of the papers and on the six o'clock news too damn many times.

"Then let security deal with it. Let them be heroes," he repeated firmly, not even trying to hide his reluctance to be involved in any capacity. Trish had to know what she was asking of him was too much. He didn't give a hoot how many favors he owed her.

"But I already told her you're a policeman," Trish pressed. "I know you're not on duty right now, but she's so scared, Nicky. Put yourself in her place. It's Christmas Eve and her little boy is lost. They just moved here, so she's all alone. It's no wonder she's freaking out. Please, you have to do something. Go into your professional mode. Ask the right questions, organize the search. That will calm her down until security can find her son. I'm sure it won't take that long."

Nick wasn't nearly as optimistic as his sister. In a crowd like this, with everyone focused on last-minute shopping, how many people would even notice a little boy on his own? His stomach continued to churn. He poked a hand in his pocket in search of the antacids he usually had with him. Unfortunately, he hadn't transferred them to Santa's costume.

"What about the line?" he asked, preferring even another hundred kids to one desperate mom whose child had gone missing in this mob scene.

"I'll tell them Santa has to take a break," Trish said at once. "It happens. They won't freak out or anything."

She regarded him with that same imploring look that had lured him into doing whatever she wanted when they were kids. It might work a hundred percent of the time on Stephen, but Nick was pretty much a sucker for that look, too.

Even in the face of his continued silence, Trish didn't let up.

"Security will be here any minute, but I need a real cop in charge, Nicky. You said it yourself. Please," Trish begged.

He compared his own credentials with those of the average mall security staffer and resigned himself to the inevitable. Even if it weren't his sister's neck on the line, he only had one choice. He'd been brought up to help anyone in need. His police training had ingrained the concept. Just because he was a burned-out mess, that hadn't changed.

"You get me out of here without all hell breaking loose and I'll calm this woman down and help her look for her kid." He gave Trish a fierce look. "If we don't have any luck in the next half hour, I want every cop in Charlotte combing this place, okay? I don't care what kind of PR nightmare it creates."

Trish threw her arms around him and kissed his cheek. "Thank you, Nicky. I'll make the announcement about your break right now, then I'll take you to her."

Nick figured his good deeds for the day ought to be racking up big points by now. Maybe his debt to Trish was paid. Maybe with any luck, as soon as he'd located the boy, he could scamper right on out the back door of the mall without one more ho-ho-ho.

Just as that cheerful prospect occurred to him, he caught a glimpse of the restless parents and disappointed kids as they were greeted with the news that Santa was taking a break and knew that plan was out the window.

He might be the lousiest Santa in the history of Christmas, but he was all these kids had. Heaven help them.

3

While she was waiting for that woman—Trish something-or-other—Amy called for Josh until she was nearly hoarse, even though Maylene Kinney told her she was only hurting her vocal cords.

"Kids only hear what they want to hear," Maylene admonished. "You save your voice so you can tell him how much you love him the second he turns up."

"Right now I just want to kill him," Amy said, though she knew the older woman was right. No matter how terrified and furious she was, she could hardly wait to hold Josh in her arms again.

How could she have lost him so quickly? She'd known precisely where he was headed—to see Santa. He had to be somewhere in this mob scene of frantic shoppers and impatient children right around Santa's village, but there'd been no sign of him for what seemed like an eternity.

Finally the harried-looking young woman who'd spoken to her a few minutes earlier returned with Santa in tow. He was tall, at least six feet, and well rounded, thanks to plenty of fake padding. She couldn't guess his age, because of the fake white hair and beard, but if he and Trish were brother and sister, then surely he wasn't that old, late twenties or early thirties, maybe. Right around her age. Maybe he even had children of his own and would be able to empathize with her distress.

"Ma'am, this is my brother," Trish told Amy. "Don't be put off by the costume. He's really a terrific detective. He'll help you find your son. You'll be back together in no time."

Amy gazed into Santa's dark blue eyes behind their fake, round little glasses and felt an odd *zing* that was totally inappropriate under the circumstances. She had the oddest desire to fling her arms around this man who was offering to help her find Josh and hold on for dear life. After all, Santa Claus represented all that was good and hopeful in the world. Add to that the fact that *this* Santa was an experienced detective and he was everything she needed in this particular crisis.

"I'm Nick DiCaprio," he told her, his somber expression far from the jolly persona usually expected from Santa.

Her mouth dropped as the irony struck her. "St. Nick?"

His face relaxed and a faint smile touched his lips, then vanished. "Hardly. Trish had a last-minute emergency and, after a lot of sisterly persuasion and blackmail, I agreed to fill in for Santa. Trust me, no one would confuse me with any kind of saint."

The young woman beside him nudged him in the ribs. "Don't be modest, Nicky. You have a few saintly traits." She smiled at Amy, then gave her an oddly speculative look. "For one thing, Nicky is one of the last genuine good guys. You can't tell it now, but he's really handsome. Hot, even. And he stays in great shape."

Santa—rather Nick—frowned and cut her off before she could cover any more of his masculine attributes. "I think maybe she's more interested in my professional qualifications, Trish."

"I already told her you're an excellent policeman," she said quickly, then turned to Amy. "He has lots of commendations. If anyone can find your son—"

"Why don't you tell me about your son," he interrupted, his tone gruff. He still seemed uncomfortable, even though his sister's unsolicited praise had turned professional. "Trish, let me borrow your clipboard and notepad." He glanced back at Amy. "What's your name?"

"Amy Riley."

"And the boy's name?"

"Josh Riley."

"Age?"

"He's five."

"Height? Hair color?"

Amy rattled off the statistics, growing more impatient by the second. She knew he needed the basic information but why weren't they looking already? By now Josh could have been swept along to the other end of the mall.

"What's he wearing?"

Increasingly exasperated, she tersely described the bright red jacket, jeans and Spiderman T-shirt Josh had put on that morning and the red and green scarf he had around his neck.

"I know you think we're wasting time, Mrs. Riley," Nick said as if he'd read her mind. "But with thousands of kids running around the mall today, it's best to know exactly what your son looks like. Giving a good description to the security staff will save a lot of time in the long run."

"I have a picture," Amy said, hurriedly pulling his last school picture from her purse. It had been taken just a couple of months before they'd left Michigan. She choked up at the sight of Josh's precious gaping smile and that untamed cowlick of brown hair that refused to stay put no matter how much gel she used to slick it down.

Handing the picture to Nick, she said, "He needs a haircut now, but this was taken not too long ago."

"Cute kid," Nick said, then turned to his sister. "Trish, how far does the sound from that PA system travel?"

"It's just for the immediate vicinity," she told him. "Some of the department stores have their own. I could write up an announcement and ask them to make it ASAP."

"Do that, and we'll give this one a try, in the meantime. Keep it simple, Trish. Ask Josh Riley to come to see Santa." He glanced at Amy. "Think that would get his attention?"

"Oh, yes," Amy said eagerly. "He was so anxious to see you, I mean Santa. That's why he took off in the first place. I wasn't moving fast enough to suit him. He wanted to see you up close, then get in line."

"Have you checked the line?" he asked.

"Front to back," Amy confirmed. "He's not in it. I just don't understand why he would have wandered away."

"Because that's what little boys do," Nick offered. "They're easily distracted and often far too fearless for their own good. Trish, let's try the PA and see what happens, then do whatever you have to do to get the cooperation of the stores."

But even after several announcements, there was still no sign of Josh. Amy gazed up at Santa. Despite the beard and makeup designed to give him a jolly look, there was no mistaking the fact that his expression was troubled.

"He really is lost, isn't he?" she whispered, her voice choked.

Nick nodded, but he took her hand in his and gave it a squeeze. "Don't you dare lose it on me now, Mrs. Riley."

"Amy," she told him.

"Okay, Amy. Hang in there. We're going to find your boy."

"Of course, you will," Maylene added.

It was the first time she'd spoken since Nick's arrival. Amy knew she'd stayed close by in case she was needed, but she hadn't intruded. Amy was grateful for her presence. With Maylene around, she didn't feel quite so alone.

"I believe I know your mother, Nick," Maylene continued. "We belong to the same Red Hat Society." She beamed at Amy. "Laura DiCaprio is always bragging about her son the policeman." She smiled at Nick. "Your mother is very proud of you."

Nick seemed as surprised by that as he'd been put off by his sister's glowing comments.

"Weren't you involved in a high-profile case just recently?" Maylene asked, her brow furrowing as she apparently tried to recall the details.

"Let's not get into that," Nick said curtly.

Maylene looked taken aback by his sharp tone, but then something must have come to her because she nodded. "I'm sorry. You're absolutely right," she said hurriedly. "I don't know what I was thinking. You need to be concentrating on finding Josh."

"That's exactly right," Nick said, his sympathetic gaze pinned on Amy. "You okay?"

"I'll be a lot better when we find Josh."

"It won't be much longer," Nick reassured her. "I can see some of the security guys coming now. We want to get this search organized the right way. Once security fans out through the mall, it shouldn't take any time at all."

Oddly enough, Amy believed him. There was something solid and reassuring about a detective who would be willing to take the time to play Santa in a mall filled with last-minute shoppers and hyperactive children. It said a lot about his character that he'd helped out his sister, when most men wouldn't have wanted to be within a hundred miles of the mall today. Of course, he had mentioned something about Trish needing to blackmail him to get his cooperation, but still…

With his warm, comforting hand wrapped around hers, Amy finally let herself start to relax. Nick might be a reluctant substitute for the real Santa Claus, but perhaps he was capable of performing at least one minor miracle and reuniting her with her little boy.

* * *

By the time Nick accepted the fact that Josh Riley was nowhere near Santa's village, a dozen mall security officers including the less experienced extras hired during the holidays, had arrived. Familiar with the mall's various wings, Nick hastily organized them into an efficient search party, showed them the picture of the boy, gave them a description of his clothes, and sent them to the areas of the mall most likely to draw an adventurous five-year-old.

All the while, he was aware of Amy regarding him with her big, soulful eyes that were shadowed by fear. Tyler Hamilton's mom had looked at him exactly like that, trusted him to bring back her boy. Nick shuddered at the memory of those harrowing hours, which Maylene Kinney had almost revealed at a most inopportune moment. Thank goodness the woman's memory had temporarily failed her. When the incident had come back to her, she'd covered well. Meanwhile, Amy seemed too distracted to notice the byplay between them. He didn't want her to start asking a lot of questions about why Nick had been in the news recently.

None of them could afford to go back and think about that tragedy right now. Amy needed to believe in him. And he had to stay focused on this mom and this boy. He refused to consider the possibility that this was anything more than a missing child. Anything else took him down a road he couldn't bring himself to travel.

That didn't mean that he didn't understand the urgency of finding Josh before his mom freaked out completely or before the situation turned into something worse. Any location that attracted a lot of children also had the potential to draw those who preyed on them.

With the security staff fanning out, he turned back to Amy.

"Let me take the baby, okay? Then we can leave the stroller here with Trish," he said lightly. The little sweetheart with her blond curls and pink bow in her hair immediately beamed at him in a way that made his heart ache.

"Who's this angel?" he asked, responding to that smile with one of his own.

"Her name's Emma," Amy said. "She's eleven months old. Are you sure you want to hold her? I can keep her."

"I don't mind. I have a niece who's not much older," he told her.

He gently patted the baby's back till she settled down again. She felt good in his arms. There was something about holding an innocent baby, smelling that powdery scent, feeling that weight relax against his chest, that always affected him and made him yearn for something that he rarely acknowledged was missing from his life.

Feeling the start of that yearning somewhere deep inside, he snapped his attention back to the current crisis.

"Is there any store in the mall that your son especially likes?" he asked.

She shook her head. "We've never been here before. We just moved to town a couple of weeks ago and we're getting settled. I wasn't even sure exactly where the mall was. I got lost getting here. We probably shouldn't have come, but it's been a family tradition to see Santa on Christmas Eve and I didn't want to disappoint Josh. It's hard enough on him since his dad's back in Michigan."

"You're divorced?" A glance at her ring finger confirmed the absence of a wedding band.

She nodded and Nick's sense of dread magnified.

"You're absolutely sure your husband's in Michigan?" he asked, his voice filled with tension.

Amy regarded him with confusion. "Of course. Why?"

"What were the terms of custody?"

"I have full custody. Josh will spend summers with his dad. What does that have to do with anything?"

"And your husband agreed to that willingly?"

"He was eager to have us leave," Amy explained. "Why are you asking all these questions about my ex-husband? He has nothing to do with this."

Nick regarded her with a penetrating look. "Are you sure about that? He wouldn't try to snatch Josh away from you?"

"No. Never," she said fiercely. "I told you, he was glad we were leaving, so he could move on with his new wife. I don't understand what you're trying to get at."

Nick recalled that Mitzi Hamilton hadn't believed her ex-husband was capable of taking their son, either. They'd wasted precious time searching for a stranger, only to determine that Tyler had been taken by his own dad, a man intent on revenge. How the hell was Nick supposed to know if Amy Riley was telling him the truth about this situation?

He looked into her eyes and tried to read her expression. She looked a bit confused, maybe even troubled by his questions, but she seemed totally sincere.

"You're absolutely certain your ex-husband wouldn't change his mind, come looking for Josh?"

"Not a chance," Amy said. She pulled a cell phone from her purse. "I could call him, if you want."

"Do it," Nick commanded. "At home, not on his cell phone."

"Why?"

"If you call his cell phone, he could be anywhere. I want to know for a fact he's in Michigan."

She looked shaken by his persistence, but she dialed. "Ned," she said eventually. "It's Amy." Her gaze locked with Nick's. "I..." Her voice trailed off, as if she'd suddenly realized that she needed an excuse for calling. Clearly she wasn't anxious to tell her ex-husband the truth, that their son was missing. After a noticeable hesitation, she said, "I was just wondering if you'd sent a gift for Josh. Nothing's come yet."

Nick sagged with relief at the evidence that Josh's dad wasn't involved in his disappearance. He barely listened to the rest of Amy's brief conversation.

When she'd hung up, she frowned at him. "Satisfied?"

He nodded. "Sorry. I had to be sure, Amy."

"Something tells me I need to know why all of this mattered so much."

He shook his head. "Just covering all the bases."

"I'm not sure I believe that," she said, studying him intently.

Nick hated seeing the doubts in her eyes, but he knew there would only be more if he explained. "Just trust me, okay?"

"I don't have much choice, do I?" she muttered wearily. She met his gaze. "Now what?"

Nick tried to think like a five-year-old boy on the day before Christmas. "Would Josh go to a store to buy a present for his dad?"

Amy frowned. "I don't think so. We sent a present last week."

"What about you? Would he want to find a last-minute gift for you?"

Her eyes, an unusual shade of amber, shimmered with unshed tears. "I don't think so. I don't think he has any money. All he wanted to do today was see Santa. He didn't even want to waste time looking in the windows at the toy store. He was so upset this morning when I didn't feel well and said we couldn't come. I felt so awful about letting him down that I got dressed and came anyway." The tears spilled over and ran down her cheeks. "We should have stayed at home. I should have known something bad would happen."

"Come on now, Amy. You couldn't predict something like that. Stop beating yourself up. This isn't your fault."

"I just don't understand why he didn't come straight here. I swear to you that he's never done anything like this before."

"With kids, it seems as if there's a first time for everything," Nick said. "My nieces and nephews are always catching their parents off guard."

"That's what Maylene said." She glanced around. "Where is she?" Regret clouded her eyes. "She must have left. I should have wished her a merry Christmas. She was so kind to me."

Nick regarded her with wonder. What kind of woman worried about wishing someone a merry Christmas in the middle of her own crisis? "I imagine she knew you had other things on your mind. And you know her name. You can always give her a call tonight and let her know Josh is home safe and sound."

"Do you think he will be?" she asked.

"I know it," he assured her, because he couldn't very well tell her anything else. There would be time enough for a reality check if the boy didn't turn up in the next few minutes.

Suddenly her expression turned frantic again. "You don't think he'd go outside and try to find the car, do you?"

Nick sure as hell hoped not. The parking lot would make a kidnapping a thousand times easier, to say nothing of the other dangers from careless drivers trying to snag a parking place in their rush to finish up last-minute shopping. "What do you think?" he countered.

"No," she admitted. "He was totally focused on Santa, but where on earth could he be? He saw where you were."

"It's one thing to see the whole Santa's workshop thing from a distance," Nick explained. "But the closer he got, probably all he could really see were people. That's what happens with kids. They're intrepid. They rush off and the next thing you know they're lost in a sea of legs."

"I should have held on to him," she lamented, looking miserable. "I tried. I told him not to let go of my hand."

"I'm sure you did," he soothed. "Tell you what. Why don't you and I take a walk?"

She regarded him with bemusement. "A walk? Why? He'll come here first. I told you all he cares about is seeing Santa."

"Which is why we're going for a walk," Nick told her. "We'll see if we can help him spot Santa a little more easily. When I came out here this morning, I was like some sort of kid-magnet walking through the mall. If

Josh is anxious to see Santa, maybe he'll see the commotion and find us."

"But what if he comes back here, thinking you'll be in the workshop seeing kids?" she asked worriedly. "He was in such a rush to get in line."

"But he didn't, did he? Which means something else caught his attention," Nick suggested, then turned to his sister who'd rejoined them after making her announcements and contacting the stores in the mall to get them to make the same announcement. "Trish will watch for him, just in case, though, right, Trish?"

"Of course, I will," Trish said at once. "I'll keep his picture with me, so he won't be scared if I approach him. Nicky, you have your cell phone?"

He nodded.

"Then I'll call you the second he shows up here," Trish volunteered, giving Amy a sympathetic look.

Nick studied his sister. She was a warm and generous woman and she seemed okay with his plan, but it had to be throwing her whole Santa photo-op thing off-kilter. As frantic as she'd been this morning over finding a Santa replacement, he couldn't help wondering if she was holding back her own emotions over this turn of events.

"Is me taking off for a little while longer going to be a problem?" he asked her.

She looked at Amy's pale face and immediately shook her head. "This is more important. I'll manage. If anyone complains I'll tell 'em Santa got stuck in the workshop elevator."

Nick grinned at her quick thinking. Her inventiveness was one of the traits that had made her perfect for this job.

"That'll work," he said just as Emma gave his beard a hard tug. "Hey there, sweet thing," he said, extricating her tiny fist from his beard. "Don't be giving away my disguise right here. We're likely to be mobbed by angry kids if they figure out they're being duped by a fake Santa."

A faint smile crossed Amy's lips, but it didn't take the worry from her eyes. She was trying so hard to hold it all together, but she had to be close to the edge. She was in a strange city, recently divorced, her kid had wandered off on Christmas Eve and a cop had been asking her all sorts of uncomfortable questions. Nick had to admire the strength it must be taking for her not to come unglued.

She gazed up at him just then, her heart in her eyes. There was no mistaking the fact that she was counting on him, that she trusted him to find her boy.

Seeing that expression on her face made Nick want to thrust Emma back in her mother's arms and take off, but he knew he couldn't. Trish had dragged him into this and now he had to see it through, for Amy's sake and maybe even for his own.

Something told him, as well, that Amy Riley could get under his skin if he gave her half a chance. He immediately sent that errant thought right back to wherever it had come from. His sense of timing obviously sucked. He could hardly hit on a woman, when he was supposed to be finding her child.

"Where are we going?" she asked him as they set off, their pace slow because of the wall-to-wall throng of people.

"Everyplace and no place," he explained. "The goal

is just to draw lots and lots of attention, so maybe Josh will find us."

As a plan, it lacked finesse, but Nick was a pro at using whatever unorthodox tactics were handed to him. And finding a kid who wanted to see Santa by putting Santa directly into his path seemed to be as smart a strategy as any.

4

Santa was definitely a kid-magnet, just as Nick had predicted, Amy concluded with wonder. They were instantly surrounded by children everywhere they went. She couldn't help wondering if Nick himself weren't a babe-magnet under that padded red costume. His sister had certainly hinted at as much and he didn't seem all that put off by being the center of attention.

Nor did the throngs of children seem to rattle him any more than Emma's attempt to unmask him had. Despite his grumblings about being coerced into taking the Santa job, he handled their awestruck silences or chattered barrage of questions with equal aplomb. He hunkered down to speak with them, listening carefully as if each child was the most important one in the world. Amy couldn't miss their childish delight after getting a private moment with Santa on Christmas Eve. Despite his patience with each child, they made good progress. Nick's gaze was watchful every second.

"Do you have kids?" she asked curiously, during a rare moment when Nick wasn't being besieged.

He seemed to freeze at the question. "No. Why?"

"You're wonderful with Emma and with all these kids who keep stopping you," Amy told him. "I'm impressed. You never seem to lose patience."

"Just playing a role," he said tersely. "What would it do for Santa's reputation if I were a grouch? Just because I'm not into the holiday thing this year, why ruin some poor kid's Christmas?"

Amy didn't entirely buy the explanation. She had a hunch he was trying to hide a tender heart, though she couldn't imagine why he would want to.

"You said you have nieces and nephews, though. Trish's kids?"

"No, our older brother's. He has three boys and a girl."

"And she's the one who's about Emma's age?"

"A little older." He gave her a penetrating look. "Why all the questions?"

Amy shrugged. "Just making small talk, I suppose, anything to keep my mind off the fact that we haven't found Josh yet." She'd strained her eyes scanning the crowds, but so far she hadn't even caught a glimpse of any boy who looked like Josh wandering around lost and alone.

"I have to admit it's getting to me, Nick," she confessed, then voiced her greatest fear, "What if we don't find him?"

Nick's expression immediately turned sympathetic. She was growing to hate that look, the pity that couldn't quite cover his own worry. And he was worried. She could see it in his strained expression whenever he thought she wasn't looking.

"Don't tell me he'll turn up any minute," she snapped before he could respond. "He hasn't yet."

"Come on, Amy," he chided. "Don't give up so easily. We haven't been looking that long."

She glanced at her watch and realized it really had been little more than a half hour since this nightmare had begun. She felt as if her whole life—and Josh's—had played out in her mind since she'd last seen him. She'd formed some sort of bond with this man in the Santa suit, a closer bond of trust than she'd had with her husband toward the end. Maybe that just proved that all kinds of emotions were heightened in a crisis.

"You're right, but it seems like an eternity. Don't worry, though, I'll never give up," she said fiercely. "In the meantime, you placating and patronizing me is getting on my nerves."

"I'm sorry," he apologized, his eyes filled with unmistakable regret.

She drew in a deep breath. "No, I'm sorry. I know you're doing everything you can. I'm just scared."

"Of course you are. You have every right to be, but we are going to find him, Amy."

She heard a giggle just then and glanced up to see Emma trying to snatch Santa's hat off. Nick grabbed it just in time, but not before she caught a glimpse of black curly hair under the white wig Emma had tugged askew along with the red velvet hat.

"Are you sure you don't want me to take her?" she asked Nick. "She has to be distracting you."

"Emma's fine right where she is," he assured her. "Besides, she's actually part of the bait."

"Bait?"

"With me holding her, she's high enough in the air for Josh to spot her. If I know anything about kids, he will not be happy that baby sister got to Santa first."

Amy recognized the truth in that. "You really must be a terrific detective."

He seemed taken aback by the comment. It wasn't the first time he'd seemed surprised or embarrassed when his expertise as a cop was touted. Amy couldn't imagine why it seemed to throw him. Was he just naturally modest or had something happened to make him question himself? Did it have something to do with that high-profile case Maylene had mentioned? Nick had gotten very uptight when she'd brought it up.

"Why do you say that?" he asked. "We haven't found your son yet."

The question only confirmed her reading that he was thrown by any praise of his professional skills. She was tempted to ask him why, but instead she merely answered the question.

"Maybe not, but you're obviously clever and intuitive about people," she told him. "At least you have my son pretty well nailed down. You seem to know how he thinks."

For an instant, the somber expression faded and his eyes twinkled behind his wire-rimmed glasses. "You met Trish. I'll bet there's the same age difference between her and me as there is between Josh and little Emma here. I was not happy when she came along. Having two brothers was bad enough, but a girl? I was not ready for that."

"But Josh loves Emma," Amy countered. "He's a terrific big brother."

"On the surface," Nick responded. "Underneath there are bound to be a few minor insecurities about having the whole order of his universe disrupted."

"Somehow I can't imagine you being insecure about the arrival of a baby sister," she scoffed.

"I was five," he said with a shrug. "It didn't take much to shake my world. The fact that my folks wanted a girl so badly was very apparent to me. After three boys and a whole lot of trucks and sports equipment, suddenly the house was filled up with dolls and frilly dresses and way too much pink."

She smiled at the image and at his exaggerated shudder of disdain. "How did your brothers react? Were you the only one green with envy?"

"Rob—he's the oldest—was okay. He was nine and already into sports and barely noticed a new baby in the house. Stephen, who's between me and Trish in age, seemed to take it in stride, too. He just ignored her, though I have to wonder in retrospect if that wasn't the moment he started to rebel to get attention."

"What did you do?"

"I alternated between being fascinated by this tiny creature with all her pink ruffles and bows and hating her guts because she was taking up all of my mom's time. I hadn't felt that way when Stephen came along. He seemed to fit right in." He gave her a wry grin. "Must have been all that girlie-girl stuff."

Amy regarded him with amusement. "And now? Do you still have mixed feelings?"

"Yes, but the princess back there rules the world. Otherwise, can you think of any reason a sane man would agree to step in as Santa on Christmas Eve?"

"Not many," Amy agreed. "Unless the pay was very, very good."

"No pay. I'm here as a favor," he said, then added,

"At least it's a favor if you don't take into account her particular techniques."

"Blackmail?"

Nick nodded. "Afraid so."

"Care to explain?"

"Not at the moment."

"Then I think I'll just go on believing that Trish has you wrapped around her finger," Amy replied. "I like what that says about you."

"That I'm a wuss?" he asked, clearly amused.

"No, that you love your sister. What about the rest of your family? Are you close to all of them, too?"

"Yeah, I guess so," he admitted. "I spend a lot of time with my folks, just so my mom can nag me about being a policeman. It bothers her a lot, so I make sure she sees me enough to know that I'm still all in one piece, but not so much that her commenting drives me insane."

"That's why you were so surprised when Maylene said your mom brags about you being a cop," she concluded.

"Exactly. I never wanted to be anything else, but she and my dad did everything they could to dissuade me. I've been on the force for nearly ten years now and they still take every opportunity to suggest other career options. If I complain about anything work related, they're all over it. My charming sister used that to get me here today."

Amy studied him curiously. "How? Are we back to the blackmail?"

He smiled, though he looked as if he regretted saying anything about it. "Maybe I'll tell you sometime, but not today. We need to concentrate on finding Josh."

Amy could hardly argue with that. The whole time

they moved slowly through the mall, she was scanning the faces of the children who were staring in wide-eyed wonder at Santa. Where was Josh? Why hadn't someone found him by now or why hadn't he found them?

Just then Nick's cell phone rang. He answered it, then glanced around as if to get his bearings. "Got it," he said eventually. He explained exactly where they were located. "We'll start in that direction."

"What?" Amy demanded, her heart in her throat.

"Security found a boy wandering around by himself. He says his name is Josh."

Amy's heart turned over. "He's okay?"

"He's scared and crying, but otherwise he's just fine."

"Where is he?"

"All the way down at the other end of the mall. Security's going to pick us up in a golf cart and take us to him. In the meantime, let's start heading that way."

Amy took off at a run in the direction he'd pointed.

"Hey," he said, catching up to her. "Stick with me. I'm the one the guard's watching for, remember?"

"Of course," she said. "I'm sorry."

He touched her shoulder. "It's okay. Here he comes now."

The golf cart cruised to a stop beside them and Amy climbed in. Still holding Emma, Nick sat on the seat in back.

"Were you there when they found him?" Nick asked the security officer.

"No. I just got a call to come pick you up."

The golf cart made slow progress, especially when kids spotted Santa riding in it. In fact, at times Amy wanted to leap out and run ahead to get there faster, but she restrained herself. As Nick had pointed out, the driver knew where they were going. She didn't. She'd only waste precious time if she got lost herself.

Her heart was pounding so hard in anticipation of seeing her son, she thought it would burst. Apparently Nick sensed her restlessness.

"We're almost there," he told her, his gaze locked with hers.

The golf cart made a sharp turn to the left down another corridor, then slowed.

Amy glanced around frantically looking for Josh, but rather than spotting him, she saw only a very young security officer walking their way, his expression chagrined.

"I'm so sorry," he said, barely able to look her in the eye.

"What?" Amy demanded, her heart sinking. "He run away again?"

"What happened?" Nick demanded.

The officer shook his head. "It was the wrong boy," he admitted, looking miserable. "His name *was* Josh, but not two seconds after I called you, his folks turned up." His gaze met Amy's, then shifted away. "I'm so sorry, ma'am. I've already put out a call. Everyone's searching again. We didn't lose more than a couple of minutes."

The last faint shred of strength Amy possessed seemed to snap in that instant. Tears tracked down her cheeks and her chest heaved with sobs. She was barely aware of Nick shoving Emma unceremoniously into the arms of the startled security guard. Then he was gathering her close.

"Come on, Amy," he murmured. "I know how strong

you are. Don't fall apart now. It's going to be okay. This was just a small setback."

"I know," she whispered in a choked voice, but she couldn't seem to stop the tears or to let go of him. Nick might think she was strong, but he was wrong. She needed to absorb some of his strength before they went back to search some more. "I'll be fine in a minute, okay?"

"Okay," he said gently. He rubbed her back as he had Emma's earlier. There was nothing sensual about the gesture. It was meant only to calm, but it had been so long since anyone had touched her so tenderly that she wanted the contact to go on forever.

Not once during her divorce had she let herself lean on anyone, not her family, not her friends. She'd wanted all of them to see that she was handling it all right. But this…this was too much to expect. She didn't have any reserves of strength left. She needed someone else to share the burden. Nick, a virtual stranger to whom she owed no apologies, filled a terrible void in her life. So what if she held on for just a short while?

With her face buried against his padded chest, she could smell the faint scent of mothballs—the costume, no doubt—and a mix of clean aftershave and mint mouthwash. The velvet texture of the Santa suit felt good against her cheek, though she couldn't help wondering how his fake beard would feel. The lyrics of an old Christmas song about mommy kissing Santa Claus came to mind and made her smile.

"What's that for?" Nick asked, tucking a finger under her chin and looking into her eyes.

Amy blushed. "What?"

"The smile," he reminded her. "Not two minutes ago you were soaking my costume with your tears."

"I just remembered something," she said evasively. "It isn't important."

His gaze locked with hers and something simmered in the air between them. "It is if it put a smile back on your lips," he said quietly.

She didn't want him talking about her lips or looking at them or thinking about them. Frantically she searched for something to throw him off track. "I was just thinking about how mad Josh will be that he didn't get to ride in the golf cart."

Nick didn't look as if he believed her, but he didn't press her on it. "Then we'll see that he gets a ride. You ready to go for another stroll through the mall?"

Amy blotted up her tears with the last of the tissues Maylene had given her and forced a bright smile. "Absolutely," she said. She looked at the damp spots on Nick's costume and winced. "Sorry about that."

"No big deal." He shrugged. "It'll dry out."

When he would have taken Emma back from the security officer, Amy put her hand on his arm and felt the muscle clench. "I'm sorry we've caused such an uproar."

"You have nothing to be sorry for," he said tersely, his expression suddenly distant. "But let's not waste any more time, okay?"

Startled by his abrupt change in mood, she merely nodded, then set out to keep pace with him when he strode off with Emma back in his arms. One of these days she might not mind trying to unravel the many contradictions in Nick DiCaprio, but now certainly wasn't the time. With his quick withdrawal still fresh in her mind, she couldn't help wondering if the timing would ever be right.

Nick had just descended straight into hell. He'd had a woman in his arms who'd felt exactly right there, but unless he found her son and did it soon, she would wind up hating him. He imagined Tyler Hamilton's mother didn't have a lot of nice things to say about him these days and for good reason. He'd failed her—and her boy—and this whole episode with Amy Riley was beginning to feel the same way…as if it were skidding downhill at a breakneck pace.

The emotional roller coaster of thinking her son had been found, only to realize it had been another lost child had to have been devastating. It had nearly torn him apart watching the hope in her eyes fade and the despair return.

"Let's stop back at Santa's village," he said, praying that maybe there would be news there. Of course Trish had promised to call if Josh turned up, but Nick was starting to run out of ideas except for the kind that didn't bear thinking about. He'd have to start considering those possibilities soon enough.

"Sure, whatever you think," Amy agreed, once again sounding defeated.

Nick didn't even try to dream up some lie just to bolster her spirits. She obviously knew as well as he did that the longer Josh was missing, the more danger he might be in. Besides, he was fresh out of good cheer and he wasn't sure he could fake it. He was almost as worried as Amy must be by now.

A minute later as they approached Santa's workshop,

Trish spotted them and met them before they could get too close and cause a stir. Her worried gaze shifted from him to Amy, then back again.

"Nothing?" Trish asked.

"Not yet," Nick admitted.

Trish turned to Amy. "I am so sorry about the false alarm. You must have been heartbroken. Would you like to go freshen up or anything? Get something to drink or eat? You could get off your feet for a few minutes in my office, while Nicky continues the search for Josh."

"I'm okay," Amy insisted. "I have to keep looking." She faced Nick. "But shouldn't you go back to work? Santa's been missing a long time now. The kids must be losing patience and driving their parents nuts."

"I'll go back, but not until we've found your son," he said.

"But all those kids." She gestured toward the line that still snaked down the mall's main corridor. "They're going to be so disappointed."

"They'll survive," he insisted. He gave his sister a speculative look. "But with some extra padding, Trish, you could probably pull off the Santa thing yourself."

Amy chuckled at his outrageous suggestion, which was what he'd hoped for.

The sound made his spirits lift fractionally. He grinned at her. "I wasn't kidding."

Trish frowned at him. "Well, it's not going to happen, big brother, so get over that idea. You're going to find Josh any second, then get right back into Santa mode. If I didn't know for a fact that Amy really does have a son and it's obvious that she's worried sick about him, I'd suspect you of putting her up to this just to help you sneak away from Santa duty."

Amy's eyes widened. "Would he do that?"

"In a heartbeat," Trish confirmed. "I could tell you stories about my brother—"

Nick decided these two had bonded enough. "Amy doesn't have time to listen to you go on and on about how badly I've mistreated you and how I've misbehaved through the years," he said. "Her son's missing, remember?"

Amy's intrigued expression immediately faded, but she cast a last glance over her shoulder as Nick led her away. "Later," she told Trish. "I want to hear everything."

"That's a promise," his traitorous sister replied.

Nick shook his head. If he had his way, these two wouldn't spend five minutes alone together. It was a toss-up whether his sister would sell him out…or just try to sell him. He'd seen that matchmaking glint in her eyes a few other times over the years, beginning way back with Jenny Davis. It never boded well.

5

Nick tucked his hand under Amy's elbow and started away from Santa's village, then hesitated. As much as he hated it, there was something that had to be done. He'd waited too long as it was. To wait any longer would be totally irresponsible. He could only imagine what his bosses would have to say if this whole search blew up in his face because he'd been trying to prove something to himself. He had to stop thinking about his shattered ego and do what was best for the boy.

"Wait here a sec, okay?" he told Amy, as he held Emma out to Amy. "There's something I forgot to tell Trish."

"Sure," she said, taking the protesting Emma from him.

Warmed by the baby's reaction to parting with him, he slipped back through the crowd and found his sister. En route, his good spirits had given way to grim reality. Trish apparently sensed his mood.

"What's up?" she asked, regarding him with concern.

"I didn't want to say this in front of Amy, but I think it's time to call in the police," he told her. "I don't like the fact that we haven't had any sightings of the boy at all. I'd think even on a day as crazy as today some-one would have noticed a kid alone and stopped a se-curity guard."

Trish's worry turned to dismay. "You don't think...?"

Nick cut her off before she could voice the thought. "I'm trying not to jump to any conclusions. Maybe Josh is just a self-possessed kid who isn't the least bit afraid to wander around in a strange place alone, but it's not likely. Most kids start to worry when their mom's been out of sight for this long. I don't want to upset Amy any more than she is already, but I'd feel better if there were some more professional cops on the scene or at least watching things in the parking lot to see if anything looks suspicious out there."

"You're absolutely right. I'll call nine-one-one," Trish said at once, clearly grasping the urgency.

"Tell the dispatcher I'm on the scene in an unoffi-cial capacity and that I need some backup over here."

His sister nodded and pulled her cell phone out of her pocket.

Nick felt awful for Trish. He knew how important this job was to her and that a Christmas Eve story with an unhappy ending was the last thing she needed, but he didn't have a choice. Josh's safety came first. If they did everything right, there was still hope that the ending would be the happy one they all wished for.

"I know this is exactly what you were hoping to avoid, Trish, but I don't want to take chances. I hope you understand that."

"Of course I do," she said readily. "Without a doubt, finding Josh is far more important than the mall's PR. I'd never forgive myself if something were to happen to that boy and we hadn't done everything we could to find him."

"Tell me about it," Nick agreed grimly.

She gave him a penetrating look. "You holding up okay, Nicky? I know this can't be easy for you and I'm sorry I put you in this position. Maybe when your backup gets here, you can walk away and let them handle this."

"No way," he said tersely. "Amy's counting on me."

"That's what worries me," Trish said gently. "I know how you'll react if you think you've let her down."

"I'll be fine," Nick insisted. "Or I will be, as long as we find that boy safe and sound."

Amy bounced Emma in her arms and tried not to lose her patience as she waited for Nick to return. She kept consoling herself that they weren't the only ones searching for Josh, but she needed to be doing *something, not just standing idly by while others looked for her son.*

"Sorry that took so long," Nick apologized as he joined her. "Let's try this corridor over here on the left. We didn't go this way earlier."

"Your sister must be tearing her hair out over having Santa disappear on the busiest day of the season," Amy said. "I could look by myself."

"I thought we'd settled that. I still think we'll have a better chance of finding him if I'm with you. Do you have another picture of Josh in your wallet? I think we should start showing it to some of the shop employees. Maybe they've spotted him if he's been doing some shopping. A kid that age on his own would definitely leave an impression."

"I really don't think he has the money to shop," she

said, though Nick's plan was probably as good as anything else they'd tried.

"No telling what a kid might have saved up for Christmas," Nick countered. "Is he a thoughtful boy?"

Amy recalled the breakfast he'd tried to make her for Mother's Day and the brightly painted lump of clay with an imprint of his hand he'd given her for her birthday. "He tries to be."

"Then he might have spotted something he wanted to buy for you," Nick said. "Have you mentioned anything in particular you want?"

Amy shook her head.

"Nothing?" he asked as if it were impossible for a woman not to want something.

"I've been totally focused on getting settled in our new place," she said with a shrug. "And I've never much cared about accumulating things."

"You haven't spotted a sweater in a newspaper ad or some earrings you might have mentioned around Josh?"

She glanced down at her comfortable, well-worn jeans and the warm red sweater she'd owned for four years at least. "I've never exactly been a fashion plate," she told Nick. "I dress better than this for work, but my wardrobe's not fancy. Just some suits and blouses. I can't imagine Josh shopping for those."

Nick surveyed her with an appreciative once-over that heated her cheeks. "You look good to me," he said, his gaze lingering on the soft red wool clinging to her chest. Then he jerked his gaze away. "Okay, then," he said, his voice a little choked. "If not clothes, what about candy? Do you have a weakness for chocolate?"

Amy laughed. "Do you know a woman who doesn't? But I'm happy with a bag of mini candy bars from the grocery store. I don't crave the gourmet stuff. It's definitely not in our budget."

"Still, a kid might spot those big gold boxes of chocolates and check them out," he said, turning into a candy boutique.

Amy reluctantly followed him inside, where she was immediately assailed by the rich scent of fine chocolate. She couldn't help staring at the selection of truffles in the glass case, the piles of elegantly wrapped holiday boxes on the display tables. Her mouth watered despite her claim that ordinary candy satisfied her cravings. The last time she'd indulged in anything this decadent had been before her marriage when Ned brought one of the small boxes for her as a Valentine's Day gift. It was one of those rare thoughtful gestures that had convinced her he was the right one for her.

She was so absorbed in reading the labels on the trays of individual candies that she was barely aware of Nick chatting with the salesclerk, then showing the woman a picture of Josh. Only when they were back outside did she notice the small gold bag in his hand.

"Here," he said. "You need to keep your strength up."

Startled, she met his gaze. "But I told you I don't have to have the decadent kind of chocolate."

He grinned. "Maybe not, but you were practically drooling all over the case. I had to buy something."

She was too tempted by the decadent scent of that chocolate to turn him down. She opened the bag and found four different candies inside. She took a deep breath just to savor the aroma.

He watched her with amusement. "I hear they're even better when you actually eat them."

She held out the bag. "Would you like one?" she asked politely.

Chuckling, he replied, "I am not risking life and limb by trying to take one of those away from you."

"I offered," she said, though she drew the bag back.

"But the look in your eyes is daring me to accept," he teased.

Embarrassed, she held out the bag again. "No, really. Have one."

"Watching you enjoy them will be treat enough for me," he said.

She couldn't totally hide her relief. She reached in the bag, drew out one with a dark chocolate coating. If she remembered correctly, it had a chocolate raspberry filling. Very slowly she bit into it, then closed her eyes as the flavors burst on her tongue.

"Oh, my," she murmured.

When she opened her eyes again, Nick was regarding her with an odd expression. In fact, he looked a little dazed.

"What?" she asked.

"Just thinking what it would be like," he began, then cut himself off. "Never mind. We need to keep looking for Josh."

"Nick?"

He grabbed her hand. "Come on, Amy. There are a lot of stores left to cover."

He moved so quickly, she practically had to run to keep up with him. Emma jiggled in his arms, giggling happily at the unexpected adventure. He whipped in and out of half a dozen stores before he finally slowed down again.

Amy regarded him wearily. "I feel as if we're just spinning our wheels. Josh could be anywhere."

"What have you told him to do if he ever gets lost like this?" Nick asked.

"To look for a security guard or policeman, then stay put and wait for me to find him."

"Do you think the lesson took? Has he ever gotten lost before?"

"No, he's usually very good about sticking close to me."

"Would he talk to strangers?"

"Not unless it's a policeman or somebody like that. I know he's listened to me and his dad about that. He never answers the door unless he knows who it is. And he absolutely wouldn't get in a car with anyone he doesn't know. He even asks for permission before he'll accept a ride home with a friend's parent."

Nick nodded. "That's good. Would he kick up a fuss if someone approached him that he didn't know?"

"Absolutely," she said with confidence. It was the one thing she was sure of. No one would snatch Josh from the mall without someone noticing a struggle of some kind. Outlining all the safety measures they'd taught Josh reassured her.

"You know, I'm beginning to think you're right about him shopping," she told Nick, clinging to her newfound conviction. "He probably doesn't even think he's lost and he's probably completely forgotten about the time. I'll bet something in some store caught his attention and off he went without a second thought. Maybe it's not even me he's shopping for, but Emma. I saw a baby store somewhere. And there was a toy store when we first came in the mall."

Nick gave her an encouraging smile. "Let's hope you're right. We'll work our way back to those. If what you say is true, if he's just gotten distracted, he could still find his way over to Santa's village very soon."

"Yes," she said eagerly, ready to seize on the slim hope. "I'll bet that's exactly what will happen."

They went into another half-dozen stores with no luck, then started down the other side of the corridor. The canned Christmas music, barely discernible over the hum of conversation, seemed to mock their somber mission.

"How did you end up in Charlotte?" Nick asked as they walked past a wall of display windows for a department store.

Amy regretted more than ever that Josh wasn't with them as she glimpsed the elaborate displays of snow-covered villages and mechanical elves and reindeer. She dragged her gaze away and concentrated on answering Nick.

"Things were pretty bad after my divorce," she told him. "I'd been working for a bank that has headquarters here. My boss knew what I'd been going through and asked if I'd be interested in a transfer. I grabbed at the chance."

"Was Josh happy about the move?"

"No," she admitted. "He misses his dad. I've tried not to let him know how I feel about my ex, because I don't think it's fair for a kid to be caught in the middle between parents."

"I couldn't agree more," Nick said with feeling. "You'd be surprised how many times I see parents using their children as weapons in their grown-up wars. It's always the kids who suffer most." He studied her intently. "I'm a little surprised, though, that your ex-husband agreed to let you bring the kids this far away."

"I never said he deserved the love Josh has for him," she said wryly. "He was reasonably attentive when Josh was underfoot. The same with Emma. But he's remarried and he has another baby on the way. Our kids are extraneous to his new life. I figured in the long run Josh and Emma would be better off in North Carolina, than they would be in Michigan where they'd experience their dad's growing disinterest on a daily basis."

"He sounds like a real jewel, this ex of yours," Nick said with evident disgust.

"He was that and worse," Amy confirmed. "But he gave me two great kids, so I can't hate him completely." She met his gaze. "Why were you so worried earlier that my ex-husband might be involved in Josh's disappearance?"

"It happens sometimes in divorces," he said. "Custody might be settled in a courtroom, but parents don't always agree with the decision. Then the noncustodial parent decides to do something about it."

His answer was too pat and the way he avoided meeting Amy's gaze told her there was more to it. "Have you handled some of these custody battles?"

"From time to time," he affirmed, his expression more strained than ever.

"How ugly have they gotten?" she pressed.

"Pretty damn ugly," he said. "Let's not go there, okay? Your ex is back in Michigan, so that's one less thing for us to worry about."

Amy recognized that he'd closed down the subject, but that only made her want to pursue it more. Before she could, Nick deftly changed the subject.

"It must be hard being in a new place at Christmas," he suggested. "Especially with kids."

Amy gave him a knowing look, but decided to let him get away with it.

"I don't think I realized until today how hard it would be," she admitted. "The Santa thing was a big tradition with us, at least for Josh. And we always went to church on Christmas Eve to the children's service, then went home and had hot chocolate, put out cookies and milk for Santa, and watched Christmas movies till Josh fell asleep. Then Ned would carry him upstairs and we'd put all the presents under the tree, then eat the cookies."

Nick smiled. "You didn't drink the milk?"

Amy wrinkled her nose. "Warm milk? Yuck. We dumped it out and left the glass sitting there with the empty cookie plate." She sighed suddenly. "I wonder what traditions we'll have now."

"You'll make new ones," Nick said. "And keep the old ones that work, just like coming to the mall today to see Santa." He hesitated, then said, "You know, you could come to church with my family tonight if you wanted to. I wasn't going to go, but I will if you think Josh would enjoy going and keeping another tradition alive."

Amy's eyes turned misty at the suggestion, as well as at his confidence that Josh would be safely back with her before long. "You'd do that? You don't even know Josh and you can't have a very good impression of him—or me—after what's happened today."

"He got lost. He didn't commit a crime," Nick told her. "As for you, there's no mistaking the fact that you're a loving mom. Even the best mothers can't stop kids from slipping away in the blink of an eye."

"Thank you, but I'd hate to have you change your plans for us. You said you hadn't planned on going. What were you going to do?"

"Nothing in particular," he revealed.

Amy regarded him with surprise. "You were going to spend Christmas Eve alone?"

"People do," he said gruffly. "It's no big deal."

"Of course, it is. Surely you'd rather be with your family."

"Thus the invitation to church," he said wryly. "I'd definitely get points with my folks. Besides, I think maybe going to church would be as good for me as it would be for Josh. Maybe I need to stick with tradition, too."

She studied him curiously. "Why is that?"

"Just some demons that need to be laid to rest," he said evasively.

Amy sensed they were finally cutting close to whatever Nick was struggling with. He'd been so kind to her today, she wanted to return the favor. "I don't want to pry, Nick, but is it anything you want to talk about? You've been dancing around something ever since we started searching for Josh."

For an instant it looked as if he might open up and tell her, but just then the color washed out of his face and he abruptly whirled around as if he were trying to avoid someone.

"Nick?" she said, startled by his behavior. "What is it? Did you see someone you know? Someone you'd rather not see?"

"Let's check out this place," he said brusquely, dragging her inside a men's shoe store.

Amy scanned the faces outside to see if she could

figure out who had sent Nick fleeing. All she noticed were families, some laughing, some obviously stressed by the mad rush. A few men hurried by looking thoroughly harried. And a few women—young and old—passed, laden down with packages. There was even one group of teenage girls who seemed more intent on looking for boys than shopping. They preened and pretended nonchalance whenever a boy passed by. No one jumped out at Amy as the possible cause of Nick's sudden panic, and that's what it had been, she realized. He'd been thoroughly spooked by whomever he'd spotted.

She turned back to Nick, who was chatting with the clerk behind the counter, his actions now briskly professional again.

Only after they were outside and walking toward the next store did she meet his gaze. "What happened back there, Nick?"

He regarded her with a neutral expression. "I don't know what you mean."

"You're not a good liar," she accused. "Was it an old girlfriend? A current one?"

"Not that it's any of your business, but it was nothing like that," he snapped.

His tone was like a slap. She felt oddly saddened by his refusal to confide in her, but what had she expected? He was right. She hardly knew him. He was a policeman helping her out in a crisis. She had no right to pry into his personal life.

And what about his questions, she asked herself. Were all of those strictly professional, the mark of a thorough detective? She didn't think so.

Nor was the invitation to church. No, there was something between them, some spark that might be explored sometime in the future. That spark went beyond the intensity of the situation. It was definitely personal. The surprise was that after all her vows to concentrate on her new job and her kids, she'd wanted to see where that spark led.

Or, she amended, she'd wanted to until the moment when Nick had deliberately lied and shut her out. She'd already been with a man who'd been a master at keeping her in the dark. She wouldn't knowingly get involved with another one who was capable of the same kind of deceit. It hurt to think that there might be any comparison whatsoever between her ex-husband and this man who'd been only decent and kind to her, but she couldn't take the chance.

Not that she could spend even one more second worrying about such things when Josh was still missing. Nick was her best hope for finding her son. She needed his help. And when Josh was safely with her, then she and Nick DiCaprio would go their separate ways.

Even with her mind made up, though, she couldn't help feeling as if she'd just lost something important, something good that had almost been within her grasp.

6

Nick knew he'd been too abrupt and sharp with Amy. He'd immediately recognized the hurt in her eyes when he'd dismissed her well-meaning questions, but what other choice had he had? How could he explain to her that he'd just seen the mother of a child who'd died while he was supposed to be rescuing him? Not only was it something he could barely stand to remember, but it would be the worst possible testimonial to his skills as a police officer. Amy would be justified in demanding that someone else take over the search for her son.

For reasons he didn't care to examine too closely, Nick didn't want that to happen. As he'd told his sister, he wanted to see this through. Not only did he want to spend more time with Amy, but he needed redemption and this seemed like fate's way of giving him a chance for it. He needed to prove to himself that he could find this boy and return him safely to his mother, that the tragedy with Tyler Hamilton hadn't destroyed him. Otherwise he'd never be able to go back on active duty on the force. And if he wasn't a cop, who the hell was he?

Okay, so his motives were partly selfish. He admitted that without shame. He didn't want his career going up in flames. He knew in his gut he was *still* one of the best cops in the department. All modesty aside, his skills were superior. He had the citations and job performance reviews to prove it. He just had to tamp down his anger and get his confidence back. The shrink was right about that much. But finding Josh—not endless hours baring his soul—was the answer.

Although he believed wearing this hot and bulky Santa outfit would work to their advantage eventually, he had to admit that right this second he would have preferred being in street clothes so he could blend in and move more quickly. Then, again, the costume may have been the only thing that had kept Tyler Hamilton's mom from recognizing him and for that he was grateful. A confrontation with Mitzi Hamilton was the last thing he needed. He still had nightmares about the bleak expression on her face when he'd had to tell her that Tyler was dead.

"Nick?"

He gazed down into Amy's troubled eyes. "What?"

"Are you okay?"

He forced a reassuring smile. "Fine. Let's get back to work."

Once again, she looked disappointed by his response, as if she'd been expecting—or hoping for—something more. Unfortunately, until they found Josh, he was fresh out of revelations he could make without having her doubt him and scaring her to death.

Amy reevaluated her earlier dismay over Nick's reticence. It was evident he was genuinely troubled by something, something more than their unproductive search. Maybe she should force the issue, no matter how reluctant he seemed. Maybe it would do them both good to think about something other than her son. Whatever those demons were that Nick had mentioned, maybe she could help him deal with them.

"You know, Nick," she began casually. "You can talk to me."

He glanced at her with a questioning look. "We've been talking."

"Not about anything significant," she said.

"Oh, I don't know about that," he protested. "You've told me all about your son and about your divorce. I know about how hard it is being away from your family for the holidays. I'd say we've scratched below the surface."

"Up to a point, that's right," she agreed. "You know all that about me, but I know very little about you, other than how many siblings you have and that your folks don't like you being a cop."

"That's my life in a nutshell," he said glibly.

She looked away and thought back over their conversation. One comment stood out. She was pretty sure it held the key to understanding Nick.

"I don't think your life can be summed up so easily," she said quietly. "For instance, I think there's a very specific reason you planned to stay away from church tonight." She stared directly into his eyes. "Are you mad at God? Has something happened to make you question your faith?"

He turned away, but not before she saw that her questions had struck home.

"What was it?" she prodded. She connected the dots and realized that whatever it was that had happened was somehow work related. "Did something go wrong on a case you were handling?"

His hard expression, a stark contrast to the rosy tint of his cheeks and thick white beard of his Santa costume, told her she'd hit on it. Somehow, though, she didn't have the sense that Nick admired her detecting skills.

"Leave it alone," he commanded, his tone like ice. "I'm not discussing it with you or anyone else, especially not when we're in the middle of a search for your son."

"Something tells me this is exactly the time you should talk about it," she countered. "It's weighing on you now. Is it interfering with your ability to help me find Josh?"

"Absolutely not. I don't let anything interfere with my job, not even a woman asking too many pesky questions about things that are none of her business. Now will you get your priorities in order? Stop trying to dig around in my psyche and pay attention to the people around us. You could walk right on by Josh and never see him."

The harsh accusation stung, but unfortunately Amy couldn't deny it. She'd needed a temporary distraction and she'd seized on fixing Nick, whether he needed it or not. She still believed he did, but that wasn't the point and it wasn't her job, particularly not this afternoon.

"Okay," she said softly. "I apologize for prying."

"Whatever," he said, avoiding her gaze.

Nick's attention was deliberately focused on scanning the crowds around them. Amy sighed, then followed suit, looking into the face of every child they passed. With each one that wasn't Josh, she grew more and more discouraged. With each second that passed without a call from one of the security guards or Trish, her heart ached a little more.

Then, just when she was losing all hope, she spotted a familiar-looking shock of brown hair sticking up on the back of a boy's head. He was too far away for even a glimpse of his face. Even so, a faint spark of recognition made her spirits soar. She tried to tamp down her excitement. Too many times before her hopes had been dashed seconds later.

Then her eyes locked on a red and green scarf that had come unwound from around the boy's neck. It was dragging on the ground behind him. There was no mistaking that scarf. She'd knit it for Josh herself just last Christmas.

"There!" she screamed, seizing Nick's arm and pointing across the mall. "I see him, Nick. He's right over there, going into that store. You were right all along. He is shopping."

Nick stared in the direction she was pointing. "Where did you see him, Amy? Are you sure it was Josh?"

By then Josh had disappeared into the store, so rather than answer she started to dash across the mall, dragging Nick with her. Trying to cut through the crowd bordered on impossible until Nick cupped a hand under her arm and guided her through. Whether it was his size, his determination or the Santa costume, the crowd gave him room to pass.

"Which shop?" he asked when they reached the other side. "I still don't see him."

"Right here," Amy said, her cheeks burning as she stopped in front of a display window filled with mannequins clad only in lacy underwear. "He went into the lingerie shop."

Nick gave her an odd look. "Your five-year-old son went into a lingerie shop?"

"Hey, you asked what he might buy me for Christmas. His dad used to give me fancy lingerie. It never occurred to me when you asked, but I suppose Josh got the idea from that."

Nick still looked vaguely disconcerted. "I see."

As they reached the store's entrance, she sensed Nick's hesitance and thought she knew the cause. Most men loved to see women in sexy, lacy undergarments, but they'd rather be caught dead than be seen shopping for them. Amused, she looked into his eyes. "You're not scared of a few bras and panties, are you?"

He frowned at the question. "Nope, just the women swarming around in there buying them."

"It's Christmas Eve," she reminded him. "Take another look inside. Most of the shoppers today are desperate men. I'm the one who ought to be embarrassed."

"You're absolutely sure Josh went in there?" he asked, still hanging back, though his alert gaze continued to scan the customers.

Even amidst the crush of much taller men inside the shop, she could see Josh…or at least the tail end of that dragging scarf. Filled with relief at the realization that her boy was safe and sound, she nodded. Then the crowd parted and she saw him clearly, head to toe, totally absorbed by a table full of sale items.

"I can see him from here," she said excitedly. "Right there, Nick! He has a pair of red thong panties in his hand."

At her claim, rather than looking into the store,

Nick's gaze sought hers and never left her face. His eyes darkened with unmistakable heat. "Red, huh?"

Amy couldn't help it. She laughed. "It's not becoming for Santa to drool. You look a little like I must have looked in the candy store. Will you come on? Let's not let him slip away from us."

"It's probably not a good idea for Santa to be seen ogling ladies' lingerie, either," he commented. "Why don't I just stand right here blocking the doorway with Miss Emma, while you retrieve your son? I'll be backup in case he tries to scoot off again."

"Chicken," she accused lightly, able to tease because the nightmare was almost over.

"Damn straight," he agreed without apology.

Amy didn't waste another second arguing. She made her way through the mobbed store till she was right beside Josh. For a second she simply stood there, drinking in the precious sight of him. Finally she spoke.

"Young man, you are in so much trouble," she said, hunkering down to draw him into her arms in a fierce embrace. She was so relieved, she wanted to never let go.

"Mom!" he protested, pulling away. "You're not supposed to see me."

She shook her head. He was oblivious to her distress and to the relief that was now spilling through her.

"And why shouldn't I see you?"

"'Cause I'm buying your present," he said reasonably. "It's supposed to be a surprise."

As desperately as she wanted to hug him and hold on forever, she had to make him understand that what he'd done was not acceptable.

Keeping her expression stern, she demanded, "Present or no present, Joshua Riley, did you stop to think for one second that you might scare the living daylights out of me by running off to go shopping?"

He blinked hard. "You were scared?"

"Well, of course, I was," she said, giving him a gentle shake. "When have I ever let you go off shopping all by yourself? More than that, you've never been to this mall before. When you let go of my hand, I thought you were going straight to see Santa, but you never showed up. I had no idea where you were. You've been missing for a very long time."

He regarded her earnestly. "I did go to see Santa, but the line was really, really long and I wanted to get you a surprise, you know, something like Dad would get you so you wouldn't be sad."

Touched more than she wanted to admit, she asked, "How did you know where to look?"

"I knew the kind of store, 'cause I went with Dad last year," he explained. "First I had to find the directory thing, because I knew you'd be mad if I asked a stranger. I looked and looked, but I couldn't find one, so I just kept looking for the store. There are lots of stores and it's hard to move 'cause there are so many people. It took a really long time, but this is just like the one where Dad used to shop."

He sounded so proud of himself, it made Amy want to cry. She blinked back tears. "Oh, sweetie, I don't need a present like that. Besides, where did you get that kind of money? Even on sale, these things are expensive."

"I saved the money Dad gave me before we left Michigan." He held out the red thong panties. "Do you like these?"

In Amy's opinion they looked uncomfortable, just as

the ones Ned had given her through the years had been. Those had stayed tucked in her lingerie drawer most of the time. She was not letting her son waste money on another pair that would be consigned to the bottom of her dresser.

"What I think is that you are an amazing boy to want to buy me a present like that, but I want you to save that money for something special for you, just like your dad intended." She regarded him seriously. "Though, it will be a very long time before you get to spend it, because after this stunt you're going to be grounded till you're thirty."

His expression faltered. "But, Mom, I just went shopping for you," he protested. "I thought you'd be happy."

"While buying a present is a thoughtful thing to do, running away to do it is not. A policeman and an entire mall security team have been searching for you for more than an hour," she responded.

For the first time, Josh seemed to grasp the magnitude of what he'd done. "Uh-oh," he whispered. "Are they gonna be mad at me?"

"I think they're going to be relieved that you're okay," she said. "And I know they'll appreciate it when you apologize to each and every one of them."

"Okay," he said meekly. "I'll tell 'em I'm really sorry. Maybe we could go home and get some Christmas cookies for them."

Her point seemed to have sunk in, at least enough for now. She'd spend the next ten years driving it home. With a boy this precocious, she was sure she'd have lots of opportunities.

"Now that you understand that what you did was wrong, I think there's somebody here you might want to meet. He needs to see for himself that you're safe and then let everyone know we've found you. Put those panties back, and let's go."

Josh parted with the panties reluctantly, then dutifully took the hand she held out.

"Who is it?" he asked as they walked through the store. "Who wants to see me?" His eyes widened. "Is it Dad? Did Dad come for Christmas?"

She was seized by momentary anger at her ex, who hadn't even made a phone call to Josh for over a week now. But what was the point? Ned was Ned. She was tired of covering for his lack of consideration.

"No, sweetie," she consoled Josh, biting back the desire to make excuses. "It's not your father."

"Oh," he said, his tone flat with disappointment.

"Come on now. I think this will be just as good," she told him.

"Grandma and Grandpa?" he asked, but without as much enthusiasm.

Before Amy could reply, Josh spotted Santa holding Emma. His cheeks turned pink and his eyes lit up. Whatever disappointment he'd felt that it wasn't his dad vanished in a split second of recognition.

"Santa!" he shouted, clearly thrilled. "You brought me Santa!"

For the second time that day he jerked free of Amy's grip and made a dash for it, but this time Santa was right there to scoop him close in a hug.

7

Nick's gaze had locked on Amy as she'd traveled through the store and reunited with her son. Emma had laughed and pointed, clearly recognizing her big brother and delighted to see him. Something inside Nick melted as he watched the reunion.

This was what should have happened with Tyler Hamilton. His mom should have had a joyous moment just like this, but she hadn't. Instead, there had been only the awful news that her boy was dead, news Nick had insisted on delivering himself. He had to stand by helplessly as the color had drained from her face. He'd caught her as her knees gave way and she'd been racked by grief-stricken sobs. He couldn't imagine that memory ever fading, not even with this far happier memory to replace it.

When Josh spotted him, whooped joyously, and let loose of Amy's hand, Nick dropped to his knees so he could catch the boy as he barreled straight into his knees. For at least a fraction of a second, all he felt was relief. *This* search had ended well. *This* boy was back with his mother and Nick had played at least a small part in making it happen.

His gaze stayed on Amy's. She looked as if she'd been given the very best Christmas present ever.

"Thank you," she mouthed.

Before Nick could respond, Josh wiggled free and studied him intently. "I met Santa last year," he said. "You don't look like him."

Nick bit back a smile. "Santa had a rough year. I'm older."

Josh didn't look convinced. "You don't sound like him, either. You sound funny, like you live around here instead of at the North Pole."

"Well, you see, Josh, that's the thing. Santa has to adapt to his environment," Nick improvised as Amy chuckled. "I've been here at this mall for a while now and everyone talks like this. They expect me to sound just like them."

"I guess," Josh said doubtfully. Then his expression brightened. "Can I tell you what I want for Christmas right now? That way I won't have to wait forever in line. That's how come I got lost, 'cause the line was too long and I didn't want to wait in it."

Nick exchanged a glance with Amy, who looked as if she'd give the boy the sun, moon and stars now that he was safely back with her. He wasn't inclined to be as lenient.

"Let's talk about this," he suggested to Josh. "Man to man."

"Okay," Josh said eagerly.

Nick barely contained a grin. "I'm not so sure little boys who run away and scare their moms ought to be getting presents from Santa," he said. "What do you think?"

"You're asking me to decide if I should get presents?" Josh asked incredulously.

"Yep."

Josh's expression turned serious as he pondered Nick's—*Santa's*—question. "Okay, here's what I think," he told Nick earnestly. "I didn't mean to scare Mom. And I only went to buy her a present. That's a good thing, right? Mad as she was, even Mom said I was amazing."

Nick swallowed a laugh. Amy must have her hands full with this one. He had well-developed reasoning powers for a boy his age, or else it was just a strong sense of self-preservation. Nick had been very much like that as a kid, able to fast-talk himself out of most trouble. And his mother had been every bit as tolerant as Amy. His father had been the disciplinarian. Josh didn't have anyone around to fill that role. For today, at least, maybe Nick could do it.

He looked Josh in the eye. "It was a very unselfish thing to want to do," he agreed. "So, yes, that does count as a good thing. But running away, even with the best intentions, is never good. Lots of people have been very worried about you."

The boy regarded him with genuine dismay. "I know. Mom said." Then his expression brightened with hope. "But I'm going to apologize, so it'll be okay."

Nick glanced up at Amy. "I'm sure an apology will be appreciated, but I want to be sure you understand why what you did was wrong."

"Because I scared Mom," Josh said at once.

"That's one reason," Nick confirmed.

He tried to find a way to drive his point home without scaring Josh and robbing him of his astonishing fearlessness. It would be a good trait later in life, though in the meantime it was likely to give Amy frequent anxiety attacks.

He regarded Josh with a somber expression. "But there's another one and it's just as important. It's very dangerous for someone your age to be alone in a crowd like this. All sorts of things can happen to children when there's not an adult around to keep an eye on them."

Josh studied him intently, absorbing his words, but clearly not ready to take them at face value. "Like what?"

Nick debated how specific to get, then decided on another tack. "You believe in Santa, right?"

"Sure."

"Well, Santa sees a lot of things, like when boys and girls are good and bad."

Josh nodded. "That's why I'm really, really good." He glanced at his mom, then amended, "Well, most of the time, anyway. Until today."

Nick hid a grin. "Okay, then, if you understand that Santa knows a lot about what happens all over the world, then could you just take my word for it that it's dangerous for you not to be with an adult in a busy mall like this?"

Josh still looked vaguely skeptical. "But nothing bad happened," he protested.

"This time," Nick emphasized. "You were very lucky today, Josh, but it's not a chance you should ever take again. Do you understand that?"

"I guess so."

"Then here's the deal. If you want Santa to reconsider discussing presents with you, you have to promise never to do anything like this again."

With presents on the line, Josh nodded solemnly. "Okay. I promise." He turned to his mother. "I'm sorry, Mom."

"Santa will know if you go back on your word," Nick warned him. "So you have to keep that promise forever."

Josh gazed at him with dismay. "Like, till I'm a teenager or something?"

"No, forever is even longer than that. It's till you're all grown-up and even then you should never do anything that might make your mom worry. Okay?"

"I guess," Josh said. "I'll try, but that sounds like a long time to be good." He studied Nick closely. "Do you have a mom?"

Nick nodded.

"Does she still worry about you?"

"Oh, yeah," Nick said fervently. And unfortunately he worried her all the time, though he wasn't about to tell Josh that.

"But you're Santa!"

"Moms never stop worrying, no matter who you are or how old you get," Nick told him. "I know forever seems like way too long, but I think you can do it."

"Maybe," Josh said, his voice filled with doubt.

"Why don't you think about it for a while and we'll talk about it again when you come through the line to tell me what you want for Christmas?"

Josh started to break away. "I'll get in line right now," he said, clearly about to make a dash for Santa's village.

Nick snagged his hand. "Hey there, what did we just talk about?"

Josh winced. "Oh, yeah. Mom, can we get in line now?"

Before Amy could reply, Nick glanced at the endless line. He figured if he was going to have to deal with all these kids who'd been waiting patiently to see him for more than an hour, there should be a reward for him at the end of it. Besides, something compelled him to make sure he had a chance to spend more time with this family. He wanted time to persuade Amy to go to church with his family this evening. He sensed that with them beside him tonight, he might start down the path to something special.

"Tell you what," he said to Josh. "Since the line's so long, why don't you, your mom and Emma here, go grab a snack and then come back? Then you can tell me what you want for Christmas."

"Will there still be time?" Josh asked worriedly.

"I won't leave till you've come back," Nick promised. He glanced at Amy. "Is that okay with you? You look as if you could use something to eat. The food court's right across the way. I highly recommend the pizza."

She seemed uncertain for a moment, then her expression brightened. "Actually I'm starving. I had a touch of the flu earlier, but it seems to be gone. To my amazement, pizza sounds great. Can we bring you anything?"

Nick shook his head.

"Then we'll see you in a little while," Amy concluded.

She started away with Emma in one arm and Josh holding her other hand, then turned and came back.

Before Nick realized her intention, she stood on tiptoe and pressed a kiss to his cheek.

"Thank you for helping me find Josh," she whispered, her eyes damp with tears. "You have no idea…" Her voice broke.

He touched a finger to her cheek, wiped away a single tear. "I think I do," he responded. "And I'm glad I was able to help."

Her gaze locked with his. "I'll never forget what you did for us." Then her lips slowly curved. "Or all the unanswered questions I asked you."

Nick knew she'd meant it as a mild threat, but he couldn't help chuckling. "You may be the most persistent person I know."

She grinned. "Remember that. Now, are you sure you don't want me to bring something back for you? A soda? A slice of pizza?"

"Nothing," he said again.

Not until she was moving through the crowd did he murmur, "Just yourselves."

He uttered the telling words just in time for Trish to overhear them.

"Find something more than a lost boy, big brother?" she taunted.

"Who knows?" he said, sounding only slightly defensive. "I might have."

"I saw the kiss, by the way. And I couldn't miss the thunderstruck expression on your face." She smiled. "Apparently, it's a season for miracles, after all."

Just then their mother, Laura DiCaprio, rushed through the crowd and joined them. "There you are," she said, sounding slightly winded as if she'd run through the mall. She looked Nick over from head to toe. "Nicky, you make a wonderful Santa," she said approvingly.

His mother's arrival was not a development he'd anticipated. Nor was he particularly overjoyed to see her. He couldn't help wondering what had brought her here, especially since she looked as if she'd interrupted her Christmas baking to come. He frowned at his sister, convinced she was somehow behind this, but Trish merely shrugged.

"Don't look at me," she said. "I haven't spoken to her all day."

He turned back to his mother. "What are you doing here, Mom? Don't tell me it's a coincidence, because I know you finished your Christmas shopping a month ago."

"I finished in September, as a matter of fact," she informed him.

"Not a direct answer," he accused.

"And I'm not some suspect," she retorted.

"Mother!"

"Okay, if you must know, Maylene Kinney called me. She told me about the missing boy…" Her voice trailed off as she studied him intently. "Well, I'm sure you understand why I had to come, Nicky. I wanted to see for myself that you're okay. Your father's outside cruising around looking for a parking place. I imagine he'll be in here eventually." She regarded him hesitantly. "Is it over? Is the boy okay?"

"He's fine," Nick said tersely.

None of this was good, Nick thought wearily. If news of another missing boy, even one that had been found already, got out, the mall was going to be crawling with reporters. He pinned his sister with a look. "If any of the media show up, keep them away from me, okay? Tell them it was a false alarm. Or tell them the truth, that Josh is back with his mom and it's all over, but leave me out of it."

Trish regarded him with dismay. "I'll do my best, but, Nicky, there's a reporter here already, doing a story about the last-minute holiday shoppers. I'll talk to her, but you know she may not give up easily. It's a great story. Family reunited by Santa on Christmas Eve."

"If that's all there was to it, it would be one thing, but we both know better," he said.

"But, Nicky you'll be a hero," his mom spoke. "Wouldn't that be a good thing after…well, after what happened before?"

"I don't want to be a hero and it would take more than this to turn me into one. Hell, I don't even want to be Santa." He shook his head. "I never should have answered my phone this morning."

Then he thought of meeting Amy and that precocious boy of hers. He remembered how it felt to have sweet Emma in his arms. He wouldn't have missed that for anything.

He caught the expression in his sister's eyes and knew she understood. "I'm going back to work before these kids start a riot," he said grimly.

Then he was struck by another thought. "Trish, maybe you ought to find Amy and warn her about that reporter. I don't know if anyone would recognize her or Josh and point them out, but she ought to be prepared. Tell her to stay in the food court till you come back for her. I promised Josh he could visit with Santa before the mall closes."

His mother's eyes brightened with curiosity. "Amy?

Is that the woman whose boy you found? Maylene said she was lovely and that she's new in town and a single mom. And Josh must be her son."

"That's right," Nick said, aware of the matchmaking wheels spinning into action.

"I'll go with you, Trish," his mother declared. "I'd like to meet her. Maybe she'd like to bring her family to Christmas dinner tomorrow."

Trish couldn't seem to hide her amusement. He doubted she'd even tried.

"Any comment, big brother?" she inquired.

He sighed. "What would be the point? You two never listen to a word I say, anyway."

"That is not true, Nicholas DiCaprio," his mother scolded, then winked. "Sometimes we just read between the lines, too. Come, Trish. Let's go find this woman. Nicky, when your father turns up, you tell him where to find me."

Nick watched them go. He swallowed hard. If it weren't for the jostling throng of kids waiting for him, he would have tried to stop his mom and sister, or at least gone with them to protect Amy. He had a hunch she'd be safer with a whole battalion of news-hungry reporters than she would be with his mom and sister when they were on a mission to give him the priceless Christmas gift of a new romance.

Amy bought slices of pizza and soft drinks for herself and Josh, then searched for a place to sit. Every table was jammed with shoppers taking a break from the frenzy. She could barely maneuver Emma's stroller between the chairs. She watched with her heart in her throat as Josh tried to balance the tray with their food.

"Over here," Trish said, waving and greeting her with a smile. "My mom's holding a table for you."

"Thank you so much," Amy said, relieved. "Did Nick get back on Santa duty okay?"

"He's on the job, but he wanted me to warn you to stay put here till I come back for you."

Amy paused in midstride. "Oh?"

"I'm so sorry," Trish apologized. "We think word may have gotten out about the missing child. Because of Nick's involvement, it could turn into kind of a big story. I'm going to do what I can to fend off any reporters, including the one who's already here on a different assignment, but Nick didn't want you guys to get dragged into the middle of it." She gave Amy a questioning look. "I'm assuming he's right, that you'd prefer not to be interviewed?"

"He's absolutely right," Amy said, filled with dread at the prospect. Now that the incident was over, she didn't even want to think about it again.

Unfortunately Josh overheard them. "But, Mom, we could be on TV," he said excitedly. "That would be so awesome! We could tape it and send it to Dad and Grandma and Grandpa."

"You don't get a say in this," Amy said firmly. "Besides, do you really want your dad to know you ran away? You're in trouble, remember? You have a lot of apologies to deliver."

"But I could say I'm sorry on TV and then everyone would know," Josh countered.

Amy merely shook her head as Trish tried to stifle a grin.

"Let's just sit here and eat our pizza, and be grateful things turned out okay," Amy told him. "And I need to feed Emma."

"My mom will be glad to help with that," Trish offered. "She's great with kids. She's right over here."

Trish led the way to an empty table that was being held by a woman who looked to be in her midfifties, about the same age as Amy's mother. She looked as if she'd run out of the house in the midst of baking. She still wore an apron over her slacks and sweater and there were streaks of flour on her clothes. The coat she'd flung on looked as if it might be her husband's hunting jacket. Her hair was mussed, as if it had curled while she was working around a hot stove. Despite her disheveled appearance, she gave Amy a warm smile.

"You must be Amy," she said as they approached. "Maylene Kinney described you perfectly." She beamed at Josh. "And you must be the little boy who got away."

Josh nodded. "I'm in trouble," he said, awkwardly balancing the tray of pizza and drinks.

"I imagine you are," she said. "But you're safe and that's what counts."

Mrs. DiCaprio rescued the tray of food and set it on the table. "Oh, that looks good. I think I'll run and get a slice for myself. I've been baking all day and haven't had a minute to eat anything. Don't wait for me."

Amy stared after her. She felt as if she'd been caught up in a whirlwind, then set back down in the calm that followed. "Is she always like this?"

Trish chuckled. "Pretty much. Look, is it okay if I leave you in her hands? I need to go and check on Santa. He was a bit surly before."

"Sure," Amy said, then thought of her earlier conviction that something had happened to Nick on the job recently. That fit with what Trish had mentioned about his involvement in Josh's search being newsworthy. "Trish, before you go, can I ask you something?"

Trish's expression turned cautious. "About?"

"Your brother." She moved away from the table and out of Josh's hearing so she wouldn't completely destroy his illusion of Nick as Santa. "Is there some reason reporters would be all over this story, other than it being Christmas Eve and Santa helping to find Josh?"

Trish hesitated a long time before answering. "You'll have to ask Nicky about that," she said finally. "I really do have to go now. He'll be over to get you soon, I'm sure. Or I'll come back myself. In the meantime, Mom will be around if you need anything."

She took off, leaving Amy's question unanswered. But even without Trish's confirmation, she knew she was right. There was something about Nick she needed to know before things went any further between them. Everything pointed to the fact that he was a great guy and he was certainly surrounded by a wonderful family, if Trish and his mom were anyone to judge by. But he had a secret and she'd had her fill of men with secrets.

8

It had been a day of astonishing ups and downs, Amy thought as she and Mrs. DiCaprio slowly ate their slices of pizza and listened to Josh going on and on about everything he'd seen while he was on his own in the mall. Nick's mom seemed highly amused by his nonstop chatter, which was all Josh needed. He liked nothing more than an appreciative audience. More worrisome to Amy was the fact that he sounded as if he still thought it was all a huge adventure.

"You do remember what you promised Santa, right?" she asked eventually.

"That I won't ever run away from you again," he said at once. "But, Mom, I wasn't lost, not really. You were right here."

"But I didn't know where *you* were," she explained. "That's what counts."

"I get it," he said impatiently as he stuffed the last of his pizza into his mouth. "Can we go back now?"

Amy thought of Trish's warning and cast a helpless look toward Mrs. DiCaprio, who immediately grasped her dilemma.

"Josh, I think your mom needs to rest a bit longer," Nick's mother said. "She wasn't feeling well this morning and then she had quite a scare when you disappeared."

His expression turned into a pout that set Amy's teeth on edge.

"Young man, don't give me a look like that or we'll leave this mall and you won't see Santa at all," Amy threatened. "You need to sit here and behave yourself while I feed Emma. Thank goodness I thought to stick some baby food and a bottle in my bag when we left home. I must have had some instinct that seeing Santa wouldn't go as planned."

"Can't I go see Santa while you feed her?" he pleaded. "Mrs. DiCaprio could take me." Apparently he recognized his mother's exasperated expression, because he sighed heavily. "Okay, okay, I'll wait."

"Smart decision," she commended him.

"Josh, what's on your list for Santa?" Mrs. DiCaprio asked him.

"I can't tell," he said. "It's like a birthday wish. If you tell, it won't come true."

She grinned at him. "But I happen to know Santa very well," she confided in him. "Maybe I could put in a good word for you."

Josh's expression turned thoughtful, but then he shook his head. "That's okay. I think me and Santa are pals. I'll just tell him myself."

Mrs. DiCaprio chuckled. "You know something, Josh. You are a very self-possessed, confident young man. You remind me of another boy."

"Your son?" he guessed.

"Exactly." She pointed to the strands of gray in her

hair. "You see all this gray hair? He's the reason I have it. Every time I turned around, he was getting into some kind of mischief. I have four children, all grown now, but only one of them threatened to turn me old before my time." She winked at Amy. "He still has that effect on me, thanks to that job of his."

"What kind of job is it?" Josh asked, regarding her with a rapt expression. "Maybe I could do the same thing when I grow up."

"He's a police detective, as a matter of fact," Mrs. DiCaprio said. "And while he's very good at it, I worry about him."

"Santa says all moms worry about their kids, no matter how old they get," Josh told her.

"That's very true," Mrs. DiCaprio confirmed.

"Do you worry about Trish, too?" he asked.

"Sometimes," she told him. "She works too hard and she could use a little more fun in her life, but at least her work isn't dangerous like my son's."

Amy thought of Nick and envisioned him as a mischievous boy a lot like Josh. It gave her a whole other perspective on the man. She considered asking Mrs. DiCaprio about whatever might be troubling him these days, but decided Trish was right. The answers needed to come from Nick himself.

"Amy?"

Startled, she met Mrs. DiCaprio's gaze. "I'm sorry. Did you say something?"

"I asked if you and your children have plans for tomorrow."

"It's Christmas!" Josh said, interrupting. "We're opening presents."

The older woman smiled. "I meant after that, of

course," she assured him, then met Amy's eyes. "Would you like to spend the afternoon at our house and have dinner with us? It'll be a madhouse, but Rob's sons are about Josh's age. I think he'd enjoy meeting them, don't you? And he has a little girl—Annie—who's only a little older than your Emma."

Amy appreciated the woman's kindness, but surely their presence would be an intrusion. "I'm sure Josh would love meeting them sometime, but we wouldn't want to impose on your family's holiday."

"Don't be silly," Mrs. DiCaprio said at once. "It's no imposition at all. I always cook enough for an army. The turkey's huge, so everyone can take home leftovers. And I've been baking for a month now." She cast a chagrined glance at her flour-covered clothes. "I'm still at it, as you can see. I'm hoping to get one more batch of cookies done before church tonight. There's a reception after the early service."

"Then we shouldn't keep you," Amy said. "We'll be fine here till Trish comes back for us."

"A little while longer won't make a bit of difference," Mrs. DiCaprio responded. "The dough's in the refrigerator chilling. All I need to do is slice the cookies and put them in the oven, while I get dressed for church."

"We used to go to church on Christmas Eve," Josh said.

"Aren't you going to a service tonight?" Mrs. DiCaprio asked.

"Actually we haven't had a chance to find a church since we moved here," Amy admitted. "Nick mentioned something about us coming with you."

"Really?" she said, a speculative glint in her eyes. "What a wonderful idea! Then you'll get to meet everyone before tomorrow, so you'll have no excuse not to join us for Christmas dinner."

"Can we, Mom? Please!" Josh begged.

Amy recognized that Mrs. DiCaprio had an agenda, but Josh looked so excited that she couldn't bring herself to say no. "If you're sure it's no trouble, we'd love to. The prospect of just the three of us for Christmas dinner didn't hold a lot of appeal."

"I'm sure it didn't," Mrs. DiCaprio sympathized. "The holidays are meant for families to celebrate together." She glanced up. "Ah, here comes Trish now." She stood up. "I'll leave you in her hands and see you this evening. If my husband's still circling around in the parking lot after all this time, he may never bring me here again."

To Amy's surprise, she leaned down and gave her a warm hug. "It was wonderful to meet you, Amy. I think fate had a hand in everything that happened today."

With that, she gathered up their trash, tossed it away, then rushed off with a merry wave in their direction.

Trish gave Amy a speculative look. "I imagine we'll be seeing you at her house tomorrow."

Amy nodded. "She doesn't take no for an answer."

"Not when it's for the greater good," Trish agreed. "Which is?"

"Giving my brother exactly what he needs for Christmas."

Amy blushed when she realized that Trish was referring to her. To change the subject, she asked, "How did it go with the reporter?"

"She understands," Trish said. "Everything should be fine."

Amy smiled. "Is it okay for Josh to visit with Santa?"

Trish nodded. "That's why I came back for you now. With a half hour to go till the mall closes, there's still a short line. I figure you guys will blend right in. There's no reason for anyone to link you to the big story of the day."

"What about Nick? Was he interviewed?"

"Nope," Trish said grimly. "I told her he'd refused. He had a lot going on as it was—the kid on his lap was screaming bloody murder." She grinned at the memory.

Amy smiled. "How did Nick take that?"

"Stayed right on script," Trish said proudly. "He never missed a beat with the ho-ho-ho's and asking what the kid wanted for Christmas."

"Mom!" Josh interrupted, clearly tired of waiting. "Can we go *now!*"

"Okay, okay," she said, regarding Trish ruefully. "Let's go."

As she put an exhausted and unprotesting Emma back into her stroller, Amy was filled with an unexpected sense of anticipation. It had been a lot of years since she'd been this eager to pay a visit to Santa.

The line was shorter now and they were at the end of it. No one came along to wait behind them. Exhausted shoppers were leaving the mall now in droves.

When Josh's turn came, he was still the last in line. The instant he climbed onto Santa's knee and Amy had placed Emma beside him, the photographer snapped their picture, then handed the instant photo to Amy. "No charge," he said as he packed up his things and left in a rush for whatever holiday festivities awaited him.

Emma leaned contentedly against Nick's chest and closed her eyes. The sight of her daughter in Nick's arms brought an odd tightness to Amy's heart. She had a feeling this image would linger inside her long after the photo had faded.

"So, young man," Nick said to Josh in his booming Santa voice, "what do you want Santa to bring you for Christmas?"

She tuned out the sound of her son's words as he recited not only his own list, one with which she was thoroughly familiar, but Emma's. It was a modest enough list by most standards and she knew that everything on it would be under the tree. The only wish she couldn't grant was his longing to see his dad on Christmas morning.

When Josh's consultation with Santa was over, Nick left the village with Emma in his arms and joined her. "Are we still on for church tonight?" he asked. "I can give you directions and meet you there, and then introduce you to the rest of my family." He gave her a hard look. "Or was meeting my mother more than enough?"

"Your mother is incredible," she told him. "She's invited us for Christmas dinner tomorrow."

He didn't look all that surprised. "I had a hunch that would come up."

"You didn't put her up to it?"

"My existence as a bachelor is enough to put her up to it," he said dryly. "Keep in mind she's scheming."

"I gathered as much," Amy admitted.

"And?"

"And what?" she asked.

"How do you feel about her scheme?"

"I told her we'd be there tomorrow." Her gaze locked with his. "How do *you* feel about her agenda?"

A grin spread across his face. "Better than I did a few minutes ago," he revealed. "How about giving me a moment to get out of this costume and I'll walk out with you?"

Amy glanced pointedly at Josh. "Not a good idea," she said succinctly.

"Of course not," he said at once. "What was I thinking?"

He looked around till he spotted Trish. "Sis, any problem if I wear this home?"

Laughing, she merely waved him away. "Go."

Josh looked from Nick to Trish and back again. "Is she your sister?" he asked, his expression puzzled.

Nick winced. "She is."

"Then that lady, Mrs. DiCaprio, is your mom, too?" Josh pressed.

Nick nodded.

Amy held her breath as Josh absorbed that information.

Finally Josh looked Nick in the eye. "Awesome! I know Santa's real mom! The kids back in Michigan will freak when I tell 'em. Can I call tonight, Mom? Can I? They're not going to believe this."

"Sure, you can call as soon as we get home," Amy told him, relieved that the whole Santa illusion hadn't been ruined. If anything, it had been reinforced and improved on.

"Then let's go," Josh said, trying to hurry her along. "I'll push Emma's stroller."

"Just don't get too far head of us, okay?"

"Okay," he said, glancing repeatedly over his shoulder to make sure she and Santa were close on his heels.

"I guess your lecture got through to him," she told Nick. "I think it made more of an impact coming from you."

"He'll forget it soon enough," Nick said. "I'll have to stick around to keep reminding him."

"I imagine I could remind him," Amy said, though the thought of Nick being around to do it held a whole lot of appeal.

"You don't have the Santa factor on your side," he told her.

"And you'll look pretty strange wearing that costume in July," she countered.

"Think I'll be around you guys in July?" he asked.

"I guess we'll just have to wait and see."

"You know, there's something I forgot to ask you earlier," he said.

"Oh?"

"What do you want for Christmas, Amy?"

She met his gaze and her heart gave a little lurch. "I have everything I need," she told him. "My kids are safe and happy."

"And that's enough?"

"It is for now," she told him, unable to tear her gaze away from the intensity and heat in his eyes.

He leaned down and brushed a kiss across her lips, then came back and lingered a second longer.

"Then maybe that will give you a few other ideas for your list," he said when he finally pulled away.

Oh, yeah, she thought. It most certainly did. But having X-rated ideas on Christmas Eve would shove her out of nice and straight into naughty. She wondered what Santa would have to say about that.

One glance into Nick's mischievous eyes told her the answer to that. They were working from the very same list.

Before she could examine how she felt about that, a

woman tapped Nick on the shoulder. When he turned around, his expression froze. It was exactly the look he'd had on his face earlier, when he'd dragged Amy inside that shoe store.

"Nick," the woman said softly. "Could I please speak to you for a second?"

"Sure," he said, but there was no mistaking his reluctance.

The woman cast an apologetic look in Amy's direction. "I'm sorry to interrupt, but this is the first chance I've had to speak to Nick since…" Her voice caught. She shook her head. "Sorry. I still can't talk about it."

"It's okay," Nick soothed. "Really, you don't have to say anything."

To Amy, he sounded almost desperate, as if he were willing the woman to remain silent.

The woman drew in a deep breath. "No, it's important. I tried to call you at the station, but they said you were on leave."

Nick nodded.

"Because of what happened," she guessed.

"Yes," he said tightly.

"I'm so sorry," she told him. "It's all my fault."

Nick regarded her incredulously. "Your fault? How can you say that?"

"If I'd told you right away about my ex-husband, if I'd warned you…" Her voice fell to a whisper. "Maybe things would have gone differently."

Nick put his hands on her shoulders and looked into her eyes. "No, Mitzi, nothing that happened was your fault. If anything, it was mine. I just stood by…"

"No," she said harshly. "That's just it, that's why I had to talk to you. I knew you were blaming yourself."

"Who else should I blame?" he asked heatedly.

The woman sighed heavily. "Maybe it was no one's fault, not even my ex-husband's. He had to be sick, right? To think that taking our boy and hurting him would somehow make me love him again." She shuddered. "Or even that it was a way to pay me back for leaving him. That's not right. He needs help."

"Hopefully he'll get it while he's locked up," Nick told her. "The important thing is that he'll never get another chance to hurt anyone else."

Amy listened to the exchange with mounting horror. She realized now why Nick had been so desperate to find Josh, so determined to stay right by her side until her son was safe. He was trying to make up for not being able to help another little boy, this woman's son. No wonder he was tormented. No wonder he'd asked so many questions about Ned. The search for Josh must have dredged up a thousand terrifying moments for him.

The woman spoke to Amy, "I'm sorry to intrude, but when I saw that Nick was here, I wanted to tell him that I don't blame him for anything that happened. I thought he might need to know that."

Nick did, indeed, look as if a huge weight had been lifted from his shoulders. "You have an amazingly generous heart," he told her.

"If I do, it's because I had an incredible boy in my life for a few brief years. I'm so grateful for that. It was far too short, but he taught me so much. That's what I want to remember. Not the way he died, but the way he lived." She hugged Nick fiercely. "Merry Christmas, Detective."

"Merry Christmas," he whispered, his voice choked.

After she'd gone, Amy reached up and touched the tears on his cheeks. "I am so sorry that you had to re-live all that today."

He met her gaze. "I'm not," he said eventually. "Not if it brought you, Josh and Emma into my life. How could I possibly regret that?"

He turned to Josh, who was rolling a laughing Emma in circles nearby. "Hey, guys, let's get going. It's Christmas Eve and Santa's got a very busy night ahead. I have toys to deliver."

His gaze shifted to Amy and he lowered his voice. "And maybe, if I'm lucky, I can even sneak a kiss or two under the mistletoe."

Amy laughed. "You can try. I've been wondering all day if that beard tickles. I couldn't tell earlier."

Grinning, Nick called out to Josh. "Don't look, okay?"

"Don't look at what?" Josh asked.

"Do as you're told," Amy instructed, laughing. "Mommy's gonna kiss Santa Claus."

Josh's expression immediately brightened. "Cool!"

Yeah, Amy thought, as Nick's mouth settled on hers. It was definitely cool. No, she concluded an instant later, actually, it was hot. Very, very hot.

Outside the mall, the air was icy and snow was fall-ing, but Amy was still overheated from that kiss. North Carolina might be in for some sort of rare blizzard, but for her this was quickly turning into the hottest Christmas on record.

Epilogue

Christmas, one year later

"So, young man," Nick said to Josh in his booming Santa voice, "What do you want Santa to bring you for Christmas?"

Amy had no idea how Trish had persuaded Nick to play Santa for a day once again this year. He still claimed he'd hated every minute of it when she'd coerced him into it the year before. Maybe it had something to do with knowing that Amy would once again be bringing Josh and Emma to the mall for their Christmas Eve visit.

Josh studied Santa intently, then seemed to reach some sort of decision. He cast a quick glance toward Amy, then pulled Santa's head down so he could whisper in his ear.

Nick immediately glanced at Amy, a grin spreading across his face. "Well, now, I don't know about that, son. Maybe your mom should have a say about something that important."

Amy sighed. A puppy? He'd asked for a puppy. Josh

knew they couldn't have one where they were living. What was she supposed to do now?

"Sweetie, I told you we can't have a puppy till we move to a house," she said, which oddly enough only seemed to make Nick's smile grow. She regarded him with confusion. "He didn't ask for a puppy?"

"Nope," Nick said, carrying Emma down to join her. "What then?"

"A new dad," he told her. "And he seems to think having Santa for a dad would be pretty awesome."

Amy's cheeks flooded with heat. "Oh, no. I am so sorry."

"Don't be. I'm thinking it's something to consider."

She stared at him in shock. "Excuse me?"

"Not today, of course, but you know, down the road."

"Say sometime after you've actually had a chance to think about it?" she asked dryly.

He laughed, not the fake, booming laugh of Santa, but the amused chuckle of a man she'd discovered had a wonderful sense of humor.

"Oh, I've been thinking about it for some time now," he told her. "How about you? Has the thought crossed your mind?"

It was her turn to chuckle. "How could it not, with your folks and Trish pressuring me every chance they get?"

"So, what do you think?" Josh demanded impatiently. "Is he gonna be my new dad or not?"

"I think maybe we ought to give your mom a little more time to think about this," Nick told him. "She might even want a real, romantic proposal."

"What's that?" Josh asked.

"Candlelight and stuff," Nick told him. "Keep it in

mind. You might need to know about things like that later. In the meantime, why don't I walk you all to your car. I've heard a rumor and I want to check it out."

"What kind of rumor?" Amy asked, confused by the hint of mystery in his voice.

"You'll see."

They walked to the same exit where Amy, Josh and Emma had entered the mall on that fateful day a year ago. When Nick pushed open the door, she immediately saw what he'd been talking about. Once again, snow was falling. It had already covered the ground and turned the rapidly emptying parking lot into a winter wonderland.

"Snow!" Josh screamed, running ahead and twirling around, his head thrown back and his mouth open so he could catch the fat snowflakes on his tongue. Suddenly he ran over and threw his arms around Nick's huge, padded waist. "Thank you, thank you, thank you."

Nick winked at Amy. "Sorry, kid, Santa can't take credit for this."

Maybe not, she thought, but he had a lot to do with the joyous expression on her son's face. He was also responsible for the amazingly lighthearted feeling inside her.

As far as she was concerned, Santa—*Nick*—had given them everything they needed and the promise of much more.

* * * * *

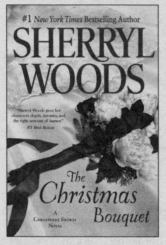

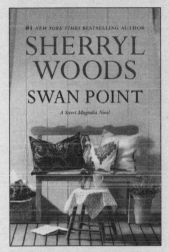

Life In Icicle Falls

SHEILA ROBERTS

Life in Icicle Falls doesn't always go as planned...

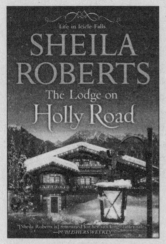

James Claussen has played Santa for years. But now that he's a widower, he's lost interest—in everything. So his daughter, Brooke, kidnaps him from the mall for a special Christmas at the lodge in Icicle Falls, owned by long-widowed Olivia Wallace. Brooke wants Dad to be happy, and yet...she's not quite ready to see someone *else's* mommy kissing Santa Claus.

Single mom Missy Monroe brings her kids to the lodge, too. Lalla wants a grandma for Christmas, and her brother, Carlos, wants a dog. Missy can't provide either one. What *she'd* like is an attractive, dependable man. A man like John Truman... But John's girlfriend will be joining him in Icicle Falls, and he's going to propose.

Of course, not everything goes as planned. But sometimes the best gifts are the ones you *don't* expect!

Available now, wherever books are sold!

Be sure to connect with us at:

Harlequin.com/Newsletters

Facebook.com/HarlequinBooks

Twitter.com/HarlequinBooks

www.Harlequin.com

MSR1661

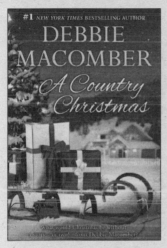

REQUEST YOUR
FREE BOOKS!

2 FREE NOVELS
FROM THE ROMANCE COLLECTION
PLUS 2 FREE GIFTS!

YES! Please send me 2 FREE novels from the Romance Collection and my 2 FREE gifts (gifts are worth about $10). After receiving them, if I don't wish to receive any more books, I can return the shipping statement marked "cancel." If I don't cancel, I will receive 4 brand-new novels every month and be billed just $6.24 per book in the U.S. or $6.74 per book in Canada. That's a savings of at least 22% off the cover price. It's quite a bargain! Shipping and handling is just 50¢ per book in the U.S. and 75¢ per book in Canada.* I understand that accepting the 2 free books and gifts places me under no obligation to buy anything. I can always return a shipment and cancel at any time. Even if I never buy another book, the two free books and gifts are mine to keep forever.

194/394 MDN F4XY

Name _____ (PLEASE PRINT) _____

Address _____ Apt. # _____

City _____ State/Prov. _____ Zip/Postal Code _____

Signature (if under 18, a parent or guardian must sign)

Mail to the Harlequin® Reader Service:
IN U.S.A.: P.O. Box 1867, Buffalo, NY 14240-1867
IN CANADA: P.O. Box 609, Fort Erie, Ontario L2A 5X3

Want to try two free books from another line?
Call 1-800-873-8635 or visit www.ReaderService.com.

* Terms and prices subject to change without notice. Prices do not include applicable taxes. Sales tax applicable in N.Y. Canadian residents will be charged applicable taxes. Offer not valid in Quebec. This offer is limited to one order per household. Not valid for current subscribers to the Romance Collection or the Romance/Suspense Collection. All orders subject to credit approval. Credit or debit balances in a customer's account(s) may be offset by any other outstanding balance owed by or to the customer. Please allow 4 to 6 weeks for delivery. Offer available while quantities last.

Your Privacy—The Harlequin® Reader Service is committed to protecting your privacy. Our Privacy Policy is available online at www.ReaderService.com or upon request from the Harlequin Reader Service.

We make a portion of our mailing list available to reputable third parties that offer products we believe may interest you. If you prefer that we not exchange your name with third parties, or if you wish to clarify or modify your communication preferences, please visit us at www.ReaderService.com/consumerschoice or write to us at Harlequin Reader Service Preference Service, P.O. Box 9062, Buffalo, NY 14269. Include your complete name and address.

ROM13R

SHERRYL WOODS

32979	MOONLIGHT COVE	___$7.99 U.S.	___$9.99 CAN.
32976	ALONG CAME TROUBLE	___$7.99 U.S.	___$9.99 CAN.
32975	ABOUT THAT MAN	___$7.99 U.S.	___$9.99 CAN.
32947	DRIFTWOOD COTTAGE	___$7.99 U.S.	___$9.99 CAN.
32927	THE BACKUP PLAN	___$7.99 U.S.	___$9.99 CAN.
32895	MENDING FENCES	___$7.99 U.S.	___$9.99 CAN.
32893	FEELS LIKE FAMILY	___$7.99 U.S.	___$9.99 CAN.
32845	SWEET TEA AT SUNRISE	___$7.99 U.S.	___$9.99 CAN.
32814	RETURN TO ROSE COTTAGE	___$7.99 U.S.	___$9.99 CAN.
32753	AMAZING GRACIE	___$7.99 U.S.	___$9.99 CAN.
32751	HOME AT ROSE COTTAGE	___$7.99 U.S.	___$9.99 CAN.
32641	HARBOR LIGHTS	___$7.99 U.S.	___$9.99 CAN.
32634	FLOWERS ON MAIN	___$7.99 U.S.	___$9.99 CAN.
31679	THE DEVANEY BROTHERS: DANIEL	___$7.99 U.S.	___$9.99 CAN.
31630	THE DEVANEY BROTHERS: MICHAEL AND PATRICK	___$7.99 U.S.	___$8.99 CAN.
31607	THE DEVANEY BROTHERS: RYAN AND SEAN	___$7.99 U.S.	___$8.99 CAN.
31589	HOME TO SEAVIEW KEY	___$7.99 U.S.	___$8.99 CAN.
31581	SEAVIEW INN	___$7.99 U.S.	___$8.99 CAN.
31512	TWILIGHT	___$7.99 U.S.	___$8.99 CAN.
31466	AFTER TEX	___$7.99 U.S.	___$9.99 CAN.
31446	SEA GLASS ISLAND	___$7.99 U.S.	___$9.99 CAN.
31442	WIND CHIME POINT	___$7.99 U.S.	___$9.99 CAN.
31436	SAND CASTLE BAY	___$7.99 U.S.	___$9.99 CAN.
31414	TEMPTATION	___$7.99 U.S.	___$9.99 CAN.
31391	AN O'BRIEN FAMILY CHRISTMAS	___$7.99 U.S.	___$9.99 CAN.
31359	CATCHING FIREFLIES	___$7.99 U.S.	___$9.99 CAN.
31348	MIDNIGHT PROMISES	___$7.99 U.S.	___$9.99 CAN.
31326	WAKING UP IN CHARLESTON	___$7.99 U.S.	___$9.99 CAN.
31309	THE SUMMER GARDEN	___$7.99 U.S.	___$9.99 CAN.
31262	A CHESAPEAKE SHORES CHRISTMAS	___$7.99 U.S.	___$9.99 CAN.

(limited quantities available)

TOTAL AMOUNT	$ _____
POSTAGE & HANDLING	$ _____
($1.00 for 1 book, 50¢ for each additional)	
APPLICABLE TAXES*	$ _____
TOTAL PAYABLE	$ _____

(check or money order—please do not send cash)

To order, complete this form and send it, along with a check or money order for the total above, payable to Harlequin MIRA, to: **In the U.S.:** 3010 Walden Avenue, P.O. Box 9077, Buffalo, NY 14269-9077; **In Canada:** P.O. Box 636, Fort Erie, Ontario, L2A 5X3.

Name: _____
Address: _____ City: _____
State/Prov.: _____ Zip/Postal Code: _____
Account Number (if applicable): _____
075 CSAS

*New York residents remit applicable sales taxes.
*Canadian residents remit applicable GST and provincial taxes.

HARLEQUIN® MIRA®
™ www.Harlequin.com

MSHW1114BL